"You'll learn more about Thailand and Thai people than you could from any tour book—and have fun doing it. It's gritty and sad, but with an overlay of hope and love. . . . Hallinan enchantingly captures the life of a Bangkok bar girl. . . . Enlightening, educational, and hugely entertaining."
—*San Jose Mercury News*

"The most moving [book] yet in an exceptional series. . . . A thriller with a heart, as well as a haunting and insightful portrait of a strong and courageous woman who manages to escape her destiny and help others to do the same."
—*Denver Post*

"Hallinan takes his Poke Rafferty series to the next level with this taut, offbeat, and fast-moving thriller. . . . Hallinan's writing really shines: Readers can feel the grime and poverty of village life, smell the streets of Bangkok, taste the fear. . . . Hallinan's unlikely hero shines in this sometimes funny, always engrossing, and undeniably authentic story that explores a dark and fascinating side of Thailand."
—*Kirkus Reviews* (starred review)

"I have loved all of Tim Hallinan's Bangkok novels, and his latest, *The Queen of Patpong*, is the best yet. Hallinan is a wordsmith of the first order, and he puts his great narrative skills into overdrive on this one. A great personal story with universal themes and even a dash of Shakespeare. You won't read a better thriller this year!"
—John Lescroart, *New York Times*
bestselling author of *Treasure Hunt*

"Tim Hallinan is one of the great unsung mystery writers. His latest in the Poke Rafferty series is his best yet. Not only a terrific mystery but writing so fine, you want to read it aloud. *The Queen of Patpong* opens with the beguiling chapter heading 'Caliban.' And from there it takes off like a stealth bomber, a narrative-soaked novel that screams to be filmed. For shamefully too long, Hallinan has flown under the radar. This novel alone deserves to place him up there with the heavyweights. John Burdett writes about Bangkok. Tim Hallinan *is* Bangkok. I adore this book."
—Ken Bruen, author of *London Boulevard*

THE QUEEN OF PATPONG

THE QUEEN

of

PATPONG

TIMOTHY HALLINAN

HARPER

NEW YORK · LONDON · TORONTO · SYDNEY

To my first listener,
Munyin Choy-Hallinan

HARPER

This book is a work of fiction. The characters, incidents, and dialogue are drawn from the author's imagination and are not to be construed as real. Any resemblance to actual events or persons, living or dead, is entirely coincidental.

A hardcover edition of this book was published in 2010 by William Morrow, an imprint of HarperCollins Publishers.

HarperCollins books may be purchased for educational, business, or sales promotional use. For information please write: Special Markets Department, HarperCollins Publishers, 10 East 53rd Street, New York, NY 10022.

FIRST HARPER PAPERBACK PUBLISHED 2011.

The Library of Congress has catalogued the hardcover edition as follows:

Hallinan, Timothy
   The queen of Patpong : a Poke Rafferty thriller / Timothy Hallinan. — 1st ed.
     p. cm.
   ISBN 978-0-06-167226-2
   1. Bangkok (Thailand)—Fiction. I Title.

PS3558.A3923Q44 2010
813'.54—dc22

2010002112

ISBN 978-0-06-167227-9 (pbk.)

11 12 13 14 15 OV/RRD 10 9 8 7 6 5 4 3 2 1

PART I

CALIBAN

1

Temporary Honeys

Old cigarette smoke, cheap perfume, sweat. The proven architecture of soft pink light on soft brown skin. Bad rock and roll, some mercifully forgotten tight-pants, stadium-rock anthem from the 1980s, still being played in Bangkok, the town where bad songs last forever. Shredded speakers, probably blown for fifteen years. The bass notes like tearing paper.

The girls on the stage.

And there she is: Number 27.

The tall man sees her the moment he reaches the top of the stairway, the symbolic barrier that prevents Bangkok's finest from enforcing Thailand's strict anti-nudity law, news of which has clearly not reached this room. Thanks to an elaborate, almost courtly, system of graft, the cops pause downstairs long enough to let the doorman slip them a couple thousand baht as he pushes a buzzer, and then they shuffle slowly upward while the girls onstage wrap themselves in the cheap taffeta slips that are normally knotted around their upper arms to display the merchandise.

They're almost all naked now, four of the five on the stage and most of the eight or so who sit on customers' laps, arms languidly draped around the suckers' necks. The girls dazzle their temporary honeys with honest, open Thai smiles and whatever lie will open a pocket. The tall man at the top of the stairs does a quick scan of the room, making sure no one he knows is there. Then he returns his gaze to Number 27.

She's tiny, plump-cheeked, sullen-mouthed, with cupcake breasts, a child's round tummy, and straight black hair in a blunt schoolgirl cut that's grown out just enough to brush her shoulders. Of the five women on the platform in the center of the room, she is the youngest by at least five years, and the only one who isn't naked.

The tall man stares at her long enough to draw a glance, but she quickly turns her back. He crosses the dark, narrow room to the banquette in front of the mirrored wall. Once he's seated, with little squares of light from the revolving mirrored ball above the stage chasing each other across his shirt, he glances down. The photo in his hand is a smudged photocopy of a high-school identification card. The girl in the picture faces the camera with the hopeful insecurity of adolescence. She had risen to the occasion with a smile.

She isn't smiling now. She dances as though she is underwater, her eyes fixed unblinkingly on her reflection in the mirror. She might be stoned, drunk, suicidal, or just exhausted. Her short, salmon-colored slip, a loop of elastic holding up a yard of some cheap synthetic, has been tugged down below her baby's belly to bare the upper half of her body almost to the pubic area. The round LAP BAR button with the number 27 on it is pinned to the elastic band of the slip, directly over her right hip bone. The number is her only identification, but the tall man knows her name, which is Toy.

In the six months since the photo was taken, she has grown the schoolgirl hair an inch or more and plastered her face with makeup so she looks older, but no matter. The tall man knows her age. The tall man is here, in the Lap Bar on Bangkok's Patpong Road, *because* of her age.

Today is Saturday, the twenty-fourth of April. Two days ago Number 27 turned sixteen.

IN THE STREET below, the short, crowded road called Patpong 1, the street market has sprung into noisy life. Beneath the smoky half glow of the night sky, two straggling lines of overilluminated stalls offer curios, jewelry, eel-skin and leather goods, preserved tarantulas and scorpions, and an impressive variety of forgeries: watches, sunglasses, fountain pens, computer software, games, compact discs, mislabeled designer clothes, acrylic amber, and plastic ivory that's been buried in water-buffalo manure for that convincing patina of age. In a few booths, less brightly illuminated, the discerning shopper can pick through an assortment of Tasers, flick knives, brass knuckles, switchblades, and other instruments of intimate aggression.

They're mostly male, the florid horde for whom these treasures gleam. Ranging from half drunk to barely ambulatory, grim-faced and dripping sweat, they push their way between the stands, checking the rows of counterfeits with one eye and keeping the other eye on the open doors to the bars. Patpong Road at night is almost all bars: Kiss, Lipstick, Safari, King's Castle, Supergirls, Pussy Galore. Through the open doors, chilly air pours into the streets, pumped by the heartbeat rhythms of trance and techno. Bar girls in cheap, fake-satin wraps stand in the doorways and call out cheerful, indiscriminate Thai greetings to the nameless darlings in the street, pushing the paradise inside.

At the end of the road, where Patpong empties into Silom Road, a man wearing reflective Ray-Bans and the tight-fitting brown paramilitary uniform of the Bangkok police lounges against the window of a nondescript restaurant. The uniform sets off broad shoulders and narrow hips while also making way, with a certain amount of strain, for a small but ambitious potbelly. There is nothing soft about the potbelly: it looks like something to avoid bumping your head on. He glances at a heavy steel watch on a too-large band, flips it around from the front of his wrist to the back, and then checks it again as he realizes he's forgotten to look at the time. Satisfied, he folds his hands over the round belly—a practiced, comfortable gesture.

The policeman has a hairline receding on either side of a stubborn widow's peak, medium-dark skin, a disappointed mouth that turns down at the ends, and broad, almost muscular nostrils. Behind the mirrored Ray-Bans—genuine—he lazily scans the crowd, straightening only when he catches sight of a heavyset white man in a loose shirt, patched with sweat, who roughly tows a young Thai girl through the throng. The girl—dark-complected, tangle-haired, flat-nosed, dressed in a knotted T-shirt and cutoff jeans—pulls back, distracted by a bright row of bootleg DVDs, and the heavyset man gives her hand a yank that almost jerks her off her feet. Feeling the policeman's eyes on her, the girl turns and frowns at him before breaking into a smile. After a moment the policeman smiles back. The heavyset white man snags a *tuk-tuk*, a three-wheeled open-air taxi, and hauls the girl onto the backseat behind him. He doesn't barter the fare, so he's in for at least one unpleasant surprise during the evening. The *tuk-tuk* driver swerves into traffic with a fine disregard for the possibility of death. The policeman leans back against the window of the restaurant and looks at his watch again.

"THANK YOU," SAYS the young woman with the wandering eye. She's in her middle twenties, plain and plump, with a wide Isaan nose. A fall of red-dyed hair has been combed forward over the left side of her face to mask the errant eye. She has tugged the elasticized slip modestly up to her armpits. A thin gold chain around her neck disappears into the slip. The tall man knows there will be a Buddhist amulet at the end of it, which the woman will drag around to hang against her back when she dances, so as not to expose it to the goings-on in the bar. She will also remove it when she services a customer.

She puts the cola the man bought her on the round table in front of him and gives him an expert glance. There is an Asian smoothness to his features. He has straight black Asian hair and uptilted eyes that are almost black, the color of dangerous ice.

He says, "What's the baby's name?" He indicates Toy with a lift of his chin. One of the other dancers leans over, laughing, and yanks the girl's slip down, and now she dances with the slip pooled at her ankles and her hands folded protectively over her shadowy pudenda. She seems miles away.

"Toy," says the plump girl grudgingly. She leans forward and puts a hand on his wrist as a demand for attention. "You no good for her. She too young for here. You have good heart, you give me thousand baht, I give five hundred to mama-san for bar fine and five hundred to Mai, and she go home. You take other girl, I help you find pretty girl, not like me. She baby, you unnerstan'?"

"Yes. Tell Toy I want to talk to her."

The plump girl has picked up the cola, but now she puts it down and pulls the hair back from the wandering eye. It searches the mirror behind the tall man as the other eye studies his face. Whatever she sees there, she lowers the hair over her face again and turns her back on him, heading for three very drunk Japanese men who have just staggered in, their bright red faces upturned toward the stage. They brush past the plump woman as though she isn't there, and she stands where they've left her, hands hanging loose at her sides, looking at a spot on the floor. One of them points at Toy and says something, and the others laugh.

The tall man checks his watch, sits back, and smiles at Toy.

AT 9:22 by the policeman's watch, two beer-sodden Australians begin to clobber each other in the street in front of a stand selling fake amber beads. The Aussies throw their punches slowly and deliberately, as if rehearsing for a fight that will be filmed later, but the blows land with a flat, heavy sound, like cuts of meat falling to the floor. The prize over which they are fighting—a slight, narrow-shouldered, heavily tattooed Thai female of twenty or so—chews thoughtfully on a hangnail as the larger of the two men grabs the smaller by the hair and slams his head against the edge of the booth. The small man starts to bleed immediately, even before the beads hit the pavement and begin bouncing among the feet of the onlookers. The girl scratches her shoulder, snags the offending fingernail on her T-shirt, and looks down at it with irritation.

The bleeding man emits a high, reedy, choked sound. He rips off his football jacket and hands it to the girl and then leaps forward, wrapping his fingers around his friend's neck. The two of them begin to topple over. The policeman steps forward, arms spread wide, thoughtfully clearing a space in the crowd for the struggling men to fall through. He steps over the fighters without a downward glance and begins to help the vendor pick up her beads. The girl takes a quick look at the fighting men and rifles the pockets of the jacket. Whatever she finds there, she slips it into the pocket of her jeans. She drops the jacket onto the street, and her eyes meet the policeman's. He gives her a shrug, and she melts into the crowd.

HE SITS BACK, watching her not look at him. Her glazed fascination with her own reflection has been broken. She's even picking up her feet a little, although she's turned her back to him, almost shyly. But he can still see her face in the mirror on the opposite wall, and her eyes come back to him again and again, and then they slide away and search the room as if she's looking for an ally.

He orders a Singha beer from the mama-san, a thickset, brightly dressed woman with gold on her wrists and fingers and nothing merry about her. The Lap Bar is a typical upstairs joint. The bar is at one end of the room, the women dance on a raised platform in the middle of the space, and the customers sit either at stools pulled directly up to the stage or on a long, cigarette-scarred bench against the mirrored walls, with a small table every few feet to hold their drinks. The tall man is on the couch, and he keeps his eyes on Number 27.

Chased by his gaze, the girl has worked her way down the stage until she's directly in front of the three drunk Japanese. One of them calls out to her, placing both hands over his heart in a gesture of exaggerated romanticism and then forming a circle with his right thumb and fore-finger and pushing his left index finger in and out of it. His companions burst into raucous laughter, an explosion of sound that the tall man can hear even over the loud music. The girl misses a step, as if she's tripped on the laugh. She stands still for a long moment, not looking at the Japanese men, not looking at the tall man who watches her, and then she turns and trudges the length of the stage until she is in front of the tall man again. She walks as though she weighs five hundred pounds.

The three Japanese men are drumming their hands on the bar, a roll-ing rhythm over the music, to call the girl back down to them. They flash fingers in the red light, playing a game of rock-paper-scissors to see who will have her first, and Number 27 makes her decision. She turns and forces a smile at the tall man.

It isn't much of a smile.

THE AUSTRALIANS HAVE their arms wrapped tightly around each other's shoulders. Their anger has been redirected.

"Bloody hell," says the smaller one. He wears the blood on his face like a veil, like a disguise. "She buggered off and took my money."

"Is that so?" says the policeman, clutching a fistful of fake amber like a talisman.

"You're wasting your time," the larger one tells his bleeding friend belligerently. "You think he's going to help you? He probably gets a cut of everything she steals." He leans down toward the policeman, bringing his big red face so close that he can see his own eyes in the policeman's Ray-Bans. "'At's right, innit, mate? You pocketing the proceeds?"

"Bangkok police are very honest," the policeman says, not wasting much conviction on it. "Fortunately, finding her will be easy." He releases a smile into the night air to show how easy it's going to be. "You remember her name, of course."

"Name?" asks the larger man. He takes a drunken, involuntary step backward, dragging his bleeding friend with him.

"Her name." The policeman looks from the larger to the smaller man, his eyebrows high and querying. "You know. What everybody called her." He waits. "The short, one- or two-syllable sound to which she answered when others spoke it." The policeman has developed a faint British accent. "Name," he says again, and smiles encouragingly.

"Who the fuck knows?" asks the bleeding man.

"I see," the policeman says. "Listen. Let me give you a tip." The policeman lowers his voice confidentially. "In case this happens again."

"I'm bleeding," the smaller man says.

"We are poor in Thailand, compared to you," the policeman says, dropping his voice even further. They lean in to hear him. "There are many things you take for granted that we do not have. But all of us—" He reaches out and taps the larger man on the chest. "Every one of us—even the poorest, even the destitute, even the beggars, *even the girls who work in the bars*—every one of us has a name." He places the false amber beads on the counter from which they have fallen and catches sight of his watch. "Oh, my," the policeman says. "Look at the time."

THE TALL MAN goes down the stairs first, with Toy trailing a few steps behind. He can smell her, a damp, sweetish mixture of makeup and perspiration. When he'd put his arm around her shoulders after the mama-san accepted the five-hundred-baht bar fine—worth about fourteen dollars in California, where the tall man used to live—she'd shrunk back. She hadn't met his eyes since she stepped off the stage.

At the bottom of the stairs, he turns and watches her come, now wearing a T-shirt, a bright orange skirt that ends midthigh, and lizard-skin cowboy boots. He gives her a smile, but she's got her eyes on the stairway, as though she's never gone down one before.

"Here we go," he says. "I hope you're ready."

He opens the door.

THE POLICEMAN'S SUNGLASSES reflect the words LAP BAR. The words are written in fuchsia neon set into the center of a bright heart, a cheap electric valentine sizzling fifteen feet above the Patpong sidewalk. He takes a final look at his watch and then leans against a metal pole that once had some sort of sign atop it, now amputated. The crowd, sweating, wrinkled, and ripe-smelling, divides on either side and flows by.

The boy who has been assigned to watch the door to the Lap Bar looks at the policeman and fails to recognize him. Patpong is a very profitable beat, and the police assigned to it have paid dearly for the pleasure. They know the rules. A new cop means trouble. The boy abandons his post and does a discreet fade, stopping a few yards away to watch. From that vantage point, he sees the policeman climb two of the four steps to the door. The door swings open, pulled from the inside, and a tall man comes out, followed by the youngest and newest of the girls in the bar—what was her name?—Toy.

And the policeman puts an arm up, resting his hand against the edge of the door, to block Toy and the tall man from coming all the way outside. Toy makes a scrabbling move backward, but the policeman snakes his other arm out and grabs her wrist. This is completely outside the boy's frame of reference: a policeman interfering with a customer and a bar girl at the door the boy is supposed to be guarding.

The boy decides it is time to go home.

THE POLICEMAN LOOKS past the *farang*, directly at Toy. "How old are you?"

"She's eighteen," the tall man says.

"Shut up," says the policeman in English. "I asked her."

"Hey, listen," the foreigner begins, but the policeman stops him with a look. Then, deliberately, he reaches down with his free hand and unsnaps his holster.

"No problem," the customer says immediately, bringing his hands up in front of him, palms out. "You want her, she's yours."

"Come out here," the policeman says. With one hand resting on the butt of his pistol, he backs slowly down the steps leading up to the door, dragging Toy with him, and waits on the sidewalk. After a long moment, during which his eyes remain locked on the policeman's face, the tall man comes down the steps.

"This is ridiculous," he says, but his voice is thin.

"I told you to shut up," says the policeman. "Put out your hand." A crowd has begun to form about them, mostly Thais drawn by the spectacle of a policeman actually enforcing some sort of law on Patpong. His eyes darting around the circle of faces, the tall man puts out his right hand, and the policeman snaps a cuff on it, a chilly metallic click in the tropical air. The other end of the cuff closes around the metal pole against which the policeman had been leaning. The tall man stands as though dumbfounded, and a murmur runs through the group of Thais.

"I asked how old you were," the policeman says in Thai.

"Eighteen," Toy says. She seems even more disoriented than the customer by the turn of events.

"Give me your card," the policeman says in Thai. Each bar girl who is legally employed must carry an identification card.

Toy looks for support at the circle of faces on the pavement—surely nothing very terrible can happen with so many people watching. Her tongue explores her lower lip. "I left it at home."

"You don't have one," says the policeman. "You don't have one because you're not old enough to have one. Do you know what the penalty is?"

"I don't care," she says, but it's almost a question.

"Two years in the reformatory. Up-country. No Bangkok, no movies, no discos, no bright lights, just big paddies for you to work in. Full of leeches. Nowhere to hide from the sun. Snakes everywhere. Spiders as big as dogs. They'll cut your hair off, like a boy's. No cosmetics. No pretty dresses. Rotten meat and rocks in the rice. There are girls there who will bother you. If you don't do what they want, they'll beat you up. Do you understand me?"

She starts to say yes, swallows, and then says it.

"Two years from now, you'll be black as a boot and your gums will bleed when you smile. You'll have wrinkles around your eyes. No one will even recognize you. You'll be lucky to make two hundred fifty baht a trick."

"I'm eighteen," Toy protests faintly. Her eyes go to the faces of the people gathered on the sidewalk, seeking help.

"Look at this man," the policeman commands, indicating the hand-cuffed customer. "What do you know about him?"

This is a safer topic. "He bought me out for the night," she says, eager to please. She glances at the handcuffed man, who is regarding the crowd uneasily. "He lives at the Tower." She lapses, her fund of knowledge exhausted.

"Look at him," the policeman says. "You're lucky to be alive."

"Oh, no," Toy says. "Mama-san told me I should always leave my shoes by the door so—"

"He hurts girls like you." The tall man stops trying to worry his wrist out of the cuff and begins to listen. "Last month he bought out a massage girl, almost as young as you. He took her to an apartment in Thonburi, and he used a razor to cut her face. From here," he says, letting go of her arm and placing a finger below her right eye and drawing it straight down to her chin, "down to here. You could see her teeth through her cheek."

Toy has forgotten the crowd; her eyes, on the policeman, fill half her face. "*This* man?"

"And then he cut her throat." His throat-slashing gesture, operatic in scale, draws appreciative gasps from the crowd. "He would have killed her, but she jumped though the window. She's not pretty any-more, but she's alive. You're a lucky girl." He lifts her chin with his fingertips and studies her face. "Now, get out of here. Go home. And I mean all the way home. If I ever see you in Patpong again, I'll make sure you're in the monkey house until you're a twenty-year-old farm girl with feet like shoe boxes."

The girl takes a step back.

The tall man handcuffed to the sign clears his throat. "Fifty thou-sand baht," he says.

"Wait," the policeman says. He reaches out and takes Toy's wrist again. Then he turns to the crowd. "Go, go. There's nothing to see here. You have things to do." The group backs up a few steps, and he advances on them, pulling the girl in his wake, and they retreat several paces more. When the policeman is sure he cannot be heard, he says to the American, "For what?"

"For letting me go," the customer says. His eyes travel to Toy. "And for letting me keep her."

The policeman knots Toy's T-shirt in his fist and forces her several steps in the tall man's direction. "You are insulting me," he says.

"You have me confused with someone else," the tall man says. "It's not surprising. Many men look like me. The salary of a policeman is small, and the hours are long. You're probably very tired. It was my fault that I have embarrassed you by taking this girl when you were on duty."

"You apologize," says the policeman thoughtfully. "And yet you offer so little."

The tall man doesn't even blink. "One hundred thousand baht," he says.

"No," says Toy, straining against the hand that holds her shirt. "Please."

"One hundred thousand baht," the policeman repeats. He shakes the girl like a puppy. "Stop it."

"Now," says the customer with some urgency. "In cash."

"Suppose you hurt her," the policeman says conversationally. He winds Toy's T-shirt tightly around his fist. "Suppose you hurt her and she reports it. It could interrupt the upward movement of my career. You understand, of course, that I could never seriously entertain a request such as this one."

"Hundred twenty," the tall man says.

"There is still the problem of the girl," the policeman says. "Not that I care personally what happens to her. You would have to guarantee she would not complain."

The American looks at Toy. "I do."

The policeman turns his head to regard the watching crowd. "How will you get her out of here?"

"You help me walk her to the corner. Handcuff her if you have to. I have a car waiting there."

"But, but . . ." Toy says.

The policeman swats her on the head. "Let me see the money."

Toy begins to scream. As people in the street stare, she twists against the hand grasping her shirt, striking out with both fists, hammering at the policeman's wrist and forearm, and then the nails come out and she rakes his skin. He grabs at her with the other hand, and she raises one of her heavy, steel-tipped cowboy boots and kicks his shin with all the force she possesses, so hard she staggers back after the kick lands.

The policeman releases her and grabs his shin in both hands, hopping up and down and swearing a blue streak in both English and Thai, and Toy leaps backward, bolts into the crowd, and disappears from view. A ripple in the movement of the heads, visible down the bright street, tracks her path. Some of the people who are watching from a safe distance applaud approvingly.

The policeman ignores them, focusing instead on the man handcuffed to the pole.

"Spiders as big as dogs," says the tall man.

The policeman straightens. "Are you giving me a problem?"

"Feet like shoe boxes." The handcuffed man makes a sound that could be mistaken for a snort. "The girls will *bother* you."

"Everybody's a critic," the policeman says, bending to rub his shin again. "Goddamn Bangkok cowboy boots. Steel tips. They should be outlawed. I'm going to have a lump the size of an egg." He gives the tall man a severe glance. "I've got half a mind to leave you here. Nobody told me I was going to get kicked."

"Yeah, and nobody told me I was going to be Jack the Ripper. 'Her teeth through her cheek.' Jesus."

"She's scared, right? Wasn't that the point? Isn't that what I was supposed to do?"

"Well, I think you succeeded," says the tall man, rattling the cuff against the signpost. He yanks at it a couple of times. "Arthit," he says, "tell me you haven't lost the key to these things."

2

All the Devils Are Here

Miaow looks up from her plate. "Hell is empty," she says in English, "and all the devils are here."

"Hello to you, too," Rafferty says. He looks at the half-eaten dinner spread across the table. "Thanks for waiting."

"We were going to," Rose says in Thai. She puts down her ever-present cup of Nescafé and adds in careful English, "But we are hungry." She's been studying English six hours a week, trying to leave bar-girl Thaiglish behind, but the past tense is a problem, since the Thai language lacks it. Then she says to Miaow, in Thai, "What was that you said?"

"It's from the play," Miaow says. "The first act. I get to say it."

Rose says, "What are 'devils'?"

Over the noise of the restaurant, Miaow launches into an energetic explanation in Thai that involves one of the more baroque Buddhist visions of hell, and Rafferty squeezes past his adopted daughter's chair to get into the banquette so he can reach under the table and put a proprietary hand on Rose's leg. She pats his hand and then laces her fingers through his, listening to Miaow, who finally has to pause for breath.

"Not a nice thing to say about Poke," Rose says.

"Oh, I don't know," Rafferty says. "Compared to some of the things Arthit just said about me, it's a birthday card."

"He didn't come back with you?" Rose asks. She glances around the restaurant, an American steakhouse on Silom, as though she's worried she might have missed him. The mention of Arthit puts her into anxiety mode, as it has for the past eight months, since his wife, Noi, died.

"He wanted to go home," Rafferty says. "I tried to talk him into joining us, but . . . well, you know. He's going to get through this alone. If it kills him."

Miaow says, "*Guys*," in a world-weary tone that almost makes Rafferty sit up straighter.

Rose apparently doesn't see anything precocious in the remark. "I wish I knew someone I could introduce him to," she says. "My girls wouldn't work." Rose's "girls" are former dancers from the Patpong bars who have left the life to work with the agency Rose co-owns, which finds them jobs as housekeepers. And Rose is right, Rafferty thinks; they'd be disastrous matches for Arthit.

"Speaking of your girls," he says, "you can tell your friend Fon that Toy is probably still running. Arthit scared her silly."

"Serves her right." Rose pushes a full water glass toward Miaow and makes a "drink up" gesture. Miaow rolls her eyes but picks up the glass. In keeping with some health advisory she read somewhere, Rose has the two of them drinking more water than they want, although she herself continues to subsist on the instant coffee Rafferty loathes with such intensity. "The little idiot," she continues. "I've never seen Fon so angry. Here she is, slaving in other people's houses all day, *not* working the bars but still sending money home every month, and her stupid little sister decides to come to the big city and give it a try. Probably thought it was all cell phones and fancy clothes, gold jewelry, going out to dinner with foreign gentlemen. When what it really is, is dancing around dressed in almost nothing and letting fat men grunt on top of you a couple of times every night."

Miaow darts a look at Rose and then looks away.

"Toy didn't seem happy," Rafferty says.

"I'm sure she didn't," Rose says. "And to make things worse, she decided to work in an upstairs bar."

"Why does that matter?" Miaow asks. "What happens in upstairs bars?"

Rafferty says, "Nothing that you need to—"

Rose says, "Upstairs the girls dance naked."

Miaow says, "Oh." For at least the third time since Rafferty sat down, she runs her hand through her hair, which is now chopped to within four inches of her scalp and bleached a sort of margarine yellow with a slight orange cast at the roots, the stubborn remnant of the midnight black that's her natural color. The haircut cost all of Miaow's allowance for five weeks and looks like it was done with a broken glass. She came home with it ten days ago and announced that it was for the play, her school's production of Shakespeare's *The Tempest*, in which she's been cast as the spirit Ariel. Ever since the time, four years earlier, that Rafferty had first seen her selling chewing gum on a Patpong sidewalk, she'd worn her hair severely parted in the center and pasted down, a hairstyle he'd come to think of as unchangeable, quintessentially Miaow. And now she looks, he privately thinks, like a very short Sid Vicious. He's still startled every time he sees her. She gives her new hair a tug and says to Rose, "Why would they want to dance naked?"

Rose says, "Money. They get paid a little more."

Miaow absorbs it for a moment. "You never did that." It's not a question, but it is.

"I didn't have to," Rose says. "I was beautiful."

"You still are," Rafferty says.

Rose leans in his direction and says, "What did you say?"

"I said—"

"Oh, I heard you." She shakes her head. "I'm ashamed for wanting to hear it again. Poor, dumb little Toy."

"She believed every word Arthit said. She'll probably run all the way to the train station."

"Just like my sister, Lek, when you and Arthit chased her away," Rose says.

Rafferty says, "We're thinking of opening a business."

"I was that innocent," Rose says. Her eyes roam the restaurant, as though she's surprised to find herself there. "When I first came down to Bangkok, I believed everything. I had no idea how things worked. If it hadn't been for Fon, I don't know what would have happened to me. I was frightened, I was sad, I was stupid. I did everything anyone told me to do. A girl would take me over to a customer—a customer who'd *asked* for me—and then she'd tell me I owed her ten percent for introducing me. Girls borrowed money they never paid back. One of them stole my shoes, and I had to go out barefoot and buy some flip-flops on the sidewalk. I stepped on a burning cigarette butt."

Miaow says, "I did that, too, once."

"And you were just a kid," Rafferty says. "Both of you."

"I was seventeen," Rose says. "And that's *village* seventeen, about as sophisticated as a Bangkok ten-year-old. I remember the first time I went shopping with my own money. I'd never owned anything except T-shirts and shorts, and those were secondhand. And here I was, in Bangkok, on my own, with money in my pockets, more money than I'd ever had in my life. And there were stores *everywhere*. I bought toys, stuffed animals, little plastic pins that lit up. A Santa hat, a ring with a big red plastic jewel in it that I thought looked like a ruby, and a bracelet made of little plastic fruit. The most terrible things—blouses with big buttons and hearts all over them, teddy-bear hair ornaments, brand-new, stiff, dark blue jeans that were loose and too short to be stylish. I was so proud of them. I got all dressed up to go to the bar that night, and the girls just laughed. Everybody except Fon. Well, she laughed a little, but not the same way. She's the one who taught me that you were supposed to spend ten times as much money for a pair of jeans that look like a whole village wore them for a year and that are so long you're walking on the cuffs. That you have to wear real rubies if you're a Bangkok girl. I was a hick. I didn't fit in at all. And some of the girls just hated me because I stood out."

"You certainly stood out when I came in," Rafferty says. Out of the corner of his eye, he sees Miaow fidget. For the past eight or nine months, Rose's past, which she'd previously taken for granted as part of the family landscape, has become an object of both interest and a certain amount of embarrassment. In the relatively exclusive private international school Miaow now attends, a former street child whose adopted mother was a prostitute is conspicuous in all the wrong ways. Eight months ago she'd had Rose lighten her hair to a dark red, and she'd bought skin-lightening cream. Next was her name. She's already told them that the play's program will inform the audience that Ariel is played by Mia Rafferty.

Rafferty has to face the fact that his daughter is turning into a petit bourgeois. Surrounded every day at school by kids from middle-class and upper-middle-class families from all over the world, Miaow has been looking for the magic that would transform her into one of them. And she seems to hope that the play will help her make the transition.

"Sir?"

Rafferty looks up to see a waiter, maybe eighteen years old, with a carefully trained flop of reddish hair over his forehead, fine high cheekbones, and a waist narrower than Scarlett O'Hara's. His eyes go to Miaow's hair, widen for a split second, and then bounce back to Rafferty.

"Do you need a menu?"

"No," Rafferty says. "Miaow, what did you have?" Miaow is more a red-meat expert than Rose, who thinks all beef should be cooked gray the whole way through, and then cooked again. And served to someone else.

"The rib eye," Miaow says, pushing the remains toward him for inspection, although there's not much left. "It was good."

"The same," Rafferty says to the waiter. "Medium rare. With some french fries. Cook the french fries until they scream."

The waiter says, "Sorry?"

"I want them very crisp. Burned, even. And a Singha."

"Rib eye medium rare and a Singha, and french fries that scream," the waiter says. His English is much better than Rafferty expected it to be, yet another sign of the ways in which Bangkok is changing. When he first got here, most people's English was rudimentary at best. "Do you want them to scream in French?"

"If you can arrange it, I'd like them to scream '*Sacre bleu.*'"

"Of course, sir. Singha, coming up." He leaves.

Watching him go, Miaow says, "He's cute."

"He's an old man," Rafferty says.

"He liked your hair," Rose says. For the first couple of days, she'd looked at Miaow's blond chop with horror, but lately her gaze has grown speculative.

Rafferty says, "Don't even think about it."

Rose puts both hands at the nape of her neck and lifts the long, heavy fall of hair, then lets it drop again. "Do you have any idea how long all this takes to dry?"

"To the second. I've spent some of my happiest hours waiting for it to dry."

"Look at Miaow," Rose says. "She washes it, dries it with a towel, and then messes it up with her fingers. How long, Miaow?"

"Three or four minutes," Miaow says. "But then I have to keep messing it up all day."

"Of course," Rose says, as though it were the most obvious thing in the world.

"It has to be messed up *right,*" Miaow says.

Rafferty says, with some nostalgia, "It's amazing how your part's disappeared."

"It hasn't," Miaow says. "That's why I have to keep messing it up. Andy says it's—"

Whatever Andy said it was, Miaow decides not to share it. She clamps her mouth closed and starts pushing around the remnant of her steak.

"Who's Andy?" Rafferty says, exchanging a glance with Rose.

"This guy," Miaow says. Nobody says anything, so she adds, "He's in the play."

"When the play's over—" Rafferty begins.

"No." Miaow ruffles her hair. "I won't keep it blond, but I'm not going to start parting it again. I looked like a baby." As long as she's ruffling it, she grabs a tuft and tugs, as though she's hoping to get another half inch of growth. "What do you think about it for the play?"

"I think it's great," Rafferty says truthfully. "For the play."

"Since Ariel's sort of a he," Miaow says.

"I guess so," Rafferty says. As the only professional writer among the school's parent population, he'd been asked by Mrs. Shin, the Korean drama teacher who's directing the play, to cut it down to seventy minutes or so, mainly to get the roles to a length the kids could memorize. As a result he's spent several months immersed in *The Tempest.* "But Ariel's a spirit, not a person," he says, "so I think it's right for the character to be, you know, not really a girl or a boy. The costume and the hair—I think they're going to be great."

"Caliban, though," Miaow says, "Caliban has to be a boy, right? Even though he's kind of magic, too. Because he tried to mess around with Miranda, and Prospero is pissed—I mean, angry—at him."

"*Miaow,*" Rose snaps.

"Sorry," Miaow says. "The kids all talk English, and they say that all the time."

"Well, *you* don't."

Miaow changes the subject, asking Rafferty, "What's an anagram?"

"It's a word that has the same letters as another word but in a different order. Like 'eat' and 'ate.' Or 'life' and 'file.'" Rafferty watches

Miaow visualize the words in her head and move the letters around. "Or 'vile' and 'live' and 'evil.' Is this about Caliban?"

"Yes. Mrs. Shin says it's an anagram for . . . for—"

" 'Cannibal,' " Rafferty says. "It isn't exactly, not the way we spell it now. But the Elizabethans were kind of adventurous about spelling."

"But if he meant 'cannibal,' it means he didn't like Caliban, right?" Miaow says.

"When Shakespeare wrote the play, new kinds of people were being discovered all the time," Rafferty says. "There were all sorts of ideas about them. Some Europeans didn't think the savages, as they called them, were human. The English were snobs, and as you know, a snob is someone who dislikes anyone who's not like him." He's trying clumsily to make a point about Miaow's school, but it sails past her. "Mrs. Shin is interpreting the play so it's about colonialism. Remember, we talked about interpretation, how people at different times find different meanings in Shakespeare's work. From a modern point of view—one point of view anyway—Caliban is the original inhabitant of the island, and whether he's evil or not—"

Rose drops her fork with a clatter on top of her cup, which tips over and spreads coffee across the tablecloth.

A man's deep voice says, "Well, well. *Rosie.*"

Rafferty looks up to see a tall, very solid-looking white man looming over their table. He's at least six-two, mannequin handsome, broad-shouldered and narrow-hipped, with a jawline so square it looks like a caricature. His pale hair is perhaps half an inch long and has been allowed to grow in front of his ears in squared-off sideburns. It looks like a helmet.

From behind the man, another man, almost as big, says, "This the one that got away?"

Rose hasn't said anything. Rafferty looks over at her and sees astonishment and, behind it, like an electric current, a buzz of fear.

"I suppose this belongs to you," the man says, his eyes flicking to Rafferty and then away again. "The little hubby, maybe? The kid can't be yours, though, can she? I mean, you'd have had stretch marks, and I remember real good you didn't have stretch marks."

Rafferty starts to get up, but the man pushes the table back against him, trapping him partway up, without even glancing at him.

The man says to Rose, "I think you met John." He turns his head a quarter of an inch toward the other man. "Oh, that's right, you didn't. But you talked to him on the phone, remember? Out on the rocks." Finally looking at Rafferty, he says, "Stay down, Hubby,"

Rafferty shoves the table back and pushes himself the rest of the way up. He says, "I always stand when a lady comes to the table."

The man grins and extends a hand as though to shake. "Howard Horner," he says, and there's a blur of movement and a glint of silver, and Rose stabs Horner in the hand. She holds her steak knife close to her chest, ready to use it again.

For Rafferty, time shudders to a stop. He sees Rose, motionless, the knife pointed outward, sees the blood flowing very slowly down Horner's hand, sees Miaow, her mouth half open and both hands on the edge of the table as though she's about to bolt and run.

"Rosie," Horner says, without even pulling his hand back. It's dripping blood onto the tablecloth, but he doesn't give it so much as a glance. The other man has taken a couple of steps forward and then stopped. "This is how you say hi?" Horner asks.

A noise draws his eyes. Miaow is holding her steak knife, too, the serrated cutting edge facing Horner.

"The kid knows more about knives than you do," Horner says. "Slash, don't stab." His uninjured hand streaks out, so fast Rafferty barely sees it move, and Rose gasps and snatches her own hand back, but when the blur is over, Horner is holding Rose's knife. He leans forward, and Miaow's knife comes up. "Remember that," he says to Rose. "From an expert, remember?" He puts the knife back on the table, handle politely extended toward Rose. She makes no move to pick it up.

"I think the ladies would like you to leave," Rafferty says.

"*Ladies,*" Horner says over his shoulder to the one called John. Then he brings his pale gaze back to Rafferty and holds Rafferty's eyes for a full minute without blinking, his expression absolutely flat.

Rafferty says, "I'll bet you giggle before I do."

Horner holds up the bleeding hand, his fingers spread out, the blood running down his wrist. "Pick a finger," he says to Rafferty. "I'll kill you with it."

Suddenly strangled with rage, Rafferty shoves the table back and starts to force his way around it as Horner, looking pleased and sleepy, takes a step back to let Rafferty come at him, but Rose, in a single sweeping gesture, pulls the tablecloth off, and plates, glasses, and silverware crash to the floor.

The restaurant goes silent. Everyone in the place is looking at them. Horner glances around the room, sees the attentive audience, and nods appreciatively at Rose. He bends down, picks up a folded napkin from the floor, and wraps it around the bleeding hand. "We in your neighborhood?" he asks, backing away. "Great, great. See you again sometime. Got a lot to catch up on. We never finished our last conversation."

The restaurant manager and some of the waiters and busboys are on their way over. Horner says, "Bye, Hubby." He looks at Miaow and makes a pistol with his unwrapped hand, points it at her, and drops the thumb that represents the hammer. "Keep your eyes open, cutie." The two men turn and walk toward the front door, Horner in the lead. Watching them go, watching their carriage and the roll of their shoulders, Rafferty thinks, *Military.*

Miaow is staring after them, wide-eyed, and Rose is apologizing to the manager, but all Rafferty can manage to say is, "Who the fuck was *that*?"

Rose says, "Someone I thought I'd killed."

3

The Black Lake

They sit for twenty minutes at the barren, grease-stained table, enduring the stares of the other diners. Rafferty and Miaow have been forced into silence by the intensity of Rose's anger. She's rigid with it. She sits with her back absolutely straight, both hands flat on the table with the fingers spread, the right hand resting on the handle of the knife, her breathing fast and shallow. She doesn't look at either of them. Her eyes are focused on something invisible that's one foot in front of her.

When some internal clock tells her it's time, she waves the waiter over and sends him out to secure them a taxi and then insists that three of the restaurant's male employees follow them onto the sidewalk and surround them as they get into the cab. Once in, she orders the driver to lock the doors, including his own, before she allows him to pull away from the curb. The car feels pressurized to Rafferty, as though the emotion trapped inside it might blow out the windows. When they've gone four or five blocks, Rose orders the driver to pull over fast without signaling, hands him fifty baht, and hurries them all out of the cab. To Rafferty's amazement, she grabs Miaow's hand and drags her into traffic. Rafferty trails helplessly behind his wife and child as they thread their way between speeding cars and trucks and motorbikes and *tuk-*

tuks to the center island, where they clamber over the knee-high barrier that divides the opposing streams of traffic on Silom. Then they dodge suicidally between vehicles, setting off horns all the way, to the far curb, where Rose flags a second cab. All the while she is looking back to see whether anyone is making a U-turn at the divider break. When she's satisfied that no one did, she tells the new driver to make the first turn that's a through street.

"You look behind us," she says to Rafferty.

"Who *was* he?" Miaow asks, her voice well into its upper register. She sounds eight again. "You thought you *killed* him?"

"I hoped I had," Rose says. "Anyone back there, Poke?"

"As far as I can tell, no," Rafferty says. "But, you know, headlights are headlights."

"They would have had to cross Silom if they were on foot." Rose says in Thai. Her voice is almost mechanically flat, the words precise and uninflected. "Or make a U-turn if they were in a car. I didn't see anybody cross the street, and I know nobody made a U-turn."

"Well, then," Rafferty says.

The driver says, "Somebody following you?"

Rose, in the front seat, says, "Let's say yes."

"No problem," says the driver. He punches the accelerator, and their backs bump against the seats. After a couple of blocks, he makes a sudden left onto a narrow street where only a pair of run-down restaurants, so chalky with fluorescent light they might be a chain of competing morgues, show any sign of occupancy. No lights follow them. The next right takes them onto an even narrower street, a vista of dark windows and padlocked gates except for a gaggle of hostess bars that signal their presence with pink neon and bored-looking clusters of evening-gowned girls, all curled hair and bare arms, sitting on plastic chairs. The cab turns right again and then makes another left immediately, this time onto a street parallel to Silom that runs behind a row of apartment houses, set above cavernous, sunken concrete garages. The driver peels, tires squealing, down a sloping driveway into one of the garages, takes a spiral ramp up one level, and then exits the garage on the front side of the building, which puts them on Silom again, a good mile or so from the restaurant.

"Nobody back there now," he announces. "Where do you want to go?"

"Soi Pipat," Rose says. Then she says, without turning to face Rafferty and Miaow, "Don't ask me any questions, because I won't answer them. I'll talk when I'm ready."

Rafferty says, "Sure, sure. I had a wonderful time."

Miaow says, "You cut him."

"I said no questions."

"That wasn't a question," Miaow says.

This time Rose's head snaps around. "Then what do you want, Miaow?" she demands. "Do you want me to agree with you? Fine, I agree with you. I cut him. Is there anything else on your mind?"

Miaow says, in English, "Jeez."

"That goes for me, too," Rafferty says.

"Both of you," Rose says. "*Stop.* If you don't stop, I'll get out of this car and you'll see me whenever you see me."

The driver says, "Want me to pull over?"

There is a long pause, and then Rose says, "I guess not."

They make the rest of the trip in a chilly silence. At the apartment house, Rose orders the driver to take them down into the underground garage and all the way to the elevator so they're not exposed on the street. After Rafferty pays the man, he turns and sees their eighth-floor neighbor, Mrs. Pongsiri, gowned and made up for the night, coming out of the elevator, on her way to the bar she runs. She smiles at Rafferty, but it's a puzzled smile, and he looks beyond her to see Rose holding the elevator door open for him. Miaow is pressed against the elevator's back wall as though she wishes she could push herself through it. Clutched in Rose's right hand is a steak knife.

THEY MOVE SILENTLY through the apartment, turning on lights in every room: three people, Rafferty thinks, who look like they barely know each other. The air in the living room feels as thick as syrup. Miaow stalks into the kitchen and takes a Coke out of the refrigerator, pops it open defiantly in front of Rose, who would normally tell her to drink water instead, and heads for her bedroom, chin up and back stiff. The door closes behind her, not particularly gently.

Rose stands at the opening to the hallway, her eyes on the point where it ends at Miaow's door. The knife dangles heavily in her hand, elongating the smooth muscles in her forearm. Rafferty wants to touch her, but she seems to be at the center of a sizzle of negative energy. If the lights went out, he wouldn't be surprised to see sparks chasing each other over her skin.

"Sooner or later," he says.

Rose says, "Later." He can barely hear her. She shakes her head slowly, as though it weighs a great deal and it hurts her neck to turn it, and then she goes to the couch and sits heavily, leaning forward like someone who's going to put her head between her knees until a spell of faintness passes. Instead she straightens and tosses the heavy steak knife onto the glass coffee table, which has the good sense not to break. She studies the knife for a long moment, looking like she can't remember how it got there. When she shakes her head again, it's a decisive side-to-side snap, bringing herself into the present, and she widens her eyes, blows out a big breath, and opens her big leather bag. She paws through the clutter until she comes up with a pack of Marlboro Lights.

Rafferty goes automatically to the sliding glass door that leads to the balcony and opens it. They've been on what he thinks of as a very limited health program: Rose has been trying to get them to drink their weight in water, and he's been trying to rid the apartment's atmosphere of some of its secondhand smoke. Standing in the flow of humid air from outside, he turns back to her and says, "I need to know whether we're in danger. For Miaow's sake, especially."

"Yes," Rose says. She strikes a match, takes an enormous drag, and holds on to it, then blows it out all at once. "Yes, if he finds us, we're in danger."

"What you're not telling me," Rafferty says. "What I'm not supposed to ask you about. If I know it, will it help me keep us safer?"

"No. You just need to know that he'll kill me if he gets a chance. And he might try to get me through you and Miaow. But he can't fly or lift automobiles or walk through walls. He can't read minds. He's a guy. He's a very dangerous guy, but he's just a guy."

Rafferty hears a kind of compressed control in her voice that he's never heard before. She's fighting to keep it steady. "How good is he at finding people?"

"Good enough that I ran all the way to Isaan, and not to my own village either."

Rafferty files that for later and says, "Does he know where your village is?"

"Yes. I told him everything, back then."

Back when? Rafferty thinks, but he knows the answer. "He's military."

"He's worse than military. He's crazy."

"Always a good combination." He turns again to look out across the city, glittering with the fraudulent optimism of big cities everywhere.

"Poke?" Rose says. He looks back to see her studying the tip of her cigarette. He waits, despite the fact that she seems disinclined to say anything else. He notices she doesn't have an ashtray and gets the one that's on the counter that separates the kitchen from the living room. He takes it to her and puts it beside the knife, then picks up the knife and carries it over to the counter and puts it where the ashtray was. He's moving, he knows, just to be doing something, just to compensate for the words that aren't being said, and he's about thirty seconds away from rearranging furniture, so he goes back over to the table, pulls the white hassock close to the couch, and sits on it.

"You have to believe me," Rose says. She is not looking at him, not even near him. She is looking at her knees. "I never, ever thought this would happen. I was absolutely sure it was over. I was sure he was dead. If he wasn't dead, I knew he'd come back. And I *waited* for him to come back, for more than four years. Every time I got onto that stage at the King's Castle, I thought I'd see him. Every time I turned a corner on the street, every time I went through a door at night, every time an elevator opened. Every time I went into my own room alone. Every time I saw a crowd of faces, I thought he'd be there. And he never was." She checks the length of the cigarette in her hand and takes another drag, squinting against the thread of smoke.

"I used to dream that I'd flag down a taxi and get in back, and when the driver turned around, it would be him. I dreamed of a dark village where he was behind every house. He stepped out of mirrors, he bled through walls. He came up at me out of black water. Especially the water. He was always rising toward me through dark water."

"He, him, him, him," Rafferty says. "He's got a name. Howard Horner. Why don't you use it?"

She shakes her head. "I didn't even let myself think it. For years it was just 'him.' He was less real when I didn't think his name." She hears herself and almost smiles. "Like thinking or saying his name would bring him. Village-girl magic."

Rafferty just waits.

"It took me a long time to let myself get close to you. When you came into the bar, when you started talking to me, I was still waiting. I'd already waited for years, and then, when I knew I wanted to be with you, I waited a few months more. And he still didn't come. So, because I wanted to be with you, I made myself believe he was dead. If I hadn't been able to do that, if I'd thought there was any chance he was alive, I never would have gotten involved with you."

Miaow says from the hallway, "This is because of your old job, isn't it?"

"That's right," Rose says, and sighs heavily. "It's because I was dancing at the King's Castle."

"Not just dancing," Miaow says.

"No, Miaow," Rose says. She stubs out the cigarette. "Not just dancing. Thank you for reminding me of that."

"I thought you went to bed," Rafferty says.

"You were wrong," Miaow says. "I went to my bedroom to drink a Coke and think about getting killed. And I came back out."

"Well, you might as well come all the way in," Rose says. "I'm not going to throw anything at you."

Miaow trudges in but doesn't get close to them. Instead she hugs the wall as she crosses the room, pulls out one of the stools at the kitchen counter, and sits. She puts the can of Coke down with a sharp sound.

Rose says, "I'm not contagious, Miaow."

"Everything was all right," Miaow says. She sounds like she does when she's working on her lines for the play, as though she's practiced what she wants to say, and she swivels the stool back and forth, not looking at either of them, just getting through it. "We were all happy. You had your business, Poke was making money from his book. My school was okay, there was the play."

"There still is," Rafferty says.

"And now there's this," Miaow says, finishing her speech as if no one had spoken. "Just when I think we can finally live like everybody else, without being *different* all the time. Without anybody chasing us. Without being frightened."

"You don't have to be frightened," Rafferty says.

She gives him the look of pure, concentrated scorn that the lie deserves. "I saw that guy. And there wasn't just one of them. There were two. Maybe there are a lot more."

"There aren't," Rose says.

"You can't know that," Miaow says, and now she's glaring at Rose. "I heard you talking to Poke. This happened when you were . . . *dancing* or whatever you call it. And you worked in the bar *four years* after the last time you saw him. You've been with Poke for five years now. How do you know he hasn't got a hundred friends by now? How do you know anything?"

Rose leans back on the couch and looks regretfully at the smashed cigarette butt. Miaow's gaze drops to a spot on the carpet about halfway across the room, but her mouth remains a tight line. Rafferty fights the urge to take hold of the conversation, try to turn it away from the black lake that seems to have opened up between them. All his instincts, developed by years of listening as his mother and father sharpened their razors on each other, push him toward trying to find a safe common ground, somewhere they can smile at each other and pretend that nothing happened tonight.

But he can't do it.

"Miaow," he finally says. "Nobody is happy about this. But either you can be polite to your mother or you can go back to your room."

Miaow says, "Fine." She grabs the Coke, downs what's left in a single long series of gulps, and then tosses the empty can over the counter and onto the kitchen floor with a clatter that makes Rose straighten galvanically. Miaow pushes herself off the stool and leaves the room without a glance at either of them.

Rose is very focused on getting another cigarette. Although Rafferty hasn't moved, she says, "Let her go."

He gets up in the silence and goes into the kitchen. Miaow had crumpled the can in her hand. He picks it up and puts it, very quietly, into the plastic recycling bag. A thought knocks on his head, goes away, and comes back, so he gives it voice. "Do you want something to drink?"

From the living room, Rose says, "Whiskey. A big one."

"I'll join you," he says, although he never drinks whiskey and Rose rarely takes anything stronger than a few sips of beer. At the back of one of the shelves above the counter, he locates a bottle of Crown Royal, a gift from somebody, still unopened in its blue velveteen bag. He's been moving it to look behind it for more than a year. Now he takes it down, tussles thick-fingered with the bag's tightly knotted drawstring, slips the bottle out, and opens it. Two eight-ounce water glasses, soldiers in

Rose's hydrating campaign, are drying upside down in the drainer. He fills each of them about one-third full. As he picks them up, tucking the bottle beneath his arm, he realizes that one reason he doesn't drink whiskey is that he hates the smell.

He comes back into the living room to find Rose firing up the new Marlboro. Two in ten minutes is heavy, even for her, but this doesn't seem like the time for Mr. Healthy Habits to make an appearance, so he just puts down the glasses and the bottle and sits beside her. She looks at the glass, and her brow furrows doubtfully for a moment, but then she picks it up.

Rafferty extends his own, feeling like a character in a 1940s film. They clink rims, and Rose tosses back almost an inch's worth. She lowers the glass to her lap and sits back, blinking as her eyes water. "Oh," she says, mostly breath. "Oh, that's awful."

"Here goes." Rafferty gulps some down. The two of them sit there, squinting at each other in shared misery.

"Together this time," Rose says, and there's a glint of grim humor in her eyes. "On the count of three. One. Two. *Now.*" The glasses come up, the heads go back, and then the glasses come down again and the two of them stare across the living room with the kind of expression they might wear if the floor had disappeared. Rose opens her mouth wide and breathes out to clear the fumes, then says, "Why do people *do* this?"

"Well," Rafferty says, "why are *we* doing it?"

"Right," Rose says, and drinks again. Rafferty joins her.

"Or"—Rose makes a face—"maybe it's not worth it." She puts the glass on the table.

Rafferty says, "Actually, I'm getting the hang of it." He takes another slug.

"He couldn't have followed us here," Rose says. She lets the sentence hang in the air for a moment and then reaches forward and picks up the glass. She sips it this time, but she takes three sips. She pats at her sternum until she can talk, then says, "For now, we're safe."

"If he wanted to find us, how would he do it?"

"He'd start at Patpong," she says. He'd go into every bar on the street. He has—or anyway he had—pictures of me. He'd show them to people and ask if they know where I am now."

They both drink to the idea, and Rafferty says, "He'd find someone who knows you in ten minutes."

"Especially because of the employment agency," Rose says. "Lots of girls know about Peachy and me. They think about us as someone they can come to if they ever decide to quit."

"But they'd know where the office is, not the apartment." He leans over and picks up the bottle, pours some for Rose, and then drinks directly from the bottle's mouth, feeling a fine line of fire burn its way through the center of his chest.

"Most of them don't even know the office," Rose says. She takes the bottle out of his hand and pours a couple of fingers' worth into his glass. "They've got a telephone number written somewhere. Half the time they won't even have that—they probably wrote it on the palm of their hand and then washed their hands before they copied it onto anything."

"Okay, but let's say he gets the number," Rafferty says.

"Because he will," Rose says.

"He dials it. Either he gets Peachy in person and he asks her for the address, which she gives him, or he gets the answering machine, which tells him he's called your agency. Then he goes to a phone book, and he's got the address. Either way he knows where the office is."

"Then he waits there," Rose says, and they both drink.

"So you don't go," Rafferty says.

"But Peachy would. And Peachy's been here."

"Peachy wouldn't tell—"

"Peachy would tell him anything he wanted to know." She raises the glass and lowers it again, the whiskey untasted. "You don't know him, Poke. He'd make her tell. He can make anyone tell him anything."

There's a sniffle in the hallway, and Miaow says, out of sight, "He'd hurt Peachy?"

"You might as well know, Miaow," Rose says. "He'd hurt anybody."

Miaow sticks her head around the corner and looks at them. The teary look gives way to the aspect of her personality Rafferty calls the Disapproving Executive. She says, "You're drinking that stuff?"

"It's an anesthetic," Rafferty says. "It makes us braver."

"Then I want some," Miaow says, coming the rest of the way into the room. "And don't tell me I'm a kid. I'm more scared than you are."

Rafferty can't think of a good enough reason to say no, so he gets up and goes into the kitchen to get Miaow's special glass, which has a color picture of the South Korean pop star Rain printed on it, his shirt strategically open to display the best set of abs on earth. The image bothers Rafferty, but not enough to make an issue out of it. When he comes back into the living room, Miaow is sitting on the couch, leaning against Rose with her eyes closed, and Rose is smoothing her choppy hair. Rafferty guesses he missed the apology.

Miaow opens her eyes as he sits. He holds up the glass and says, "Are you sure?"

Miaow says, "Why not?"

Rose gives Rafferty a disapproving glance. "You'll learn the answer to that question in a minute."

Rafferty pours a splash into Miaow's glass.

Miaow says, "Up to his belly button."

"Taste it first," Rafferty says, and hands it to her. He and Rose pick up their own glasses, and the three of them, in response to some psychically shared impulse, hoist and drink at the same time.

Miaow says, "*Eeeeeewwwwww.*" Her face is so twisted it looks like it's being wrung out.

"It doesn't get better," Rose says.

Miaow lifts the glass again and sniffs, then quickly puts it down. She scrapes her tongue against her top teeth, trying to get rid of the taste. Then she says, "I'm still scared."

"He's not going to find this place tonight," Rafferty says. "And tomorrow we'll start making it harder for him to find it at all. But tonight we're okay. We'll wake up early tomorrow and get to work."

"And I'll tell you about it then," Rose says. "In daylight."

"Anybody want more?" Rafferty has picked up the bottle. When no one answers, he grabs his glass in his other hand and goes into the kitchen. He turns from the sink to see Miaow standing behind him, holding the other two glasses. He takes them from her and puts them into the sink, and she wraps her arms around his waist and presses the side of her head against his side. He looks down at the raggedy-yellow crop of hair. Sure enough, he can see her part.

"We're okay," he says. "Go to bed, and everything will be fine."

Miaow says, "I want to sleep with you and Rose."

"Fine," Rafferty says, hoping she can't hear his heartbeat double in fury. "We've got lots of room. But don't worry. He won't find us."

IT'S A SHARP smell, one he knows he should recognize, but he's functionally impaired until the coffee electrifies his nervous system, and he's still muzzy from the evening's whiskey. The flat, dead reek of Rose's cigarettes takes the edge off the smell and makes it an irritant, like a word he's used a million times and suddenly can't remember. So he stands in the kitchen, his bare shoulder against the cool refrigerator door, and watches the coffee drip.

He's halfway through the first cup when he thinks he knows what the smell is. At the same moment he hears a knocking at the front door.

He goes quickly into the bedroom and opens the sliding door in the headboard of the bed. He'd quietly unlocked the safe last night, while Rose was in the bathroom and Miaow was changing for bed, and the Glock is unwrapped and waiting for him. There's no school today, and Rose and Miaow are both asleep, Rose's arm thrown over the child's shoulders. He puts his coffee on the bedside table, transfers the gun to his left hand so it'll be out of sight behind the door, throws Rose's towel over his shoulders, and goes shirtless into the living room. He tries the peephole in the door, but it's blocked, so he racks a shell into the gun's chamber and opens the door a crack with his foot against it. The smell becomes a blunt-force object, almost overwhelming.

Mrs. Pongsiri stands there, wrapped in a silk kimono, holding a cup of what smells like hot cinnamon. She apparently slept in her bar makeup, and it's smeared on the side of her face that she'd sunk into the pillow. It makes Rafferty feel like he's looking at her through a rippled window.

"Mr. Rafferty," Mrs. Pongsiri says in English, "do you know about this?"

"About . . . ?"

"*This.*" Mrs. Pongsiri indicates the door with a scarlet-tipped hand in a vertical sweeping gesture, top to bottom, bottom to top.

Rafferty pulls the door toward him and freezes when it's about a third of the way open.

A thick X runs from corner to corner in a deep blood red. Taped over the peephole is a small, uneven square of cardboard, no more than half an inch to a side, clipped with scissors from something larger. Printed on it in dark gray is the claw of a bird of prey.

A raptor.

4

Wampire

e's having *fun*," Rose says, giving the word a bitter twist. "Terrifying people, threatening them. Playing with them. This is his idea of a joke."

It's a few minutes after 10:00 A.M., and the day is well into its long, slow sizzle. The living room is bright enough to make Rafferty, whiskey-sensitive, wish he were wearing dark glasses. Rose is curled on the couch, brown knees drawn up protectively, wearing a man's T-shirt, size quadruple-X, with a picture of Wile E. Coyote on it, above a pair of cutoff jeans. Circles are thumb-smudged beneath her eyes. Miaow, who's barely spoken all morning, sits perched on the edge of the chair at Rafferty's desk, decked out in one of her usual immaculate weekend outfits: pressed lemon-yellow jeans and a severely white T-shirt, unsullied by anything as vulgar as a design. Rafferty can't see himself, and he has no idea what he's wearing.

Sunday or not, Arthit is in uniform. For the past eight months, he's been putting in six- and sometimes seven-day weeks. His face looks crumpled. He's lost at least six kilos, and the lines on his forehead and around his eyes and mouth have deepened. He could probably slip four fingers inside the buttoned collar of his shirt.

For the first time since they met, Rafferty thinks, his friend looks old.

"Howard Horner," Arthit says. "And you think he's military."

Rafferty looks to Rose, but she says nothing, so he says, "Has to be."

"He never talked about it," Rose finally says. "He said he was in business, but he looked like a soldier."

Arthit says, "Do you actually know whether that's his name? Did you ever see anything with his name on it? A passport, driver's license, anything?"

"No," Rose says. "But that was his name. His cell phone rang all the time, and he answered it, 'Horner.' Not hello or anything, just *Horner.* Like he was the only one in the world."

"That's all?"

"No," she says, after a moment. "They called him Mr. Horner at his hotel." She plucks the bottom of the T-shirt and looks down at Wile E. Coyote. "At all the hotels."

"Need a passport to check in to a hotel," Rafferty says. There's a faint pulse beating at his right temple. "So he's got a passport that says 'Horner' anyway."

"And he came and went, you said." Arthit is on the hassock with his notebook positioned in front of him on the glass-topped table. He's made half a page of notes.

"He'd usually stay a month or so," Rose says. "Then he'd be gone for a while and come back."

"How long between visits?"

"Maybe three months, maybe more." She squints into the past. "Maybe less. It's hard to say. I hadn't been in Bangkok long. Everything was new to me. Some weeks felt like months, some months felt like days. I was fighting for my life in the bar, trying to figure out how to tell friends from enemies, trying to get over being terrified all the time. I wasn't keeping track of anything, just trying to get through the nights."

"Don't think about that one for a minute," Arthit says. "Maybe it'll come. When did you first see him?"

Rose rubs her upper arms as though she's cold, although the living-room temperature is into the eighties. "A few weeks after I got here. I know that because it was near my birthday. I got here in July, and my birthday is in September."

"That's how many years ago?"

"Thirteen." She glances at Rafferty. "No. Fourteen. I've been with Poke five years."

"So he came into the bar," Arthit prompts.

"I don't want to talk about that. I mean, I do, but I need to explain things to Poke and Miaow, not just answer questions like this."

"Fine," Arthit says. "Can you remember anything he said about himself? What he did, where he went when he left here, anything like that?"

"He told me he came from England."

"He's American," Rafferty and Miaow correct her, almost in unison.

Rose straightens, looking from one of them to the other. "*I* know," she says. "I didn't know then that there was a part of America called England."

"There isn't," Miaow says. It's nearly a snap.

"*New* England?" Arthit asks.

Rose nods but doesn't speak. She's gazing at Miaow, who's searching for something in her own lap. Finally Rose says, "Yes. New England. Someplace with a *V.* I remember that because he laughed at the way I pronounced it. I said"—her face clears for a moment as she remembers—"Wermont. I called it Wermont."

"Like wampire," Arthit says. "Thais say *wampire.*"

"Like that," Rose says, the animation fading from her face. "Wermont." She makes a knot out of her fingers. "Wampire."

"When he was here for these—what?—one-month stays . . ."

"Something like that. Sometimes longer."

"Did he ever leave the country for a short time, a few days, and come back? Would we find multiple entries in immigration?"

"No," Rose says.

"Here a month or more, every time. No need to go back to wherever he earned his living. You're sure."

"I'm sure," Rose says, and buries the lower half of her face in her coffee cup.

"How?" Arthit asks.

Rose looks at Miaow and then lets her eyes slide to the floor. "Because I was with him."

"The whole time?"

"Yes. He paid the bar fine for a month in advance every time," she says.

Arthit makes a note, but Rafferty recognizes it as just something to do, a way of masking his discomfort. Rafferty, who is standing beside the kitchen counter, goes into the kitchen and tops up his cup, which is still full. He doesn't want to go back into the living room. What he wants to do is leave the apartment, go out into the oven of the day, find Howard Horner, and kill him. Kill the other one—what was his name?—John. Kill John, too.

But he breathes several times all the way to the depth of his belly and goes back in. Instead of stopping at the counter, he goes to the couch and sits next to Rose. Puts a hand on the smooth warmth of her thigh. Rose doesn't seem to notice.

"Why is this important?" he asks Arthit. "Whether he came and went, I mean."

"It's a pattern," Arthit says. "It feels military, or quasi-military. So many months on, a month off."

"Either he's military or he was," Rafferty says. "All you have to do is see him walk."

"Rose stabbed his hand," Miaow says suddenly. "He didn't even pull it back. You know, when you touch something hot, the way you yank your hand back? He didn't do that. He just left the hand there, like he was waiting for her to stab it again." Her voice is higher and younger than usual.

"It was a display," Rafferty said. "It was a macho, four-testicle display. Like that old bullshit about holding your hand over the fire. 'I've got more testosterone in the cleft in my manly chin than you have in your entire body.' "

"It isn't something many men could do," Rose says. "It might be a display, but you should take it seriously, Poke."

"Yeah, Rose?" Rafferty's voice is more truculent than he would like it to be. "What's it supposed to tell me?"

"That you can break his bones but he'll keep coming at you. You're not going to win a fight with Howard, because he won't stop until you're dead."

Rafferty says, "We'll see."

"Poke," Rose begins, but she lets the energy fizzle out and shakes her head.

"So," Rafferty says to Arthit, around the ball of heat in his chest. "Can you talk to immigration?"

"Sure I can," Arthit says. "Whether they'll answer me is another issue. What do you want from them?"

"Confirmation that Howard Horner is his name. A photo, if they keep the ones those cute little cameras take at passport control. What he lists as his occupation. Where his flights originate. How often he comes. Whether he's left."

Miaow says, "Left?"

"We were wrong last night," Rafferty says. "He *could* find the apartment. But he didn't do any real harm, did he? Assuming that he meant to. You could knock that door over with a blunt remark, but he didn't come in and kill anyone. Maybe that would have been too easy. Or maybe he didn't have time to play with us. Maybe he had to leave the country, go wherever the hell he goes. So he buys a can of paint and he and his jerk friend paint the X on the door just to make us sweat, and then they go and get their plane. Maybe hoping we'll move by the time he gets back and he can have the fun of finding us all over again."

Arthit says, "Maybe he already knew where you lived. Maybe he spotted Rose months ago and followed her here, did a little research, maybe paid a cop. Maybe the meeting in the café was part of his game."

Rose says, "And maybe he's down in the street right now, enjoying the fact that he frightened us. Maybe he'll be back tonight. This is what he does. He plays with people before he— *Before.*"

Miaow gets up as though she has somewhere to go and then sits down again.

"I can request all that information from immigration," Arthit says. "They won't have today's records. If he left today, that'll still be in the computers. And I can show that bird's claw around, see if it means anything to anybody," There's a drag of unwillingness in his voice. "And I know this feels serious to you. To all of you. But you're making this guy sound like a maniac."

"A what?" Rose says in Thai.

Arthit translates.

Rose says, "That's what he is, Arthit. A maniac."

ARTHIT HAS GONE back to the station to start asking questions, and Miaow has retired to her room with her copy of *The Tempest* to work on her lines and, Rafferty thinks, to get out of whatever room Rose is in. The pressure of the silence in the apartment chases him out of it, and it's almost noon when he comes back up from a short random wander, capped by a stop at the sidewalk restaurant a block away to pick up everyone's favorite food, a gesture that feels futile even before he's paid for it. He finds Rose sitting out on the balcony with the door open behind her, smoking and looking at the city.

He puts the take-out containers on the kitchen counter and goes to the balcony door. "Are you hungry? It's a thousand degrees out here."

"I'm Thai," Rose says without turning. "This is how it is in Thailand."

"That doesn't mean it's not hot."

"So it should be cooler? Has the climate made a mistake?"

"Sorry?"

"It's hot," Rose says. "That's how it is. Life isn't fair sometimes either. That doesn't mean that it's supposed to be or not supposed to be. That's just how it is."

"You don't believe that."

"I do. You'd believe it, too, if you hadn't grown up with all those choices." Her back still to him, she lifts a hand and starts ticking off fingers. " 'Let's see, shall I go to college or run away to Asia and try to find my father? Or write books? Or live here? Or there? Or get married? Or adopt a daughter? Or do it all at once?' "

"That's not what it felt like when it was happening."

"Not to you. It wouldn't. You have no idea how privileged you were. You could choose this or that, and it wouldn't matter much if you chose wrong. '*Uh-oh*, better go back and give it another try.' Nobody pulled you out of school at harvest every year so you could help raise the kids and work in the fields. Nobody was waiting for you to earn money so they could keep their house or feed your brothers and sisters."

"Poor little farm girl," he says. "Are you done?"

"I don't know. I don't even know why I started. My own daughter is hiding from me."

"That's not like the heat," Rafferty says. "That's something you can do something about."

"Maybe."

Impatience crests inside him. "Of course it is."

She starts to says something, then shakes her head and says, "Leave me alone."

"Fine." He steps back into the room. "If you get hungry, come in and eat."

She says, "Close the door."

He slides the door closed, with a little more force than required, and stalks down the hall to Miaow's room. She has the frowny face out, just a rectangle of shirt cardboard that features an unhappy-looking, crayon-scrabbled roundhead, traced around a pie tin. The other side, the smiley face, means come in, and this side doesn't. Rafferty hasn't seen either face in almost a year. He thought she'd thrown them away a long time ago.

He hesitates and then knocks.

"Go away," Miaow says.

"That's what everybody says. I'm lonely."

"Ohhhh, phoo. Just a minute."

He waits, and a moment later he hears the door unlock, and Miaow pulls it open about four inches and looks up at him. "What?"

"Are you hungry? I brought back some larb kai, extra spicy."

She pulls her mouth to one side. "What else?"

"Vietnamese spring rolls, the ones you like, that aren't cooked, with mint and shrimp in them."

"Coke?"

Rafferty draws a breath to slow himself down before he replies. "You mean, did I buy Coke or is there some Coke left?"

"*I* don't know," she says. "I just want Coke."

"Then you'll probably get some. Seems to me you usually get what you want."

"Boy," she says. "Everybody's really awful today."

Rafferty says, "I hadn't noticed."

5

Those Are Pearls That Were His Eyes

F ull fathom five thy father lies,'" Miaow says. She's mumbling a little, embarrassed to speak the lines in this small apartment living room. In rehearsal at school, when she's on the big stage, she belts it to the back row.

"What's a fathom, Mia?" Mrs. Shin asks. As always, it takes Rafferty a beat to realize that "Mia" is Miaow. His child has been reincarnated while he was busy elsewhere.

"About six feet," Miaow says, with a sideways glance that stops just short of Rafferty, who had asked her what a fathom was in the taxi on the ride across town and then provided the answer. "So he's thirty feet underwater. Pretty deep."

"His bones are becoming what?" Mrs. Shin asks.

"Coral," Miaow says immediately. The corners of her mouth lift as she gets to the line she likes best. "And his eyes are pearls." She waves the words away with her hands. "I mean, 'And those are pearls that were his eyes.'"

"No 'and,'" Rafferty says. Neither of them gives him a glance.

Mrs. Shin leans forward. "Can you envision that, Mia?"

"Yes," Miaow says, her own eyes drifting past Mrs. Shin. "I see white sand with flickery ripple light on it, light coming through water, and the king lying there on his back all alone with a gold crown on and pearl eyes, and he's holding one of those sticks with a jewel on the top."

"A scepter?" Rafferty guesses.

"One of those. And he's turning into something sort of fishy. Not fishy, oceany."

"Exactly," Mrs. Shin says. "A 'sea-change.' It's a wonderful speech, isn't it? We're going to give you a special light when you say it."

Miaow's eyes come back to the teacher's. "Special like what?"

"You'll cross all the way downstage, to the edge of the orchestra pit, and you're going to look down as though you're seeing him through the water. We'll have a blue-green spotlight aimed up at you."

"How will you make it watery?" Rafferty asks, interested in spite of his preoccupation with Rose and Horner.

"We'll shine it up through a big round glass baking dish, Pyrex because of the heat, with about three inches of water and food coloring in it, and the kid who's holding it will slosh it around a little."

Miaow says, "Cool," which is one of the many words that's followed her home from school lately.

"I thought of it yesterday," Mrs. Shin says. She picks up her teacup and glances down at it. "A sea change." To Rafferty, she says, "Mia has some of the best lines in the play."

"Yes, and I get to hear them over and over."

"More tea?" Her cup is empty.

"No thanks. It's great, but I'm topped up." Rafferty loathes tea but has forced down two cups to be polite. He has drunk more tea in the six weeks he's been condensing *The Tempest* with Mrs. Shin than in his entire life before they met.

"More Coke, Mia?"

"No." Miaow feels the force of Rafferty's glance and corrects herself. "No thanks."

"It's a surprise to see Mia, but I'm glad you brought her," Mrs. Shin says, standing and bending down to pick up her teacup. This is one of their regular Sunday rewrite meetings, where Rafferty proposes ways to condense and simplify and Mrs. Shin thinks of something better. His first inclination was to cancel today's session, but it gave him a chance to get out of the apartment. When he'd invited Miaow, hoping to help her shake her mood, she'd actually jumped into the air. He'd meant the invitation to demonstrate that life was going on in spite of everything, but to Miaow it was mainly about getting away from Rose for a while.

"She wouldn't let me come without her," he says truthfully.

"Well, I'm happy she's here. She's a lucky girl, having a father who's a famous writer."

"Huh," Miaow says.

Rafferty says, "Not so famous."

As always, they're seated on the beige carpet in Mrs. Shin's living room, around a little black-lacquered table, inset with mother-of-pearl, that's about ten inches high and is almost the only piece of furniture in the room. Floor sitting is a trial for Rafferty, but Miaow can stay cross-legged forever, just one more benefit, he thinks, of being ten, or maybe eleven, years old.

Mrs. Shin goes to the counter that divides the kitchen from the living room and puts her cup in front of an electric hot-water pot. "I don't know about you," she says as hot water streams into the cup, "but I feel as though I've been through a sort of sea change myself, little bits of me getting less Korean and more Thai every year."

"How many years have you been here?"

"Twelve." She picks up the cup and inhales the fragrance, a brisk, trim, short-haired woman in her late thirties or early forties, wearing a brightly striped blouse in hard-candy hues, tucked into fawn-colored slacks. "And you?"

"Six," he says. "I'm becoming Thai by marriage."

"That's a good way to do it," Mrs. Shin says. "Twenty-four-hour tutoring. And you're becoming Thai through fatherhood, too, of course."

"That goes without saying," Rafferty says.

Miaow says, "Does not."

"When I first got here," Mrs. Shin says, "I was only supposed to stay a year, and for the first three or four weeks I thought I wouldn't make it. I hated it. Everything was so *different* from Korea. Bangkok felt like a mess—more than a mess, it felt like complete chaos. The traffic, the heat, the noise, the dirt." She shakes her head. "And I was dripping sweat, waking up with a headache from the exhaust, and wondering why everybody *smiled* all the time. I was suspicious. What did they want from me? After eight or nine days, I noticed that the muscles in my cheeks ached a little because I was smiling back at everybody. So that was the beginning of my sea change—sore cheek muscles."

"Mine was a keen awareness that my teeth weren't very good."

"Your teeth are fine," she says without a glance. It's a very Thai response. She sips her tea and looks down at Miaow. "And the people, they . . . Well, from a Korean perspective the Thais are a little . . . haphazard."

"We are?" Miaow says.

"From a Korean perspective." Mrs. Shin emphasizes the words. "Koreans tend to be highly organized. We're planners and list makers. Not particularly spontaneous, unless we've been drinking, and then we're *too* spontaneous. The Thais, on the other hand, sort of flow." She sees the confusion in Miaow's face and laughs. "Don't worry, I'm not saying anything bad about the Thais. It's actually about me, and it has to do with the play." She crosses the small room again, barefoot, as are Rafferty and Miaow. One of the things Rafferty loves about Asia is how close everyone is to being barefoot all the time. When the two of them came into the apartment, they kicked off their shoes beside a plumb-straight line of Mrs. Shin's, just inside the door, and the backs of all the shoes were flattened, stepped on repeatedly to make them easier to slip on and off. After all his years in Asia, the sight still cheers him.

"As a Korean, I didn't think the Thais measured up to me," she says, sitting down on her heels in a posture Rafferty has never been able to attain. "And now here I am, twelve years later, slowly turning Thai and delighted about it. And it makes me think about Caliban."

Rafferty says, "Ah," and Miaow says, "Why?"

"We don't like Caliban. We're not supposed to. Shakespeare doesn't like him. Caliban is the only non-European on the island, except for Ariel, who's clearly an upper-class spirit, almost English. But Caliban . . . well, Caliban is definitely not English, and Prospero treats him like a dog."

Miaow says, "And he's . . ." She falters and puts both hands on the table.

"He's what?" Mrs. Shin asks.

Miaow shakes her head. "I'm not smart like you."

"You're one of the smartest children I've ever known," Mrs. Shin says.

Miaow's mouth opens at the praise and stays open. She looks as if she's just been hit on the head.

"So what is it?" Mrs. Shin prompts. "What else is Caliban?"

Miaow grabs a breath and plunges in. "He's the only one who doesn't get off."

Rafferty says, "By 'get off,' you mean—"

"Nobody forgives him. Prospero forgives everybody, even after they tried to kill him and his daughter. He sets Ariel free. But nobody forgives Caliban."

Rafferty and Mrs. Shin sit there looking at Miaow. Then Mrs. Shin says, "Miaow, I am so happy you're in this play."

Miaow says, "Really?" She's blushing.

"Really, totally, completely, one hundred percent, absolutely. But why doesn't Prospero forgive Caliban?"

"He tried to fool around with Miranda," Miaow answers. "She says so herself."

"Actually," Mrs. Shin says, "I think we may take that speech away from Miranda."

Miaow starts to smile but whisks the expression out of sight. She's deeply envious of Siri Lindstrom, the Scandinavian-goddess-in-waiting who's playing the magician's daughter and who gets all the production's beautiful gowns. Behind the envy, Rafferty thinks, Miaow is half in love with Siri. If Miaow had her most secret wish, she'd be blond, blue-eyed, willowy, and named Siri Lindstrom.

"But Siri loves it," Miaow says piously. "It's the only time Miranda says anything interesting."

"She's got lots of scenes," Mrs. Shin says.

"Yeah, but they're all sappy." Miaow clasps her hands together in front of her chest. "'Oh, Ferdinand, *Ferd*inand.'"

"Siri will be fine, Mia," Mrs. Shin says. "Every play needs a love story."

"I'd rather whoosh around doing magic," Miaow says.

"Well, you've got the right part. And look at you. You figured out, all by yourself, what the play is really about." Mrs. Shin sits back on her heels, looking pleased.

"What?" Miaow asks, as though she suspects a quiz. "What's it about?"

"Forgiveness. It's about the healing power of forgiveness. And do you know why I think Prospero doesn't forgive Caliban at the end of the play? Because Prospero doesn't *understand* Caliban."

Howard Horner's face flashes into Rafferty's mind. "That's a very liberal attitude."

"Well, I believe it. I believe it's impossible to hate anyone you understand. Don't you feel the same way?"

Rafferty's pause is all the cue Mrs. Shin needs. "Well, perhaps not. But I'm the director and you're the condenser, so you have to help me make this work."

Rafferty says, "At the end. We could do something at the end. After everybody's gone, maybe Caliban becomes more human."

Mrs. Shin has a habit of squinting at nothing when she's thinking about the stage. "Could be. Let's ponder it." She sticks out her lower lip, completely unaware she's doing it, and then she turns to Miaow. "I've got something for you."

"For me?"

"And it solves a problem. A problem with Ariel. Mia, think about the stage direction in the play just before you do the 'Full fathom five' speech. The one that says 'Enter Ariel, invisible.' Have you wondered how we're going to do that?"

"Well, sure," Miaow says. "I mean, how can the audience see me if I'm invisible? And if they can see me, how do they know I'm invisible?"

"That's the problem," Mrs. Shin says. "Let me show you how we're going to solve it." She pushes herself back on her haunches and rises effortlessly with a grace that Rafferty, whose legs have gone numb, can only envy. "Maybe I thought of this because you're so bright. I'll be right back."

She goes past the kitchen and into the hallway to the rear of the apartment, and Miaow leans over to Rafferty and says, "I know who you were thinking about. When she said about understanding the people you—"

"Well, let's keep it to ourselves, okay?"

"Jeez," Miaow says, pulling back, all the happiness gone. "I'm not stupid."

"Miaow, I didn't say you were—"

"Mia," Miaow says in a sharp whisper. "My name is Mia."

"How about giving me a little time with that? You've been Miaow the whole time I've known you, so just let me have a few weeks—"

"It's *been* a few weeks. It's been a few months."

"Well, I need a few more. I actually have some other stuff on my mind."

"Look at this," Mrs. Shin calls from the hallway, although they can't see her yet. "No, wait. Mia, go turn on the overhead lights. That's the switch right inside the door."

Miaow gets up and hits the switch, and the apartment brightens somewhat.

"Okay," Mrs. Shin says, "look here."

She comes into the room with something hanging over her open fingers, a glittering strip about ten inches long and six inches wide. It flashes when it catches the halogen lights recessed in the ceiling.

Still at the light switch, Miaow narrows her eyes and says, "What is it?"

"Look at yourself," Mrs. Shin says proudly. "Well, I know you can't actually look at yourself, but feel how you're squinting to see what it is? That's what everyone's going to do." She comes to the table and holds out the glittering hand, and Rafferty sees that the strip is made up of rectangles of mirrored plastic, each about two inches square. Small holes have been bored in each side and white thread passed through the holes so the squares could be sewn together.

"This is your cloak of invisibility," Mrs. Shin says. "Bigger, obviously. It'll hang from your shoulders to the floor, and we'll put a couple of white spotlights on you. You'll just be a dazzle, a sort of moving sparkle."

"Ohhhh," Miaow says, coming to the table. Rafferty hasn't seen her face this open and this rapt in months. "It's beautiful."

"Siri's going to want it," Mrs. Shin says, and then she laughs. "But it's all yours."

Miaow reaches out and passes her fingertips over the surface of the mirrors. She swallows before she speaks. "A sparkle. I'll be a sparkle."

"You're already a sparkle, Mia. That's why you're playing Ariel."

A deep flush darkens Miaow's face, and she quickly looks down at the table. Rafferty watches the reaction with a twinge of jealousy. It's been a while since anything he said or did made his daughter this happy.

"Oh, I hoped you'd be pleased." Mrs. Shin gives Miaow the strip of mirrors, and Miaow turns it over in her hand.

"You're good," Rafferty says.

"They deserve good," Mrs. Shin says. "They're wonderful kids. And it's a wonderful play. An enchanted island, spirits, a magical storm, a shipwreck, revenge turning into forgiveness. How could you not love it?"

"I'll work on Caliban."

"Please. You know, there's one clue that Shakespeare might have known that Caliban had a better side than the one we see, although you have to look at the play on the page to find it. He speaks in verse, Caliban does. The clowns speak in prose, but Caliban speaks verse, and he's got that beautiful speech about waking up from good dreams and wishing he could dream again."

"I can identify with that," Rafferty says.

"Oh, don't be silly. You're drowning in blessings. You're living in a city you love, you have a beautiful wife and an amazing child. Oh, and speaking of your wife—her name is Rose, right? This play is eating me alive. Look at this place, it's filthy. I need somebody to help me clean."

"No," Miaow says immediately. "Her girls—I mean, they . . ."

"They'd be great," Rafferty says, fighting down an urge to kick Miaow in the shins. "I'll give you the number for the agency."

"But . . ." Miaow is rocking back and forth in sheer anxiety. "Those girls, they're not . . . they're not really . . ."

"I know all about it, Mia," Mrs. Shin says. "I think you should be proud of what your mother is trying to do. Giving those women a chance at a different kind of life."

Miaow says to Rafferty, "You *told* her?"

"Sure," Rafferty says. "I'm proud of Rose. You should be, too."

Miaow's face is as closed as a stone. "Fine," she says, snipping the word at both ends.

"We'll be going," Rafferty says. He stands, and his numb legs hold him up. "Thanks for the tea. Come on, Miaow."

Miaow says, "Mia," but she reluctantly lays the mirrored fragment on the table and follows him to the door.

Mrs. Shin says, "You're going to be beautiful, Mia."

"Not as beautiful as Siri," Miaow says. She's not meeting anyone's eyes.

"You'll be beautiful in a different way."

"Yeah."

"What she means to say is thank you," Rafferty says. "We're finding our way through a little snag in the growth process. The politeness area of her brain has shrunk."

Miaow says, *"Poke."*

"Don't tease her," Mrs. Shin says, opening the door as they slip into their shoes. "I need her to be in good spirits, no pun intended."

"I'll do what I can," Rafferty says.

"I can take care of myself," Miaow says.

"Yeah, well, don't trip over your lower lip on your way out. Thanks again, Mrs. Shin."

"You take care of my little Ariel." Mrs. Shin gives Miaow a fingertip wave, which Miaow acknowledges with a nod that borders on curt. With a quick glance at Rafferty, Mrs. Shin closes the door.

Rafferty and Miaow walk to the elevator in complete silence. He pushes the button, and Miaow slips in between him and the closed doors, facing them with her back to him. They wait without a word until Rafferty says, "This won't do, Miaow."

"You told her," Miaow says.

"I don't know how to break this to you," Rafferty says as the elevator doors finally slide open, "but the school knows pretty much everything about us."

"Omi*god*," Miaow says, sounding so American that Rafferty almost does a double take. "Everything?"

"There were about five thousand forms to fill out just to get you in. And then interviews." The elevator starts down.

"But suppose Siri finds out." She's got her fingers knotted together, chest high, just barely not wringing her hands. "Suppose *Andy*—" She breaks off and abruptly closes her mouth.

"Who's Andy? That's the second time you've mentioned him."

Miaow's response is a savage kick to the elevator wall. "Skip it."

"Absolutely no problem," Rafferty says. The two of them ride down in an elevator that feels like a diving bell. They endure an ear-popping silence until the car shudders to a halt and the doors open. "And whoever *Andy* is, either he'll like you for who you actually are or he won't. And if he doesn't," Rafferty says with a sudden surge of heat, "fuck him."

Miaow helps the doors slide open with a shove and stalks across the lobby, her shoulders almost as high as her ears. The day gleams painfully bright through the glass doors. They're halfway to the door when she stops and whirls on him.

"I don't have *any* friends. Not any, not real friends. Everybody looks at me like I'm a black peasant kid. And I am. Siri asked me . . . she asked me whether I was a scholarship student. Like *charity*. Like I came down from some farm somewhere, so some rich person could make merit. Like my mother and father raise pigs in the mud and I usually wear rags and have snot on my lip. What am I supposed to say? I don't know who my mother and father are? I used to live in the street? My mother, my stepmother, used to be—"

"That's enough," Rafferty says. He puts his hands on her shoulders, and she stiffens, so he kneels down until their eyes are level. Her upper lip is shining with sweat, and her eyes are all over the place. "Nobody loves you more than Rose does," he says. "Probably nobody ever will. She'd die for you. Do you know that?"

Miaow grabs a breath, holds it for a moment, and then lets it out in ragged spurts. She finally meets his eyes, and at that instant she starts to cry. She wraps her arms around his neck and presses her hot, wet face against his. "I just want . . . I just want to . . . to be like everybody. I want people to like me. I don't want to get up every morning with my stomach all feeling like it's got ice and glass in it, and have to smile at you and Rose before I go to school, and wish all day I could be back in bed and pull up the covers. I'm not big like you. I'm not brave. I need friends. I want . . . I want . . ."

"You are brave," Rafferty says. "You're one of the bravest people I've ever met. And you know what? About those kids? They'll like you when they know you better. Look at you, you're younger than they are because you skipped a grade, and you're not real tall yet, so you look even younger. And so maybe they're kind of snobbish, you know? Maybe they think it actually means something that their parents have money. Maybe they've had little tiny lives and all they're comfortable with is stuff that's familiar to them. And you're different. Maybe they're a little afraid of you." He holds her at arm's length. "Do you know what I'm saying?"

"I'm not brave," she says, but she's not crying anymore.

"What you have to do," he says, "is remember that you've had four or five lives already, compared to them. They're the babies. You know more about the world right now than they will when they're thirty.

Just go to school in the morning, knowing that you understand things about real life, not just school life, that they've never had a hint of. And know that you're big enough to forgive them, without them even knowing you've done it."

She stands there, all four feet of her, waiting for something Rafferty isn't sure he has to offer. What he says is, "And play Ariel all the way to the back row, because there isn't another kid in the school who has the magic to do it."

Miaow sniffs. Her eyes are downturned but flicking back and forth as though she's reading a page, and he knows she's sifting his argument for weak spots. He also knows it's full of them. But if he says anything else, it's just going to get weaker.

She nods and scuffs her right shoe over the marble floor, producing a squeal that bounces off the walls. She does it again. Then she says, "Let's go."

Rafferty rises, looks down at the thatch of short yellow hair, and ruffles it. She immediately scrubs her fingers through it to disarrange it her way. He says, "I love you," and she reaches up and takes his hand. She slides her feet over the marble until she reaches the door, producing a long, agonizing string of squeals.

Mrs. Shin's apartment house is tucked away off Sukhumvit Soi 11, and there's no traffic on the little street, not even any vehicles except for a couple of motorcycle taxis parked in the building's shade. The drivers are out cold, balanced on their seats with their bare feet on the handlebars, demonstrating the Thai genius for sleeping anywhere. Since Miaow hasn't yanked her hand back, she and Rafferty hold hands as they head for the boulevard to flag a taxi. It's after three, and the buildings and road surfaces have had all day long to absorb heat. It radiates from the walls and sidewalks, wrapping them in a claustrophobic personal climate that's rich in perspiration. There isn't even a whisper of a breeze.

"I like Bangkok best from high up," Miaow says.

What Rafferty hears is a roundabout acknowledgment that she's grateful to live in their eighth-floor apartment. It's oblique, but that doesn't mean it didn't cost her anything. He gives her hand a little swing. She resists and then gives up and takes exactly one skip. His heart lightens.

On Sukhumvit he signals a cab and opens the door for Miaow. He has his hand in the small of her back as he leans down to tell the driver where to go when he feels Miaow turn to stone. He looks at her and finds her staring across the street. He can see the pulse slamming at the side of her throat.

"Look," she says.

He follows her eyes and sees a long blue bus lumbering past on the other side of the street and then, as it passes, the only man on the busy sidewalk who is standing still, the man who is looking at them.

Horner's friend, John.

Rafferty throws forty baht at the driver, says, "Go away." He steps into traffic with his arm upraised and his palm down. A motorcycle taxi swerves sharply, barely missing him. Before the bike is fully stopped, Rafferty passes the driver a hundred baht, picks Miaow up—not even feeling her weight—and plops her onto the backseat, facing back. He takes her hands and puts them behind her on the grab bar between her and the driver's seat, and says, "Face this way. If you see anything you shouldn't see, any car or bike that's back there too long, have him take you to Arthit at the Lumphini police station. Got it?"

Miaow nods, her eyes on the opposite sidewalk. Rafferty slaps the driver's helmet and says, "Take her to Soi Pipat, unless she tells you to go to Lumphini. As fast as you can." The teenager on the bike looks down at the bill, shoves it into his shirt pocket, and jams the throttle. The bike does a little wheelie and lurches into traffic.

Rafferty dives into traffic himself, pushing his way across the street, trying to get there before John disappears.

6

Beer Garden

He jumps when it becomes inescapably clear that he can't possibly run fast enough, and that the truck driver has no intention of slowing. His leap carries him to the center island, the truck's wind on the back of his neck and traffic screaming by in front of him and behind him, and he stutter-steps to keep from pitching face-first onto the pavement. When he's got his forward momentum under control, he stands there gasping carbon monoxide and heat from the pavement, and he checks the far sidewalk. Fifteen yards to the right, an old man is down on his knees and elbows on the sidewalk, crumpled like a swatted spider above a spill of groceries. A knot of Samaritans is beginning to form around him, and one man is shouting up the street, hurling curses after John.

Who has to be running. Rafferty lets his eyes roam right, and there he is, about two-thirds of the way down the boulevard to Soi 10: John, hauling ass at a good clip, running effortlessly, as though it were something he could do all day. Rafferty checks the traffic and plunges into the stream of vehicles, zigzagging through the moving maze to the curb and then loping along in the street, right at the edge, jumping up onto the sidewalk whenever a car comes too close. He's gaining on John, who looks to be in much better shape but is forcing his way through the inevitable Sukhumvit pedestrian throng.

On the other side of the boulevard, the side Rafferty just left, the vendors have already built their brightly lighted obstacle course, selling flick knives, pornography, Buddha images, and brass knuckles, the everyday Bangkok mix of veneration and violence. John obviously chose this side of the road, which is relatively vendor-free, in case he had to run, since it's impossible to maintain even a brisk walk on the other side. So he'd thought he might have to run. Or maybe he'd set it up so he *would* have to run and so Rafferty would chase along after him, a good little lemming, into whatever snare Horner has prepared.

But what's the alternative? Rafferty picks up his pace.

Ahead of him, John bulls his way to the curb and steps into the street, looking left—an American's most dangerous Bangkok mistake—and just barely misses getting run down by a motorcycle, which swerves around him with only inches to spare. John does a little "can't stop" dance, windmilling his arms and turning his head the other way to see what's going to kill him, but he catches sight of Rafferty before his head has whipped all the way around, and the sight makes him pause just long enough for another bike to tear by, the driver giving him a gravelly horn. Then he looks in the correct direction, assesses the traffic, and dives in.

He's not even breathing hard. Where Rafferty feels as though the asphalt is jumping up to meet him, jamming his joints and making his teeth click like castanets, John seems to glide, running beside a car occasionally to get the speed he needs to slip between it and the one behind, and then he's made it to the median divider, which has a thigh-high fence running down the center of it. He vaults the fence effortlessly, and a horn screams in Rafferty's ear, moving up the scale as the source approaches in a lethal-sounding Doppler effect, and something clips his elbow—a Jeep, he sees, as it speeds past—and leaves him cradling an arm that's suddenly gone numb, not a good sign, and as he plows toward the divider he cups the elbow in his hand and feels something wet and warm.

Also not a good sign.

Well, *sure* it's blood—what did he expect?—but there's no time to stop and survey the damage now, because John is off the divider, running with the traffic instead of through it, sticking to the edge of the divider and heading for Soi 9 and the lower numbers beyond. Rafferty gets to the island without knowing how he did it and runs on his side of it, watching John and leaving to the oncoming drivers the challenge of not running over him. He gets a lot of horns and some shouts, but everyone manages to avoid damaging their paint jobs, and Rafferty is feeling a burning under his lungs by the time John angles off to his right and into traffic, heading for the far side of the street.

And the numbness in his arm is wearing off. It hurts significantly.

But there's nothing he can do about it, and he speeds up. John will have to slow for the vendors' stands, but Rafferty continues his accelerated plod on his side of the road divider as John charts a course on toward the booths. John's made another Bangkok duffer's mistake, though, because he doesn't know, until his ignorance almost kills him, that traffic in the curbside lane of Sukhumvit goes *in the opposite direction* from all the other traffic on that side of Sukhumvit, and a taxi misses by a couple of inches the opportunity to spread him over the pavement. John stumbles into the rear of a stand and nearly goes down.

And Rafferty's up on the divider, clearing the low fence without difficulty, figuring that John's misstep has got to be good for five or ten yards. But the other man is already up and lengthening his stride. Rafferty figures he's lucky if he gained ten feet.

And now he has to keep up.

The knot under his heart and the cramp in his side remind him that he hasn't been going to the gym, but he discovers he can forget the cramp and the knot in his chest if he just concentrates on his arm, which hurts like hell. He risks a glance down and sees lots of blood running along the underside of his forearm and making a red octopus over the back of his hand. For a moment his head goes kind of bubbly and light and the day seems to brighten at the edges.

Well, there isn't time to faint, so he concentrates on his breathing—suck big gulps of air in, empty his lungs completely on the out breath—and he feels the weight returning to his body, and he registers again the solidity of the street beneath his feet. The elbow hurts like a newly orphaned son of a bitch, and he focuses on the long train of pain running up his arm and uses it to push him forward.

He stumbles along for two more blocks, his breath in tatters and the clot of pain beneath his heart gradually narrowing into something focused and hot. Just as he thinks he'll never catch the man, he sees John charge the curb and head to his right, into Soi 7.

Rafferty knows Soi 7 from his earliest days in Bangkok, pre-Rose, when he occasionally browsed the city's meat markets for temporary companionship. He's at the mouth of the *soi* less than a minute after John entered it.

But there's no John in sight. Rafferty stands there gasping at the day, while he orients himself. Just behind the first row of buildings and shops, an alley angles off to the left, leading into a warren of little streets that are perfect for getting lost in. Directly ahead the *soi* stretches into a straightaway, and John's not in it. To the immediate right is a large outdoor restaurant. A couple of billiards bars face the street through darkened windows, one on each side of the *soi,* and halfway down the block on the left is the Beer Garden.

If John's spent much time in Bangkok, he hasn't spent it wandering around on his own. He almost got clipped in the street because he forgot that Thais drive on the left, so he's probably not aware that the alley leads to a maze. Scratch going left, at least as an operating hypothesis. Rafferty doesn't see him at any of the tables in the outside restaurant, and he's not dwindling into perspective down the *soi.* That leaves the pool-table bars and the Beer Garden.

Most guys who come solo to Bangkok learn about the Beer Garden within a few days. In a town where the nighttime action is literally overwhelming, the days can seem positively dreary. For a man who's in the market at 3:30 P.M., the Beer Garden is a shining exception.

And a dangerous place to chase someone into.

The problem is that there's only one official entrance, and every seat in the place faces it. That wouldn't be such an issue if there weren't three hundred seats. The Beer Garden is enormous. On any day of the week, there are likely to be a hundred to a hundred fifty *farang* men and as many as two hundred women, many of whom are standing or circulating, looking for a free drink, a meal, or a welcoming lap. Plenty of room for old John, plus Howard and a dozen of their friends to be sitting there, watching the door, waiting for the rabbit to stroll into the trap.

Rafferty pushes open the door of the pool-table bar to his right and sticks his head in, letting his eyes adjust to the dimness as the hostesses hurry toward him. There's a herd of them, and a quick look around makes it clear that Rafferty will have all their attention, because there's not a customer in the place. He waves off the women who are nearest and yanks the door closed.

He turns, irresolute for a second: Check the other bar or brave the Beer Garden? The day brightens again, and he closes his eyes and feels the street start to move beneath his feet. As he opens his eyes, looking for something—anything—that's standing still instead of spinning, he feels a tug at the back of his shirt.

He whirls so fast that he nearly goes down, and the person behind him takes a panicked leap backward. The two of them topple sideways simultaneously, Rafferty coming to rest in a semi-standing position against the wall of the bar and the girl yelping as one of her towering platform shoes rolls sideways. When she finally stops moving, she's bent double, both hands on her left ankle, going, "*Oooo-oooo-ooooo.*"

"I'm sorry," Rafferty says. He pushes himself off the wall and raises both hands to show he's harmless, but she's already taken a little hop away. She lands on the newly sprained ankle and emits a squeak so high it's at the upper limit of Rafferty's hearing. Then she drops to one knee and wraps both hands around her ankle again, looking up at him through a dry frizzle of badly dyed red hair.

"You arm," she says in English. "You arm no good." She raises her right hand and points at his injured elbow as though he might be unaware of it, then grabs her ankle again and says, "You arm. You know you have problem you arm? You know you have ow?" She's short and plump and dark-skinned and ridiculously young, maybe eighteen, wearing a chopped-off T-shirt, red hot pants with a wide white vinyl belt studded with rhinestones, and makeup so thick it looks like she put it on with the lights out.

"I know," Rafferty says. "No problem." Just then his elbow lets loose a giant twinge of contradiction, and he catches his breath and expels it with a chuff like a steam engine. "What about you?" She looks up at him, clearly working on an internal translation. "Your ankle," he says in Thai. "Is it okay?"

"Not okay," she says in English. "But not have . . . not have . . ." She thinks for a second and then rubs her heavily lipsticked lower lip with a fingertip, makes a red smear on her bare arm, and points to it.

"Blood," Rafferty says.

She nods eagerly. "Not have blood." She sticks out a pink tongue and licks the lipstick on her arm, then rubs it away with the palm of her hand.

"Look," Rafferty says, "I have to go over there for a second." He points to the dark-windowed billiards bar across the street. "You get up and walk a little." Although he's speaking Thai, she just looks at him, so he imitates a limp for a moment. "You need to walk on it, before it swells up. Take your shoes off and move around. I'll be right back."

She says okay to his back, and he turns at the sound of her voice, but she just smiles at him and says okay again. He starts across the *soi,* and when he glances back over his shoulder, she is watching him go as if he were her only friend on the playground. She waves but makes no move to get up.

Rafferty nods at her, feeling oddly formal, and crosses the street. One last look reveals her still in a crouch, her hands still cupped around her ankle. When she sees him turn, she smiles again. Her little belly pouches out over the top of her hot pants, her belly button looking like the world's deepest dimple.

He pushes open the door of the billiards bar. It's cool and dim, and neither of the two *farang* hunched face-to-face over one of the tables is John.

Rafferty shakes his head to slow the approaching hostess and turns back to the street, hearing the door sigh closed behind him. It hits his elbow, and his arm blooms with pain. He grabs his shoulder, which seems to ease the pain slightly, and leans forward, blowing out all the air in his lungs. He stays there, staring at the sidewalk, until the tide of pain has receded to the point where he can breathe regularly. When he straightens and looks across the street, the plump little apprentice tart is right where he left her. She's on one knee, with the injured ankle stretched in front of her, and she's slowly wiggling the foot back and forth. The platform heel on the shoe she's removed has to be six inches high. Rafferty stands there, waiting for the red heat in his arm to subside further, and sees a group of four cigarette-puffing women, older and more seasoned than the one across the street, go through the open space that leads into the Beer Garden. Then come the usual high-frequency cries of delight from their friends, who probably haven't seen the newcomers for at least an hour.

And here Rafferty is, halfway up the block. If he'd been right beside the door, he might have been able to slip in with the women, maybe hunched over a little. Maybe whoever is watching the entrance would have registered the girls and looked away, maybe turned to the person next to him to say—

No. Not these guys. If John's supposed to be watching the door, he'll be watching the door.

Rafferty pulls out his cell phone and pushes the speed dial for Miaow.

"Nobody's behind me," she says, without waiting for his hello. "I'm getting sick, riding backward."

"Sick is better than dead. And you're keeping your eyes open."

"What else have I got to do?" Miaow says. "But there's nobody back there."

"Good. How long until you get home?"

"I'll get home about ten minutes after I throw up." She disconnects.

Across the street the plump girl wobbles to her feet, arms spread as though she's on a tightrope. She takes a step, but when she puts her weight on the bad ankle, she straightens quickly, and Rafferty can hear her shrill squeak over the traffic from the boulevard. With a certain amount of relief, he resigns himself to not confronting John and goes back to her.

The girl leans against the wall of the bar and watches him come. The *soi* is completely in shadow now, and multicolored lights begin to blink in the boughs of the enormous tree that grows just inside the entrance to the Beer Garden.

She stands like an egret, the foot beneath the injured ankle raised slightly, letting the wall take all her weight. Rafferty kneels in front of her and slides his hands over the ankle, feeling the warmth of the swelling. "This is no good," Rafferty says. "You have to walk on it."

She says, "Too many ow."

"It'll feel better if you put some weight on it. Come on." He gets up and thinks for a second about how to help her without further damaging his bad arm, then goes around to her left side and puts his right arm around his waist. "Lean on me," he says in badly pronounced Thai. "Put about half your weight on the ankle." He starts to walk her in a circle.

"*Ooo,*" she says. A moment later she says "Ooo" again, and he can hear the wince.

"It'll get better."

She says "Ooo" yet again. She has the salty smell of sweat, mixed with something that Rafferty can't place, slightly fragrant, slightly medicinal. Talcum powder, he thinks, with menthol in it, the poor person's cure for prickly heat.

"In a circle," he says, guiding her. "Come on. Put some more weight on it. Don't just put it down like that. Bend it a little when you step on it."

"Buy me drink," the girl says, stopping. "Hot."

"Make a deal. You walk another two minutes by yourself, just keep going in a circle, while I run over to the pharmacy and get some aspirin and a bandage, and I'll buy you whatever you want."

"Want cola," she says.

Someone comes out of the Beer Garden, and Rafferty slows his pace to watch, but it's not John. It's a lanky scarecrow with a pair of women in tow, and Rafferty can almost see the thought balloon above his head, saying, *Wait'll I tell them about this back home. God, am I a stud.*

"Two lady," the girl says flatly. "Two lady no good."

"Why no good?"

"Ugly," the plump girl says. "One lady, one man okay. Two lady, one man ugly."

"I agree. Walk a minute while I go over there. Then I'll get you your Coke and you can go inside."

"Lady in there no like me," she says, showing no sign of wanting to let go of him.

"Why?"

She shakes her head. "Don't know. No like."

"Because you're young," Rafferty says. "Most of them are getting older. They're aunties."

"But lady in there," she says, and pauses, and he thinks she'll switch to Thai, but she finds her way in English. "Pootiful. Many lady Beer Garden pootiful. Have jewel, have watch. Have tattoo. Me no pootiful. Me fat."

"You're fine," Rafferty says.

"You take me?" She looks hopeful.

"No," Rafferty says. "I'm married."

"Ugly," the girl says. "Fat. Black."

"Oh, give it a rest," Rafferty says in English. In Thai he says, "Walk. Watch the door to the Beer Garden for me. Look for a man. Taller than I am." He lifts his hand, palm down, a couple of inches above his head.

"Very short hair, flat on top. White shirt with blue stripes. This wide." He holds up thumb and forefinger, half an inch apart.

"Friend you?"

"No. He's not your friend either. If he comes out, don't get near him. Just watch where he goes, so you can tell me. And keep walking, okay?"

He waits until she starts to limp in a tight circle, toting her shoes in her hands and squeaking like a chipmunk, and then he turns and jogs to Sukhumvit. The pharmacy is about half a block to the right, exactly where he remembered it. He comes out a couple of minutes later, dry-chewing four aspirin and carrying a plastic bag containing some more loose pills, a roll of gauze, some bandages, and a tube of antibiotic cream. The young woman behind the counter had wanted to treat him right there, but he'd fought her off, although he was unable to prevent her from soaking some tissues in water and pressing the sopping wad into his hand. It drips down his bloody arm and onto his shirt as he works his way back through the crowd on the sidewalk, making pink stalactite-shaped stains on the front of his T-shirt like a souvenir of the Cave of Blood.

When he reenters the *soi,* the girl is at a table with a can of Coke in front of her, the can sweating in the humidity, and she's holding her left foot in both hands, turning it this way and that. She gives a little start when she sees his ruined shirt and then holds out both hands for the bag and the tissues. Even before he's fully seated, she's gently wiping his forearm with the wet tissues, folding them to get a clean surface and wiping some more, then patting the skin dry with napkins.

"Ankle better?"

"Small ow," she says. She places a hand on his upper arm, and with the other she takes his wrist. With a practiced air, she bends the arm at the elbow and then straightens it, taking it through the full range of motion and ignoring Rafferty's grunt of pain.

"Him not come," she says, indicating the Beer Garden with her chin. She returns her attention to his arm, pushing it so the elbow forms an acute angle. "This okay. Not break." To prove it she yanks the arm open and then closes it again, bringing Rafferty three or four inches into the air. "Baby," she says. "All man baby."

"Yeah, well, thanks for the help." He reclaims his arm and opens and closes it gingerly, the pain slowing him like rust on the joint, and then he rotates it for a look at the elbow. He's got a swelling the size of a tomato, and the skin is torn in a jagged three-inch pattern that looks like lightning.

"No problem," she says. "Only dirty. I clean."

"Wiggle your foot around," Rafferty says. "I mean, as long as we're playing doctor."

"Foot okay. Ow, but okay. Same you." With considerable precision she inverts the cap on the tube of ointment to puncture the top, lays a thin line of cream along the zigzag of the tear, and uses a small piece of gauze to spread the ointment on either side. She examines her work and then takes the roll of gauze and begins to mummify his elbow with it.

He says, "Not so tight."

She tugs the gauze a bit tighter and passes it under his arm again. Without looking up she says, "Name you?"

"Poke," he says. "And you?"

"Pim." She rolls the gauze around his arm four more times, nips the edge with small white teeth, and rips it neatly across. Then she folds the end under once, so no loose threads are exposed, smooths it flat across the mound of gauze swathing Rafferty's elbow, and expertly tapes it in place with two elastic Band-Aids. She eyes her work critically, smooths it again, and drops everything back into the bag. "You no die," she says.

"You've done this before," he says.

"Have," she says without meeting his eyes. "Have many baby, my house."

"In the bag," he says. "Three aspirin for your ankle."

"Not like."

"Nobody likes. But they'll keep it from swelling. Take them."

She grimaces in protest but scrounges in the bag until she comes up with the pills. Then she gives them a dubious glance, looks at the Coke in her hand, fills her mouth with Coke, and drops the pills in. Then she swallows convulsively and immediately burps, her free hand splayed out over her sternum.

"There," Rafferty says. "You did great, but don't make it a habit."

Pim puts the can down, blinking fast, and picks up the roll of gauze.

"I'll do it," Rafferty says. "Give me your foot." She puts her foot in his lap, and he starts to wrap the ankle.

"More harder," she says, and he tightens the spiral of cloth.

"Friend you, in there—" She jerks her head back, toward the entrance to the Beer Garden.

"Not a friend," Rafferty says.

She says, "No good?"

"No good." He tugs on the roll, passing it under and over her ankle. "I don't want him to see me, but I need to know where he goes."

"Short hair," Pim says. "Shirt same-same . . ." She draws vertical stripes down Rafferty's T-shirt, then burps again. "Old, not old?"

"Not old," Rafferty says, and puts in the little barbed clamps to hold the gauze in place. "But I don't think you should—"

"I look," Pim says. She gets up and then squeaks, both hands grabbing at the back of her chair. Says, *"Oooo."*

"Skip it," Rafferty says. "Not a good idea."

"You say I walking, yes?" Pim says. "So okay, I walk."

"Look." He gets up. "If you're going in there, make me a promise. Don't get anywhere near him. Go in, look around like you're supposed to meet somebody and he's not there. If you don't see him, come out and tell me. If you do see him—" He breaks off. "You've got a cell phone, right?"

"Sure," she says, slightly affronted. "Have."

"Give it to me."

Her lower lip pops out, and for a moment he thinks she will refuse. She has no jewelry yet, no expensive clothes, just cheap, badly sewn junk from the vendors out at Chatuchak Market. At this stage of her life in Bangkok, her phone—the symbol of freedom, the first thing every girl buys—is the only trophy of her new career. She makes a sour face, forces a hand into a pocket in her hot pants, and brings up a thin silvery cell phone that Rafferty recognizes at once as the one Miaow's been asking for.

He has to tug on it twice before she releases it. He keys in his number, then hands it back. "This is me," he says. He puts a hand on her shoulder, a bid for full attention. "If you see him, just turn your back to him and push 'send.' I won't answer—just let it ring once or twice and then hang up. That way you don't have to go right back out again, or get anywhere near me, or talk on the phone, or do anything that might catch his attention. Don't get close to him, don't talk to him, don't do anything that makes him notice you. You go in, look around, and if he's there, you press 'send' and you hang up, understand?"

"Go in, look around, press 'send,'" she says with exaggerated patience, reminding Rafferty that she's just a kid. It's gotten darker now, and her makeup doesn't look quite so garish. He can see the mildly pretty, still-developing face beneath it. Not beautiful, not unforgettable, just the sweet, unassuming transitional prettiness so many young women share. She reaches up and pats the hand on her shoulder, then twists away and out from under it. "I go."

"Hold it," he says. "You had any customers today?"

She opens her mouth, closes it, and then says, "No."

"Okay." He pulls a fold of money out of his jeans and peels off a reddish note. "Here's five hundred baht."

She avoids looking at the money and shakes her head.

"It's for taking care of me. And for checking it out in there. Why should you do all that for free?"

She raises her upper lip and sucks air through her teeth, making a little squealing sound. Then she takes the bill and says, "Thanks."

"Tell me what you're going to do when you get in there."

She shakes her head, fills her cheeks with air, and puffs out. "You same-same my mama. I go in. I look like I want find somebody. If I see, I call you. Hang up. Not go close. Not look him. *Okay?*"

"Okay." He fights down the urge to tell her again to be careful and stands there watching her limp barefoot across the street, shoes dangling from her left hand, a girl from the northeast who'd been a village teenager six or eight weeks ago. Now she's been cast on the surface of the Bangkok ocean like chum. Food for sharks.

She's inside, and Rafferty fights off a wave of uneasiness. He picks up her can of Coke and finishes it without tasting it, his eyes on the entrance. Without looking down he puts his phone on the table so he'll see it light up in his peripheral vision. It doesn't, and he knows he's got to move or he'll jump out of his skin.

She'll be fine, he thinks, crossing the street. The Beer Garden is full of people. She'll be one girl among a couple of hundred. She's not going anywhere near him. Go in, look for somebody, push a button. It's simple. And even if *everything* goes wrong, even if John has somehow seen them together outside the Beer Garden, what could he do to her with all those people around?

Rafferty positions himself about half a block to the right of the door, on the Beer Garden's side of the street. He figures John will head right, toward Sukhumvit, once he comes out. He'll be able to get a cab more easily there. Rafferty settles in to wait.

The phone doesn't ring. He has an irrational impulse to shake it.

And then it does.

He checks it and sees UNKNOWN NUMBER, which is what he expects, so he puts it in his pocket and prepares to settle in and wait for John. But it rings again, and again.

He fishes it out of his pocket, but it stops. Then, just as he starts to put it back, it rings again. He opens it and hears nothing, then a high, thin *"Oooooo"* and a choking sound, and then a clatter like the phone hitting a hard floor. Then it disconnects.

7

Nam Pla Prik

He's already running when the phone vibrates and then rings again, and he stops and answers, but no one is there. Instead he gets one of those twirling barber-pole lines that means something is downloading, and a moment later he's staring at an out-of-focus close-up of Pim, her eyes taking up half her face, looking like someone who's just opened the door to death.

He runs across the *soi* and jumps up the steps to the open-air restaurant where he and Pim had sat. The woman who waited on them looks apprehensive as she watches him come, moving behind her counter just in case.

"Nam soda," Rafferty gasps. "Soda water. In the bottle. Orange juice to go. *Hurry.*"

"You take bottle? Extra baht if you take—"

"Yeah, yeah. Here." He throws another hundred-baht note on the counter and shifts helplessly from foot to foot as the woman opens the cooler at Thai speed and pulls out a bottle of soda.

"Not so cold," she says doubtfully.

"I don't care. Open it and give it to me. Get the orange juice."

The woman pops the cap, releasing a spurt of soda, a sure sign that it's warm. Rafferty snatches it from her right hand and plucks the cap from the counter. As she prepares the orange juice, he pours out about a third of the soda, making a bubbling puddle at his feet. He snaps the bent cap back on as tightly as he can, shoves the bottle into the center of the back of his pants, against the gully of his spine, and tugs the T-shirt free so it hangs loose over his jeans. In the meantime the woman has taken a clear plastic bag and filled it halfway with orange juice, then stuck a straw into it, twisted the bag around the straw, and with expert quickness wrapped a rubber band around the bag to create a tight seal. She hands it to him and watches openmouthed as he undoes the rubber band, pulls the straw out, and pours the orange juice onto the concrete floor. Then he turns to the selection of condiments and picks up a clear glass bowl of nam pla prik, fish sauce with hundreds of tiny, fiery red and green peppers floating in it. He upends the bowl of chili sauce into the bag, replaces the straw, and reseals the bag with the rubber band. He wraps his right hand loosely around the bag and takes off at a dead run toward the Beer Garden.

He veers left, into the alley. John and his friends, if he has any with him, will be watching the entrance. If Rafferty goes in through the entrance, he'll have no options at all.

As he tears around the corner of the second alley to the right, he finds himself at the base of the eight-foot wall at the back of the Beer Garden. The Beer Garden is essentially open-air, although a roof has been built over the central area, covering the bar and the restaurant booths to the right of the door. But the roof is raised on poles; it doesn't join the walls in most places, and back here, where the kitchen and the restrooms are, there's a gap between the top of the wall and the roof, to let out heat and odors.

If Rafferty can get in here, he'll be at the back of the establishment, near the kitchen and the restrooms and behind everyone in the main room who's facing the doorway.

But the wall rises eight feet, and eight feet is too high. He could jump and get his hands on top of the wall, but there's no way he could hold on, much less climb up.

The area at the base of the wall is shaded by the umbrellas of vendors—a shoeshine man, a guy who repairs disposable lighters for a few pennies, a barber, complete with chair and mirror. About five feet from the wall, a woman carefully sews the hem of a skirt that's apparently been plucked from an overflowing basket beside her. She's using an antique sewing machine powered by a foot treadle. It's a heavy machine, and the old oak table it rests on looks like it's supported its burden for decades without so much as a creak of protest. Rafferty grips the bag of nam pla prik between his teeth, setting the tip of his tongue on fire, says "Shorry," grabs the table, and drags it to the base of the wall.

The woman calls after him, but by the time anyone has registered what he's doing, Rafferty is balanced on the table, feet on either side of the sewing machine. The table is a little more than three feet high, so he can get both arms over the top of the wall and haul himself up. The woman is still yelling at him and drawing a crowd, so he extracts yet another hundred-baht bill and lets it flutter down.

Because of the bottle tucked into the back of his pants, he has to go over the wall on his stomach. He hears women's voices, indignant and scolding, behind him, and when he turns, he sees a group of eight or ten Beer Garden regulars, women of various ages and shapes, tightly clustered around an open door. They look angry and upset, and some of them are trying to push others forward, through the door. The women at the front hold back, obviously unwilling or afraid to go in.

One of the women at the rear spots Rafferty and waves him to hurry. He palms the bag of chili sauce and covers the distance at a run. The women part, and he's looking into the men's room.

It's not much—a row of urinals with those round pink cakes in them that somebody somewhere thinks smell better than piss, a filthy once-white tile floor, a couple of sinks to the left of the door, and three toilet cubicles with a great many words scratched into them.

John is standing with his back against the wall of the center cubicle. He's sweating heavily, and there's a mean-looking six-inch knife in his hand, which he's using to try to get the crowd of women to back up. Crumpled on the floor beside him, leaning against the door of the right-hand cubicle, her face a twist of pain and her left arm hanging uselessly in her lap, is Pim. Her shoes lie on their sides next to her, and the bandage around her ankle is soiled from the floor. Tears have eroded deep, wet tracks through her cakey makeup from her eyes to her jawline. A teardrop dangles from her chin.

Rafferty eases the last woman aside and says to John, "Get away from her."

"The hero," John says. "Send in a girl. What an asswipe. Come on in here, asswipe."

"You're fucked," Rafferty says. "I don't think Howard is going to like this at all."

"The hell with Howard," John says, but he sounds less certain. "Get in here."

"Yeah? What do you think you're going to do? Cut me in front of all these ladies? Fight your way out of here with me bleeding in the bathroom? Howard will love that, his fifth-rate jerkwater backup in jail, charged with stupidity. What were you supposed to do? Follow me. Find out where I went. Get a little information. Report back to Howard, wherever Howard is. Instead here you are, stuck in a toilet with a knife in your hand." Rafferty comes just inside the door. "Where's Howard?"

John says, "Fuck yourself," and flourishes the knife, doing a gleaming, professional-looking, little back-and-forth razzle-dazzle, but Rafferty ignores it. Either the man will use it or he won't.

"I asked you a question."

John puts the tip of his tongue to his upper lip and then retracts it. "And I told you what you can do, if your dick is long enough to stick it up your ass."

"I also told you to get away from her."

"Man," John says, "you are *so* not listening."

Rafferty's got no moves that will protect him from a blade. What he can do, if he can work up the courage, is to offer John another target. He takes a longer look at Pim, who is staring up at him wet-eyed, slumped slightly to the side to try to ease the weight of her damaged left arm. He flips a mental coin, and it comes up heads: John would prefer not to use the knife. So Rafferty grabs a deep breath and brushes past the man as though he's not there, barely bothering to sidestep the knife, and bends down over Pim, practically waving in John's face the freshly bandaged left elbow.

John seizes the advantage, grabs the bandages, and squeezes for all he's worth, with explosive results. Rafferty lets out a bellow of pain, straightens convulsively, and through a sort of red haze he brings his right hand, with the plastic bag in it, up into John's face. When the straw is pointed at the other man's eyes, Rafferty squeezes the bag.

His own cry is still ragged in his throat, but even so he can hear John howl. John yanks his head back, slamming it against the wall of the toilet cubicle and scrubbing at his eyes with his forearm as Rafferty reaches back, lifts his T-shirt, and brings out the heavy soda bottle, clutching it by the neck. With an effort that begins at the soles of his feet, he slams the bottle against the side of John's head, so hard that the bottle almost flies out of his hand. There's a surprising *crack*, a sound that nearly persuades Rafferty he's broken the man's skull. John's knees accordion outward like he's doing a dance step, and he goes down. Rafferty whacks him again for insurance as he drops, hitting his ear this time. John crumples on the floor like a loose sack, looking as though he has no muscles in his body.

Rafferty stands over him, panting, making sure the man is out. From beneath John's head, blood begins to pool across the tile floor. The women standing in the doorway break into applause.

Taking it one deliberate step at a time, Rafferty puts the bottle down carefully, not spilling the remaining soda, and kneels beside John. He pries the knife from the man's hand, tosses the blade against the opposite wall, and puts a couple of fingers over John's pulse, which is reassuringly strong and steady. As if on cue, the man moans, and Pim lets out a squeak of terror and scrabbles away from him, using her good arm to pull her along.

"I need a belt," Rafferty says in Thai to the women in the doorway. They're pushing at each other now, peering in at the flattened man and the injured girl. A woman in front, older and tattooed and somehow familiar, unbuckles her belt, slips it free of her jeans, and throws it to him.

She says, in English, "Here, Poke," and Rafferty takes his eyes off the belt to look at her, and it falls at his feet, the heavy buckle making an echoing clank as it hits the tile.

"Move," Rafferty says to Pim, and when she's scooted farther away, he rolls John over onto his stomach, yanks his arms behind his back, and makes a tight figure eight with the belt, wrapping it around and between the arms just above the elbows, Khmer Rouge style, where John won't be able to reach it with his hands. When he's tugged it as tight as he can, he secures the buckle and takes a quick look at John's scalp. The bottle broke the skin, but there doesn't seem to be any real damage, just the usual aggressive bleeding from a scalp wound. He rolls John onto his back again.

"Hold still," he says to Pim. He puts his hand on her left shoulder and probes it gently. She lets out a shrill yelp. "Dislocated," he says. "Stay where you are."

Pim says, around a sniffle, "But—"

"Do what I say. If you move around, it'll hurt more." He turns to the woman who threw him the belt. He's suddenly immensely weary. "I'm sorry. I know you, but I can't remember your name."

"Lan," she says. "I dance King's Castle long time. Before, me friend for Rose."

"Right, right. Sorry, Lan. Where's security? They should be here by now."

"You want?"

"No, I don't. If they come, try to keep them out, okay?"

"Okay. Him." She points her foot at John, a gesture of contempt. "Him boxing her. *Bang,* take her hair, pull her."

"Well, he's not going to enjoy the next few minutes." John moans again, and Rafferty gets up, turns on the water in the sink, cups his hands beneath the spout, and throws the water at John. He does it three or four times, and then John's eyes are open. He struggles once against the belt, takes a quick look around the bathroom—at Rafferty, at the huddled Pim, at the band of angry women. His eyes find the knife on the other side of the room, and he goes still. He's not even looking at Rafferty.

"What's your full name?" Rafferty asks, kneeling beside him again.

"Fuck you," John says. He's looking past Rafferty at the wall.

Rafferty picks up the soda bottle, which feels like it weighs ten pounds. "If I hit you in exactly the same place, it's going to get your attention." He wiggles the bottle by its neck.

John closes his eyes and slowly opens them again. "Bohnert. John Bohnert."

"Spell it."

"B-o-h-n-e-r-t."

"What did you think you were doing today? When I saw you on Sukhumvit."

"Looking for a library. I'm a big reader."

"Who else was following us?"

The question provokes a surprised contraction of Bohnert's eyebrows, quickly smoothed away. Then he shakes his head.

"Was somebody else following Rose?"

Bohnert squirms for a moment, testing the strength of the belt, and Rafferty puts an open hand on the man's throat and presses down, hard. "Stay put and I'll let you breathe. I asked whether anyone was following Rose."

Rafferty lifts his hand, and Bohnert coughs. "Who's Rose?"

"Be like that," Rafferty says. "But listen. You're going to tell me what I want to know, and you really ought to do it the easy way. So I can feel good about myself when this is over."

"Have I said 'fuck you' yet?"

"Well, it's a good thing my self-esteem is solid," Rafferty says. "Otherwise I might regret doing this."

He picks up the bottle of soda and holds it to the light, checking the level. Still about two-thirds full. John winces at the sight of it and draws his head away, but Rafferty pops the cap with his thumb, puts the bottle down again, and pulls the straw out of the bag of chili sauce.

There's a murmur among the women gathered at the door. Three or four of them are whispering to others.

"You know this one, do you?" he asks them. Even Pim is watching now, although she looks puzzled. She hasn't been here long enough to learn the trick, which owes its existence to the limitless imagination and limited resources of the Thai police.

"A friend of mine who's a cop told me about this. It's not a complicated recipe," Rafferty says to Bohnert, who's working on looking impassive, his eyes once again on the wall. "The trick is to get the proportions right. Also, it works better if you can grind the chilies to a paste, but this is an improvisation."

He gathers the open end of the bag of chili sauce into a tight bunch and works it into the neck of the soda bottle. Then he upends the bag and squeezes on it again so the nam pla prik flows into the soda water, turning it the color of weak tea with lots of little red and green bits floating in it. To Bohnert he says, "You following this?"

Bohnert says nothing.

"One more chance," Rafferty says, hoping the man will cooperate. He's seeing little bright flashes at the corners of his vision, and he can hear his blood singing high and thin in his ears. His voice sounds distant, as though he's hearing it through a wall. "One more chance for us both to walk out of here feeling relatively okay. Where's Horner?"

Bohnert says, "You're dead. You and the whore and the midget. You're dead."

Rafferty says, "I'm sorry you feel that way." He puts his thumb tightly over the top of the bottle and shakes it vigorously as the women's voices rise in expectation. When he can feel that the pressure's increased as much as it's going to, he brings the Coke bottle up to Bohnert's nose, removes his thumb, and jams the bottle into the left nostril.

Coca-Cola spurts out of Bohnert's nose and over Rafferty's hand, and John's knees unbend spasmodically, scissoring in both directions. Rafferty rises and steps back as Bohnert thrashes on the floor, coughing and choking, and then the chili hits, and he roars and jackknifes and then straightens, kicking his feet out so fast that he cracks both shins against the vertical support of the toilet cubicle, and he twists back and forth, rocking on his bound arms, hacking and spitting and sobbing simultaneously.

Rafferty's voice feels like it's being forced through a sieve. "Where's Horner?" His phone begins to ring.

Bohnert's eyes are streaming water, but he pulls his mouth tight and spits at Rafferty.

As his phone continues to ring, Rafferty bends over John and says between his teeth, "There's lots left. Let's try again." He puts his thumb over the bottle and starts to shake it.

"No," Bohnert says. It's mostly breath.

The phone stops ringing. "Why were you following us?"

"See . . . where you went. Who you know."

"Why?"

Bohnert's nose is running, and he sniffs, which is a mistake that registers instantly. He blows out explosively and makes a retching sound that turns into another fit of coughing. When it's over, he lies still except for deep, shuddering breaths, and Rafferty says again, "Why?"

"Pressure points," Bohnert says. "Looking . . . for pressure points."

Rafferty's phone rings again. He looks at it and sees ROSE.

"What does Horner want with her?"

"Don't know."

"Fine." Rafferty puts the phone into his pocket and shakes the bottle again. John is pushing back with his legs, trying to scrabble away, under the wall of the toilet cubicle. A couple of the women laugh.

"He . . . he says she tried to kill him."

"Why?"

"Don't know. Really, *really.* He wanted—Howard wanted—to marry her."

"He . . ." Rafferty stands there, the bottle dangling heavy in his hand, feeling as if a building just fell on him. "*Marry* her?"

"He asked her, she said yes. That's what he says."

"True or false?" He shakes the bottle again,

"True, true. Ask her. Ask *her,* not me." Bohnert's voice breaks like an adolescent's.

"And where is old Howard?"

"I . . . I can't."

"Sure you can. Unless you want to sneeze blood for the next week."

Bohnert's face softens, and he starts to cry like a child, and Rafferty, with no pleasure, recognizes a self-shattering sense of shame. "He's in . . . he's in Afghanistan," Bohnert says.

"CALL DR. RATT," Rafferty says into the phone. "Tell him—"

"You went after him, didn't you?" Rose demands, her tone as sharp as broken glass. "That man, the one who was with Howard. How *stupid* can—"

"I'm not up for an argument." The sweat he smells now is his own, his T-shirt wet and heavy beneath his arms. "Call Dr. Ratt. Get him and Nui there now."

"And you got yourself hurt," Rose says. "You *saw* them, you saw how they were, and now—"

"It's not me. And will you please—" Beside him, on the backseat of the cab, Pim shifts her weight away from him and whimpers.

"Then who?"

"Goddamn it, will you please do what I'm asking you to do?" He is suddenly so furious that his mouth tastes like metal. "Will you just fucking do what I want?"

Pim pulls farther away, leaning against the door.

There is a long pause. Then Rose says, in a voice he's never heard before, "You sound like a customer."

He is trying to think of something to say when he hears her disconnect.

ROSE'S EYES ARE stones when she opens the door, but the moment she sees Pim, her face softens. "You poor baby," she says in Thai. "You've been crying." Her eyes flick to Rafferty's bandage, but she makes no comment, just gathers Pim in.

Behind Rose, Dr. Ratt's wife, Nui, gives Pim a sharp-eyed glance. "It's a new one," she says in English, calling toward the kitchen. Rafferty can hear water running, so the doctor is probably washing his hands.

"How long have you been in Bangkok?" Rose has wrapped a long arm carefully around the girl. Pim's chin is dimpling at the sympathy.

"Three weeks," she says. Even less time than Rafferty had guessed.

"And what's the problem?" Rose asks in Thai. "Did my husband beat you up?"

"No," Pim says. "He was wonderful. He stuck a bottle right up the man's nose."

"Did he?" Rose says, without a glance at Rafferty. She guides Pim toward the counter between the living room and the kitchen. "Sometimes he's nice by accident."

"Ahh, our patients have arrived," Dr. Ratt says in what he imagines to be a soothing tone but has always sounded to Rafferty like the voice of an amateur who's somehow gotten on the radio. "Who needs to be looked at first?"

"Sorry to disappoint everyone," Rafferty says, "but this is nothing." He raises the bandaged elbow. "I'm fine."

"Oh, well. That won't last long, the way you live. Who's our little friend here?"

"My name is Pim," Pim says, looking dazzled. Dr. Ratt and Nui are dressed like a cross between medical personnel and slumming angels, he in a white tunic that looks like something Nehru might have worn if Nehru had been a doctor, with a stethoscope gleaming around his neck for effect, and Nui in the latest of a long line of hand-tailored all-silk nurse's outfits. The two of them have made a fortune by defeating Bangkok's fearsome traffic, putting multiple teams of doctors and nurses in cars twenty-four hours a day on the assumption that often enough, when a call comes in, there will be a team nearby. A lot of the profit has gone into clothes. Faced with their soigné urban elegance, Pim folds her arms around her middle to cover some of her bare brown skin and appears even more uncomfortable than before.

"Mmmm," Dr. Ratt says, giving her a closer look. "Dislocated, is it?"

"It is," Rafferty says.

"When I need a layman's opinion." Dr. Ratt says, without glancing up, "you probably won't be the layman I ask."

"When everyone hates you," Rafferty says, "drink beer." He goes into the kitchen and pulls the refrigerator door open.

"Well, now," Dr. Ratt says, with a "come here" glance at Nui. Between them they maneuver Pim onto one of the stools at the counter and then swivel the stool so she's got her back to the kitchen and is facing into the living room. She sits there, hunched over protectively, looking from one of them to the other, as though she's trying to decide which of them will bite her first.

"This is going to hurt," Dr. Ratt says, taking her left wrist. "Only for a second, though, and then it'll be fine."

"But—" Pim says, just as Dr. Ratt brings the arm up, twists it slightly, and pushes, and it pops into the socket, accompanied by a squeal from Pim that goes through Rafferty's ears like a smoking wire.

"There," Dr. Ratt says. Pim is bent double, holding her shoulder. "Better?"

"Yes," she says, "but it hurts."

"Well, I lied about that. It'll be sore until tomorrow. But it doesn't hurt like before, does it?"

"Oh, no."

"He did this to her?" Rose asks. It is an accusation.

"John," Rafferty says. "The other one. John Bohnert. He's not as dangerous as he thinks he is."

"Don't you fool yourself," Rose says.

"He told me something interesting."

"Hard to believe," Rose says. Dr. Ratt, Nui, and Pim are watching the two of them, unwilling to interrupt.

"What?" says a new voice, and Rafferty looks around the kitchen door to see Miaow. "What was that noise?" Miaow gives Pim a glance that takes in the garish makeup and the cheap clothes, then dismisses her. "And who's *this*?"

"Her name is Pim," Rose says, all ice. "Not 'this.'"

"You're grumpy," Miaow says, turning back toward her room. "And he's got bandages on and he's drinking beer. Call me when dinner's ready."

"Hello," Pim says, but Miaow keeps walking.

"You were just spoken to," Rose says to Miaow's back.

"Well," Dr. Ratt says, "if no one else is hurt, we should probably be going."

"Yeah, hello," Miaow mumbles, without slowing.

"You turn around *right now*," Rose says. "Who are you to be so rude?"

"It's all right," Pim says.

Miaow stops, wheels around, and impales Rose with a glare. "Why are you so *mean*?"

"That's it," Nui says, grabbing her husband's arm. To Rafferty she says, "Call us if this gets medical." She hauls Dr. Ratt toward the door.

"I haven't paid you," Rafferty says.

"For that? Forget it." Nui is already opening the door, but the doctor puts a hand on the jamb to keep from being towed out of the room. "If you get a chance," he says, "mention us in one of those magazines you write for." He nods to Pim. "Nice to meet you, young lady."

Pim gives a high *wai* of respect to the door, which is already swinging shut behind him. She calls out, "Thank you," but the closing of the door cuts the phrase in half. To Rafferty she says, eyes shining, "He's a real doctor."

"He is," Rafferty says. "And he's got manners, too."

"Oh, blah, blah, blah," Miaow says. "Why doesn't *everybody* just yell at me?"

"Miaow," Rafferty says, "I know it's hard, at your age, to believe that there's anything that's not about you, but it's true."

"Oh?" Miaow says, and her chin juts out in challenge. "So you're yelling at me because of what? Because of Rose? Or maybe *her*?" She flips a thumb at Pim. "Or the guys in the restaurant? Or whoever hurt your stupid arm? Like, what, it's an accident that *I'm* the one you're yelling at? If someone else was standing here, would you be yelling at them instead of me? Fine. I won't stand here anymore. One of *you* can stand here and let him yell at *you*." She turns and stalks down the hall, and a moment later the door to her room slams.

Rose stands, looking after her as though she'd vanished through a wall. She seems distant enough to be reconsidering her entire life. Rafferty drains his beer and thinks about getting another. Then Rose says to Pim, "We're not usually like this."

Pim glances at Rafferty, looking for help, but he's staring into the refrigerator. She says, "Oh." She makes fluttering gestures with her fingers, but no words come.

"This is not a good job," Rose says, her voice flat. "What you've come to Bangkok to do. It's not good for you."

"My parents," Pim says. "And there are five kids." She puts a brown hand flat on her bare knee, fingers spread wide, and stares down at it. She swivels on the stool, and her hot pants glitter. "Everybody needs money," she finally says.

"I know," Rose says. Then she says, "Poke. Get me a beer."

"Gee," Rafferty says. "You're speaking to me." He pulls a Singha out of the refrigerator and says to Pim, "Want one?"

She shakes her head. "I don't drink."

"See?" Rose says over the hiss and fizz as Rafferty pops the cap. "You're a good girl. I know it feels like there's nothing else you can do, but you're wrong. You have no idea how wrong you are. You think you'll do it for a while, a few years, and then it'll all be over, but you're wrong. It's never really over. I haven't danced in more than five years, I'm married, I have a husband and a daughter, and it still comes up and kicks me in the teeth."

"*You* danced?" Pim says. She blows out a deep breath of admiration. "You must have made big money. I'll bet you got all-nights, maybe even weeks. I'm not beautiful like you. I usually have to wait until they're drunk before one of them picks me, and then it's a short-time. Nobody ever wants me to stay all night." She rubs her palms over her thighs as though she's cold. "I hate going home after, at three or four in the morning with money in my pocket, dressed like this. It frightens me."

"It should *all* frighten you," Rose says, taking the beer from Rafferty. "You see how disrespectful my daughter just was? That's because she's ashamed of me. My *daughter*. She could barely look at you because of what you do. And she was a street kid just a few years ago, so it's not like she shits silk. Is that what you want? Someday, after you fuck a thousand drunk men, and defend yourself against the ones who hate women, and avoid getting AIDS, and save your money, and maybe even buy a little house, if you're not like all the other girls who spend the money as fast as it comes and lose it at cards and give it to boyfriends who beat them up. If all that happens, if you live through it and take care of everybody and keep a little money somehow, then your daughter is disgusted with you."

"Miaow's a kid," Rafferty says.

"What do you think Pim is?" Rose says, just this side of a snap. "And don't say 'Oh, that's different,' because it wouldn't have been, not if you hadn't come along. What do you think Miaow would have been doing at— How old are you, eighteen?"

"Sort of," Pim says.

"What would Miaow have been doing at seventeen or eighteen, do you think?" Rose demands. "Running for office? *Look* at her, Poke. She even looks a little like Miaow."

Rafferty looks at the girl, and Rose is right. They're both small, brown, and shaped by the distinctive gene pool of the northeast, with rounded features, broad nostrils, and the fine, dark, flyaway hair that Miaow used to part and slick down with water. "A little," he says.

"Miaow is your daughter?" Pim says. "She's prettier than I am."

"It'll change you," Rose continues, as though no one else has spoken. "Now you're a good girl, you're a village girl who's never hurt anybody. Two, three years from now, you'll lie, you'll tell men you love them when you can't stand the sight of them. You'll steal their money when they're in the shower, then tiptoe out of the room. You'll tell your friends to look for them outside the club so you can hide when they come in. You'll drink and smoke and take *yaa baa* and nobody knows what else. You won't be Pim anymore."

"*You* haven't changed."

Rose tilts her head back and drains most of the beer in three or four long swallows. "I don't even have my own name," she says. "Now I'm Rose. Before, in my village, my name was Kwan. I came to Bangkok as Kwan, who bathed in the river under a long cloth and washed my hair in rainstorms with all my clothes on. I kept my voice down to be polite. I was a good daughter and granddaughter. I was embarrassed to be so tall. It took about six months before I turned into this person called Rose, who danced nearly naked every night and gave big smiles to men when what she wanted to do was to kick them in the face. I ate *yaa baa* like candy, and I smoked"—she looks down at the cigarette in her hand—"about as much as I smoke now. I let one of the men rename me. A man gave me the name Rose—you didn't know that, did you, Poke?" She hasn't turned to face him. "He said, this man, he said that Kwan was too hard to remember, even though it's a good name and it means 'spirit,' and that the rose was the queen of flowers and I was the queen of Patpong." She laughs, rough as a cough. "The queen of Patpong. A kingdom of whores and viruses. Death with a smile. Every dick every night, every guy who wants to go bareback, maybe he's the one who'll give it to you. So you visit the temple and you pray and you say no when they don't want to wear one, and they slap you around until you say yes, and then you go to the temple and pray harder, and you're terrified next time you get tested. Except you learn, when you've been here for a while, that all the tests are negative. Even if you're positive, the tests are negative." She inhales the rest of the cigarette as though she'd like to bite into it and spit it out. "Did you know that, Poke? All the tests are negative. Positive tests are too expensive for the bars."

"I don't think that's true anymore," Rafferty says.

Rose backs across the living room, drinking as she goes, still looking at Pim. When she feels her legs touch the couch, she collapses and tosses the almost-extinct cigarette butt into the ashtray. "True or not, who cares? You." She tosses the word toward Pim as if it were a rock. "You want to spend your life worrying about condoms? You want to ride up in elevators with guys who might decide to break your fingers? You want to learn to pee on guys who need that? You want to do threeways and four-ways and five-ways and whatever way the guy wants? You want guys to put it in your butt?"

There's a moment of dumbfounded silence, and Pim bursts into tears. She puts her right hand on her injured shoulder and cradles it, then reaches down and grabs her ankle and just lets the sobs come. They're big, gulping sobs, minor-key foghorn tones, sobs that lift her back and lets it drop, and they come from someplace very deep.

Rafferty says, "Great. You've cheered her right up."

"I wasn't trying to cheer her up," Rose snaps. "I was trying to— I was trying to . . . save her. *Save* her, okay? Is that too dramatic for you? Does all the talk make you uncomfortable? You want to leave it unspoken? What do you want to believe? You want to believe that I lived on the tips from colas? That I turned down guys for all those years, just waiting for you to come in off the street?"

"It's a little late for that," Rafferty says, and he feels an immediate and blood-hot wash of shame.

A door bangs against a wall, and a moment later Miaow stalks into the room. Without looking at either Rose or Rafferty, she goes to Pim and rests a hand on the back of the girl's neck. "Come on," she says. "You can cry in my room. She'll leave you alone in there."

Pim gets up, looking even younger than Miaow, and Miaow puts an arm around her and leads her out of the room. This time she closes the door quietly.

Rafferty stays where he is, listening to the silence reestablish itself in the room. Rose is as still as a mannequin for the space of nine or ten breaths, and then she pulls back her arm and slings the beer bottle, end over end, spewing beer, at the sliding glass door to the balcony. The bottle explodes in a skyrocket of brown sparkles, and the pane of glass in the door cracks from corner to corner. By the time Rafferty has torn his eyes from the damage, Rose is already up and heading for the bedroom, her spine as straight as a bullet's path, her hands balled into fists. She shoves the door aside with her shoulder and kicks it closed behind her.

IT TAKES PIM a few minutes to stop crying, or at least to lower the volume to the point at which it's not audible from Miaow's room. There's a single crash of something hard and heavy in the room Rafferty and Rose share. Then there's nothing at all, just the steady sigh of the air conditioner, and the city dark and sparkling behind the crack in the glass door, turning the jagged seam into a long, narrow prism, shining with color like a frozen rainbow.

It seems like a good idea to clean up the broken glass. This is an area in which he can be helpful. He can think of no reason that anyone would get angry at him for cleaning up the broken glass.

He goes into the kitchen and pulls open the door of the narrow pantry, which is next to the stove, tugging it gently to keep the catch from making its snapped-finger sound and opening it only partway so it won't bang against the handle of the oven.

A loud noise right now would, he thinks, break him in pieces.

The dustpan and the broom are exactly where they should be. There's a sort of smugness to them, an implicit criticism of everyone and everything else in an apartment where nothing seems to be where, or the way, it should be. He picks up the items carefully, as if they were made of hundred-year-old crystal, and carries them into the living room, making a detour to the door to slip into his shoes. The shards of brown bottle glass cover a roughly semicircular area of carpet in a radius of about two feet. Some larger pieces glitter even farther away. The neck, widening at its base into a jagged crown, would make a formidable weapon. He picks it up. If he'd broken the soda bottle on John's head, he would have been holding something as lethal as this. It's easy to imagine bringing it up, the neck clenched firmly in his fist, to cut long, deep, bleeding scores in John's flesh. Parallel, like rows in a field, spouting blood wherever the furrow intersected an artery.

On the whole, he decides, looking down at his knuckles, gone white on the bottle's neck, he's glad the soda bottle remained intact. He'd been angry enough to cut John, cut him badly. Instead all he'd done was inflict temporary damage on the man's mucous membranes. And he wasn't happy with himself even about that.

He isn't really happy with anyone.

A bag. He needs a paper bag now, doesn't he? There's not much fucking point, he thinks—and then goes back and deletes the "fucking"—there's not much point in picking up a few hundred pieces of broken glass without having something to put them in.

He gets up, hearing his knees pop in a way they didn't used to, and returns to the kitchen. The paper supermarket bags are neatly folded into thirds and pressed flat, then jammed by Rose into the space between the side of the stove and the counter, in such high numbers that they've reached the kind of superdensity that Rafferty associates with collapsed stars. It takes him three or four minutes to tease one out, and when he's worked the corner free and is tugging it, it promptly tears off in his hand. The rest of the bag remains, pristine and unmolested, in the cramp of brown paper between the oven and the counter.

He crouches there, the kitchen floor vaguely tacky under the soles of his shoes, and looks down at the little corner of bag in his hand. Then he gets up, deliberately drops the tiny piece of paper on the floor, and grinds it beneath his shoe. That chore done, he puts both hands against the edge of the stove and shoves it with every ounce of strength he possesses, into the side of the pantry.

The stove has only a couple of inches to travel, but it accelerates surprisingly and creates a rewarding *wham* when it hits the pantry wall. The smell of old grease wafts invisibly upward. Lazily, as if in slow motion, the bags that had been jammed between the counter and the side of the stove fan out like a hand in gin rummy and then spill onto the kitchen floor in a slippery cascade. Some of them manage to slide all the way to the counter on the room's far side.

Isn't gin rummy an alcoholic-sounding game? Rafferty thinks as he uses the soles of his shoes to stretch, mark, and tear as many of the bags as possible. Gin *and* rum, all in one game—and a game that kids play, at that. Have to look into the origins of the name sometime. This is precisely the kind of thing the *Oxford English Dictionary* is for, not that he has an *Oxford English Dictionary*. What he has, at the moment at least, is an apartment that is easy to visualize as a map, complete with borders, heavily defended borders, dividing the independent nations that fight over the space: Roseland, Miaowistan, and the Kingdom of Poke. Crossing these borders involves negotiation, checkpoints, and body-cavity searches. And even then you might be turned away.

"I didn't sign on for this," he says aloud.

He picks up the single bag that's survived his shoes—obviously the sturdiest bag of all, and it *has* to be sturdy to hold this much broken glass without shredding, so he can tell Rose, assuming he ever speaks to her again, that he was testing the bags to find the one that would keep them safe from the shards. Safe from the shards, safe from the shards. He totes the shard-safe bag into the living room, where he sees the broom and dustpan right where he put them a year or two ago, and he sets the bag down, sweeps some glass into the dustpan, tries three times to sweep in one larger piece that doesn't want to be swept, bends down to *shove* it into the dustpan, and . . .

. . . slices the pad of his thumb.

In one white-hot movement, he drops the piece of glass, drops the dustpan, grabs his thumb and squeezes it, all the while straightening his knees and his back, coming up until he's standing and whirling in a circle against the pain, swinging the bleeding thumb fast enough to create a zigzag Jackson Pollock lighting strike of blood on the white wall beside the door. He steps sideways and bangs his bandaged elbow against the wall to his left, and the next thing he knows, he's kicking the dustpan as hard as he can and it's sailing across the room straight and true, shedding splinters of glass as it gains altitude, until it bangs up against the door to the bedroom. It flips over and spills all the glass he's swept up, directly onto the carpet in front of the bedroom door.

A moment later the door opens, and Rose stands there. She sees the blood on the wall, sees him folded over in pain, and steps into the room at the precise instant he realizes that she's barefoot.

"No!" he shouts.

Rose says *"Uuuuiiii, uuuuiiii!"* and grabs her right foot. She looks at the bottom of the foot, and she's bleeding.

Rafferty feels something swell inside him, low in his belly, and then there's some kind of pressure forcing its way up, and suddenly he's laughing. The laughter reaches down and brings more laughter with it, and he's standing there, still bent over, injured elbow tight against his side, squeezing his sliced thumb, simultaneously laughing like a fool and blinking away tears as Rose, her foot still in her hand, glares down at the hazardous litter on the carpet in front of her, clenches her teeth, bends the knee of the leg she's standing on, and jumps over the spill of glass. She lands on one leg, windmills her free arm to stay up, and manages to remain standing, and then she's laughing, too, and Rafferty moves crablike, still bent forward, across the room to her, and he puts his unbandaged arm around her, pointing the bleeding thumb away to keep the blood off her clothes, and the two of them lean against each other and laugh until Rose starts to cry.

Very slowly, very carefully, Rafferty maneuvers her to the couch, Rose taking small, backward, one-legged hops, and gets her seated. He kneels in front of her and cups her face in his hands, painting a bright brushstroke of blood across her cheek, as she closes her eyes and weeps, bringing her own hands up to hold his wrists. He leans toward her until their foreheads are touching, his hands still cradling her face. She makes an enormous snuffling sound, and he laughs again, although his own cheeks are cool and wet. Rose's sobbing turns into a laugh and then a hiccup, and Rafferty says, "Look at us."

Rose pulls back enough to pass her arm over her cheeks and sees the blood she's smeared on her arm. "We're both bleeding."

Rafferty says, "Are we ever."

He feels a presence and turns to his left to see Miaow and Pim standing there, staring at them, eyes wide and faces wide open.

Rose snuffles again and then wipes her nose on the back of her hand. "Okay," she says. "It's time."

Pim backs away from the crying, laughing people on the couch. She puts a hand behind her for the doorknob and says, "Thank you for a nice afternoon."

"You might as well stay," Rose says. "You need to hear this as much as they do."

"But I have to—"

Rose sails over her with a single breath. "No you don't. You need to know about this. You must be hungry, right? Well, Poke's going to bandage his thumb and bring me a bandage for my foot, and then he's going down to get us all some takeout from the street vendors. You and Miaow can go down with him to help him carry it all. Get a lot, because this is going to take a long time."

Miaow looks suspicious. "What're *you* going to do?"

Rose reaches over and brushes Rafferty's hair off his forehead, then raises her hand as though she's going to swat him. "Be Poke's wife," she says. "Wipe blood off walls. Sweep glass."

PART II

1997

THE SEA CHANGE

8

The Shoes

Afternoon sunlight sparkles off the stones on her fingers and at her wrists.

Kwan watches as the young woman leads a small parade of children, the bolder ones pushing forward for a closer look as though she's fallen to the dust from outer space, as though some of them hadn't known her when she was as brown and filthy as they are. The children wear patched shorts and dirt-brown T-shirts, liberally ventilated with holes. Their feet are bare or slap along on rubber flip-flops. Scabs define their knees, and their legs are lumped and mottled from insect bites. One of them, not one of the bolder ones, is Kwan's next-youngest sister, Mai. At thirteen, Mai is one of the tallest children in the queue, but that's because she's older than most of them. She hasn't yet had the growth spurt her mother dreads, the spurt that says that Mai may yet become as freakishly tall as Kwan.

As tall as the Stork.

The boy bringing up the end of the line proudly tows a small bright pink suitcase. It has wheels, and they get snagged in the holes that pit the road every few feet, so the boy doing the honors has to yank the wheels free every time and then catch up with the parade. In the background, at the village's edge, the dented orange taxi that first drew the children's attention finishes a jerky turnaround—back and forth, back and forth, trying not to bump two rickety houses it could bulldoze flat without denting its fenders—and bounces over the rutted track leading back toward the railroad station, kicking up a plume of reddish dust that drifts across the village in a dry parody of fog.

The woman the children follow shimmers like an exotic tropical bird that's landed among the rice sparrows. She wears a loose blouse the color of sunset—silk, from the way the air drapes and redrapes it—and a short, tight, glittery black skirt. Shiny high heels in a leopard-skin pattern puncture the dust of the road between the houses. The woman's skin, paler than Kwan remembers it, looks polished, as though it's been slowly rubbed smooth. The highlights in her shaped and tapered hair, bright enough to have been shellacked, are almost blinding in the slanting sun. She pays no attention to the kids, but as she passes Kwan's house, she looks up and smiles.

Kwan feels like she's been caught spying. She pulls back, ducking behind the damp clothes that hang on the line strung above the deck around her sagging wooden house. The deck and the house are raised about a meter above the dirt to keep the floors dry in the rainy season. Kwan reads the name of the rice company printed on the inside of one of her mother's dresses before she realizes how rude she's being, and she pushes aside the stiffening and now-dusty clothes and does her best to return Moo's smile.

"We should talk while I'm here," Moo says, looking up at Kwan Then, as though she's remembering something, she says, more politely, "Are you well? Have you had rice yet?"

"I'm fine, thank you," Kwan says. She knows she's blushing. Moo has never once spoken to her in the four summers since she went down to Bangkok, never even seemed to notice her. Now that they're speaking, Kwan has no idea what to say.

"Straighten up," Moo says severely. "You're tall. You can't fool anybody by bending over like that. You just look crippled. Stand up and be proud of it. Some men will like it."

Now Kwan's face is aflame. This is her least favorite topic. "Nobody likes it," she says. "I look like a giraffe."

Moo nods, but she's not listening. The nod is polite dismissal. "Maybe tonight," she says. "We'll talk." She starts to move away but stops, and some of the kids who were already in motion behind her bump into each other. She reaches up to her left ear and fiddles with something for a moment. Then she mimes a little underhand throwing motion, and Kwan brings her hands up, and on the second pass Moo actually does throw something, something that flashes blue in the air as it flies and then lands, small, hard, and sharp, between Kwan's panicky, hurriedly clasped hands. An earring.

A sapphire earring.

The stone is the size of a small raisin, dark blue as the new-moon sky, mounted on a straight gold post. A little tangle of gold wire that looks like one of the symbols in written music that Kwan has seen in school—a clef, the bass clef, for low music, Teacher Suttikul calls it—is stuck on the post, where it secures the earring to the lobe and holds it in place. The earring probably cost more money than her father earns in two years.

Kwan says, "Oh, Moo. I can't—"

"*Not Moo,*" the woman says, and her smile goes muscular, just something her face is doing, with nothing behind it. "Not Moo anymore. My name is Nana."

"Nana," Kwan corrects herself. She *knows* that. Moo has called herself Nana for years now, ever since the first time she came back. Kwan wants to kick herself. She never gets anything right. Tall, awkward, tall, stupid, tall.

"Put it on," Nana says. "After we talk, I'll give you the other one."

"No, no. You don't need to give me anything just to talk to me. I'm happy to—"

"When somebody gives you something, you take it," Nana says, without smiling. "They don't teach you that in school, so I've made this whole long trip here to say it to you. And this way we'll be sure to talk." She makes a little side-to-side bye-bye wave, more brisk than friendly, checks the location of the child hauling her suitcase, and resumes her procession down the red ribbon of dust that separates the run-down houses on Kwan's side of the village from the run-down houses on the other side. The children are towed into motion behind her, like ducklings.

Kwan tears her eyes from the blue stone in her hand to Moo's leopard-spotted shoes. Yellow and black, impossibly pointed in the toe, they send thin yellow straps spiraling almost all the way up to the knee. They seem to have been made by someone who has never seen a foot.

How does Moo—*Nana*—how does Nana walk in them? The heels must be five inches high. The village road is uneven, with holes everywhere, hidden beneath the dust. How does she keep from breaking her ankles?

Something warm seems to flood through Kwan's veins. Unconsciously, she slides her foot out of her rubber flip-flop, a man's size medium, worn cardboard-thin beneath the ball of her foot, and points her toes straight down. How would it feel to wear shoes like that?

Tall is how it would feel. Even taller than she is now. Tall enough to talk to birds. Tall enough to see the sun rise half an hour before anybody else, to eat the tender top leaves of trees. Tall enough to have men tilt their heads way back to look up at her and then grab their necks in pretended pain. And then laugh.

Of course, they already do that.

THE PARADE IS long gone, and the street is settling into the slow cooling that ushers in the evening. The warped, mismatched wood of Kwan's house, and of the houses on both sides of the street, begins to rehearse its little orchestra of groans and creaks, just a tune-up for the ensemble piece of contracting and settling to come, when the sun is down. Her house makes so much noise that it seems to Kwan it must shrink two or three inches every evening. She wishes it were that easy for people.

Longer shadows, stiller air. The late sun scatters reddish light across the tops of the trees. Some people are finishing the sleep in which they hid from the day's hottest time, and a few voices, pitched low in conversation, create a sort of ribbon of sound, a little like the murmur of the stream behind the houses during the months it flows—here now, gone a moment later, then back again. No words, just voices, tones, laughter, lazy emotion. Across the street, above a sprawled dog, a sparse column of flies spirals slowly, its members probably half asleep on the wing. A sudden sharp smell of garlic tossed into hot oil.

The weathered wood of the railing beneath her elbows is warm and smooth, but her back hurts. The railing, comfortable for everyone else to lean on, is too low for her. The tops of the village's doors, some of them, are too low for her. When the young people gather in the evening to watch the village's one television, Kwan is pushed to the rear so people don't grumble. And she can barely see the screen from back there. She has a suspicion, growing stronger over the past few years, that she needs glasses. Glasses. They might as well be diamonds for all the likelihood she'll ever get them.

If it weren't for Teacher Suttikul seating her in front of the class and to the side, she wouldn't be able to read the blackboard either. The other kids call her desk "the Stork's nest."

School. The thought cuts through her like a red-hot knife.

The blue earring that Moo—Nana—threw to her is punching a hole in her palm, and she relaxes her fist. She doesn't dare put it in her ear. Her father would probably rip it out to sell it.

Kwan knows that the town is pitifully small and poor, not from having been anywhere else but from the few times she's been able to get near enough to the television to turn the shifting, blurred patterns into identifiable shapes. She's seen the bustling sidewalks and spiky skyline of Bangkok, watched the gleaming cars glide through the streets, seen rich, beautiful, unhappy people double-cross each other in palatial bedrooms and candlelit restaurants where she doesn't even recognize the food. She's seen other, even richer and *more* beautiful but equally unhappy people double-cross each other in a paradise that's apparently called Korea, where all the women are ravishing and wear astonishing clothes, nicer even than Nana's, and all the men are impossibly princely, and some of them even seem to be tall. Some of them—not the women, but the men—seem as tall as Kwan.

How could people who have everything be unhappy? Kwan wants to know, but there's no one she can ask, since no one she knows has anything.

Except Nana, and she hardly knows Nana anymore.

She has no idea how long she's been standing there, but the stiffness in her back says it's been an hour or more. So she's not completely surprised when she hears the low voices from the other side of the house and then the feet on the steps leading up to the door.

Her mother's voice, raised in greeting, is unfamiliar in its bright friendliness. She's using the voice that's her version of dressing up for company. She never unpacks it for use with her family.

They're here.

Kwan's stomach knots as though she has to go to the outhouse, and her T-shirt is suddenly wet beneath the arms. Moving as silently as a breeze, she rearranges the hanging wash behind her so it completely covers the window, making her invisible from inside the house. She hopes nobody saw the motion. She wishes she were small enough to creep into one of the pockets of her mother's dress, hanging a few inches away.

When her teacher told her that she wanted to have this meeting, Kwan's heart had leaped in hope. Now that the moment has come, though, the hope seems transparently thin, too thin even to hold a patch. If anything, the meeting will make matters worse, not better. It will put an end to the hope.

She smells the whiskey on her father's breath before she hears him behind her.

"Stork," he says. "Your teacher. And some *farang* man."

She doesn't turn. She tries to stay away from him when he's been drinking. For the past two years, that means all the time. "I don't care," she says.

"Don't talk to me like that. You're big, but you're not too big to hit." He leans toward her, the smell growing stronger, and lowers his voice. "They want to talk about you, and they want you in there."

"There's no point."

"They don't know that," her father says. "They need to hear you say it."

"Maybe I won't say it."

"Maybe you won't eat dinner tonight. Maybe you won't eat breakfast tomorrow. It costs a lot to feed you."

Kwan's clenched fist again drives the post of the earring into her hand. She squeezes harder, inviting the pain in, and then she wheels around and sidesteps, grabbing the clothesline and feeling her father's hand slide over her back and down toward her rear. As it reaches the sensitive skin at the small of her back, she lets go of the rope and hears it snap against his chest.

"Sorry," she says without turning around.

Rounding the corner of the small house, she smells smoke. Someone down the street is burning trash. She thinks hopelessly of the rooms she has seen on the television screen, the careless litter of nameless possessions owned by people who have forgotten they have them, and she wonders what could be useless enough, in this village where there's a third and fourth use for everything, to feed to the flames.

There's a knot of brothers and sisters around the front door. Kwan pushes through them and enters the darkness of the single room they all share.

Teacher Suttikul is short and wide. She's not fat, just broad in the shoulders and hips, and she wears clothes that make her look even wider. Today's outfit is a loose blouse with black horizontal stripes above a straight white skirt. Without ever having owned nice clothes herself, Kwan has known from the first time she saw her teacher that the woman dresses all wrong. Somehow it's endearing that a woman who knows so much about so many things has no idea what clothes she should wear.

"Here she is," Teacher Suttikul says brightly as Kwan comes through the door. "Isn't she pretty?" she asks the man who's with her.

One of Kwan's brothers on the deck snickers.

"This is Mr. Pattison," Teacher Suttikul says, using the English honorific. "Mr. Pattison is from the Children's Scholarship Fund."

Kwan, acutely conscious that her jeans end high above her ankles, conscious of her thin arms and sharp elbows, gives Mr. Pattison a respectful *wai,* palm to palm as though in prayer, at the level of her forehead. Mr. Pattison smiles. He is taller than she and frayed in the way some older people are, with peeling, papery skin, thinning hair, and eyes of a faded ghost-blue.

"Very pretty," he says in thickly accented Thai, followed by a pale blue glance that silences the laughing boy. "And she looks smart, too."

The room—the only room in which Kwan has ever lived—contains two large pieces of furniture: the bed on which her mother and father and the three youngest children sleep, and a table surrounded by mismatched molded plastic chairs in dark, scuffed primary colors. On top of the table is a scattering of chipped and faded dishes and bowls and a stack of spoons. Above the crockery hang two shelves lined with jars of spices, sugar, and oil, tightly closed against ants. A length of faded cloth dangles diagonally across the far right corner to create a cramped space for people to undress and dress in before and after a bath and, at night, a place for Kwan to sleep. The cloth has been pulled partway aside, and the thin, soiled mat of rags that make up Kwan's bed is in plain sight. The sight stops her in the doorway. Why didn't they just hang her dirty underwear in the middle of the room?

Kwan's mother has pulled the two best chairs away from the table for the teacher and the *farang* to sit on and has claimed the edge of the bed for herself. She looks up at Kwan and, with her eyes, indicates the high metal stool that's been positioned in the middle of the room. Kwan goes and sits on it as Mr. Pattison and Teacher Suttikul take their seats. Perched there, halfway between them and her mother, she feels like the pile of small money that her father and his drunken friends play cards for, sitting all day on the raised wooden platform outside, next to the street. She catches a glimpse of herself in the cracked mirror hanging beside the door, averts her eyes from the geometrical schoolgirl chop that cuts her straight hair off just below her ears, making her neck look even longer than it is, and ducks her head apologetically, with no clear idea of what she's apologizing for.

"Thank you for letting us come," Teacher Suttikul says.

"Don't thank her." Kwan's father comes into the room, rubbing his chest as though it stings. "If you've got to thank somebody, thank me." He takes a small, inadvertent jog to the right but stops himself before it turns into a lurch, raking the visitors with his eyes to see whether they noticed it. Both of them are looking at Kwan, whose gaze is fixed on her lap, her spine as curved as a cello. Her father goes to the bed, waves his wife to move down although there's plenty of room, and sits heavily.

Teacher Suttikul smiles so appreciatively he might have spouted poetry. "We want to talk about Kwan," she says. "You know, you have a very smart daughter."

"So what?" her father says. He's at the near edge of very drunk, and his consonants are approximate. "She's a girl."

"There are lots of good jobs for girls these days. She'll earn plenty of money if she stays in school."

"What good does that do anybody? If she makes money, it'll go to her husband's parents, not us." He lifts his chin toward Kwan, not even bothering to look at her. "If she can ever find anybody to marry her."

Teacher Suttikul keeps the smile in place, although her eyes have gotten smaller, an expression that has chilled many classrooms full of children. "She'll always take care of you. And I know she can get a good job. Someday she'll—"

"Someday," her father says heavily, as though the words are in a foreign language. "Someday. My children need food now. The roof needs to be fixed before the rain comes. We need money now."

The words ricochet back and forth, past Kwan, who ducks her head and tries to sink farther into the stool, which is high enough to make her almost as tall as she is standing up. Nana's earring feels so hot in her hand that she wouldn't be surprised if its glow were visible through her skin.

"Now," her father repeats, as though the word were an unfamiliar one.

"We're *talking* about now," Teacher Suttikul says. She has locked eyes with Kwan's father, and she holds his gaze for a moment before politely dropping her own. "Mr. Pattison can tell you what he wants to do." She adds, as an afterthought, "For you, I mean. What he can do for you."

"The money in the scholarship fund comes from people all over the world," Mr. Pattison says, very much with the air of a person who is beginning something that could go on for a while. His Thai is slow and badly pronounced but correct, and he speaks like someone who is unused to being interrupted. "They give us money so we can help promising students stay in school—"

"While their families starve," her father says.

Mr. Pattison puts up a hand, and the gesture startles Kwan's father so much that he stops talking. "We understand that families need money," Mr. Pattison says with weighty geniality. "We know they want their children to begin to work as soon as possible." A slow blink. "So they can help the family."

"It's their duty," Kwan's father says, jumping into the pause and holding tight to the edge of the bed as though he's expecting to launch himself into an argument. "We've taken care of her her whole life."

Pattison nods. "Of course you have. But we also know that in the long run it's better for children to be educated, so they can make even more money."

"That's for sons," Kwan's father says. "Weren't you listening? Daughters leave. They take care of their husband's—"

"If you'll let me," Mr. Pattison says without raising his voice, "I'll tell you how Kwan can start bringing money into the house right now."

Kwan's father rubs the bristles on his chin with the backs of his fingers, then nods to Mr. Pattison to continue.

"What we do," he says, "is give small amounts of money to the families while the children are still in school, in exchange for them letting them continue—"

"Stork? Money for Stork?"

"For Kwan," Teacher Suttikul says in a voice that could snip tin.

Kwan's father purses his mouth. "Small amounts. How small?"

Mr. Pattison licks his lips and looks at Teacher Suttikul. Teacher Suttikul says, "Kwan is seventeen. She needs to go to school for one and a half years more—"

"And then what?" her father says.

"Then she can go to college," Teacher Suttikul says, and despite the sheer impossibility of it, Kwan's heart leaps at the word "college." She holds herself absolutely still, trying not to betray her reaction.

"And I can die of old age," her father says.

Before she can stop herself, Kwan says, "It won't be old age."

"You see," her father says to the teacher. He looks almost pleased. "She's probably good when she's at school, probably got a sweet mouth, but here she's just another sharp edge. Just looking for a slap."

"Thirty-six thousand baht a year," Teacher Suttikul says. She glances at Mr. Pattison and says, "About nine hundred dollars U.S."

Kwan's father sits back. Her mother stares at the teacher as though gold dust has just poured from her mouth. Out on the deck, there's a little ripple of words from the brothers and sisters. This is more than the whole family earns in a year.

"Okay," her father says. He licks his lips. "Give it to me." He actually stretches out his hand, but he leans too far forward and his wife has to grasp his shoulders to keep him from falling off the bed. He shrugs her off indignantly. "Now."

"It doesn't work like that," Mr. Pattison says. He smiles, but not broadly. "We have to make a piece of paper that says you promise that Kwan will stay in school, and then we give some of the money every month to Teacher Suttikul, and she gives it to you if Kwan's been in class. By the end of the year, you'll have the whole nine hundred."

Her father has screwed up his face, trying to see the numbers. "So in a month . . ."

"About three thousand baht."

"Three thousand baht? Are you joking?" Kwan's father lifts both hands and slaps them down on his thighs. "No more talking." He leans forward as if to rise, and his wife reaches for him, just in case.

But before he can push himself up, Teacher Suttikul says, "That's more money than she could earn in most jobs."

"Tomorrow," her father says. "Tomorrow I can get—" He stops talking, although his lips move for a moment. Then he shakes his head and tries to get up.

"How much?" the teacher asks. Her mouth is all muscle. "Thirty thousand baht? Forty? And for what?"

"Sixty," her father says, with the satisfaction of someone playing a trump. "For working in Bangkok. And then she'll be sending more money home right away. Sixty is just to start. A lot better than a few thousand a month, and nothing more coming in, while she learns things girls don't need to know."

"And what job would that be?" the teacher asks.

Kwan's father shows her the back of his hand, flapping it in her direction in a way that's nothing short of scornful, certainly nothing like the respect Kwan believes a teacher is owed. Her spine folded forward, her chin practically touching her chest, Kwan has reached her limit. She can't endure another moment of humiliation—her teacher, whom she has worked so hard to impress, being insulted like this. She raises her head, glares at her father, and puts a foot down to stand.

Teacher Suttikul's voice almost takes the skin off her back. "Kwan. You stay right there."

Kwan turns to her and is startled by the fury in her teacher's face. She sinks down on the stool again, and for the first time she feels a lifting in the center of her chest. Something good may happen here after all.

"I asked what job you were thinking of," Teacher Suttikul says. Her tone is sinuous as a snake. "Sixty thousand baht is a lot of money. For what? Waitressing? Down in Bangkok, you said?"

Her father swallows, clears his throat, and pats his shirt pocket for a cigarette. "Something like that."

"Sixty thousand baht." The teacher settles back in her chair. "For a waitress."

"It's a good restaurant." He's already arguing.

"For a village girl, still dusty, just down from the paddies. Someone who's never even *eaten* in a good restaurant."

"So what? You think waitresses eat in nice places? With gold plates and, and ice cream, and lace on the table? They eat noodles in the street, like everyone else."

"What I think is that waitresses in good restaurants come from city families. I think they get the job because somebody knows somebody who knows somebody—"

"That's me," Kwan's father says. He stops and makes her wait as he pulls out a pack of cigarettes, extracts one between his index and middle fingers, tweezers style, and lights up. "I know somebody."

"Who?"

He regards her, blinking through a cloud of smoke. "What?"

"Who do you know?"

"What does that—" Kwan's father's face is suddenly deep red. "What does that have to do with you? Who do you think you are, coming in here and asking questions like this?"

"I think I'm Kwan's teacher. That means I'm in charge of her welfare."

"You just stop there." Kwan's father is standing, wobbling a little, but standing. "Stork is my daughter, not yours. She'll plow fields if I want her to, she'll wash floors, she'll shovel buffalo shit. She'll go where I want and do what I want. Did you bring her into the world? Have you worked all your life to feed her, even though she eats like an ox? Have you given her a roof and a place to sleep? Here's what you can do, you and your *farang* boyfriend. You can get out of my house, that's what you can do. And you can keep going. Kwan's out of school right now. You won't see her again. I don't want to see *you* again." He stamps toward the door, trailing smoke like a locomotive. At the door he wheels and says, "You have to get up before you leave. Come on, up, up, *up*."

"You can leave if you want," Teacher Suttikul says, waving him out. "We'll keep talking."

"You should stay," Mr. Pattison says.

Kwan's father grabs the doorjamb on both sides. "This is *my house—*"

"My *job*," Teacher Suttikul says, and her words cut through his. Although she has not raised her voice, there is a glittering edge to it. "My job says that I have to tell the police when a girl is taken out of school before she's eighteen. If she's not in school and I report it, they have to go looking for her. This is the first place they'll come. If they don't find her, there can be trouble."

Kwan's father says, "Police?" and fails to hear Kwan ask the same question at the same time.

"Some people," Kwan's teacher says, eyes wide, "actually sell their daughters. Into prostitution, I mean. They can get quite a lot of money, I'm told."

Kwan's father starts to say something, darts his tongue into the corner of his mouth, and says, "You don't—"

"Of course not," Teacher Suttikul says. "It's hard to believe, isn't it? But it happens. And there are laws against it now. It's not like it used to be. I've known families, close to here, who sold their daughters and got caught, and the police took all the money away—fifty, sixty thousand baht—put the father in jail, and then sent the girl home. Good for nothing by then, of course, not even a dowry. Ruined. Nobody would marry her. And then the father had to buy his way out of jail *and* pay the gangsters back. Took them years."

Kwan's mother lets out a quiet moan. Kwan feels like she's been nailed to the stool. *Sold?* There's a thin, high mosquito whine in her ears, and the room seems to tilt a little. *Ruined?*

It's growing dark outside.

"May I light a lamp?" Teacher Suttikul asks, indicating the kerosene lantern on the table. "We can all see each other better."

Kwan's father shakes his head, then nods. To the kids clustered around him, he says, "What's wrong with all of you? Go somewhere. Do something. Clean under the house." He flaps his hands at them. "Go on, go on." They back up a couple of feet.

"Thank you," Teacher Suttikul says. She reaches into her old straw purse and brings out a disposable lighter, removes the lamp's chimney, and lights the wick. It catches and sends up a thin, dark thread of smoke. "Needs trimming," Teacher Suttikul says, replacing the chimney. The light, shining directly beneath her chin, emphasizes her broad, strong cheekbones but leaves her eyes in shadow. "There," she says, resuming her seat as though nothing has happened. "Isn't that better?"

Nobody says anything. "What I think," she continues, "is that you should forget about Bangkok. It's probably not a real offer. They'll find a way to cheat you, and then they'll make her"—her eyes flick to Kwan—"*wait on* people for free. What could she do? Alone, miles from home. What could you do? The people who run . . . mmm, restaurants can be very rough. Instead, permit us to give you money to let Kwan stay in school." She glances questioningly at Mr. Pattison, who nods about a quarter of an inch. "You've got a lot of children to feed," she says. "We'll offer you something special. Forty thousand baht, and since you need money now, we'll pay you the extra four thousand when you sign. So that'll be seven thousand baht, and then three thousand a month for eleven more months."

"Ten thousand," her father says.

Teacher Suttikul shakes her head. "If we give you ten when you sign, you won't get anything for the last month."

Kwan realizes she is holding her breath. She lets it out in a rush that draws Mr. Pattison's faded blue eyes.

"That's a year from now." Her father comes back into the room and reseats himself on the bed. He scratches at the side of his nose. "I don't need to think about that yet." He puts his cigarette butt between thumb and forefinger and snaps it through the open door. Children scatter out of the way. "Ten thousand."

"Just so you understand . . ."

"I'm not stupid. When do we make the paper?"

"We can do it tomorrow," Mr. Pattison says.

"And you'll give me the money tomorrow?"

"Will you be able to read it?" Mr. Pattison asks, not unkindly. "We need to know that you understand what—"

"She can read it," Kwan's father says, glancing at Kwan. "If she's so smart, she can read it."

"Then I don't see any problem," Mr. Pattison says. "We'll come tomorrow evening, about this time."

"With the money."

"With the money."

"Cash," Kwan's father says.

Mr. Pattison's face doesn't change, but he glances away, out through the door. It looks to Kwan like he is eager to be out of the room. "Of course."

Teacher Suttikul stands up. "I'm so glad we could talk," she says. "I know how much you love Kwan, and this is the best thing for her. You should be proud that you've reached this decision."

Kwan's father nods brusquely, but his wife gets up. She's beaming. "Thank you," she says. "Thank you so much. Kwan is—" She looks at her daughter. "Kwan is my first baby. Even though she's bigger than I am, she's my first baby."

Everyone laughs except Kwan and her father.

Teacher Suttikul holds out an arm, and Kwan gets up and goes to her. It seems to take five minutes for her to cross the room, and she can feel her father's eyes on her every step of the way. When she's finally side by side with Teacher Suttikul, the teacher barely comes up to Kwan's shoulder, and Kwan is amazed all over again that such a small, unassuming person has such strength. The teacher puts an arm around Kwan's waist and gives her a squeeze.

"That's finished, then," she says.

Kwan can't say anything. She feels as though her throat has been tied in a knot.

Her teacher pulls a little flashlight from her purse. "Come on," she says. "You can walk us past the dogs."

The children scatter in front of them as they come through the door. Only one of them, Mai, is slow to move, and that's because she's staring up at the teacher. Teacher Suttikul slows and touches Mai's shoulder. "Your name?"

Mai glances at Kwan for reassurance. "Mai."

"Good, good. How old?"

"Thirteen."

Teacher Suttikul beams at her. "Then I'll see you next year." She turns back to the room and calls out, "I'll look forward to seeing Mai next year."

Mai bobs her head and backs away. With Mr. Pattison in the lead, Kwan and her teacher go down the four steps and turn right, around the house, to get to the dirt street. Once they're out there, the stars running like a spangled river between the dark trees, Kwan whispers, "Please turn off the light."

Teacher Suttikul snaps off the flashlight, and Kwan throws her arms around the woman. Hugging her teacher with all her strength, and with her own heart pounding in her ears, Kwan still hears Mr. Pattison stop to wait for them, standing alone in the dark.

9

The Broad Black Door

She can't even smell the exhaust of Mr. Pattison's motorbike anymore. She's been sniffing for it, but it's gone.

The last she saw of them was the wide cone of light from the bike's headlamp, bumping away from her, leaving her by herself, dead center in the red dirt of the road, staring after them. Staring at the black and white stripes of Teacher Suttikul's terrible blouse as it recedes into the darkness and the fuzziness of the nearsighted. Gone now, leaving Kwan more alone than she's ever felt in her seventeen years.

They're far enough away now to take with them even the sound of the bike, and here she is, ducking into the undergrowth to the side of the road just beyond the village, out of sight of anyone who might come looking for her, anyone who might say any word at all to her, have any kind of plan for her. She's thinking about ghosts and wishing she could have gotten on the bike. Just climbed up, wrapped her arms around her teacher's thick, solid waist, and zoomed through the night. Away from the broad black door that's just swung open in front of her.

Sold. Ruined.

Her father's eyes when her teacher talked about prostitution, about families who—

She's the center of a vortex of mosquitoes. Something moves, back in the bush. Everyone knows there are ghosts outside the village.

A breeze rattles the dry leaves on the bushes near her. If whatever made that noise is still moving, she won't be able to hear it. She can smell herself, the salty smell of shock and fear.

She can't stay here all night.

She feels like she's turned to stone. Her feet are too heavy to lift. And even if she could lift them, where would she go? She can't force herself to go home. She can't be in the same room—she can't even share the same light—with her father.

What she wants to do is drop to her knees and cry as she cried when she was a child, her throat wide open, her eyes running, and her nose streaming, letting out some of the grief that's built up inside her, like smoke with no outlet. She wants to slice open the skin on her cheeks and forehead with her fingernails and then scrub dirt into the cuts, dirt that could never be washed out, that would scar her, and then nobody would ever want to . . . buy . . .

She realizes she has her palm pressed hard over her lips and that a moan is building behind them. She straightens. Pulls her hand away. She will *not* moan.

And as she feels her will strengthen, a new thought, even colder than the others, breaks over her. What had her mother known? How long had she known? Her *mother*.

An hour ago, Kwan thinks, *I was worried about staying in school.*

She's aware again of the door, broad and even blacker than the night that surrounds her. She imagines something on the other side, holding out a hand to her. Or maybe it's not a hand.

The image makes her back prickle, and she turns slowly, seeing the dark, foamy shapes of bushes and, behind them, something bent and spavined, and she inhales quickly, the hand that had been over her mouth now pressed to the center of her chest, fingers splayed.

From the direction of the village, off to her left, a motorbike coughs a couple of times and roars into life. Kwan looks again at the twisted shape, sees that it's not moving, and backs deeper into the brush, farther away from the road. She keeps her eyes on the road, trying not to imagine the twisted thing opening long-fingered hands behind her. As much as she needs to know what's coming down the road, she looks over her shoulder at the dark shape. At first she can't give a form to anything, but then the bike's headlamp is turned on and the darkness thins, and she can see the bushes behind her, with nothing behind them but a spindly, dejected tree, and the roar increases in volume and whips past, dwindling into the distance. Two boys from the village, a little older than she, boys who are always in trouble for drinking and fighting. Boys without money. No one knows where they got the bike.

There is something in her left hand, the clenched hand. She lifts it to see what it is but then remembers. It's Nana's earring. Brought all the way here from Bangkok.

She sees her village with sudden clarity: Two rows of slanting, leaking houses, stinking latrines, badly chewed dogs. Dust and heat. People who are sometimes kind and sometimes cruel. Old people, young people. Working and living and dying. At the mercy of the weather, at the mercy of the rich. At the mercy of alcohol. Trapped in circles of karma that none of them can perceive, sentenced to a life of numbed endurance, voluble about nothing they care about, but slinging words bright and sharp as razors when tempers flare or the whiskey speaks. Mute as fish about the things that matter, the things they think about all the time. Hunger, work, injustice, endurance, the empty bellies of those they love.

The problem of their daughters. The opportunity presented by their daughters.

She could, Kwan imagines, just turn and walk down the road with the village behind her and never look back. Walk through the night until she sees a lighted window with someone behind it who needs her, someone who will take her in and let her help, let her wash and scrub and lift and carry. And never speak to her, never ask her anything. A smile in the morning, work through the day, a clean floor to sleep on at night. No one coming to the door. No one knowing her name.

Right, she thinks. *Life is a movie.*

She takes three deep, silent breaths. She'll be able to go to school. Teacher Suttikul won. She's got what she wanted. School, learning, working to make herself better. The story she's been trying so hard to write, the story of a village girl who is led to a treasure by the ghost of her dead grandmother. How happy the treasure makes the girl's poor family. The story Teacher Suttikul likes. The word Teacher Suttikul said: "college."

Her father's eyes. The way he watched her when she crossed the room to get to Teacher Suttikul. Their cold weight on her back as she and her teacher paused in the doorway to talk to Mai.

And she knows, deep in the pit of her stomach, that the wide dark door is still open and that school is not on the other side of it.

The moon has begun to lift itself above the hills to the east, just a sliver of silver so far, a crack in the black sky, not much thicker than a pencil line. It brings a chill, chalky light with it, and Kwan uses that light to look down at the earring in her hand, sparkling cold blue. To her own surprise, she reaches up and, working by feel, removes the little steel stud in her left ear and puts the sapphire in its place.

It seems to throw off a sort of warmth. She imagines she can feel it, not only in her ear but down the side of her neck and across the top of her shoulder. Like a soft fall of light. She likes the feeling. Something about it loosens the tangled knot that's squeezing her heart—not much, but some.

Her father will not take the earring from her. She will wear it, even if people laugh at it. She's used to being laughed at. It hurts, but it doesn't scar.

She has fingernails. She has teeth. She has fists. The house is full of knives. Her father will find it hard to push her through the dark door. Pocketing the stud she removed from her ear, Kwan pushes her way through the brush and takes the road back to her village.

SHE SEES the dark shape on the wooden platform by the side of the road, the platform on which her father and his friends drink and play cards. She stops, hoping she has not been seen or heard, hoping it is not her father who sits there, but then the figure speaks.

"Where have you been?" Nana's voice.

"Down the road," Kwan says. What she felt there, what she thought there, is her secret, not to be shared even with those she trusts. And she doesn't trust Moo. Now, with all that has happened, she remembers that she didn't much like Moo—Nana—when she lived in the village. Moo was five years older than Kwan, a hot-tempered girl who fought with other girls frequently, usually girls smaller than she. She was fat then, and she used her weight as a weapon, bulldozing her opponents to the ground and kneeling on them, digging her knees into the most sensitive spots and bearing down. She once put her hand in a plastic bag and used it to pick up some dog droppings, which she rubbed in a smaller girl's face. Kwan finds it difficult to see the angry fat girl in the self-possessed, attractive woman who has come back, at least temporarily, from her years in Bangkok.

Nana says, "I've been waiting for you."

"Why?" Nana hadn't even seemed to notice Kwan on her earlier visits to the village.

"To talk." Nana's voice is silky, even friendly, but it doesn't sound personal. Nana could be talking to the night, to the rising moon. "Don't you ever just want to talk to someone?"

With the moon a little higher in the sky, Kwan can see that Nana is wrapped in a light blanket, probably to protect herself from mosquitoes. "I'd think Bangkok is full of people to talk to."

"Bangkok is . . . I can't even tell you what Bangkok is like. You have to see it for yourself. You'd love it. But it's not the same, the people there. They're not from here. They don't know what our lives were like."

"*Are* like," Kwan says. "I still live here. And I thought all the girls like . . . like you . . . came from Isaan."

"Most of them do." Nana wastes no energy on resolving the contradiction. Instead she picks up a pack of cigarettes from the platform and puts one in her mouth. She lights it with a slender, gleaming lighter not much bigger around than the cigarette. As she draws in the smoke, she glances up at Kwan and then lifts the lighter for a better look. "You're wearing it," she says.

Kwan's hand flies to her ear. "Please put out the flame."

"Sure." The lighter clicks off. "Who don't you want to see you?"

"Everybody. I mean, anybody. I don't want anybody to see me."

Nana draws deeply on the cigarette, her face gleaming a dull red in the coal's glow. Then she releases the smoke slowly between her lips and inhales it through her nostrils. To Kwan it looks like a magic trick. "Want one?" Nana blows the smoke out and extends the pack.

"I don't smoke. My father smokes all the time, and then he coughs all night. I think it's stupid."

"Up to you." Nana's eyes remain on Kwan's face. "I remembered right," she says. "You're getting very pretty."

Kwan has to review the sentence in her mind before she actually understands its meaning. "Me? Pretty?"

"Maybe more than pretty." Nana slides aside and pats the platform. "Sit. You can't stand there all night."

"I don't know." Kwan doesn't want to go home, but she's not comfortable with Nana either.

"I won't bite you," Nana says. She smiles. "I'm not even hungry." Then she reaches into the pocket of her blouse, finds something, and extends her hand. "Here's the other one."

"Why?" Kwan makes no move to take it. "Why are you giving it to me?"

Nana pauses and then says, "You didn't listen to me this afternoon. When someone offers you something, take it."

"That's not the way I am."

"You have so much?" Nana says. She sounds like a purring cat. "All your jewel boxes are full? You're so overloaded that you couldn't force the lid closed on a nice pair of earrings?" She drags on the cigarette again, and Kwan sees that Nana is wearing new earrings, earrings that have stones dangling on the ends of fine, thin chains.

"How many pair do you own?" Kwan asks.

Nana tilts her head to one side and looks up at Kwan. The little stones sway back and forth on their chains. "I have no idea."

"Oh." Kwan stands there, trying to wrap her mind around the idea of not knowing how many you have of anything. Finally she says, "More than five?"

Nana laughs with a lungful of smoke, then bends forward, coughing pale clouds into the night. When she's got it under control, she waves her open hand side to side in front of her face, clearing away the smoke, and then wipes the corners of her eyes. "Many more than five. Probably thirty or forty. Please. Sit down. My neck is getting stiff. And take this thing or I'll get irritated."

Remembering what Nana was like when she got irritated, Kwan sits. After a moment she reaches for the earring, but Nana withdraws her hand, just out of Kwan's reach.

"Let me," she says. Very gently, she removes the stud from Kwan's ear, drops it into her own lap, and inserts the post that holds the sapphire. Her hands are soft and smooth, not hard with calluses, like Kwan's. When she's slid the backing into place against Kwan's lobe and the earring is secure, Nana pulls away a little and studies Kwan as if Kwan were something she had just made and she wants to check the quality of her work. Kwan drops her eyes in embarrassment. Eventually Nana nods. "Get rid of that rice-bowl haircut, feather it a little, and then let your hair grow a couple of feet," Nana says. "Put about five kilos on you, get some decent clothes. Find some platform shoes that make you even taller."

Kwan says, *"Taller?"*

"You idiot." The word would hurt, but Nana is smiling. "You have no idea what you look like. I mean, just *look* at this." Nana puts out a thumb and sculpts the air just above Kwan's cheekbones, then down over her nose and across her lips. "I'd give a hundred thousand baht for your cheekbones," she says. "You'd stop traffic in Bangkok."

Kwan pulls her knees up and wraps her arms around them, curving her spine into the comfort of its familiar C. "You're making fun of me."

"Is that so?" Nana sticks her cigarette into her mouth. Then she puts one hand on the nape of Kwan's neck and pulls Kwan's head back, using the other hand to push the base of her spine forward. Kwan straightens, surprised at the contact. "There," Nana says. "Like that." She turns away and surveys the night, making sure no one is close enough to overhear. Then she hits on the cigarette again and flicks it into the darkness. It lands six or eight feet away with an eruption of red sparks. She leans toward Kwan so she can whisper into her ear. What she says is "If I'm making fun of you, why are you worth sixty thousand baht?"

The knot around Kwan's heart tightens again, and she feels her mouth drop open.

"Because you're ugly?" Nana continues, ignoring Kwan's reaction. "Because men won't like you?"

"It's not—" Kwan says. "That's not— I mean, it won't happen."

"It will, you know." Nana sounds neutral, as though she's talking about a third person, someone who's not there and whom they know only slightly. She's turning the steel stud over between the fingers of her right hand and combing the fingers of the left through her shoulder-length hair.

Kwan wants to argue but instead says, "How do you even know about this?"

"I didn't until I got here. I'll tell you the truth, though: I came back to talk to you."

"About what?"

"What do you think? About going back to Bangkok with me."

Kwan is searching Nana's face, looking for a hint of the joke. "Me?"

"You don't know," Nana says. "Foreign men will go crazy for you."

"You mean . . . I'd be doing what . . . what you do?"

Nana fills her cheeks with air and blows it out with a brusque little pop. "I was *exactly* like you," she says. "I forget sometimes how much I was like you. How could those girls *do* all that? How could they dance around in front of men and go with them? To hotels, I mean. And in the rooms? How could they do that, with men they don't even know? Aren't they . . . ashamed? When they think about their lives, don't they want to die?"

Kwan says, "Don't you?"

"Actually," Nana says, "I've never had so much fun in my life." She holds the stud up between thumb and forefinger and sights the moon past it. "I was terrified at first. So they let me go slow. They had me stand outside the bar for two weeks, dressed like a schoolgirl, just trying to get men to come in. 'One beer, eighty baht, have many beautiful girl, one beer eighty baht.'" She is speaking English. "Do you understand what I just said?" She takes a cigarette that's been bent slightly, straightens it between her fingers, and fires it up.

"Most of it."

"Well, I didn't, not then. But that's right, you're good at school, aren't you? All I ever did in school was think about getting out of this town. But the mama-san in the bar said the English words over and over again until I could repeat them, and then, after about a week, I got brave enough to take men by the arm and lead them into the bar. They'd be speaking English to me, or Japanese, or German, and I'd just say, 'Yes, yes, yes,' and sometimes, 'You so handsome,' which one of the dancers taught me, until one of the mama-sans got hold of the man's other arm and took him away from me. Then I'd stand there for a minute and watch the girls dance, thinking how beautiful they were, until somebody waved me back out into the street."

"You can do that?" Kwan asks. "That's allowed? You just stand there? Without having to, you know, to . . ."

Nana is studying the side of the cigarette, where a tendril of smoke is escaping. She licks her forefinger and presses the wet finger against the tear in the paper. When she's sure she's sealed it, she says, "Sure. But a door girl doesn't make any money. Just enough for noodles in the street and a bare room you share with six other girls. And they make you buy the schoolgirl's uniform, too, and they subtract part of that money from your pay every week, so you wind up with even less."

"Ah." Kwan hugs her knees more tightly but remembers to keep her back straight.

"And you couldn't do it anyway," Nana says. "You'd look silly in a schoolgirl's uniform."

"I look okay," Kwan says, stung.

Nana blows out, wafting the argument away with the smoke. "Oh, sure, for *here*. Who cares about here? Down there, where there are beautiful girls everywhere, you'd look stupid, like somebody too dumb to get out of seventh grade. With your height you need to be glamorous, not all little-girly."

Kwan says, *"Glamorous?"*

Nana faces her full on. "Kwan, you have to get used to this. You're beautiful. With a little work, I mean. You're tall, but in Bangkok that would be good. You'd stand out, and that's what matters. There are a lot of girls, and you have to stand out somehow. The girls who work down there learn to make as much as they can out of what they've got. That's their job. They have to figure out what their best look is. Some girls are short and plump, so they act cheerful, with little bows in their hair and big plastic bracelets, teddy-bear knapsacks, things like that. Some girls are little, and they try to look young, pigtails and bangs. A lot of men like young girls best. The prettiest girls get great haircuts—I know somebody who could make your hair look amazing, by the way, even while it's growing out." She reaches over and rubs the ends of Kwan's hair between her fingertips. "Perfect hair." She stops. "What was I saying?"

"About the pretty girls, how they—"

Nana pats the air to show she doesn't need the prompt. "Right, they get their hair cut just so, and they find someone to teach them about makeup, and they just go out there and look beautiful. But you—you could be the star of any bar you worked in."

"A *star*? You make it sound like the movies."

"It is," Nana says. "Sort of. I mean, it's like there are stars and there are those other actresses, the ones you see all the time, but they never play the girl the hero loves, and then there are ordinary girls, the girls who stand around in the background in the big scenes. Some girls never get taken out until everybody else is gone. Other girls, girls as beautiful as you, they've got men fighting over them, they're doing three or four short-times a night. Making big money."

"What's a short-time?"

Nana closes her eyes for a second, and Kwan has the feeling she's reproaching herself for having said too much. "A trip to a hotel. With a customer."

"Four of them in one night?" Kwan can feel how wide her eyes are. "You mean, with different men?"

"Honey," Nana says, "if there's a man anywhere in the world who can do it four times in one night, I hope I never meet him."

"I have to go now," Kwan says, and she puts both feet on the ground.

"Two hundred dollars," Nana says. "Maybe more. That's how much those girls make. In one night."

Kwan's head is ringing. "My father doesn't make five hundred dollars in a year."

"Three nights," Nana says. "You'd earn more in three nights than he does in a year. And you can send most of the money home. Your parents could build a new house."

"That's . . . that's *twelve men.*" A new house?

"Those are the best girls. And you might not have to do that. You might be able to get more every time. But I think you'd get that kind of attention."

Kwan turns away, unwilling to let Nana look any more deeply into her eyes. "I could never do that. I've never . . . I mean, I've never even . . ." She can't finish the sentence.

"I was going to ask you about that," Nana says. "Have you or haven't you?"

"Of course not."

"Lots of us had. Before we went down, I mean. I had, twice. Well, okay, four times. But it's better if you haven't."

"It doesn't matter—"

"Oh, yes, it does. You could get five hundred, six hundred dollars, twenty or twenty-five thousand baht for the first time. Maybe more."

Once again, for the fourth or fifth time during the evening, Kwan has the sense that people are speaking some form of Thai she doesn't understand. *The first time? Six hundred dollars?* "That's not what I meant. I mean, I'm not going."

Nana takes the neck of Kwan's T-shirt and gives it a sharp tug. "Listen. You have to think about this, because if you don't, your life might as well be over. You can come with me, to Bangkok. Day after tomorrow, we have to go day after tomorrow. I'll pay the train fare, I'll lend you five thousand baht. You come with me, I'll take you into a bar, and you can start out as a waitress. All you have to do is give people their drinks and collect the money. Smile once in a while. You don't have to go with anybody."

"I wouldn't."

"I just said you wouldn't have to." Nana's voice has sharpened. She pauses before she goes on, and then she takes a corner of the blanket and drapes it over Kwan's shoulders, too, so they're both covered. She smooths it down gently. "You can see the way things work. Get to know the girls. I'll be there. I'll take you to the bar where I work, so you'll already have one friend. You can watch the girls, talk to them, see whether you think you can do it. See how much money there is down there. You can't *imagine* how much money there is. See how well the girls live." She thinks for a moment, feeling the focus of Kwan's attention, and says, "See how much it means to them that they can help their parents and keep their brothers and sisters in school."

"Keep them in school?"

"If you're sending money home, there's no reason for them not to stay in school."

"My sister Mai," Kwan says slowly. "She's very pretty. Not like me, *really* pretty."

"Three or four years from now, your father is going to start looking at her and seeing money."

"But he can't," Kwan says. "My teacher, she says that the police—"

"Forget the police. I'm telling you, you have to come down to Bangkok with me. And you need to make up your mind right now, because you have to leave the day after tomorrow."

"But tomorrow he'll get the money to keep me in school. Then I won't have to worry about—"

Nana's hand lands on top of Kwan's. "Be quiet and listen," she says. "Tomorrow he'll get the money to keep you in school. The day after tomorrow, he'll sell you."

10

The Moon Below

The colony of small frogs that makes its home in the little creek behind the houses, somehow staying alive even during the long dry season, chooses this moment to start a conversation. The two girls sit there, still as a painting, wrapped in the chirping and thrumming from the creek bed.

At last Kwan says, over the noise, "Before you say anything else, I want an answer to my question."

Nana pulls out another cigarette, raises it halfway to her lips, and says, "You've asked a lot of questions." With a practiced flick of the wrist, she lights it, taking the first drag in a businesslike fashion this time, no fancy inhaling techniques. She blows smoke and leans back slightly, and the movement tugs the blanket off Kwan's shoulder.

"Why I should believe you. And . . . and how you know. About my father. About the sixty thousand baht."

"When I got off the train," Nana says, "somebody was there, somebody who probably knew I was coming. Not from this village, and you don't know her. But she told me not to try to take you with me."

Kwan says, "Because . . ."

"Because these people talk to each other, and somebody, most likely someone from my bar, told somebody else I was coming up here. Probably got paid five hundred baht for the information. So she—the woman at the train station—wanted to make sure I knew that you were bought and paid for."

"But I haven't been. Paid for, I mean."

"You're wrong. He's already got some of it. He'll get the rest when they come and take you."

Kwan leans forward as though that would drive her words home. "He can't. He'll sign the paper tomorrow. He'll take the money from Mr. . . . Mr. Pattison."

"The scholarship fund," Nana says, not even leaning back to reestablish the distance between them. She makes a *pfft* noise between her teeth and lower lip. "Small change."

"But . . . but Teacher Suttikul, she said she'd tell the police if I wasn't in school, and the police would come looking for me."

"Oh, they will," Nana says. For a moment Kwan thinks she is going to laugh, but she shakes her head. "They'll be here in no time. They'll drive a hundred miles an hour."

"Well, then my father can't—"

Nana's hand comes to rest on the top of Kwan's head. To Kwan it feels as if a circuit has been created between them. "Because they want the money. Your teacher will complain to the cops right away. That day. She'll want to get you back fast, before anything happens to you. So your father will still have the money, all of it. The cops will come and demand to see you. Stamp around the house and scare everybody. There will be two of them, so one can keep an eye on the other, make sure he doesn't pocket anything. When they discover you're not there, which they already know you won't be, they'll tell your father he's going to jail unless he gives them half. Thirty thousand baht, probably. It *was* sixty thousand, wasn't it?"

"Yes," Kwan says, more breath than voice.

Nana takes her hand away and turns a palm upward. "They're getting a deal. If they could see how beautiful you are, your father could hold them up for a hundred thousand, maybe more. You're a bargain because you're tall."

"But my teacher—"

Nana scrubs the air with the open palm. "Your teacher, your teacher. Your teacher can't do *anything*. Didn't you hear me? *The cops will take the money.* Then they'll go and tell your teacher that they're mounting an investigation. They'll say they'll find you wherever you've gone. They'll throw your father in jail for a week or two, but he'll get good food and they'll treat him well because it's just a show, because they're going to want more money from him later. After a month or two, they'll tell your teacher you've just vanished. By then she'll have some other girl to worry about."

The half-moon, cream yellow now, hangs at a slant just above the treetops. It looks to Kwan like it's spying on them. Lanterns shimmer through the windows of the two nearest houses, but the ones farther away, at the village's edge, gleam with the hard, bluish, skim-milk light of fluorescent bulbs. In the farthest of the houses, the light is snapped off. It's getting late. The frogs chatter in amphibian, back in the dry creek.

Kwan reaches behind her and grabs the blanket and wraps it again around her shoulder. She is surprised to find that she's shivering. The image of the wide, dark door, banished while she talked with Nana, yawns open again. "What . . . what will happen to me?"

"Here's what will happen if you go with me," Nana says. She puts the cigarette on the edge of the platform, spreads the fingers of her left hand, and ticks them off with her right index finger as she makes her points. *One.* "You'll work in a bar." *Two.* "You'll take your time before you have to get up on the stage." *Three.* "You'll make friends with the girls who work there, and they can be like your map, they'll show you what to do and what not to do." *Four.* "Once you decide to dance, you'll go with men once in a while, if you want to. Some of them are even handsome. The way you're going to look, you'll be able to pick and choose. You'll be able to get the men all the other girls want to go with. And you won't have to take the ones the other girls don't want. Remember, you don't have to leave the bar with any man you don't want to go with. If he's too fat or crazy or too drunk or anything, you can say no. Nobody can force you." She waggles the spread fingers at Kwan's face like a spider and then remembers the cigarette. She picks it up and takes a leisurely inhale. "In fact, you don't really have to go with anybody at all. You won't make much money, but you can live off the commission on the Cokes the customers buy you. You'll get fined part of your salary if you don't go a few times a month, but you're going to be so beautiful they'll never fire you. You just won't have much money to send home. You won't have money for fun."

"I don't need fun."

Nana shrugs. "You're not there yet. There are more ways to have fun than you can imagine."

"Maybe. But I'm not going."

"You're even thicker than I was afraid you'd be." Nana takes a long, angry drag that turns the coal on her cigarette a brilliant, hellish red. Kwan looks away from it, letting the darkness soothe her eyes. "You haven't asked the important question."

"What is it? What's the important question?"

"What happens if you *don't* go with me. And don't talk to me about your wonderful teacher. She can't do anything."

Kwan lifts her feet again and puts them on the bench, her long legs folded vertically in front of her, knees as high as her chin. She puts her hands, fingers spread, on top of the familiar curve of her bent knees. Nothing there comforts her. Her knees feel like they belong to someone else. "What happens?"

Nana looks down at the cigarette in her hand and then drops it into the dust. She shifts the blanket a little, making sure Kwan is covered, and slides closer, so that Kwan can feel the other girl's body warmth and smell something sweet and flowery on her loose, thin clothes.

Nana sighs. "Day after tomorrow, on your way home from school, three men will grab you. They'll wait until you're walking alone. They'll cover your mouth with tape and put these tight things on your wrists that will hold them behind your back. They might do that to your feet, too. They'll throw you into the back of a car and drive you to Bangkok. One man will drive. Two will sit in back. They'll touch you any way they want to, but they won't do anything that would cost their bosses the money they're going to make from selling you as a virgin. But they can think of plenty of things to do without that. By the time you get to Bangkok, you'll feel like filth."

"My father wouldn't do that to me."

Nana doesn't say anything. Kwan closes her eyes and listens to the frogs as they sing the songs she's heard her entire life. She feels a tear slide down her cheek. She says, "Then what?"

"You'll be taken to a house. It'll be dirty, and it'll have windows that don't open. Some of the rooms will have bars on the windows."

"Bars?"

"What do you think this is *about*? You think you're going to work in a flower shop? You're going to be in some filthy, rat-filled cement house in Bangkok with bars on the windows and a lock on the door. You're going to get put into a room with a bed in it and a bucket to pee in, and you're going to stay in that room for months without ever going out. You'll get fucked, you'll rest, you'll get fucked again. They'll bring you some food, and then you'll get fucked again. At night you'll sleep in the same bed you fucked in all day, with the sheets still dirty from all those men, and whenever a new man comes, no matter what time it is, they'll wake you up and you'll have to fuck him. Doesn't matter if he's fat, filthy, drunk, mean, ugly, smelly, toothless, diseased. Doesn't matter if he wants to slap you around. You'll fuck him. Every day, seven days a week, all year long. For two or three years, until you've paid back the sixty thousand baht they paid your father, and they'll cheat you on that. They'll charge you rent for the room they lock you in, they'll charge you for sheets and towels, for food. Whatever it costs them, they'll charge three times as much. Until you've paid back every baht of the sixty thousand, plus interest."

Nana has been whispering fiercely, but Kwan hears the creak of wood down the street. She puts a hand on Nana's wrist, and Nana goes silent and throws a protective arm around Kwan's shoulders.

Another creak, and then the slap of a rubber sandal. It's coming from the dark rectangle of Kwan's house fifteen meters down the street, its flat blackness broken only by the single window, a hazy patch of light thrown by the lantern on the far side of the room. The sound came from above the street, from the wooden deck that surrounds the house. Nana's breath catches, and Kwan whispers, "Shhhhhh."

The creaking continues, and then there's the confused thump of a stumble, followed by a slurred, muttered curse. And then Kwan hears the sound of her father's sandals on the four steps that lead down to the street.

"Stay here," she whispers, her lips practically touching Nana's ear. Kwan throws off the blanket and eases herself back so she can slip off the edge of the platform that faces away from the street. From there it's just a few fast steps to the darkness beneath the house that's behind the platform. Kwan has to bend almost double to squeeze into the space, and the rough, unfinished wood above her snatches at the threads of her T-shirt, but she keeps going until she's well past the midpoint of the house, two meters or so beyond the moonlight's milky edge. She drops to her knees, scoops dirt into her hands, and rubs it on her face. When she finally breathes, it feels as if a stone is caught in her throat.

Nana sits on the platform, one knee drawn up like someone who could sit there forever. She is humming.

"Well," her father says from somewhere to the right, out of Kwan's line of sight. "Look here. It's little Moo."

"Nana. I stopped being Moo a long time ago."

Kwan's father lurches into view. He stops in front of Nana, swaying slightly. He is as drunk as Kwan has ever seen him. He blinks heavily down at Nana as though to clear his vision. "Still Moo. Got nice clothes now, got pale skin, not so fat, but you're still dirty."

"And you're still a drunk," Nana says, with a calm that amazes Kwan. She could never talk like that to an older man who's not a member of her family.

Her father takes half a step back. "Little whore. Up from Bangkok, waving around your hundred-baht ass."

Nana laughs. "A hundred baht? For a hundred baht, I wouldn't show you the bottom of my foot." She waves him off, left-handed, like she'd shoo a chicken. "Why don't you keep going wherever you were going? There's probably another bottle there."

Kwan's father clears his throat loudly and spits. Kwan thinks the spittle may have struck Nana, but Nana doesn't move a muscle. Beyond Nana's black silhouette, Kwan can see half of her father's face, rendered in pastel by the moonlight. After a moment he says, "Your round little ass." He lifts his chin imperiously and stumbles back a step. "I got money."

Kwan's heart is suddenly pounding at the side of her neck.

"Not enough," Nana says. "No matter how much you have, it's nowhere near enough."

"Got a lot."

"Fine," Nana says. "Thirty thousand baht. Special price, just for you."

Her father pulls his head back, as though someone has swung at him. "Thirty— 'At's a joke, right?"

"For thirty thousand," Nana says sweetly, "I'll let you lick my shadow. It's right down there, on the dirt."

"Little *bitch*." He takes a step toward her, raising one arm.

"Hit me," Nana says. "And then I'll scream, and when everybody comes, I'll explain how you offered me thirty thousand baht to sniff my butt. And then I'll ask where you got thirty thousand baht. In fact, you don't even have to hit me. I'll scream anyway, just for fun."

"No, no, *no*." Kwan's father looks reflexively in the direction of his house. "Don't."

"Two thousand baht," Nana says. "Right now. Two thousand baht or I scream."

A pause. "You said what?"

"Village men," Nana says, spitting the words as though they'd caught in her throat. "I always forget how *slow* they are. Two thousand baht right now, from your pocket into my hand, or I scream. Was that slow enough for you?"

Kwan's father squeezes out a bleary laugh. "Who's going to believe you? Everybody knows what you do down there."

"You're probably right. So it'll be twenty-five hundred. For reminding me."

Her father sways in the moonlight, looking down at Nana.

"All right," Nana says. "Here goes." She takes a deep breath and raises both hands to her mouth.

"*Stop.*" Kwan's father digs into his pockets, pulls out a handful of bills, and fumbles blunt-fingered through it. "One thousand, fifteen hundred, two thousand five hundred." He puts the other bills back. It's a thick wad, and Kwan's eyes follow it, something in her chest threatening to break into sharp pieces.

Nana withdraws her outstretched hand. "Put it on the platform," she says. "Do it politely. And not too close."

He releases a sharp hiss between his teeth but shuffles forward and bends down to put the bills beside Nana. The movement puts his eyes level with Kwan's, and for a heart-freezing moment she thinks he's seen her, but he straightens.

Nana picks up the money by its corners, using the tips of two fingers, and shakes it as though things are crawling on it. Then she slips it into her pocket. "Were you looking for Kwan?" she asks, as pleasantly as though they haven't exchanged a word yet.

"Was I— I was, yes. Stork, looking for Stork. Ought to be home by now."

"You take such good care of her," Nana says. "She's a lucky girl. She went that way." She points off toward the other end of the village. "Maybe half an hour ago, maybe more."

"By herself?"

"Who could she have been with? Her fiancé? Her big gang of friends? Of course she was by herself."

Kwan's father hesitates and licks his lips. "Can I have the money back?"

"Ask me again and it'll be five thousand."

He bares crooked teeth. "Ahhhh. Fuck you and your mother." He turns and shambles down the street in the direction Kwan indicated. "And your mother's mother," he says over his shoulder.

"Keep talking," Nana says. "Sooner or later you'll think of something clever." She gets up from the platform and wraps the blanket around her like a big shawl, watching him go. Hunched down in the darkness, Kwan stares at her. She has never in her life heard a woman talk to a man like that. It violates everything she's been taught about men and women, about young people and their elders, but somewhere deep inside, somewhere even deeper than the heartbreak, she wants to laugh.

"I'm going to walk the other way," Nana says very quietly, without turning toward her. "Go out on the other side of the house and take the same direction. Keep the houses between us. After the last house, I'll come to you and we'll find someplace else to sit. We have to finish talking about this."

"YOU HEARD," NANA says. "You saw. The money."

Kwan doesn't answer. They're in a small clearing fifteen or twenty meters beyond the last house in the village, a rough rectangle of pale earth, black-shadowed by trees silhouetted against the moon. This is a place Kwan knows, a place she went to sit, a place she hid in, when she was a child and wanted to be alone with her thoughts. A long time ago, before she was born, a house had stood here, but the owners went away. Over the course of years, the villagers had gradually picked the structure apart, piece by piece. Bits of it are now woven into every house in the village.

For some reason the foliage never grew back. On hot, still days when the air was thick with sun and the electric buzz of cicadas, Kwan sat and probed the soil with a stick. She unearthed broken pieces of dishes, sharp corners of old pottery, on one memorable day a tarnished spoon, and this miscellany of litter became her treasure. After days of reburying it every time she went home, she thought, *Nobody ever looks up.* And so, high in a tree behind the clearing, knotted around a branch, she hung a tattered head scarf that she'd wrapped her treasure in. Feeling Nana waiting for a response, she finds herself wondering whether the treasure still hangs there.

"He wanted me," Nana says. "What about you?" She tosses her head in the direction of Kwan's house. "Has he—"

"No," Kwan says flatly. "He wants to. When he's drunk, he wants to. He fumbles at me sometimes. But I've never even let him put his hand under my clothes." She feels the shame rise in her. "He looks at Mai sometimes, too."

"Mmmmm." Nana glances around the clearing. "I remember this place. Sort of."

"I hid treasure here once." Kwan knows it sounds silly, but anything seems safer than talking about what's happened this night, what she just saw her father do, the things Nana has been saying.

"Treasure?"

"Stuff. Broken stuff. I dug it up from where the house used to be."

Nana turns to her. "You hid it. Did you bury it?"

"No. It's back there, in a tree." She thumbs over her shoulder toward the trees behind her. "It *was* back there anyway."

Nana swallows, loudly enough for Kwan to hear it. "I want to see it."

"Nana, it's junk."

"I want to see if it's still there."

Kwan regards her. Nana's mouth is set in a line of determination. The moon plants tiny points of light in her eyes. "Why?"

"If it's still there," Nana says, and then she closes her eyes tightly, "if it's still there, maybe everything will be all right for you."

Kwan is inhaling, but her throat suddenly slams shut. She looks at Nana, her eyes still closed, and an enormous sob swells into existence inside her and pushes its way out. A moment later she is sitting on the ground with no memory of how she got there, weeping loudly, and Nana is beside her with both arms wrapped around her, saying, "Hush, hush, hush. They can hear you. Go ahead and cry, but here, here. . . ." She puts a soft hand on Kwan's wet cheek and presses Kwan's face against the lightly fragrant silk of her blouse. "Here, baby, cry here. But quietly, quietly."

Kwan laces her fingers behind Nana's neck, pressing her forehead against this girl she has never liked, and releases sob after sob into the darkness like black birds. She can almost feel them circling Nana and her, spiraling higher until they point themselves toward the moon and disappear.

"It's all right, baby," Nana whispers. "It's just time to grow up. It's just growing up, that's all. You're not going to die." She smooths Kwan's hair with one hand, and then she says, "Oh, this hair. How I'd love hair like this."

Kwan says, "You can have it," and a single laugh bubbles up. She sits back and passes her forearm over her face, blinking her eyes rapidly to force out any late-arriving tears. She's not through crying, but she'll wait until she's alone. She sniffles, loudly enough to startle herself.

Nana reaches out and wipes the side of Kwan's neck, then dries her hand on her black silk blouse. The blouse is smeared with streaks of dirt, the dirt Kwan rubbed on her face so her father wouldn't see her. "Let's look," Nana says.

Kwan sniffles again and says, "This is silly," but she's getting up as she speaks the words.

"I'll bet you don't remember where you—"

"Of course I do." She's standing, still feeling the cool dampness on her cheeks, and blots them with the backs of her hands, and then she extends a hand to Nana, who grabs hold and hauls herself upright with a little grunt, and for a moment they're both children again. Nana dusts her rear and scans the perimeter of the clearing. "Five hundred baht," she says. "Five hundred baht says you can't find it."

"Where would I get five hundred baht?"

"Then you'd better find it, or you'll owe me. And believe me, you don't want to owe me money."

Kwan takes a couple of steps and stops. The edge of the clearing is black and unfamiliar. She says, "I hid it during the daytime."

"Do I hear an excuse?"

"Quiet. I *am* going to find it." She turns toward the road and re-orients herself, then stretches an arm in front of her, her index finger pointing straight ahead, grabs a breath that seems to go all the way to her knees, and slowly rotates to the left. About three-quarters of the way around, she says, "There." Then she follows her finger, edging between a couple of low bushes and past a waist-high tree stump, Nana trailing behind, until she comes to a tree with a broad branch angling up to the right.

The flare of recognition gives way to surprise. "That limb was lower when I did this."

"So were you," Nana says.

"I can get up there." On tiptoe, Kwan gets the palms of her hands on the top of the branch, judging its height, then bends her knees and jumps. She throws both arms over the branch, anchors herself, and then starts to swing her legs side to side until she can throw one foot over the limb. Once that's done, she gets her other foot up and locks her ankles on top of the branch so she's hanging upside down like a sloth. "I feel ten years old," she says.

"It's okay," Nana says. "Come down before you break your neck. I believe you."

"I want my treasure." Kwan gets one thigh on top of the branch and hauls herself up so she's flat on her stomach. The ground looks a long way off. She balances herself and peers into the darkness of the foliage. "Oh," she says, surprised in spite of herself. "Oh, I can see it." She inches forward, pulling herself along, feeling the bark scratching the tender skin on the insides of her arms. Nana is saying something beneath her, but Kwan disregards it and inches farther up, at about a twenty-degree angle, the dark, dangling shape now less than a meter away. "I don't believe it. It's still here."

Gripping the limb tightly between her thighs, she sits up and extends both hands until they touch the rough cloth of the scarf, which feels dirty and slightly sticky. There are pointed objects inside it. Suddenly she remembers the exact knot she tied in the sunlight as the cicadas whirred, and she reaches up to undo the work of nine years ago. Her fingers find the knot and trace its shape. All she has to do is ease the scarf off the twig it hangs from and then untie the knot, but she stops, feeling her hand shake. She sits there long enough for Nana to ask a question.

"Wait," Kwan says, not even trying to reassemble Nana's words into something she understands. The moon throws patterns of light around her, dappling her bare arms and the front of her shirt, and the leaves of the tree shiver in a breeze so slight it might be the weight of the moonlight. The forest stretches off in all directions, a village here and a village there, linked by paths she can walk blindfolded, paths she explored alone, at a time when she imagined a monster waiting at every turn. A time when monsters were imaginary. She smells the sharp tang of the fire she noticed earlier, and she knows that if she were on the other side of her village, she would see the moon below her, shining up from the water in the paddies.

To Nana she says, "Can you hear this?" She strikes the hanging bundle with her open palm, and it makes a clattering sound, like someone shaking rocks in cupped hands.

"Yes."

"Well, that's it. Can you think of any other way I could have made that noise up here?"

"No."

Kwan hits the bundle twice more. It rattles and clatters. Dirt sifts down through the coarse weave of the cloth onto her other hand. She hits it harder, slapping at it now, feeling the muscles in her back tighten, feeling her jaw clench, and then tears are standing in her eyes. It's junk, just like she said. Her treasure is junk, crusted with dirt, trash that even the poorest, hungriest child wouldn't bend down to pick up. She sees the precision of the knot. Her eight-year-old fingers making sure her treasure wouldn't fall. Broken things. Useless things. Worthless, but hidden.

Like her. She reaches for the bundle again, meaning to rip it loose and throw it down, but instead, holding her breath without knowing it, she passes her hands lightly over its shape. Finding an area where the pieces bulge out beneath the cloth, she pushes them back in, tracing the teardrop form of the bag beneath her palms, patting it here and there to make it symmetrical. When she takes her hands away, it's swinging back and forth slightly, and she puts one hand up, wide open, to still its movement. She lets her fingers rest against an eight-year-old's treasure, closes her eyes, and tries to feel the magic it had all those years ago. She sits there like that until her arm feels heavy and the bag is warm to the touch.

She slips sideways off the limb and lets herself drop, feetfirst, to the ground.

Nana says, "Where is it?"

Kwan has to clear her throat before her voice will come. "Up there."

Nana's eyebrows contract and then smooth again. "And you're going to leave it up there?"

Kwan says, "Until I come back for it."

11

Nowhere in Particular

In the end it was simple. Mr. Pattison came at exactly four o'clock the next afternoon and handed Kwan's father eight one-thousand-baht bills and four five-hundreds: ten thousand baht precisely. Her father crumpled them like scrap and shoved them into his back pocket. Kwan read out loud to her mother and father the piece of paper that was meant to lock the door of the schoolhouse behind her, as though the document contained the words of the king, unquestionable and unbreakable. Her father nodded solemnly, but Kwan's mother stayed across the room, as far from the transaction as possible. She seemed as insubstantial as smoke.

Kwan's father signed the paper, some kind of mark that he thought looked like writing. Mr. Pattison folded and pocketed the document, made a *wai* to Kwan's father, and got one, more or less, in return. He patted Kwan on the shoulder and said, in English, "Glad you're going to stay with us."

Kwan said, "Me, too. I thank you and Teacher Suttikul."

"No problem," Mr. Pattison said, and then added, in his awful Thai, "We'll look forward to seeing Kwan at school tomorrow." He left, and the silence in the house was loud enough to drive Kwan outside.

Her mother never met her eyes.

The next morning Kwan left for school at the usual time, wearing her frayed uniform, the white blouse above the blue skirt with the hem her mother had let down as far as it could go to cover her daughter's endless legs, so far that there was no fold left. Stuffed beneath the papers in Kwan's book bag were two clean T-shirts and her only pair of jeans. She counted the steps down to the street while, behind her, sounding as though he were already a thousand miles away, her father asked what time she'd be home and her mother said same time as always, and her father said what time is that, and her mother said four, and her father grunted. As their voices faded, she marked the moment when she stepped free of her house's shadow and the sun struck her skin. She kept her eyes straight ahead as she walked between the rows of sagging houses, her heart beating like a drum in counterpoint to her footsteps.

When she was safely out of sight of the village, she stopped. She stood there, nowhere in particular, loose-jointed and hollow, for three or four minutes, hearing the cicadas without listening to them and looking at a spot on the road a few meters in front of her, where a small stone lay. Then she reached into the pocket of her blouse and took out the sapphire earrings, which she had removed before going home the previous evening. She put them on by feel, still looking at the spot on the road, and then she went over to the stone and picked it up and put it in her pocket. The earrings were glittering in her ears when, a little less than halfway to school, she took a narrow path between the paddies to the bigger road and climbed into the taxi that was waiting there. The door closing behind her sounded like a cannon.

Nana slid aside on the backseat to make room for her. She was dressed to travel, in the black skirt she'd worn on the day she arrived and a tight red top that looped up over one brown shoulder and left the other bare. The leopard-spotted shoes were back on her feet.

Kwan said, "You look beautiful."

"You're going to be a lot more beautiful than I've ever been."

The driver's eyes flicked to Kwan's in the rearview mirror, and then he shifted with a grinding of gears, and the car bumped down the road.

"Before I get on the train," Kwan said, leaning against the door to increase the distance between them. She had rehearsed the demand in bed the previous night. "I need to know that everything was true. About the house in Bangkok."

"It's worse," Nana said. "You remember what I told you about what would happen to your father's money."

"You mean, the—" But Nana waved her silent before Kwan said the word "police" and lifted her chin toward the back of the driver's head.

"Yes," Nana said. "Them. They would have taken half, and your father would have gone to the bank for more. To get back what he lost. Do you understand what I mean by the bank?"

"Yes," Kwan said. She turned away from Nana to look out the window.

"He drinks, he plays cards. He'd have gone to the bank three or four times. Every time he gets more money, it takes longer to pay—"

Kwan rolled down her window. "I said I understand."

SHE'S HEARD the train passing by all her life, but she's never been on one. Nana climbs on board as though the whole thing, all thirty cars of it, has been sent just for her, and she hoists her bright pink bag up onto a shelf above the seats. To Kwan she says, "The bathroom."

"I forgot." The car is dingier than she imagined it would be. The floor has the advanced filthiness of a surface that's been spit on repeatedly. The windows are so dirty that the world outside looks like she's seeing it through a glass of tea, and the seats are worn bare wood, wide enough for three narrow rear ends. Hugging her book bag to her chest, she goes to the end of the car, but there's no bathroom there. She looks back at Nana, who waves briskly for her to keep going. She's in midstride in the third car, threading the narrow corridor between the rows of seats, when the train lurches into motion and sends her sprawling back, onto a hard wooden seat on her right, the book bag squirting up from beneath her arms. She flails at it and grabs it, and a young man, not handsome but wearing immaculate clothing, looks at her in amused surprise as he scoots toward the window.

"I'm . . . I'm sorry," Kwan says, her face hot as fire.

He smiles at her, a nice smile that contains nothing to be afraid of. "Why? You didn't start the train."

"But I . . . I fell here, and you . . . um, you had to move, and—"

"It's fine. Really. Trains do that. If they didn't, we'd never get anyplace, would we?"

Absolutely no words come to her mind. "The . . . um, the . . ."

"The bathroom? Down there." He points toward the end of the car. "Put your hands on the backs of the seats as you walk. That way when the train goes around a curve, you won't fall down again."

"This thing," Kwan says, lifting the book bag as though she hasn't seen it and immediately feeling even more stupid.

"*One* hand, then," he says patiently. "Hold the bag under your left arm and use the right to grab the seat backs."

Kwan nods but still can't think of anything to say. The train is shuddering beneath her feet and making a clacking sound like something chewing rocks. She's starting to haul herself onto her feet again when he says, "Where are you going?"

Where *is* she going? She hasn't actually asked Nana. "Um," she says. "Bangkok." She manages at the last moment not to turn the word into a question.

"Where in Bangkok? It's a big city."

Kwan nods and says, "Really big." And then, since he seems to expect more, she adds, "My aunt's house."

His eyes travel to the sapphire in her right ear and then come back. "That's good. You've got someone waiting for you, then."

"Oh, yes. My . . . my aunt." She wants to fan her face, but she won't do it.

"So you said." He lifts his eyebrows and lets them drop. "Well."

"Well," Kwan says, searching desperately for something to say. "Thank you."

He smiles again. "I didn't do anything."

"You taught me . . . um, how to walk. On the train, I mean."

"You'd have figured it out. So." The eyebrows go up and down again. "The bathroom."

"The bathroom." And then she's up, the bag trapped beneath her left arm, taking it one cautious row at a time, her right hand grasping the backs of the seats.

The bathroom is tiny and dirty, and it smells sweetly awful. She has to lean against the door to get her skirt off, terrified that it'll swing open beneath her weight and she'll be standing there in her frayed underpants. Once the skirt is off, she hurries into the jeans, having some trouble with the left leg because there's nothing to balance herself against except the door, and the train is turning, as the young man said it would. With the jeans finally up and buttoned, she pulls the school blouse over her head and chooses her best T-shirt, the one that nobody else owned before she got it, and slips it on. She looks at herself in the mirror, avoiding her eyes, and smooths the wrinkles in the T-shirt with the palms of her hands. She lifts the blouse by its shoulders to fold it and feel the weight in the pocket. The stone.

She stands there, swaying with the train, holding the stone in her right hand and feeling the distance between her and her village open and stretch. She shoves the stone into the pocket of her jeans.

Then she carefully folds her school uniform and places it in the bottom of the book bag, takes a last glance at herself, and pours water over her hands so she can scrub her face and smooth down her hair. She finds herself thinking of the young man as she dabs her face dry with her spare T-shirt.

When she passes him on her way back to Nana, his eyebrows rise again and stay up as he takes in her jeans and shirt. His smile, when their eyes meet, is more measured than it had been before.

"BUT WHAT DO you *want*?" Nana has been filing her nails for the past twenty kilometers or so, but now she looks over at Kwan, who has her nose pressed to the window, watching Thailand slide by.

"Want?" She realizes that Nana has been talking for a few minutes but has no idea what she's said. "I don't know."

"There must be something."

There is, actually, something she's always wanted. "A wristwatch."

Nana laughs, a laugh as sharp as glass breaking. "In the village? A wristwatch? Why? The whole village is a clock. Sunrise is at sunrise, noon is at noon. When the sun disappears, you pee and go to bed. When it comes up, you pee and wash your face. Everything you have to do, everything everyone has to do, it's got its time, and everybody knows when it is. And if you're wrong, by a few minutes or a few hours, so what? You can do it at the right time the next day. Or the next." She looks critically at her nails, her arms outstretched and her fingers spread. "That was one of the things I hated most. Every day, every day, exactly the same, like the week was Monday, Monday, Monday."

"I still want a watch," Kwan says stubbornly.

"Well, that's easy. If that's all you want, you're going to be happy."

"That's not *all* I want."

"Then what? What else?"

A better life for my brothers and sisters. Safety for my sister Mai. Someone who will love me. Someone I can love. A place that's mine. Being clean all my life. What she says is, "Never mind."

"Oh, don't sulk. This is an adventure."

"I'm not sulking."

"Don't worry, then. There's nothing to worry about. Don't you want a cell phone? Pretty clothes? A gold bracelet? Two gold bracelets?"

"Yes," Kwan says. "All those things."

"Fine. Don't talk." Nana goes back to work on her nails.

"What time is it?"

"You really do need a watch, don't you?" Nana puts the emery board between her teeth, fumbles with the catch on her own watch, and hands it to Kwan. "Here. Put it on."

"Oh, no, I—"

"*Stop* that. I just gave it to you. Stop saying no. Life is about getting things. You get nice things, and you give them away. You make money—you never say no to money, never—and you give it to your family. You have food, and you share it with friends. You have spare change, you give it to monks or beggars. But you can't do any of that until you have things."

Kwan says, "Thank you," and tries to put the watch on, but she doesn't know how to work the catch.

"You're absolutely hopeless," Nana says, and she reaches over and snaps the catch closed. "See? You fold it here and then just fit it over the inside piece and press."

"Thank—" Kwan begins, but realizes she's just said that. She looks at the watch. "Almost four," she says. "Mai will be getting home in a few minutes."

"Your mother will be making something for her to eat," Nana says. "Isn't that sweet? And your father will be off in the woods with the three guys who are waiting to tie you up."

Kwan swivels to face her. "That's not—"

"If you're going to remember any of it," Nana says between her teeth, "remember all of it." She looks back down at her nails and frowns. "I don't have the color I want."

"Do you . . ." Kwan falls silent, and Nana makes a show of folding her hands to hide the unfinished nails and turning her eyes to Kwan's.

She waits. "Don't you ever think about it? How you used to be? The people you knew? I mean . . . I mean—what your life was like?"

"No. My life was covered in shit. I stepped in shit all day long. Buffalo shit, dog shit, sometimes human shit, someplace where some little kid took a squat. I was fat, I was angry, I was lonely, I was hungry. I didn't even know you weren't supposed to be able to be fat and hungry at the same time. Now I'm full and I'm thin. Better, right? I never step in shit. I can have anything I want. Another watch? No problem. Ten pairs of thousand-baht blue jeans? No problem. A man? Anytime I want one. And yeah, sometimes when I don't. But you know what? If that's the worst thing that ever happens to me, I'll die happy." She stops and looks beyond Kwan, at the scenery blurring past the window. When she speaks again, some of the edge is gone from her voice. "You have to wait, baby. You have to see how you feel when you've been there for a while. You're scared. You don't know what your life is going to be like." She puts her hand on her own chest, fingers flat. "You never liked me. Well, I didn't like you either, but that wasn't your fault. I didn't like anybody. So forget what you thought about me then and look at me. Do I look unhappy? Do I look like somebody who's going to jump off a bridge? Do I look like I'm about to burst into tears?"

"No."

"I lived through this. I know hundreds of girls who lived through this. And you know what? *You'll* live through it."

The train is slowing. Kwan leans against the window and peers ahead. A small station is gliding toward them. People in worn village clothes stand there, clutching plastic bags.

"Nowhere," Nana says, without even looking. "We're nowhere."

The doors open at the end of the car, and the young man Kwan almost fell on walks through them, carrying a cloth traveling bag. As he comes toward them, his eyes find her and then slide past to Nana. The smile on his face loses its energy. He looks straight ahead and passes them without slowing.

"Mr. Nowhere," Nana says when he's gone.

Kwan looks at Nana, seeing her blouse the way the young man had seen it, high on one shoulder and low above the opposite breast. Then she closes her eyes, places a hand over the stone in her pocket, and waits for the train to start again.

12

Candy Cane

She smells Bangkok long before she sees it. The train is slicing through the night, and Nana's watch—*her* watch—says it's almost nine. By now her family would normally be asleep, but her father is probably stalking the village in a rage, his pockets empty again, while the children stay out of sight. During the past hour, the dark expanses between villages have grown shorter, until now there are always lights on both sides of the train and she's surrounded by a brownish back-of-the-nose smell, like standing behind a bus, and she thinks, *This must be Bangkok,* but the train keeps going and keeps going, and the lighted windows get higher and higher, and there are more roads, and then the roads have cars on them. At one point cars pass above them on a bridge, and Kwan cranes up to stare at them.

"Getting there," Nana says. She yawns comfortably. Her nails are now a kind of tangerine color with red underneath it, like a juice mix. Kwan thinks the polish is as garish as some of the colored electric signs they've been passing for the last half hour.

Looking back out the window, Kwan says, "It's too big."

"It's still a village, once you know it. It's just that it's a *big* village." The train begins to slow, and Nana is up, yanking her bag from the overhead shelf while the world is still sliding sickeningly by. "Come on," she says. "We've missed most of the night." And she's halfway down the car, moving toward the rear of the train, before Kwan has even gotten her arms around her book bag.

Outside the train Kwan sees a rice paddy of people, a solid field of people, pressed shoulder to shoulder, too close together for light to shine between them, stretching back four or five meters from the train, where it thins into individual shapes, blurs to Kwan's nearsighted eyes. She is seeing, she realizes, more people in one moment than she has seen in her entire life. She hesitates, one foot still on the step leading up to the train, but Nana reaches back without even looking, snags Kwan's T-shirt, and drags her behind. Kwan has to dodge the wheels of Nana's pink suitcase.

Outside, in a haze of heat and fumes, Nana stops and sizes up a long, long line of taxis, all new-looking, painted every color Kwan has ever seen, plus some she hasn't. Nana opens the door of the cab at the front of the line, leans in, and says, "Patpong 1. Forty baht."

The driver says, "The meter."

Nana says, "Fuck the meter. Forty baht. With the air-con on."

The driver glances up at the rearview mirror, sees the number of taxis behind him, and does something under the dashboard. Kwan hears the trunk pop open. Without a word Nana goes to the back of the cab, raises the trunk all the way up, slides the bag inside, and slams the trunk. To Kwan she says, "What are you waiting for? Get in." She hip-shoves Kwan across the seat and, even before she closes the door, says to the driver, "Go, go, go."

Kwan has to fight the urge to press her nose against the window. Lights, cars, people, more people, more cars, buildings high enough to lose their tops in mist. No stars at all. The taxi is freezing, and goose bumps have popped up all over her arms. She glances at Nana, who is sitting there gazing at the back of the driver's seat as though a movie were being projected on it. Just as Kwan is about to speak, Nana says, "Listen. Are you listening?"

"Yes."

"Good. Here's what's going to happen. He'll drop us at the end of Patpong. There's a market set up in the middle of the street, and the sidewalk is crowded. I don't want to have to keep looking for you, so you grab the back of my blouse and don't let go. If anybody gets in the way, just shove."

"Shove someone?"

"That's what I said, isn't it? If we get separated, I could waste half an hour looking for you, and I want to get to work. Don't look at any of the men."

"Oh," Kwan says, thinking, *She* wants *to get to work?* "I won't."

"Well, don't. One of them might try to stop you, and I haven't got time for that. When we get to the bar, you just keep your mouth shut. I'll introduce you to the mama-san, and then she and I will go away to talk some business for a couple of minutes. You stay wherever she puts you. *Exactly* where she puts you. Don't talk to the customers." The taxi passes a big, brightly lighted shrine, and Nana dips her head and makes a *wai* in its direction. Kwan follows suit, and Nana begins talking as though she'd never stopped. "It's important that you *do not* look at, or talk to, any customers. You don't want to make enemies of the other girls before you even start to work."

"Enemies?"

"Think about it. They've been up there all night, dancing their feet off, trying to get one of those fatsos to buy them a drink, take them out, whatever will put some money in their pocket. Then you come in, with dew still on you, and the customer one of them has her eye on suddenly decides you're the angel of the evening. That girl is not going to be your friend. And neither are *her* friends."

"I'm not going to be anybody's . . . angel."

"See that you're not."

"Why can't I go with you and the mama-san?"

"Because I say so."

"Oh."

Nana pats her hand. "I know this is confusing, but just do what I say and stay out of trouble. A week from now, you'll feel right at home." She smiles at Kwan and then leans forward, slaps a hand on the back of the front seat, and says to the driver, "Could you move this thing? I'd like to get there in this lifetime."

THE SIDEWALK IS solid with people, almost all of them *farang*. They seem to be suffering in the heat; their shirts are as wet as second skins, their hair is matted, and their necks and faces are red and dripping. Maybe they sweat so much, Kwan thinks, sneaking quick looks at them, because so many of them are fat. They smell different from Thais, too. Some of them smell so bad that Kwan breathes through her mouth, thinking it would be rude to hold her nose. For a sliver of a moment, she tries to imagine being close to one of these men, being alone with him. Could she do it? Would it be rude to ask him to shower first? Maybe she could wash him, like a baby, to make sure he was really clean.

What amazes her is how *tall* they are. Most of them are only a little shorter than she is, and some are actually taller. For the first time in her life, Kwan doesn't feel like the one nail that's sticking up from the board. She doesn't feel like a freak. She has a brief sensation that she's walking in a trench.

To her right is a long line of brilliantly lighted booths, rich with the saturated dyes of new clothing that's never faded, never even been washed; paintings on black cloth of impossibly clean villages, full of colors where, in a real village, there would be only the leached-out, sun-bled browns and grays of old wood; big wooden frames surrounding enormous scorpions and spiders pressed into white cotton beneath glass (for whom?); and then—gleaming directly at her, as though they've seen her coming—wristwatches, dozens of them, enough wristwatches for her whole village, with a handful left over. Kwan lags, drawn by the glitter, but Nana reaches back and grabs her arm, zigging left at the same time to avoid three men walking side by side yet towing Kwan directly into their path.

"Whoa, whoa, *whoa*," says one of them, a distinguished-looking man with gray hair, maybe as old as Mr. Pattison. "Fresh fruit. And a big one."

"Virgin girl," Nana says without slowing. "Five hundred dollar."

"I'll go second," the distinguished-looking man says. Seen up close, he's not so distinguished; his lower eyelids have sagged to reveal strips of wet pink flesh, and his nose is a web of spidery red veins. "Get a discount." He reaches for Kwan's hand, but she snatches it away and grabs Nana, practically jumping into her arms, and the man laughs. "Bunny rabbit," he says to one of the other men. "Look at her, scared as shit." To Kwan he says, "Hey, Basketball, which bar?"

"Candy Cane," Nana says, not even turning her head. "Come two day, three day more."

"What's her name?" the man calls after them.

"Not have name yet," Nana says. "Maybe Basketball." And she drags Kwan away from the men, threading through the crowd as though it were a dance she's practiced a thousand times.

Above them are big colored signs like the ones Kwan had seen from the train, but she sounds out the words and reads QUEEN'S CASTLE, KING'S CASTLE, SUPERGIRLS, LAP BAR. Neon silhouettes of naked girls blink hot pink and blue.

"*Nana,*" she says.

"Not now. Just come on."

"But look. They're naked."

"That's upstairs. Don't worry, you're not going to be upstairs."

"*Really* naked?"

"Don't think about it. You'll never have to do it, unless you want to."

"*Want* to?"

"More money. But not enough more. Okay, we're here. Come on." And beneath a red-and-white sign that says CANDY CANE BAR, she turns in. Two girls in Santa hats and schoolgirl outfits, but with very short skirts that barely cover the bottoms of their panties, squeal at Nana and hug her as though they haven't seen her in a year, and then they turn to Kwan and their eyes go flat, like someone looking at an abacus and thinking about a number.

"New?" one of them says.

"We'll see," Nana says, and one of the overage schoolgirls does a final appraisal of Kwan that makes her feel like she's being checked for dents and scratches, then pulls aside a cloth hanging over the door. A wall of cold air rolls over Kwan, and then there's a shove in the center of her back, and she's inside.

The music is so loud she wants to put her fingers in her ears, but she almost stops hearing it as she looks around the room. It's long and narrow, with colored lights flashing on and off all over the ceiling. Men are packed onto benches along the walls, and more men perch on uncomfortable-looking stools at a bar that goes around the stage. In the narrow space between the bar and the edge of the stage, women busily mix and pour drinks, but Kwan barely sees them.

What she sees are the dancing girls.

There are twenty or more, two lines of them, back-to-back so that one line faces each wall. They wear knee-high boots in red-and-white, diagonally striped leather or plastic and very, very short red pants that are cut so far below the navel that Kwan thinks some of them must be shaving down there. Above the shorts is a red-and-white-striped halter top, just big enough to cover the breasts, with a single big button in the center. Some of the girls have their tops unbuttoned, but there's a string or a little chain connecting the two halves so the top doesn't fall all the way open. Eight or ten metal poles, evenly spaced, sprout at intervals around the stage, and the girls tend to congregate around these, hanging on to one or wrapping a lazy elbow around it as they do whatever dance steps come to them, although mostly they just shuffle from foot to foot. Only one pole is the exclusive property of a single dancer, and that's the pole closest to the door. Most of the women look beautiful to Kwan, but the girl dancing all alone there is the single most beautiful human being Kwan has ever seen in her life: hair to midback, perfect legs, a plump and sullen mouth, skin that shines as though it's been dusted with pearl, and enormous, slightly tilted eyes of a peculiar, dark-golden color.

Some of the women are checking out the men, picking one here and there from the crowd and smiling at him, moving on if there's no response. A few watch themselves in the mirrored walls as though they've never seen their reflections before. Others stare at their own feet or carry on conversations with the girls nearest them.

Partway down the line, one of the dancers spots Kwan and does a double take, then grabs the arm of the girl next to her and twists her toward Kwan. That girl nudges the girl next to her, and gradually the ripple works its way the full length of the stage, and all the girls are staring at Kwan, and then one of them starts to laugh. She lets go of the pole and lifts one hand way above her head, going on tiptoe and even jumping a few inches, then bends forward, laughing, and then most of them are laughing as Kwan stands there, her face burning. But the girl alone at the front pole doesn't laugh, doesn't even look at Kwan.

She just keeps her eyes on the cloth hanging over the door.

THE REST of the evening is a series of disconnected moments. A severe-looking, slump-shouldered woman in her fifties, aggressively plain-faced, her hair pulled back so tightly it looks like it must hurt, bustles up, people stepping out of her way as she comes, and leans back to look at Kwan. She does something with her mouth that looks as if she's sucking her teeth and says a few words that Kwan can't hear over the music. Nana shakes her head and then circles Kwan's face with her hand, brushing fingertips over her cheekbones and jawline as though she has a powder puff in her hand, then uses her index and middle fingers to make snipping motions around Kwan's hair.

A couple of the girls on the stage imitate the snipping, and one of them pretends she's got an ax and is chopping Kwan down. Girls clap their hands once or twice and laugh. The beautiful girl in front pays no attention to any of it.

The severe-looking woman stares up at Kwan for a long minute or two and then shrugs some sort of acceptance. Nana taps Kwan's arm as though to say, *Stay here,* and she and the severe-looking woman disappear into the rear of the bar. Kwan stands there, using every fiber of her will to keep from bursting into tears. She presses her back against the wall, holding her arms tightly at her sides, taking up as little space as possible, trying to be invisible. But she can feel eyes on her, and not just the girls'. Around the room men have turned to regard her. Some of them have girls sitting beside them, and those girls tug at the men's arms and toss sharp-edged glances at Kwan, not the glances of people who are eager to be friends. Kwan looks down at the floor.

A chubby girl in the stage uniform of boots and shorts goes out of her way to bang into Kwan, hard, with her shoulder and says, "Oh, excuse me," and some of the girls on the stage start laughing again.

The room seems to shimmer and lose its focus, and Kwan is back at school, facing yet another bully eager to humiliate the tall girl. She knows she has to bring this to an immediate stop, no matter what Nana would say. She steps away from the wall and says, "You did that on purpose."

The chubby girl puts her hands on her hips and says, "Really?"

Kwan brings up one hand, fingers curled and nails pointing directly at the girl's eyes. "Do it again and you'll have bandages all over your fat face."

The girl in the boots backs up a quick step, and the laughter on the stage stops. Kwan looks up and sees every woman onstage staring at her. Some look surprised, some look amused. A few seem angry. The beautiful girl, the one dancing alone right in front of her, turns the enormous golden eyes to Kwan and gives her the smallest smile Kwan has ever seen, more the idea of a smile than the thing itself. Then she returns her attention to the cloth hanging over the door.

A moment later Nana and the mama-san are back. Nana has an envelope in her hand, which she tucks behind her when she sees Kwan looking at it. Trailing after them is a short, cute girl dressed for the stage. "You're set," Nana says. "You'll start serving drinks tonight. Fon here"—she indicates the cute girl, who has a face like a child's doll, with plump cheeks and a tiny nose—"Fon will take care of you. Just do what she tells you to."

"But you— I mean, where are you going?"

"My bar." She glances at her wrist and remembers she's no longer wearing the watch, so she lifts Kwan's wrist and peers at it. "I've got to get to work."

"You said I'd be in your bar. When we were talking, you told me—"

"I don't think so," Nana says. "I'm at the King's Castle. Nobody starts out at the King's Castle. Only the best girls work there."

"But you said—"

"We're on the same *street,* that's what I said. Got to go. Listen to Fon, okay? Glad you're here." She reaches up and pats Kwan on the cheek. "We'll eat dinner together sometime." Nana turns away from Kwan and obviously remembers the envelope she's hiding behind her, because she shoves it into the waistband of her skirt. She pushes aside the curtain over the doorway and is taken by the current of the sidewalk. A second later she has disappeared. The curtain flaps closed.

"What are *you* waiting for?" Fon says, and Kwan turns, but Fon is talking to the plump girl who bumped her. "Go find a lap. Drool on somebody. Do whatever you want, but do it somewhere else."

The plump girl glares at Kwan for a second, as though Kwan is the one who's spoken, then lifts her chin abruptly, an angry, jerky motion, and whirls to go. Fon reaches out, index finger extended, and jams it between the plump girl's buttocks. The girl jumps and squeals but keeps moving.

Then Fon turns to Kwan and smiles. "Good," she says. "You've made the right enemy."

The Best-Looking Cut of Meat

For a week or ten days, the city pushes at her. It ambushes her, surrounds her, presses in on her everywhere she goes, not just people but smells and sounds, the never-ending clamor of engines and horns and brakes and voices, the smells of exhaust and food vendors, the pressure of heat reflecting from the buildings, the brush of people passing too closely in the street, and the eyes of people—thousands of them each day, it seems—looking at her. If they're Thai, there's always the moment of surprise and then the amused smile and the turning head as Kwan passes. If they're men—*farang* men, that is—the eyes are speculative, the eyes of someone considering a purchase.

When she thinks about her village, what she sees is the barren, abandoned patch where she dug up her treasure, the one spot where she could be alone. She's literally never alone here. The only time she doesn't feel surrounded is in the mornings, and even then she's not really alone, because there are women sleeping nearby.

And they sleep most of the day, which isn't surprising, considering what time they go to bed. Nobody heads straight home after the bar closes. The women who haven't been chosen by a man, or who went for an early short-time and came back, cluster together at 2:00 A.M. and escape to the late-night clubs, discos, and bars. They're known, often by name, and they seem to be welcome everywhere.

This might, Kwan thinks, have something to do with the enormous amounts of money they spend—enough in a single night to keep a village family alive for a month. The endless stream of talk, rising and falling across the long nighttime hours, is fueled by alcohol, since some of the girls drink too much. Everybody seems to smoke all the time. They drink and smoke and chatter, and although they've just spent eight hours at the Candy Cane, they gossip endlessly about the bar, about who's got a *farang* boyfriend who gives her money all the time, and who's got a Thai boyfriend who takes her money all the time, and who got slapped around by a customer, and who got slapped around by her boyfriend, and who's a bitch and who's a prude and who would go to a hotel room with a dog if dogs could rent hotel rooms, and how the mama-san plays favorites, and how the bar cheats on drink commissions. In between talking to one another, they shout into their cell phones with other people who seem to be up all night.

It's immediately apparent to Kwan that the girls have turned the bar into a village, with groups that dislike each other. They've separated into two main camps, as wary of each other as the two packs of dogs that roamed opposite sides of the street in front of her house. Fon's group is the smaller but more tightly knit of the two. The members of the other gang, which includes the plump girl who bumped Kwan, are generally less attractive than Fon's bunch, although that doesn't seem to mean they get taken out of the bar less often. In fact, the plump girl, who isn't pretty even by the standards of Kwan's village, goes with more men than almost anyone. When Kwan asks Fon about that, Fon says, with uncharacteristic sourness, "If you'll do absolutely anything, there will always be someone who wants it."

Then there are the remaining girls—three or four of them—who aren't members of either group, who keep to themselves or go back and forth, crossing the invisible divide as though it didn't exist. One of the women who seems to be close to no one is Oom, the beautiful girl who's always at the pole nearest the door when her shift is on the stage. The dancers are split into two shifts that alternate all evening, each dancing for about twenty minutes until the disc jockey calls for the change, when the women in the idle shift get up off the laps of the men they've been working on and shuffle back to the stage to replace the women who are climbing down to try to snare the same men. The most beautiful girl in each shift takes the pole nearest the door. Fon calls those two girls "chicken feed," like the line of seed you lay down in a village to lure the poultry into the coop.

Oom doesn't seem to be friends with any of the girls, and she barely notices the customers. When she's not dancing, she sits alone in the back room where the girls change into their show clothes. Ten minutes after Kwan began serving drinks on her first night, a customer waved her over and pointed to Oom and said he wanted to buy her a drink. Kwan stood in front of Oom at the foot of the stage, but Oom kept her eyes on the curtain over the doorway until Fon raised her arms and waved them back and forth. When Oom's shift left the stage, she went and sat with the customer just long enough to drink one Coke, quickly, and then she got up and went into the back room. Kwan has seen her do it a dozen times.

"She's waiting for someone," Fon says. "He comes back every three or four months, and he's a little late. She's crazy. Any girl who waits for anyone is crazy, but especially a girl who looks like her. For all she knows, he's been in Bangkok for weeks and he's with a girl from the bar next door."

After the Candy Cane closed on Kwan's third night in Bangkok, she and Fon and half a dozen others went to a bar full of handsome waiters, and, to her amazement, one of the girls paid one of the waiters to go home with her. The next night they chose a dim, tiny place where women who were dressed like men waited on them and flirted with them. Two of the women in male clothing, whom the Candy Cane girls referred to as "tom-toms," made a special fuss over Kwan, and when one of them brushed her fingers lightly down the side of Kwan's neck, Kwan was so startled that she knocked over the drink of the girl sitting next to her. Everyone laughed, but some of the girls didn't look happy about the amount of attention Kwan was getting. However they felt about her, though, Kwan had no choice but to tag along. No one had yet given her a key to the rooms Fon shared with two other girls, where Fon assigned her a sagging, too-short couch on the first night and gave her a blanket and pillow from her own bed. So Kwan goes where she's led, trying to remain unnoticed, lagging behind the group. By the time she follows them through the door into their rooms, she's so tired she feels like a ghost, and it's usually almost dawn.

Everyone except Kwan sleeps until 2:00 or 3:00 in the afternoon, but in these first weeks Kwan still pops awake on village-girl time, at 7:00 or 8:00 A.M. Each morning she wiggles a little deeper into the cushions of the couch, which is much softer than the rag mat she slept on at home, and tries to sort out everything that's happening to her. In front of the couch, where she barks her shins on it occasionally, is a three-legged table with a stack of beauty and fashion magazines holding up the legless corner. After a few minutes, when she knows that sleep will not reclaim her, she gets up, taking her blanket, and opens the curtains over the room's one window—the other girls grumbling at the light and then dropping back into sleep—and then she sits in the patch of sunlight on the floor. Some mornings she eases out one of the beauty magazines from the stack holding up the table and looks at the wonderful girls, but most of the time she leaves the magazines where they are. As the patch of sunlight moves, she moves with it, the blanket draped loosely over her shoulders, bathing herself in the warmth and the silence. In her hand she holds the stone she picked up the day she left the village. It takes a long time, but eventually it becomes as warm as her hand.

"OLD ONES," FON is saying, sounding like a schoolteacher. "Not too old, but old. In their fifties or so. Not handsome. Stay away from handsome men." She makes the face of someone who's bitten her tongue. "Let the other girls have them."

"Why? Nana said—"

Fon shakes her head. "Nana's not as smart as she thinks she is. *Nobody's* as smart as Nana thinks she is. Because the old ones have money. They're more grateful. They're easy to please, like little dogs. Treat them nicely and they'll come back and come back. That's good, because there's always some risk—not much, but some—when you go with a new one, and if you're extra sweet, the old guys will usually give you a present when they leave. One guy named Martin, from Switzerland, or maybe Sweden or Brazil, gave me ten thousand baht the night before he went home."

"Ten *thousand*?"

Fon shrugs as though it were snack money. "I made him feel young. I told him he was handsome. The problem with the handsome ones is that they really are handsome." She puts a cigarette between her lips. It looks so out of place in her baby-doll's face that Kwan laughed the first time she saw Fon light up. "They feel like *you* should pay *them*," Fon says around the cigarette. "They're cheap. And they're young, too, which means they can go for longer, maybe two or three times. Thanks anyway, once is fine with me. But the big reason is the money. The money's with the old guys. But not too old, because they take a long time, too." She laughs. "Different reason, though."

The two of them are sitting on the floor of the larger of the two rooms that Fon and now Kwan share with two other women from the bar. The others are out eating a very late breakfast. After her sixth night of serving drinks, Kwan put some tip money into the pool for the weekly rent, and the next morning Fon gave her a key. With the door locked behind her and Bangkok held at bay three stories down, she almost feels at home.

Kwan says, "But most of the girls want to go with the younger ones."

"Girls are crazy," Fon says, looking for the ashtray. She gets to her knees and hobbles dwarflike toward the three-legged table, stretching an arm out, and Kwan knots a fist in the back of Fon's T-shirt to keep her from falling on her face. Fon laughs and leans farther, and Kwan has to use both hands to keep her upright. When Fon has a grip on the ashtray, Kwan pulls her back, and when Fon lands on her rump, they're both laughing.

"It's a job, not a date," Fon says. "Some girls never figure that out. They keep going after the young, handsome ones, and when they get one, they lord it over girls like me, girls who make three times as much money as they do. It's as if they have to fool themselves every night that it's really about love, like the only reason they're up there is because it's the natural place to meet the solid-gold man, the handsome, good-hearted young *farang* with the big bank account who's waited his whole life to fall in love with some worn-out bar girl so he can marry her and support her whole family for the rest of his life."

"But that happens," Kwan says, feeling very young. She waits, but Fon doesn't respond. "Doesn't it?"

"Oh, honey," Fon says, putting her free hand on top of Kwan's and tapping the ash from her cigarette with the other. "Not you, too. Yes, it happens. Maybe eight or nine times a year, but it never works. The guys lie about how much money they have, or they lie about not being married already, or they lie about when they have to go back home. So some dumb girl goes through the marriage ceremony, and promises her mother and father they're going to be rich, and gives it to him for free for three or four months, and then one day she wakes up and he's in Australia. Not even a note." She takes an ambitious drag. "And then there are the girls who marry a guy just so they can steal everything he's got. They get the fool to buy a house, which has to be in her name because he's not Thai, and one day they sell the paper on the house for half of what it's worth, empty out the loving hubby's bank account, and run north."

Kwan says, "It never works?"

Fon turns the coal of her cigarette against the edge of the ashtray with great delicacy, shaving off a fine film of ash. "It didn't for me."

"Oh," Kwan says. "I'm sorry. I didn't know—"

"How could you? I didn't tell you. No reason to. It didn't matter. No broken heart. I didn't love him. I loved the idea of a passport, and a house in wherever it was, and money going up to my family every month. When he disappeared, the only thing that really upset me was that I hadn't been sending money home. I'd stopped working, and he kept telling me it took time for his bank in . . . in Germany, I think, to transfer everything he owned here. He couldn't even give my parents a dowry payment until the money arrived, and it didn't, and then it didn't some more. After a couple of months, he said he'd have to go home to handle it. And I went to the airport with him and hugged him and even managed to cry a little. And he never came back to me."

"You never saw him again?"

"Oh, sure. About a year later. I'd changed bars, but he didn't know that. He figured he was safe as long as he stayed out of my old bar. And I was in the back room when he came in, so he sat at the edge of the stage without having any idea I was there."

Kwan glances at the window. The afternoon is starting to fade, and the evening looms ahead of her, bright and full of noise. "What did you do?"

"I went onstage like always, but I changed places with the girl who was dancing in front of him, and then I leaned down and picked up his drink. He looked up and saw me, and I gave him a big, friendly smile and spit in his drink. I'd been saving spit since I saw him walk in, so there was a lot of it. Then I put the drink down and went up and down the stage, telling every girl that he was an asshole and pointing at him so he'd know what I was doing."

"What did he do?"

Fon drags on the cigarette, squinting against the smoke. "If he'd been smart, he would have left right then, but he couldn't let me see that I'd chased him out, so he waited until my shift was over and I'd left the stage, and then he threw down some money and almost ran out. By then I'd put a wrapper over my dancing clothes, and I counted to ten or something and then went out and watched him go into the Play Pen. I gave him a few minutes, just to make sure he was staying, and then I followed him in and told the manager—" She breaks off, looking doubtfully at Kwan. "Have you been into the Play Pen?"

"I've never been to any of the bars except the Candy Cane."

"I'll take you around some night when we're off. Well, the thing about the Play Pen is that about half the girls are ladyboys. So I told the manager that he'd walked out of my bar complaining because it only had girls, so he should tell the ladyboys to go to work on him. There were four of them hanging on to him when I left."

Kwan starts to laugh. Fon watches her solemnly, and then she stubs out her cigarette. "Once in a million years, it works. Getting married to a customer, I mean. Out of maybe five hundred girls I know, two of them have done it and made it last. One of them is here, one's in America. But it's nothing you should think about. This is not about love. When you finally get up on that stage, just remember, it's a market and you're the best-looking cut of meat. Get every penny you can and forget the rest of it. What time is it?"

Kwan looks at Nana's watch. "Four o'clock."

"We've got two hours before work, then," Fon says, "and I can't look another minute at that schoolgirl haircut."

14

Silk That Thinks It's Cotton

Oh, *no*." The ladyboy in front of the mirror clutches his heart as though it's stopped in midbeat. He or she is broad-shouldered and heavyset beneath the flowered gown and the cloud of scarves, and wears shoulder-length hair, dyed midnight black, curled under at the ends, 1940s style. So much black makeup surrounds his eyes that Kwan thinks he looks like he's wearing a mask. Five-o'clock shadow prickles its way through a thick layer of pancake, but his voice is a flute. "Darling," the ladyboy says in English, "what *did* they cut it with? A lawn mower?"

Kwan decides to think of the ladyboy as "she," since it seems polite to let her be what she wants to be. In English she replies, "Not understand."

"That *hair*." The ladyboy raises both hands chest high, palms out and fingers curved in, shaking them in mock terror, like a starlet confronted by the half-eaten corpse that's always lurching out of the closet in Thai movies. The gesture rattles the beads on the twelve or so bracelets that circle each wrist. "My God, my God—that's English, by the way," she tells Kwan in Thai, in a matter-of-fact tone, "and you should learn it. When anyone says something surprising or when you want to pretend some customer has impressed you by, for example, the size of his equipment, you say 'Oh, my God.'"

Kwan carefully repeats, "Oh, my God," and gets a nod of approval. Then she says, "Equipment?"

"Later." The ladyboy lifts Kwan's hair and drops it. "Terrible, terrible. Who did this to you, your *mother*?"

"Yes."

"Oh, well, excuse me. I'm sure she meant well. But look at you, just *look* at you." She puts her hands on the sides of Kwan's head and swivels her face toward the mirror. Kwan tries to look at herself but sees Fon reflected behind her, laughing, and she laughs, too.

"I don't want to hear any laughing *at all*," the ladyboy says. "This is *serious*, even *tragic*. There isn't enough beauty in the world to waste it this way. You may not be responsible for the fact that you're beautiful, but you *are* responsible for taking care of it. It makes people *feel* better, seeing something beautiful. Don't you want people to feel better, don't you want to lift them out of their gray, muffled, boxed-in lives for a minute or two and put a silvery little sliver of light in their souls? That's what beauty is, you know—it's tiny glimmers of light left over from the Creation. You're Buddhist, of course, but in the *farang* holy book, which is called the Bible, practically the first words out of God's lips, and I'm sure they were very nice lips, are 'Let there be light.' There was probably quite a lot of it, too, Him being God and all. Most of it's gone, now, of course—the light, I mean, we've pissed on the flame by living such dreary, cowardly lives—but there are still bits of it here and there. Sunsets, music, really good jewelry. A face like yours. Don't you want to share it?"

"I don't—" Kwan begins, and stops.

"What *is* her problem?" the ladyboy asks Fon.

Fon says, "She doesn't know she's beautiful."

"*Ohhh*." The ladyboy puts the tips of four straight fingers over her mouth as though warning herself not to say something unseemly. "How very unusual. Most of the time, I work on cotton that wants to be silk, and here I am working on silk that thinks it's cotton." She laces her fingers together and holds them in front of her chest, palms touching, like someone about to beg a favor. "Let's go slowly, shall we? Sit down, please." She turns the chair toward Kwan and makes a show of dusting the seat with her longest scarf.

"The hair first," Fon says, sitting on a plastic chair against the wall and picking up a magazine with a girl's face on the cover. "And, Kwan, this is Tra-La. Like singing."

"Of *course* the hair first," Tra-La says severely. "Do I come to your bar and tell you how to dance?" To Kwan she says, "But you *are* going to have to sit. I can't cut you on tiptoe."

"Sorry," Kwan says. She eases herself into the seat. "Nice to meet you."

"Yes, I'm sure it is." Tra-La swings the chair around to face the mirror. She puts her fingertips lightly on Kwan's cheekbones and tilts her head right and left, then up and down. "It really isn't fair," she says. "No bad angles at all. What's your name?"

"Kwan."

"Well, you'll have to do something about that, won't you?" She's taking out one pair of scissors after another, snipping the air with them once or twice, then replacing them in a black metal cylinder that's bristling with them.

"Why? It's my name."

"And it's a pretty name, but not for a bar." She finally chooses a very slender, very silvery pair and holds it, point upward, while she musses Kwan's hair with her other hand. She ruffles it, lifts it, and lets it fall. "It's the Kwan that means 'spirit,' right? Not exactly the world's sexiest name."

"I'm not sexy."

"Just *look* how your hair falls. Like it was blow-dried by angels before you were born. Darling, if you're not sexy, I'm an army sergeant. You just give me half an hour here and we'll discuss it further. Oh, my goodness, I'm so distracted I forgot to cover you up. Can't have you getting hair all over your awful clothes." Tra-La puts down the scissors and grabs a length of white cloth, which she tosses over Kwan's shoulders and fastens at the neck with a hair clip. Then she picks up a spray bottle, says, "Close your eyes," and begins to mist Kwan's hair.

"Smells nice."

"Lavender," Tra-La says. "I make it myself. One must do the little things, you know. Otherwise we might as well live in holes and eat roots. Have you honestly never looked at your hair and thought, 'What does my mother have against me?'"

"Never." Kwan feels a surge of loyalty toward her mother. "At school everybody's hair looks like this."

"Yes, but I was at school, too, as hard as that may be for you to accept, and believe me, darling, most of your classmates *deserve* hair like this. Oh, I wish I had another five or six inches to work with, but we'll do what we can, and then later we'll play with it some more." She begins to snip, and bits of cold, wet hair land on Kwan's cheeks.

She opens her eyes and sees herself staring back from the mirror beyond Tra-La's busy hands. "I don't want to look."

"Whyever not?"

"I don't like to look at myself."

"Fine with me." Tra-La turns the chair ninety degrees so Kwan is facing the window. "The light is better this way."

From her chair against the wall, Fon says, "Didn't they have *any* mirrors in your village?"

"Yes," Kwan says. "I just didn't look in them." To Tra-La, who seems sympathetic, she says, "Everybody called me Stork."

"Well, honey, fuck all of them *and* the dirt they sit on. You're in Bangkok now, where people can tell diamonds from dung. Lift your chin." Tra-La is snipping, very quickly, the hair that falls over Kwan's forehead, holding the scissors almost vertical, and a fine rain of hair sifts down past Kwan's eyes. "This works," Tra-La says, nodding agreement with herself. She backs up and cocks her head with her eyes narrowed and her lips tight, then wields the scissors again. "This works just fine."

As Tra-La busies herself, Kwan watches people go past the window, which faces onto Patpong. Here and there she sees groups of bar girls dart through the crowd, their hair wet and gleaming from their afternoon showers, shiny as fish, all talking at once as they go to one of the neighboring restaurants for food to take to the bar. They'll eat as they put on their makeup, and discuss last night's dreams and the lottery numbers they're playing, and say awful things about the women who haven't arrived yet. The metal pipes that frame the night-market booths have been clamped together, lights are snapping on in bar doorways, and neon is beginning to add its acid sizzle to the night. Kwan feels Fon's eyes on her and realizes that her friend has lowered the magazine and is watching with fascination as Tra-La works.

Tra-La turns and follows Kwan's gaze, and when her eyes meet Fon's, Fon smiles. "Oh, yes," Tra-La says, eyebrows arched. "I'm *exactly* that good."

Kwan says, "What? What does that mean?"

"You just sit there, Miss Thailand, and let me do my magic." The scissors snick near Kwan's ears, and the short, straight snips of hair accumulate in her lap, and after fifteen minutes or so Tra-La steps back and says, "Hmmmm." She lowers the hand with the scissors in it, takes several more steps back, then tosses the scissors onto the table in front of the mirror, where they land with a clatter. She attacks Kwan's hair with both hands, fluffing it, tugging it, yanking it on top so vigorously that Kwan feels her eyebrows lift. Tra-La keeps toying with Kwan's hair as she circles the chair, and Kwan realizes that the ladyboy is humming. Tra-La leans across Kwan to get the scissors, moving so fast she bumps the back of Kwan's head without even noticing, and waves the scissors around until she finds a spot to improve, just a snip here and a snip there, while Fon watches the process, not even noticing when the magazine slips from her lap. Finally Tra-La gets a dryer and spends a minute or two grabbing hold of bits of hair, stretching them out, curling them around her finger, hitting them with the hot air, shaping Kwan's head in a way that reminds Kwan of the way she patted her bag of treasure back into its teardrop shape.

Then Tra-La puts down the dryer and says, "Indulge me." She grabs a shoe box full of little jars and bottles, opens one, and spreads something soft and fragrant over the skin on Kwan's face. Kwan sees Fon get up and come closer, but Tra-La says, "Eyes closed, please," so Kwan closes her eyes, and for what seems like a long time she gives herself over to this stranger's fingers on her face, smoothing, patting, massaging, whisking soft brushes across her cheekbones and spreading a moistened thumb beneath them, toying with her hair again, and then doing something with a creamy-feeling pencil to her eyebrows and upper eyelids. "Open your eyes and look up," Tra-La says, and when she does, Kwan sees Fon leaning in, no more than a foot or two from her face, the tip of her tongue trapped between her teeth, as Tra-La draws a line on Kwan's lower lid. "Look at these lashes," Tra-La says to Fon. "Long as palm fronds. It'd be a sin to put goop on them." She purses her mouth, studying Kwan's eyes in a way that seems completely impersonal and doesn't make her uncomfortable at all. "Maybe just a little shine, what do you think?"

Fon says, "Yes," and Tra-La opens a slender tube that has a tiny brush in it and tells Kwan once again to look up. The brush barely touches Kwan's lower lashes before she's ordered to look down, and she feels the strokes, almost as soft as Tra-La's breath, on her upper lashes.

Tra-La screws the brush back into the tube, and she and Fon move away. Tra-La says, "Yes, yes, yes," and drapes an arm comfortably over Fon's shoulders, and the two of them stare at Kwan as though she were a photo in a magazine.

Then Fon starts to laugh, and after a surprised pause Tra-La joins in. Fon is laughing so hard that she bends forward and rests her hands on her knees, and Tra-La wipes her eyes and smears black makeup over the bridge of her nose.

Kwan feels the heat mounting in her face. With an abrupt jerk, she swivels the chair to the mirror, looks, and stops breathing.

There is no one in the mirror who looks familiar. The once-blunt, geometrical hair is jagged and spiky, no two locks the same length, and the longest ones, on the sides, have been swept forward to frame a pair of cheekbones that have been highlighted and shaded until they almost dominate Kwan's face. Her eyes are lined in a darkness that makes them seem brighter than ever before, and her mouth has been redefined in a pale pink so that its fullness is apparent. The way her hair tapers down above her shoulders makes her neck look a yard long, and she thinks, *Stork's neck,* and then instantly, *Swan's neck,* and the words strike her like lightning. She instinctively lifts her chin to make her neck even longer and pulls open the cloth Tra-La wrapped around her, to see the way her collarbones wing out on either side at the base of her throat. She has no idea how long she has been looking at herself when she says, at last, "Is this really me?"

Fon says, "It is now."

"Darling," Tra-La says, leaning on Fon as though she's exhausted. "You are going to make a *fortune.*"

"YOU ARE, YOU know. Do the job right and you'll earn so much money you can buy your whole village. If you want it, I mean." Fon pours herself an inch of white wine and offers the glass to Kwan, but Kwan shakes her head yet again, and Fon drains it. The half bottle at Fon's right hand is mostly gone, and the dishes that litter the table are empty on Fon's side and almost full on Kwan's. The food was strange to her, and anyway, she's too unsettled to eat and she doesn't want to ruin her lipstick. She feels like she's been turned into something new, like she just woke up in someone else's life.

She forces herself to remember what Fon just said. "Before I make money," she says, "I have to decide to work." Without thinking, she takes a rambutan from a pile of them in front of her and peels it by feel, her eyes roaming the room in which they sit, a room unlike any she has ever been in, although it seems familiar.

"You will," Fon says. She leans back in her chair and picks up her cigarettes.

The restaurant is a geometrical landscape of crisp, square white table-cloths and dark corners. At odd intervals, spotlighted on the walls, hang paintings of—Kwan supposes—Europe. They depict *farang* people in odd, old-looking clothes, and horses, dogs, and dark, hazy forests. Here and there, usually glimpsed in the bluish distance, is a house big enough to be a palace. One of the horses is white and has a horn coming out of its forehead, and dogs are leaping at it. She has seen pictures of paintings like these in school, but she never thought she'd see the real thing.

In the center of each table is a small golden lamp with a pale pink shade, and Kwan thinks the light makes Fon look younger and softer, her cute face restored to the freshness it probably had when she was sixteen. Waiters in white shirts and black slacks stand idly by; it's early still, and only a few of the tables are occupied. She and Fon have walked just a few blocks from the noise and glare of Patpong, but it could be a hundred miles. This is a different Bangkok. And then she knows why the room seems familiar: It makes her feels like she's in one of the television programs she watched in the village. She's at the edge of the life in which people have things.

"I don't know if I can do it," she says.

Fon says, "You can. You have to." She starts to light her cigarette, but a waiter is suddenly there with a lighter outstretched. Fon nods and smiles thanks as though it happens every day and says, "You're never going to make enough money to send some home until you start going with customers."

Kwan waits, her eyes on the tablecloth, until the waiter is gone. "It doesn't . . . bother you, talking about that in front of . . . I don't know, people like him?"

Fon laughs. "He knows what we do. How else could a couple of girls dressed in jeans and T-shirts afford a place like this?"

Kwan thinks, *What* you *do*, but doesn't say it. What she says is, "Why are we here? We've never gone anywhere like this."

"It's your Bangkok birthday," Fon says. "Today, for the first time, you look like you belong here."

"I'll pay you back," Kwan says. "For all of it. For Tra-La, for dinner, for everything."

"Really." Fon picks up the small crystal ashtray and hefts it, as though surprised at its weight. "With money you earn from what?"

Kwan says, "I should tell Nana I want some of what the mama-san paid her."

"She's spent it by now," Fon says. "She sold you. I wasn't sure you realized it."

"But she helped me, too. My *father* was going to sell me. And it would have been a lot worse than the bar."

Fon pours the last of the wine, hoists the glass, and eyes Kwan through it. "She wouldn't have lifted a finger if there hadn't been something in it for her. She'd have let them grab you without even thinking about it. Nana doesn't do favors."

Kwan pulls back her newly cut hair. "She's not so bad." She turns her head to display the earrings. "She gave me these."

Fon picks up the little lamp and tilts the shade so she can see more clearly. Then she puts it down again and says, "Real sapphires? Real gold?"

"Sure," Kwan says. "Why?"

Through a mouthful of smoke, Fon says, "Because they're turning your earlobes green."

15

Whether She's
Done It Yet or Not

"W e're late," Kwan says as she and Fon thread their way through the Patpong crowd. Their progress is slower than usual because they're holding hands. In the village Kwan had always envied the girls who were good enough friends to hold hands as they walked, and now, for the first time, she has someone whose hand she can hold. Even here, on this street, it's a comfortable feeling.

"We want to be late." Fon slows their pace and then stops, anchoring Kwan beside her. "Take it easy," she says. "I want to do this right."

"Do what?" But Fon's not listening. They're four or five meters up the street from the Candy Cane, and Fon's leaning forward, watching the two overage schoolgirls who control the curtain across the door. "When I say go, we go fast," she says. "Understand?"

"Sure. But why?"

"*Go,*" Fon says, almost pulling Kwan off her feet. One of the school-girls has stepped inside the bar, and the other is facing the other way. Fon drags Kwan to the curtain, throws it open dramatically, and then pushes Kwan in, standing beside her with both arms upraised, demanding attention.

The first girl in the bar to notice them is Oom, dancing as always at the pole nearest the door. She glances at Fon, and then her eyes travel to Kwan's face, and she looks puzzled, as though she's never seen her before. Then she stops dancing, and there's a spark of recognition in her eyes, and for the first time since Kwan met her, Oom smiles broadly. She takes a hand off the pole and gives Kwan a thumbs-up. Kwan feels herself smiling back and hears Fon smother a laugh.

Oom's gesture draws the eyes of the other women onstage. Some of them stop dancing, too, a couple of them gawking openmouthed. The women who are in Fon's group grin and nod their heads or repeat the thumbs-up. One of them puts two fingers into her mouth and whistles loudly. The girls in the other group look at Kwan and then through her and return to their dancing, their focus on the customers, most of whom are staring at Kwan. The plump girl pulls the corners of her mouth down sharply and turns her back, then slips her hand under her long hair, and flips it up in Kwan's direction, a gesture of dismissal. Some of the women who are sitting with men desert their customers and come running. Hands touch Kwan's hair, a mix of perfumes surrounds her, and two of the girls hug her. Everyone seems to be talking, but they fall silent simultaneously.

The women crowded in front of Kwan part to let the mama-san through. Small as she is, the mama-san is given a wide path, almost enough space to swing her arms on either side. She wears her usual uniform: a plain T-shirt and blue jeans. Her hair is, as always, pulled painfully back, and her face is makeup-free. She seems bent on making herself as drab as possible, in contrast with the primped and painted girls who surround her. She stops a few steps away from Kwan and lets her eyes slide slowly over Kwan's hair and face. Her expression does not change. Then she leans forward, and for a moment Kwan thinks the mama-san is going to sniff at her.

But what she does is say, "Take off those earrings."

Kwan removes the earrings Nana had given her, and the mama-san holds out a long, thin hand for Kwan to drop them into. When she does, the mama-san waves past her, and Kwan turns to see one of the women at the door tug aside the curtain. The mama-san pulls back her arms and throws the earrings over the heads of the clump of girls and into the street. One of the door girls starts to go after them, turns to check the mama-san, and finds herself impaled on the sharp end of a glare. She resumes her place beside the door and lets the crowd of shoppers and barhoppers crush the earrings underfoot.

Kwan feels a sudden sting on the inside of her elbow. The mama-san has snapped the sensitive skin there with her index finger, and she's curled the finger beneath her thumb to do it again, but when Kwan turns, she lowers her hand and stares up into Kwan's eyes. As tiny as she is, her gaze has an almost physical weight to it. Without moving closer or raising her voice, she says, "You."

Kwan leans forward, trying to hear her over the noise of the club. The mama-san says, "You will *not* embarrass me. Do you understand?" She lifts her chin in warning, and then she steps aside and looks back to where someone is standing at the edge of the group of dancers, a short, fat, pig-faced man in the brown uniform of a police captain. The uniform is wrinkled and dirt-mottled, the necktie pulled to one side, and the shirt patched with sweat. It balloons out over his pants, trapping rolls of fat. The mama-san raises her eyebrows inquiringly, and the captain studies Kwan's face, and then, slowly, he nods.

Fon says, very softly, "I think you're in business."

"BUT YOU WILL," the mama-san says. They're alone in the room the girls use to change in, just a space behind the stage with little square lockers set into one wall. Kwan stands with her back to the lockers, which are to the right of the door. The bar's main speakers hang on the other side of the wall, and she can feel the bass thumping against her rump and shoulders. The mama-san sits upright, spine vertical, at the edge of a blue plastic chair. A doorway with no door in it leads to the men's room, which stinks of piss. Men come in at irregular intervals, some of them staggering, use the urinals, and leave. Most of them take long looks at Kwan on their way out.

"I won't," Kwan says.

The mama-san doesn't acknowledge the remark. "Nana told me you were a virgin. Did she lie?"

Kwan feels herself blush, but there's also a bright tingle of anger. "No."

"Did you lie to her?"

"Of course not."

The mama-san hears Kwan's tone and lifts an eyebrow. "Good. He's expecting a virgin. If he doesn't get one, he'll tell me."

"Then find him one."

"I have. You."

Kwan feels the pounding of her heart above the bass line. "I'm not even dancing yet."

The mama-san nods as though she's finally gotten the argument she was expecting. "You will be. Not until he's finished with you, because he won't want to share you with anyone until he's tired of you. That's if you take care of him right, of course."

Kwan summons her one piece of ammunition. "Nana said I didn't have to go with anyone unless I—"

The mama-san says, "Sssssssss," and shakes her head sharply. "Don't talk to me about *Nana*. Is Nana your boss? Is Nana in this room?"

"No," Kwan says. She's searching for words, but they're jumbled and meaningless. They seem to flit past her eyes, disappearing before she can read them. She grabs onto four: "But she promised me." She breaks off as Oom comes in, damp with sweat, and looks at the two of them questioningly.

"Who promised who?" Oom says. "And what was the promise?"

The mama-san flicks a hand toward the bar area and says to Oom, "Sit out there. We're talking."

Oom takes a plastic chair, puts it against the wall, and stands beside it, one hand on the back. "I don't sit out there."

The mama-san's head comes forward like a snake's. "No, you don't, and don't think we haven't noticed. Nobody's buying you drinks, you're not getting taken out. No commissions, no bar fines. We're making no money off you. What good are you?"

Oom lifts her hair and fans the back of her neck. "I bring men in."

"So will she," the mama-san says, tilting her face toward Kwan. "And she won't be as picky as you are."

"I'm not picky," Oom says mildly. "I'm in love. And you just hate that, don't you? You've never loved anybody in your life. You don't even have a cat."

"*Love,*" the mama-san says. "Love is a stocking full of drink receipts. Love is money in the bank. Love is having a nice place to live, one that's all yours, that nobody can take away."

"Listen to this," Oom says to Kwan. "Wouldn't it be awful to end up like her?"

Kwan says, "She wants me to go with that fat policeman."

"This is not a three-way conversation," the mama-san says.

To Kwan's surprise, Oom says, "So? Do it. He's okay. Half the time he can't even manage it."

"But—" Kwan says. "I can't, I mean, I've never even . . . I've never been with a man."

"Ahh," Oom says. She picks up the chair and turns it around and straddles it, her arms folded over the back. "I should have known you were a virgin," she says. "You give it off like perfume. So this is about your hymen, isn't it?"

Kwan says, "I—"

"You get a lot of use out of your hymen?" Oom asks.

"What?"

"I mean, when was the last time you did anything with it? Do you take it for little walks? Talk with it at night? Buy it cute hats? Introduce it to your friends?"

The mama-san leans back in her chair for the first time. Kwan looks from her to Oom, and Oom returns the look with a faint smile.

Oom says, "No? Then you're saving it? Is anyone paying you interest?"

Kwan has to say something, so she says, "I don't think this is funny."

Oom shrugs. "It's not funny, and it's not *not* funny either. It's just how things are here, and here is where you've wound up. But your hymen. Let's face it. It's pretty much useless, isn't it? Like your appendix." She twists a finger through her hair and pulls a long lock forward to check the ends, apparently giving it all her attention. "But there's a big difference between your hymen and your appendix. Do you know what it is?"

The mama-san makes a chirping sound that might be a laugh.

Kwan says, "No."

"You have to pay someone to remove your appendix," Oom says. "But someone will pay *you* to remove your hymen." She glances over at the mama-san. "He *is* going to pay, isn't he?"

"You're joking," the mama-san says. "He's never paid for a girl in his life. We'll have to pay her."

Oom fans the hair to check for split ends. "How much?"

The mama-san says, "Three-fifty."

"Not enough," Oom says. "Should be five at least."

"Five what?" Kwan says.

"Five hundred dollars," Oom says. She lets the hair fall back into place.

"*We're* paying her," the mama-san says. "That means no commission to us. She'll wind up with the same amount of money. If he paid five, we'd take a hundred fifty."

"I know," Oom says. "It's the principle of it."

"I don't care how much it is," Kwan says, but Oom raises a hand.

"Of course you care how much it is. What do you think this is *about,* if it's not money? You're only going to be able to sell this once, and then you won't have it anymore. Losing your virginity is not a career. It's a onetime sale, and you should get every penny you can."

"I mean, I mean . . . I don't think I can—"

"Oh, grow up," Oom says. "You're here. You've left behind everything you know and everybody you know, just to come down here. As though this is the . . . the ocean, right? You've left your village and come to the ocean. And the only reason to go to the ocean, the only reason anyone goes to the ocean, is to get in the water, but you, you're afraid." She wraps her arms around herself and does a mock shudder. "It's too *cold.* It's too *rough.* You want to dip your toe in and give a little scream and pull it out again and have everyone tell you how brave you are, and then next time maybe you'll go in all the way up to your ankles and get splashed a little, and we'll all applaud and probably buy you dinner. Or we would if we really cared, which we don't. But, see, the *point* is that you've only got two choices. Go back home—" She stops and turns her head a bit to the right with her eyes on Kwan. "Is there some reason you can't go home?"

Kwan hesitates. "Yes."

"Then you're stuck at the ocean, aren't you? And the only thing to do is dive in."

Kwan says, "You're not diving in."

Oom laughs, and the mama-san joins in with that odd chirping sound. "I've been in so long my fingers are wrinkled," Oom says. "I've gone all the way to the bottom and brought back pearls. I'm so wet I'm half fish. It's just *now* I'm not doing it. Because I've told someone I won't. Because he pays me not to."

"Lots of girls are getting paid," the mama-san says. "They do their jobs."

"They're not in love. I am. And he loves *me,* and if you say one thing about that, I'll walk out of here right now, and tomorrow I'll be bringing customers into the Kit-Kat."

"All right, all right."

"This is not a stupid girl," Oom says, nodding toward Kwan. "And look at her. She's the most beautiful girl to come in here since I did. She's valuable. You don't want to lose her. You should explain the situation to her instead of pounding her over the head."

"Whose side are you on?" Kwan asks.

"You're thinking about this all wrong," Oom says. "There aren't any sides in here, despite the cliques Fon and those other idiots form. Now you're my friend, now you're not. I liked you yesterday, but I hate you today. There are really only two sides: us and the customers. It's us against the customers. They come in and sit down and pretend they're interesting and different in some way from every other man in the room, and we pretend they are, too, and we take their money. As much of it as we can get. And we should be helping each other, not competing. That's why I come back here between sets, that's why I don't sit with customers or let them buy me drinks. I want them to pick a girl. I'm not going with them, so they should choose somebody else. I just get out of the way."

"That's a new excuse," the mama-san says.

"Explain it to her." Oom stands up. "Or don't, it's up to you. But *you,*" she says to Kwan, "you have to get into the water or go home. And this could be a good deal for you." She moves to the door that leads back to the bar.

The mama-san says to Oom, "Don't tell me you're actually going out there to smile at someone, maybe sell a couple of drinks."

"No," Oom says. "I have to pee." To Kwan she says, "Just stop wringing your hands." And then she's gone.

Kwan tries again. "Nana told me I could *decide* whether to go with—"

"And you can," the mama-san says. She puts both hands out, palms up. "After this." She shifts impatiently in her chair. "Sit down," she says.

"I like it up here," Kwan says.

"All right, be a bitch, give me a stiff neck. Oom's right. I should tell you what's going on. After you help us this time, after Captain Yodsuwan, you can decide every time, yes or no, go or no go. But this time you've got to do it."

Kwan says, "I don't have to do anything."

"Listen." The mama-san lets her head drop forward and twists her neck left and right. She says, *Please* sit down. This is giving me a headache."

Kwan turns around the chair Oom vacated and sits.

"This is about the bar. If you go with Captain Yodsuwan, it will be a favor to the people who own the bar. They can be good friends to you. The captain can be an even better friend. He can look out for you. If you get into trouble, he can protect you. It's important to have someone like that in Bangkok. Every other girl in this bar would go with him in a minute. But naturally, since I have such terrible karma, he wants you."

"Why do the owners care?"

The mama-san slaps both knees and clenches her fists, which have come to rest on top of her thighs. She draws several deep breaths and wills her hands to relax. "Why do I have to explain this to an ignorant village girl?" She shakes her head to take the sting out. "Don't be offended. We're all ignorant village girls. The village is just farther away for some of us than it is for others. All right, to make it simple: There are three men who want this bar. They own a lot of bars already, and they've got power and money, and they want the Candy Cane."

"And?"

"And they can take it, unless someone with enormous face is on our side. Captain Yodsuwan isn't exactly that, but he can help for now. He can tell his men to start making trouble in the other bars. They have girls dancing naked upstairs. That's illegal. They have some girls who aren't eighteen. That's illegal. Some of them have short-time rooms in back. You know what a short-time room is?"

"I know what a short-time is."

She shakes her head wearily. "Well, having a room for them is illegal, too. He can cause enough problems that the men who are trying to take the Candy Cane will take another bar instead. But he wants money, of course, and the choice of any of our girls. And since you had to go to the beauty parlor today, he's chosen you."

Kwan slumps forward and rests her face in her hands. With her eyes closed, with the pressure of her fingers on her face, she can almost pretend that she has a choice. Then, suddenly, one presents itself. She sits up and says to the mama-san, "I can go to a different bar."

"Kwan." The mama-san uses her name for the first time. "Just do it for us. Don't force me to—"

"Well?" The gruff voice is not asking a question. It's making a demand. Kwan looks around to see Captain Yodsuwan standing in the doorway. His tiny eyes study her as though he's trying to see through her skin, and he's sweating so heavily that Kwan wouldn't be surprised to see steam rise off him.

"We're just talking about it," the mama-san says.

"What is there to talk about? She's a whore, whether she's done it yet or not."

Kwan feels the words like a slap. She knows that her face must be as white as paper.

"There's no problem," the mama-san says with a smile. The stiff spine is gone; she's leaning forward, tilting her face up to him submissively. "It's her first time, that's all. I'm just telling her a few things, trying to make sure you both have a good time."

"You're a farm girl, right?" The captain's hard little eyes skitter up and down her body. "Nothing you haven't seen before."

"She's . . . shy," the mama-san says, with an edge of desperation in her voice.

"Five minutes," the captain says. "And then you can keep her and the deal will be off." He goes back into the bar.

Kwan gets up. She says, "Never."

The mama-san says again, "Don't force me."

"Me? Force *you*?"

"I didn't want to have to say this, but you're not giving me any choice. I know who your father was selling you to. If you don't do this, if you don't go with Captain Yodsuwan tonight, I'll have two of the waiters hold you here until those people come and get you." She lets her eyes drop to the floor and then looks out through the door, at the crowded bar. "If I call, they'll be here in ten minutes."

Kwan feels like she couldn't move if someone lit her on fire. She's staring at the mama-san, but the face she sees is Nana's.

The mama-san says, "Well?"

Kwan can barely hear her own voice. "I'll go."

ON THE WAY out of the bar, fighting for breath as she edges through the crowd of customers with Captain Yodsuwan's fat, wet hand on the back of her neck, Kwan hears a long shriek, high enough to leave a scratch on the ceiling, and she sees Oom charge out of the women's bathroom. Oom vaults onto the stage and runs its full length, girls jumping out of her way at every step, until she reaches the far end of the stage, near the door, and she leaps off it, sailing over the women serving at the bar, clears the bar itself—two customers diving sideways off their stools—and lands in the arms of one of the tallest, best-looking men Kwan has ever seen. Oom throws her arms around his neck, both legs bent at the knees so he's supporting her full weight, and she kisses his neck and cheeks over and over again as he slowly turns in a circle, his eyes wide open, looking past Oom. Looking at Kwan.

16

Dog Tricks

The door is open, which is a surprise. Everyone should be asleep.

Kwan had found her way home through the bright morning, resolutely dry-eyed, without thinking about anything at all, without even feeling the rawness between her legs. She had looked at faces, at shop windows, at cars in the street, at the occasional scraggly bush clinging to life in a square of dry dirt on the sidewalk, giving her full attention to everything she saw. When she finally reached the building, after a lifetime of walking, she had hauled herself up three flights of stairs, leaning against the wall as she climbed, expecting to have to cope with the lock on the door, which sometimes sticks. She was steeling herself against the lock, knowing that if it did stick, she'd burst into tears.

But the door is standing open.

She starts to go on tiptoe and then thinks, *Why? What can anyone do to me now?* And drags herself the rest of the way down the hall and stops in the doorway and stares in, her heart swelling inside her until she feels as if it will push its way right out of her chest, and then the tears do come.

Sitting on some folded squares of cloth on the cold cement floor, her chin resting on her chest, is Fon. She's obviously waited all night and into the morning for Kwan to come home. In front of her is a cup on a saucer, the only matching cup and saucer in the apartment, and the cup has something dark in it. Steam rises from the cup, so Fon fell asleep only a few minutes ago.

Kwan's second sniffle brings Fon's head up, her eyes instantly on Kwan. Fon gets up and runs to her and wraps her arms around her, hugging her so tightly Kwan can hardly breathe. Kwan looks down at the top of Fon's head, and then she rests her chin on it and cries out loud, Fon patting her back like someone burping a baby.

THE FACE SHE makes when she takes the first sip from the steaming cup sends Fon into a seizure of laughter. The two of them have been sitting on the floor, with the folded cloths—clean towels, Kwan sees—between them. Fon falls sideways, onto one elbow, laughing and pointing at Kwan's face.

"It's awful," Kwan says, but she can't help smiling, feeling the stiffness of the skin on her cheeks, salty with dried tears. "What is it?"

"It's Nescafé," Fon says. "You mean you've never drunk coffee?"

"Why would I?" Kwan puts the cup down. "Why would anyone?"

"You drink that," Fon commands. "I worked hours to make it."

"Really?" Kwan reluctantly picks up the cup and sips it again, trying not to betray how bitter it is. She gets the first sip down and then takes a bigger one, hoping to drain the cup quickly.

"You don't know *anything*, do you? It's instant. You just boil water and put the powder in."

Kwan stares down at the cup. "Is there any way to get it out?"

"Yes. You drink it."

Kwan holds the cup out. "I'll share it with you."

"Smell it first," Fon says. "Smell it and then drink it."

Kwan sniffs the cup. "It smells better than it tastes."

"Well, then smell it every time before you drink. Get the smell in your nose first. But drink it."

"Why?"

"Because you need two things." Fon picks up the towels, and beneath them is a new, still-wrapped cake of hotel soap. "You need to get cleaner than you've ever been in your life, and then you need to talk. And that stuff"—she nods toward the Nescafé—"will help you talk."

"HE COULDN'T DO anything at first," Kwan says. She is on her back on the couch, with her knees drawn up because the sofa is too short for her, with her head resting on Fon's lap. Beneath her hair, wet from the cold-water shower down the hall, is a folded towel. She wears clean, fresh-smelling pajamas that belong to Fon, bright primary-school yellow, with happy teddy bears and birthday cakes all over them. It seems to be the teddy bears' birthday. The pants come to a premature halt just below her knees, although they reach the tops of Fon's feet.

"I could have told you that," Fon says. She lifts a strand of wet hair and lets it fall. "Your hair is so nice. He usually can't. He drinks too much."

"Oom said the same thing."

Fon's eyebrows go up. It makes her look even more like a child's toy. "Oom? Oom actually bothered to talk to you?"

"She asked why I was saving my hymen. Whether anyone was paying me interest."

Fon laughs, just a short syllable. "Our bar's little nun. Talking *you* into going to work."

"She's in love—"

"With that big guy," Fon says. "Too handsome for me. But for a while now, he's the only one she'll go with. He buys her out and we don't see her for three or four weeks, and when she comes back, she might as well have stayed away. She just hangs on to that pole all night and doesn't go with anybody."

"He pays her."

"Well, of course he does. Oom's pretty, but she has to eat, same as me."

The buzz of traffic from the street below floats into the room through the open window. Kwan can feel a warm energy coursing through her, a little kernel of electricity beneath her heart. She lifts her head and takes another swallow of the Nescafé. It's starting to taste better. "Oom's beautiful."

"Beautiful is easy. Keeping a good heart, that's hard. But you know what? In twenty years she won't be so beautiful, but you and I—you and I will still have good hearts."

"You think I have a good heart? How can you tell?"

"Kwan. You're as transparent as water." Fon kisses the tips of her fingers and then places them dead center on Kwan's forehead.

Kwan puts a hand over the place Fon touched. "I never had a friend like you before."

Fon is silent for a moment, but then she says, "Be careful. Lots of girls will act like . . . oh, well, you know. Nana." She smooths Kwan's wet hair. "Everybody in the bar wants something. They want to borrow money or they want some man who likes you or—this could happen because you're beautiful—they'll pretend to be your friend so they can drag you into threesomes."

"Threesomes?"

"Two girls and one man. Some of the girls who are ugly will do that, make friends with a beautiful girl so they can say to a man, 'You want me and my friend over there? Two ladies? No problem.'"

Kwan says, "That's awful."

"It's okay sometimes. It's less work, and it's a little safer. Most guys won't try anything with two girls in the room. And if he doesn't speak Thai, you can talk about him while you're working, as long as you don't laugh too much." She runs her palm over Kwan's slick hair again. "But," she says, "speaking of ugly."

"What?" Kwan holds up the cup, nothing inside but a thick black paste on the bottom. "Can I have some more?"

Fon takes the cup out of Kwan's hand and puts it on the three-legged table. "No. You're going to want to sleep eventually. *Ugly*. You know, Captain Yodsuwan. Talk about it. Get it all out, and then you can go to sleep."

"I slept at the hotel, a little. You're the one who stayed up."

"I'm used to it. You're a farm girl."

"That's what *he* called me," Kwan says, and suddenly the coffee seems to be rising in her throat. "Just after he called me a whore."

Fon puts her hand back on Kwan's forehead. "It doesn't mean anything. You're the same person today you were yesterday."

Kwan says, "Not exactly."

"Oh, well, if you never lose anything more valuable than that, you'll have lots of tears left over when you die. Why did he call you that?"

"I don't know. Because I am?"

"Oh, shut up. When? Where? What was happening?"

"We were in the bar. The back room. I was trying to decide whether I could do it."

"*That* was the mistake. You always have to make them think you want to do it."

"But . . . but they're giving us money to do it. Why would they have to give us money if we want—"

"Doesn't matter. They all want to believe you're thrilled to go with them. They want to feel like they just give you money because they're generous." Her hand, which is still stroking Kwan's damp hair, stops. "I shouldn't say 'all.' There are a few men who hate us. They're happy that we don't want to do anything. They like to force us. They love to make us feel like dirt."

"I did feel like dirt. Keep playing with my hair or I'll cry again."

"If you cry about that, I'll slap you."

"You would not."

"I would. Listen, baby sister, this is how it is. We're poor. We've barely been to school. We're doing the only thing we can to help our families. We may hate it, but we do it, and we don't do it for ourselves, at least not mostly. We do it for people we love. Them? They're rich. They have houses, families. They fly thousands of miles to come into the Candy Cane or the King's Castle so they can pay us money to fuck us. Who's dirt? Them or us?"

Kwan rolls over onto her side, her knees against the back of the couch, her nose inches from the warmth of Fon's belly. "I don't want to do it."

"Nobody does. Do you think this is what *I* dreamed about, back when I was a kid?"

"No." She looks up at Fon. "What did you dream about?"

"Doesn't matter. This is what I'm doing. Do you think it's made me into a bad person?"

"Oh, no." Kwan puts her hand on top of Fon's and presses down. "You're a wonderful person."

"Coffee," Fon says. "Maybe I shouldn't have given you coffee."

"I mean it. You've taken such good care of me. Nobody—" She swallows, hard. "Nobody in my family ever cared about me this much."

"Sure they did. They just didn't know how to show it. Kwan. You can do this job and still be a good person. You can do this job and still honor Buddha. You can do this job and keep your heart clean."

Kwan says, "He opened me with his finger."

"Because he couldn't—"

"He was too drunk, so he did it that way. Later he could, and he did. And it hurt. Then he drank some more and he couldn't anymore."

"Did you help him?"

"*Help* him?"

"Help him do it again."

Kwan turns her head to look up at her friend. "Why would I help him? And how?"

"Those are two different questions." Fon reaches over Kwan and picks up the coffee cup, looking down into it. "Was he angry?"

Kwan has to think about it. "I don't know. He didn't seem happy, but he didn't tell me to go away. He made me sleep there."

"Did he say anything about seeing you tonight?"

"No."

"Get up." Fon waits until Kwan's sitting at the far end of the couch, and then she takes the wet towel off her lap, folds it, and rises. "More coffee," she says. "This is serious. If Captain Yodsuwan is angry with you, you could have a very bad time in Bangkok."

AN HOUR LATER Kwan puts down the cup and says, "They're like dog tricks. I feel like the new puppy."

"Can you do them?"

"Maybe. Most of them anyway. If he's clean. He did take a shower last night. That's the only nice thing he did."

"Get in the shower with him," Fon says. "They all love that. And you can wash him yourself, every place you're going to have to touch."

"Or eat," Kwan says. "It's funny, the first night Nana took me to Patpong, and I saw all the *farang* and smelled them, I wondered if they'd let me wash them if . . . if I had to."

"The answer is yes." Fon lights another cigarette. She's begun to look tired. "It's a way of paying attention to them. They're always happy when you pay attention to them. The point is to make them happy, from the minute they buy you a drink in the bar until you leave and the hotel door closes behind you. You want to be their best memory." She rolls over onto her side, up on one elbow on the floor. "Okay. Here's a quiz."

"Like school."

"Just like school. Where do you get undressed?"

"Wherever he wants me to."

"But you put your clothes . . ."

"By the door. The side with the doorknob, not the side with the hinges. Fold them and stack them. Put the shoes on top so I can pick up the whole stack one-armed while I'm opening the door, if I have to get out of there."

"When do you put them there?"

"When he's in the shower, if I can. Then I can get in with him."

"What would make you run?"

"If there's another man in the room when we come in, or if one comes in while we're there. If he hurts me. Pinches me, slaps me, pulls my hair, even if he acts like it's a joke. If he wants to tie me up or put things on my wrists or anything, I tell him I want to go to the bathroom first, and then I grab my stuff and run."

Fon yawns smoke. "Where?"

"The fire stairs." She points at the sign Fon lettered in English on the back of a menu. "There's always a sign that says 'Stairs' or 'Fire Stairs' near the elevator. I look at it when we arrive and see what direction I have to run in."

"You remember the tricks?"

"Yes."

"One more time. Can you do them?"

Kwan looks down at her lap. "I can try."

"Good. Because you're going to have to." Fon gets onto her hands and knees and crawls into the other room. When she comes out, still on hands and knees, her cell phone is hanging from a cord around her neck. "I love waking her up," she says, dialing. She waits. "Mama-san. It's Fon. Yes, I know, sorry. Kwan's here. She wants to go with Captain Yodsuwan again tonight." She listens, holding the phone away from her ear. Kwan can hear syllables but can't string them into words. "No, not too good," Fon says. "But we've been working on it, and she wants to see him again, to make everything right. For the bar. Yes, she was a virgin. Hold on." To Kwan she says, "Did you bleed?"

Kwan says, "Yes."

"Yes," Fon says into the phone. "So he should be happy about that. Maybe you could call him and tell—" The mama-san is talking again, and Fon points her index finger straight up and makes circles in the air. "It'll be fine. Yes, she will. And then, later, if he'll let her—if he doesn't want to keep her to himself for a while—she'll dance."

Kwan says, so softly she barely hears it herself, "I'll dance."

17

A List of Won'ts

Four nights later, with a grinning Captain Yodsuwan cheering paternally at a corner table, Kwan stepped onto the stage for the first time and discovered it was helpful to be nearsighted. She couldn't see the men's faces. She could hear them, even over the music, and she could smell their sweat and their cigarettes, but they were a blur, and she could dance in front of a blur. She remained close to Fon on the stage, sharing a pole with her and keeping her distance from the women she didn't like. After a few nights, she realized the women weren't paying any attention to her; they were focused on the men. So she just danced and let her eyes roam the blurred faces, relaxing her own face whenever Fon said, "You're squinting."

On the sixth night, since Oom hadn't come back, the mama-san put Kwan on the chicken-feed pole, near the door. A few of the girls muttered about it, but most of them accepted it just as they'd accepted her presence on the stage. To her surprise, over the next few weeks her life acquired a routine, one she could never have imagined in the village but a routine nevertheless: wake up at three or four in the afternoon, shower, eat something light with Fon, try to smoke a cigarette without coughing, go to see Tra-La to listen to scandals and have her makeup applied, pick up something else to eat, and go to the bar around six.

Most of the girls did their makeup while they ate and talked, but Kwan just sat with Fon and a few of the other girls, talking, sharing food, and learning to smoke. She found she liked the bar when the regular lights were on. It was a little run-down, a little dirty, a little rubbed and scarred, with the ugly bits exposed, like a poor person's house. It became familiar. She found a table she liked to sit at, a length of leatherette couch she liked to lie down on. Women she liked to be with.

Friends. She had friends.

At seven, the women who weren't already in costume ran to the back room and dressed for the stage, and the fluorescents flickered off to be replaced by the colored lights blinking on the ceiling. The whomp and throb of the music kicked in, the mirrored balls began to revolve, the first men straggled in through the curtain, and she took the stage.

Tra-La and Fon were right. She made a lot of money. Being at the first pole helped; all night long, men would come in and stop just inside the door, gawking up at her and checking the number, 57, on the plastic badge she wore. Sometimes they called a waiter or waitress even before they sat down, pointed a finger at her, and ordered. When her set was over, she went and joined them, drinking watery colas and trying to follow their English, which even the Japanese tried to speak. She was almost always the first girl to be taken out of the bar, even if she turned down one or two men first. Fon taught her a set of hand signals that she and her friends had developed to tell each other that a man was no good, so Kwan spent more time squinting than she wanted to, since whoever was signaling was usually across the room. Several customers noticed the squinting and offered to buy her glasses. The third one to offer took her to an optics shop and got her contact lenses.

A WEEK AFTER she started dancing, she sent her mother eight thousand baht, most of which had been given to her by Captain Yodsuwan as a parting gift. She mailed it from Soi Cowboy, a smaller area of bars halfway across Bangkok, just for the sake of confusion, although she knew that her father could find her if he really wanted to. She thought the money would appease him, ease his anger, maybe make life easier for her brothers and sisters. Her little sister Mai came to mind often. From then on, Kwan sent money every week, sometimes as much as five thousand baht. On the day the bar paid her the three hundred fifty dollars for her virginity, she sent twelve thousand baht to Isaan. She kept almost nothing for herself, just enough to pay her small share of the rent and eat the cheapest street food. She walked the city when she could instead of spending money on taxis and *tuk-tuks*. Fon bought her a small spiral notebook, and Kwan used it every morning to write down the name of her customer and how much he gave her, along with something—a mole, a big nose, crooked teeth, an animal resemblance— that would help her recognize him next time.

"That's what they like most," Fon said. "When you act like all you've been doing is waiting for them to walk back in. When you remember their name."

Kwan also recorded in the notebook the amounts of money she sent home and the dates on which she sent it. When she'd sent exactly sixty thousand baht, she took a week's worth of money and spent it on herself, buying clothes and jewelry and a phone of her own, although she didn't plug in the charger or put any numbers into it, since she didn't have anyone to call. She just hung it on a cord around her neck, like Fon's, and felt rich. At the street market in Pratunam, with a pocket full of money for the first time in her life, she bought the kinds of things she'd wanted in the village: T-shirts with cartoon ducklings and bears and fawns on them; dark, stiff, unwashed blue jeans; big colored plastic bracelets and a ring with a plastic ruby in it. That afternoon she carried her bags home and hid them behind the couch, then waited to dress until Fon had left, so she could surprise her. Using the small mirror on the back of the bedroom door, she assembled the best outfit she could from the clothes and jewelry she'd bought, and went to the bar. The curtains closed behind her, and she stood there in her finery as the chatter of the girls died away. There were no admiring cries. Some of the girls who didn't like her started to laugh. Kwan backed through the curtain onto the sidewalk, but Fon and another girl came out and got her. They were trying to be sympathetic, but Fon looked down at Kwan's T-shirt and started to laugh, and then all three of them were laughing. The next day Fon and the two girls who shared their rooms took her to return the things she'd bought and then led her to the right places, to buy the right clothes. They were so expensive there was nothing left over for jewelry.

"You don't want jewelry," Fon said. "The girls will steal it, and you want the customers to think you're poor. It's good to be poor. It tells the men you haven't been working long."

"How long?"

"A month, maybe two. Say it no matter how long you've been here. Just don't tell it to someone who took you six months ago. And if you do, by mistake, tell him you went home to your village after you saw him, and you've only been back for a short time."

"A month or two," Kwan said, trying it on. "But it's—"

"You're not really lying," Fon said. "You're just telling them what they want to hear."

To her surprise, most of the men were all right. They treated her gently and tipped her well. Some of them bought her dinner, one of them at the restaurant to which Fon had taken her. Many of them took her three and four nights in a row, which eased Kwan's mind, because she knew what to expect from them. Some of them paid her much more than the other girls said they earned, and Kwan instinctively kept quiet about the occasional bonanza.

A few customers bought her clothes, which she returned for cash the day they left Bangkok, or jewelry, which she hid inside the cushions on the couch. Almost all the men told her she was beautiful, and a few of them seemed almost embarrassed by her beauty, as though they'd never been with anyone who looked like her and didn't feel worthy of her. These men made her uncomfortable, but not as uncomfortable as the ones who wanted to do things that she could hardly believe.

Fortunately, there weren't many of those. After one especially bad experience—one of the three times she had to run from the room, naked and clutching her clothes until she could leave the fire stairs two floors down and get dressed again—she and Fon worked out a list of *won'ts* to be recited aloud and agreed to before she left the bar with any new customer. Most of the things on the list were things Kwan hadn't known anyone did, ever, anywhere in the world. Just saying these things out loud embarrassed her when she first started to recite them, but once in a while a man would back away, disappointed, when she made herself clear.

With a twinge of malice, she started suggesting to those men that they take the plump girl who had bumped against her, and some of them did. Much to Kwan's surprise, the plump girl began to smile at her. Kwan did her best to smile back, although what she really felt was an unexpected surge of pity.

Still, despite the precautions, once in a while she went with someone who forced her to do what he wanted, who hurt or humiliated her and wouldn't let her get to her clothes. On those nights she left the hotel rooms feeling soiled and worthless, and that feeling lingered until Fon reminded her that it was the man, not she, who should be ashamed.

STILL, EVEN WHEN the men weren't abusive, even when they were people she enjoyed while she was talking with them or eating with them, the sex was a problem. It took her months to get over an almost paralyzing shyness when she had to reveal her body. She tried to get the customers to turn off the lights, or at least dim them, but only a few would agree. Most of them turned on everything, so the room seemed to her to dazzle with light, and she could feel their eyes like a touch, almost like a scrape against her skin.

Some of the men were impatient with her shyness, but more of them liked it. It seemed to Kwan that these men created a kind of drama out of it, a two-person play in which she was the novice, the just-arrived stranger in a new country, and they were the experts, the men with the map, who could lead her into hidden territory, show her the points of interest, introduce her to new sensations. They seemed to relish the role. When she pretended at last to enjoy herself, she could almost see them mentally patting themselves on the back. If they'd spoken their thoughts, she believed, they would have said, *She'll remember me.*

In fact, though, the individual man each of them had seemed to be when she first met him disappeared the moment the clothes came off. They became a kind of terrain to be navigated, some places more attentively than others. The person vanished, leaving a raspy chin, a sharp hangnail, an odor of butter or meat, too much hair on the body, fatness or flatness, a penis that needed more attention than a baby. The things Fon taught her, which she had thought of as tricks, became a kind of vocabulary, to be modified depending on the reactions they provoked. While she was doing them, she was focused only on the physical part of the man the trick involved.

She learned early not to call anyone by name during sex. While she was working on whoever it was tonight, he was indistinguishable from who it had been last night or who it was three weeks ago. Only later, when they were sitting up in the bed, he contented and satiated and Kwan with the covers tugged up to her armpits, counting the minutes until she could leave, would she venture the slightly risky Eddie or Jack.

She took Fon's advice and went mostly with older men, so she was safe from youthful male beauty. Occasionally a girl talked about how she taught her customers to get her off, how many orgasms she managed with this one or that one. They passed the best-trained ones around, either handing them on to a friend or suggesting a threesome. Kwan had no idea what they were talking about. When, about three months after she began to dance, a customer unexpectedly coaxed her into the first orgasm of her life, she lay bewildered until a flood of guilt washed over her. She had to fight tears. It felt like a betrayal, although of what or of whom she couldn't say. She guarded against it after that. For some reason enjoying the sex seemed worse than enduring it.

Most days, just after she woke in the early afternoon, she would roll over on the couch and reach down to the floor for the big leather purse she'd taken to carrying. She'd feel around in it until she found the notebook, and then she'd flip through the pages and pass her finger over all the names written there. Names, only names.

OVER TIME the new world grew familiar. She learned its rules and pitfalls, and she made decisions about how she would live in it. She bought nice clothes, but not many of them. She kept to the first friends she had made and only occasionally added new ones. She sent money weekly to her mother. After a month of hesitation, she wrote a letter to Teacher Suttikul that was almost true, saying she was safe and well, living in Bangkok and working in a bar where she didn't have to do anything bad. Teacher Suttikul wrote back, and after that they exchanged letters every month or so. Kwan asked her teacher to keep an eye on Mai. One month she sent Teacher Suttikul four thousand baht for pens and writing paper for the students. Teacher Suttikul wrote a letter of thanks but told Kwan to keep her money. Kwan knew that the letter meant her teacher understood where the money really came from and wanted Kwan to save as much as she could so she could quit as soon as possible.

And she did save money, even as she continued to send it home. Unlike Fon, unlike any girl she knew in the bar, she walked into a bank one day carrying a wad of cash and asked how to open an account. Twenty minutes later she had a passbook with her own name on it, making it official that she had thirty-nine hundred baht in her account. She hid the passbook beneath the couch when she wasn't using it and gave the bank account its own pages in the first little spiral notebook, and then the second and the third. Every time she noted a deposit, she would flip back over the pages listing the earlier ones. She became adept at dividing the amount in the account by the number of days she'd been depositing into it, then multiplying ahead to see how much she'd have in six months, in a year. She thought of the American hundred-dollar units as "Franklins" in honor of the bald old man whose face was on the bill. She was accumulating Franklins at an impressive pace. The bank became part of her routine, but she only went there alone. Even Fon didn't know about it.

Fon helped her economize by teaching her about makeup, showing her the things Tra-La had done to bring out her best features. As Kwan's hair grew, though, she visited Tra-La once a week to have it shaped and trimmed. The spiky look disappeared, replaced by a tapering fall of thick black hair, perfectly straight, that gleamed as though it had been oiled. Slowly, it reached her shoulders and then a few inches below.

One afternoon Tra-La lowered her scissors, stepped back, and said, "You know what you need?"

Kwan looked up from her fashion magazine. "Can I have a hint?"

"Hair to the bottom of your butt, blunt-cut straight across."

Kwan looked in the mirror and slowly turned her head and shoulders. Her hair reached about a third of the way down her back, black as a crow's wing, slightly fringed on the sides. "Do you think so?"

"Look at your height," Tra-La said. "And you've got the hair for it. Hardly any split ends, and it's got such good weight. Think of it. A river of hair flowing as you dance."

She looked again, visualizing it. Mirrors no longer bothered her. She was prettier than before, she thought, but she didn't know what all the fuss was about. "Hard to take care of."

"Oh, and you have so *much* to do," Tra-La said. "Wash it, let the air dry it, brush it a hundred times a day."

"That's what I said. Hard to take care of."

"You want to know what I think?"

"Always," Kwan said. "Any girl who doesn't want to know what you think is stupid."

"I think it could make you the queen of Patpong."

Kwan looked at Tra-La's eyes in the mirror and held them. Tra-La returned the gaze steadily.

Kwan broke the contact and picked up the small hand mirror Tra-La used. Then she swiveled the chair so her back was to the big mirror, and she looked into the hand mirror to study her back, to look at the way her hair fell. Without moving her head, she flicked her eyes to Tra-La.

"Really," Kwan said.

OOM NEVER CAME BACK.

About nine months after the night Oom had leaped from the stage into the arms of the big man, he came into the bar, obviously expecting to see her. He stopped just inside the curtained door, staring up in surprise at Kwan, dancing where Oom usually did. Looking puzzled, he shouldered his way between the customers to the back of the bar, to the room with the lockers where Oom always sat between sets. Kwan saw him again a few minutes later, talking with the mama-san, who was shaking her head. The big man's eyes darkened as the mama-san talked, and when she held up a hand, palm up, and moved it side to side, indicating the girls on the stage, he wheeled around and stalked out. The mama-san watched him go and then shrugged her shoulders.

"Well," Fon said into Kwan's ear, "I guess they didn't run away together." When Oom failed to return, the talk in the bar had been that the big man had paid her bar fine for four weeks and then they'd probably made some sort of permanent arrangement: married or almost married was the consensus. They were living in Bangkok, or in Chiang Mai, or in some small town, Nakhorn Nowhere, or maybe he'd even taken her out of the country with him. Oom was beautiful enough for something like that to have happened.

Three weeks later he came in again. This time he talked to several of the girls. Afterward they told Kwan he'd been asking them whether they'd heard anything about Oom. He said he'd been to every bar he knew of, all the way down to Pattaya, looking for her. He seemed worried, even frightened that something had happened to her.

That night Kwan left the bar around ten with a man who had taken her out three nights in a row. They turned right, heading for an Italian restaurant on Surawong. They were most of the way there when Kwan heard someone call her name. She turned, gasped, and grabbed the man's arm.

The woman behind her had two black eyes, a broken nose that was at least twice its usual width, and an upper lip swollen almost all the way up to her nostrils. When she tried to smile, she revealed a chipped front tooth. The man Kwan was with began to step between the two women, but Kwan tugged on his arm and said, "Nana?"

"Hello, Kwan." Nana put a hand up over her mouth as she talked, probably trying to mask the broken tooth. She said in Thai, "You've gotten pretty, haven't you?"

"What happened to you?"

"Nothing," Nana said. She looked up at the man Kwan was with, who was eyeing her uncertainly, as though assessing her potential risk to Kwan. "Tell your dog here that you know me. He looks like he's about to rip out my throat."

Kwan said to the man, "No problem," and paused as she tried to think of the man's name. "Steven," she said, finding it, "this is Nana."

Steven nodded, and Nana gave him a tenth-of-a-second glance.

"I need money," Nana said. "Have you got five thousand baht?"

Kwan said, "I want to know what happened."

Nana turned away in frustration, giving Kwan a quick view of a jagged cut on her right jaw. "Some man. He thought I was trying to steal from him, and he went crazy. Just hit me and hit me."

"Were you?"

Nana said, "What? What are you asking?"

"Were you stealing?"

Nana glanced up at Steven as though she were considering abandoning Kwan and asking him for the money, but Steven avoided her gaze and stared down at his feet, his face tight with distaste. "Of course not. I was looking for change. I only had thousand-baht bills, and I was looking in his wallet to see whether he had any five-hundreds so I could swap them."

"Where was he?"

"What do you care?"

"Up to you," Kwan said. She took Steven's arm. "Steven and I are going to dinner."

"He was in the shower," Nana said.

"That's what I thought. Did the bar fire you?"

Nana's damaged mouth tightened, and for a moment Kwan thought the girl was going to spit at her. But instead she said, "Until he's gone." Her voice was rigid with control, but Kwan could hear the lie. It was going to be difficult for Nana to find a bar that would take her. Nobody wanted customers coming in and making a scene about thieves.

Kwan said, "I see." She reached into the back pocket of her jeans and pulled out a fold of money. "I can give you three thousand," she said.

"Ask him for the rest." Nana's eyes were on the money.

"No, I won't. I like him. I want him to keep taking me." She peeled off two thousands and a pair of five-hundreds and held them out.

Nana made no move to take the money. "You've got a lot more."

"Yes," Kwan said. "I do."

"You wouldn't have anything if I hadn't brought you here." Her voice had risen, and Steven stepped forward.

In English he asked Kwan, "Is everything all right?"

Kwan said in slow English, "No problem. She want money." To Nana she said, "Are you going to take it or not?"

Nana snatched the bills from her hand. "Fucking Stork," she said. "Give me back my watch."

Kwan said, "Your what? Oh, that. It stopped working months ago. I threw it away and bought a good one." She held up her left wrist to show Nana the genuine Omega that someone—Robert, his name was Robert—had bought her after four days together. "Look, you can even get it wet."

Nana leaned in to her. "You think you're a queen," she said, her voice strung tight although the words were indistinct through swollen lips. "But you can end up in the street, too."

Kwan said, "I know." She put the rest of the money back into her pocket and said, "We go, Steven, okay?" and the two of them left Nana on the sidewalk. As they neared Surawong, as Kwan tried to find some satisfaction in what she had just done, she felt the pressure of eyes on her and looked over to see the big man who'd been searching for Oom. He nodded at her, but she avoided his gaze and snuggled up to . . . to Steven.

The man who was staring at her—what was his name? The girls he talked to had told her.

So many names.

Howard. His name was Howard.

18

Rose

"R ose," Howard announces. "Your name should be Rose."

They're curled up, Howard pressed against her back, on the endless bed in his hotel room, which he keeps so cold that Kwan always puts on a shirt before she goes to sleep. They're both fully clothed: This is one of the nights when Howard just buys her out and gives her, as he says, a vacation.

"Cannot say," Kwan replies. She tries to pronounce it, but it comes out "Lote." She pushes her rump against him. "Good, no good?"

"No good. Terrible. Listen: *Rose.* Hear it? Now: *Lote.* Do they sound the same to you?"

"Not when you talking."

"Okay," Howard says. "What's the name of the fat man in the red suit who comes and gives everybody presents?"

Kwan pauses for a moment, assembling the sounds in her head before saying them. She's been working on this one for weeks. "Santa . . . Claut. No, no, *no.* Clauzzzz. Santa Clauzzz."

"Good. And when does he come? And if you say 'Chritmat,' I'll make you eat raw red meat for dinner."

"Chrizzzmazzz," she says very carefully.

"See? You can do it. Rose."

Her face tense with effort, Kwan says, "Lozzze."

"Progress," he says. "We're making progress."

She wants a cigarette, but it seems like too much work to roll over and reach for her purse, and Howard's body is the warmest thing in the room. So she heaves a nicotine-deprived sigh and says, "Why Lozzze? Why not easy name?"

"Like what?"

"I don't know. I don't know *farang* name."

"Vicki," Howard suggests.

Rose says, "Wicki."

"Okay, no good. Tallulah."

Rose is laughing even before she tries it. "Tarrurrurru." She reaches back and slaps his thigh. "Not real name."

"Owww. Of course it's a real name. But Rose is better."

"Lozzze."

"The middle of your tongue," Howard says. "Not the end of your tongue. Just bring the middle of your tongue partway up. Not all the way, not so it touches, just partway. Rrrrrrrrrose."

"Rrrrrote," Kwan says. "Cannot. Why . . . that name? Why that name good?"

"Hold it," Howard says.

Kwan says, "Hold what? I no see it."

"Oh, great, now you're funny in English." He gets up, the bed creaking as his weight leaves it, and goes to the coffee table. The room they're in is the one he always brings her to, an enormous, overfurnished space with a king-size bed, two televisions—one on each side of the carved wooden partition that almost divides the room in two—a work desk, and a couch and coffee table. There's a refrigerator full of little drinks at prices that horrified Kwan when Howard read them to her. The room's longest wall is covered with floor-to-ceiling curtains that can be pulled back to reveal Bangkok sparkling all the way to the edge of the earth. The room is much bigger than the two rooms Kwan shares with Fon and her friends.

She's been keeping some of her clothes in the closet for weeks.

Howard leans down and grabs a magazine from the coffee table, its cover shiny and vibrant with color. Rose has leafed through it several times, checking the pictures and puzzling out some of the simpler English words. It's a magazine for *farang* tourists that pretends to tell them something about Thailand as an excuse to print advertisements for jewelry stores where the stones are artificially colored and Indian tailors whose clothes, Kwan has been told, never fit. He leafs through it. "Here," he says. "In Chiang Mai." He folds the magazine back and carries it over to her.

"Oh," she says, looking at the picture. *"Dawk goolap."*

"In English, rose," Howard says. "Rose. It's the queen of flowers. That's what *farang* people say. And you're the queen of—"

"Of what?"

Howard leans down and kisses her on the lips, very lightly. "Of everything."

"Pahk waan," she says. "Sweet mouth."

"You're Rose to me. You can be anyone you want when I'm not around, but for me you're Rose."

Kwan says, "Rrrrozzzzze." She looks up at him, and he grins and nods. "Okay. In the bar, everywhere. I Rrrrrozzze."

Howard says, "What would you like to eat, Rose? You can have anything in Bangkok."

Rose says, "We in Bangkok, *na*? We eat Thai food, okay? *Phet maak maak."* Very spicy, which Howard hates.

Howard goes to the closet to get a clean shirt. He changes his clothes all the time. He says, "What a surprise."

She tries, not very hard, to reach her purse and comes up short. "Can I have coat?"

"It's not cold."

"Have cigarette in coat."

"Make a deal. You can smoke a cigarette if I can eat American."

"No problem. You eat American, I eat Thai."

"You win." He takes the jacket off the hanger and says, "Why so heavy?"

"Oh," Rose says, remembering. "Nothing. You just bring, okay?"

But he already has his hand in the pocket. "What in the world is this?" He holds up a smooth, dark stone.

She looks at it in his hand, remembers picking it up that morning. She says, "For luck."

"Fine," Howard says. "I suppose it's lighter than a horseshoe." He starts to put the stone back in the pocket.

"Throw away," Rose says.

He stands there, jacket in one hand and stone in the other. "Are you sure?"

"Yes." She gets off the bed and goes to him, takes the stone, and drops it with a *thunk* into the wastebasket. "Now I Rrrozzze. I no need luck."

THE RAIN PELTS down outside, and the fluorescents are flickering, suggesting a power failure in the near future. Thai music stutters through the speaker system. Every few minutes a sopping *farang* opens the curtains over the doorway, peers in, sees the women smoking and putting on makeup, and backs out again. "I'm just saying it, that's all. Oom ran away from him. Maybe she knew something you don't."

Fon helps herself to some dried squid, a heap of which is creating a spreading grease spot on a fold of paper towels. All over the club, girls look into mirrors as they apply makeup or sit still with their eyes closed as their friends do it for them.

"You don't know what happened with Oom," Rose says. Unlike the others she is neither made up nor making up. She won't be working tonight, because Howard has paid the bar fine for weeks to come. She just stopped by to talk with Fon.

Fon nips off a length of squid and says, "And neither do you."

"They had a fight, just before he left the country. He didn't think it was important, but when he came back, Oom wasn't anywhere he could find her."

"A fight about what?"

"About nothing. Howard wanted to take her to Singapore, and Oom didn't want to go."

Fon regards the squid skeptically. "Why wouldn't she want to go?"

"How would I know? He'd helped her get a passport. He said she never argued about getting the passport, just about using it."

"Right. She didn't want to go to Singapore."

"You saw him. You saw how upset he was."

"I saw how fast he took you out, too."

Rose surprises herself by bringing a flat hand down on the tabletop with a *crack* that snaps every head in the bar toward her. Fon jerks back a few inches, blinking. "We didn't do anything," Rose says. "Not for months. He just wanted to talk. He bought me out and took me to dinner and talked, and then he gave me money and I went home. *You* should know, I was always home before you got there. It was eight or nine months before we even kissed each other. We just talked."

"Talked about what? About Oom?" This is the first time Fon has ever gotten angry at Rose. "What is there to say about Oom for all those months? 'Oh, no, she's gone. I looked everywhere. I miss her. I don't know why she left.' How long did that take? Five seconds? And she was pretty, Oom was, but nobody would call her interesting. So what was there to talk about all that time?"

"What's wrong with you?"

"I don't like it, that's all." Fon snatches another piece of squid as though she expects the paper towel to be yanked away at any moment. "How do we know what happened to her? She's here one night and then she's gone forever."

"They fought," Rose says patiently. "She didn't want to see him. So she didn't come back to the bar. She went someplace where he wouldn't find her."

"He loves Oom so much and then, bang, he loves you."

Rose looks away and sees rainwater seeping in beneath the curtained doorway. Drunk men will slip and fall later. She draws a slow, long breath. "One more time. Oom left him. What's he supposed to do, cry for the rest of his life?"

"There's something wrong with men who fall in love with prostitutes," Fon says. "They're missing something."

Rose feels a worm of unease in her gut, but she says, "Maybe he doesn't think of me just as a prostitute. Maybe he thinks of me as a *person*."

Fon starts to say something but shakes her head. "Up to you. Just be careful, that's all. I don't want to have to nurse you through a broken heart."

"Howard can't break my heart."

Fon studies the squid as she shreds it between her fingers. "You even let him change your name."

"Rose is better. *Farang* men can remember Rose. Nobody remembered Kwan."

"So what?" Fon says. "They just came in and asked, 'Where's the tall girl?' That worked, didn't it? We always knew who they meant."

"Not the same." Rose rummages through her purse and pulls out a pack of cigarettes. "Anyway, what do you care?"

"What do *I* care?" Fon places her greasy fingertips, widely spread, in the center of her chest. "We're supposed to be friends."

"We are," Rose says, reaching over and taking Fon's wrist, tugging the hand off her chest and stroking her own cheek with it, leaning against it and smelling the squid. "You're the best friend I ever had."

"That's not fair," Fon says, pulling her hand away.

"What's not fair?" Rose lights her cigarette.

"Going all sweet like that. I'm serious. I don't want you getting hurt. What do you really know about him?"

"I know a lot about him."

"Where he's from," Fon says, "if it's true. What he does for a living, if it's true. What he wants with you, if it's true. You don't know whether anything is true."

"I know a lot more about Howard than I do about the strangers I go with every night."

"You think."

"Fon." Rose closes her eyes and leans on her friend's shoulder. "I don't want to go with different men all the time. I hate it. I don't want to have customers staring at me while I'm dancing, wondering what I'll let them do to me in bed, or how much hair I have down there, or whether I'm wearing a padded bra. I don't want to smile at men I hoped I'd never see again. I don't want to watch men flipping coins to see who gets me. I don't want to lie to everybody about working here a month or two when it's been almost two years. I want to tell the truth to somebody, and I want to tell the truth all the time. And I don't want to remember any more *names*."

Fon plucks the forgotten cigarette from Rose's hand and knocks the ash onto the floor, then takes a deep drag. "So," she says. "What does he want with you?"

Rose says, "He wants to marry me."

Fon puts a forearm on the table and rests her forehead on it.

Rose lays a hand on Fon's hair. "It'll be fine. He'll take care of me. I won't have to work like this."

Without lifting her head, Fon says, "What about the dowry?"

"He understands about the dowry. He's going to—"

"Why?" Fon demands. "Why does he understand about the dowry? *Farang* don't know about dowries."

On the other side of the curtain, the sound of the rain doubles. "I explained it to him."

"He didn't learn about it by promising to marry any other—"

"Stop." Rose listens to the rain hammering down, wishing it were so loud that she and Fon couldn't hear each other. "We talked about it. He's going to give my parents more money than they ever thought they'd get." She caresses Fon's hair. "Fon. He's going to take care of Mai. Of my sister. He says he'll frighten my father so much that my father won't even think about doing anything bad."

"He'll even take care of your sister," Fon says as the lights go out, plunging the bar into blackness, and the music stops dead. Fon says, "He's thought of everything."

WHEN SHE ASKS herself later whether she should have known that something was wrong, she remembers a hundred things. Inconsistencies in some of the things he told her. The friends, big, fit men very much like himself, but taciturn and reserved, whom she instinctively disliked. The occasional flashes of anger over things most Thais would have laughed off.

One evening in the hotel room, she had drawn a house, just an ordinary village house. It was a daydream in pencil. Like half the girls she knew, she was hoping that she could build a new house for her parents and her brothers and sisters someday, but her imagination went no further than the kind of house she'd grown up in.

She'd been sitting at the desk, hunched over a piece of hotel stationery. Her lap was full of bits of pink eraser, from the messy, rubbed-looking spot in the house wall where she'd placed a second window, which she thought was a daring innovation. Still, the house would have fit into any Isaan village without attracting a glance: a single room raised a meter above the ground, a door in the center of one wall, a few steps leading up.

She had run out of ideas, so she'd put a sun in the corner of the sky and was drawing a dog under the house when she felt him behind her.

"For your mom and dad?" Howard asked over her shoulder.

"Maybe," she said, suddenly shy. She covered the sketch with her hand, but he slid the hand aside.

"Scoot," he said. "It's a big chair."

Rose shifted sideways, and Howard perched himself on the edge of the seat. He took the pencil from her hand, moving so fast she barely saw it, and began to make bold, heavy strokes, ruler-straight. She watched as the house got bigger, saw a second room appear, and then Howard sketched a big central window, four times the size of the one she'd drawn and all one big pane, like the windows in the hotel. Finally he tilted his head, studied the page for a moment, and added a modern roof, raised in the center, instead of the flat pitch of corrugated iron she'd visualized.

It was a real house.

"Room," she half whispered. "Mai can have a room."

"Here," Howard said, and he scrubbed at the paper with the eraser for a moment and blew on it, and in the blank space a third room appeared, with its own little door and window. He obliterated some of the deck on the left and redrew it, bigger, to accommodate the addition. "She gets her own door," he said, pointing the pencil tip at it.

"Lek, too," Rose said, looking at the door as though she wanted to go through it.

"Who's Lek?"

"Other sister," Rose said. She let her index finger hop up the stairs.

"Yeah?" Howard said without looking at her. "How old?"

"Only eight. No worry yet."

"Sure," Howard said. He drew a little stick figure in a skirt on the stairs and then rubbed the eraser on her index finger until she moved it. "She can stay here, too."

She stared at the page and at the strong hand resting at its edge. The desk light was on, and it made a reddish gold fringe out of the hairs on the back of his fingers.

Howard said, "We can do this."

Rose reluctantly stopped looking at the house and met his eyes. "Can . . . ?"

"Build this. We can build this for your family."

"I save money," Rose says. "Have. In bank." She passes a finger over Mai's room. "But this—maybe not enough."

"I can pay for it. I *will* pay for it."

She said, "Oh, no. No, no, no."

"They're going to be my family, too."

Rose leaned forward and rests her head on the pad. She closes her eyes.

Howard said, "Are you okay?"

"Yes," she said. "Just happy. Want to stay like this."

He put his hand on the back of her neck and rubbed, and she lifted her head and saw his other hand, still holding the pencil, only inches from her face. "You hand," she said. "You hand have hair too much."

"Because I'm a guy," Howard said. "More guy than a roomful of cops."

"Hair too much," she said, and she picked up his hand, closed her teeth on a few of the hairs growing on the back of his ring finger, and yanked them out.

"*Shit!*" Howard said, and he shoved her away, so hard she slid off the chair and hit the floor. "God*damn.*"

She looked up at him, amazed, and found him shaking his hand in the air, and she thought it looked funny, until she saw his eyes. When she saw his eyes, she backed away, two or three feet across the floor, without even getting up.

He looked down at her and through her, and it seemed to take a few seconds for him to bring his eyes out of the hole he had stared in her so he could focus on her face. When he did, he grinned. "That hurt," he said. "Did I push you off?"

She nodded, still watching his face.

"Well, you had it coming." He looked down at his hand and then blew on his fingers. She had taught him how to blow on what hurt, to make it feel better. "There," he said. He shook the hand as though it were wet. "All fine now." He extended the other hand. "Come back up here. I'm sorry. And look, I have a new idea for the house."

She stayed where she was, so he sat and began to draw. After a moment she got onto the chair again, leaving an inch or two between them, and watched the pencil as he sketched a litter of puppies gathered around the dog she'd drawn.

"That one's Donder and that one's Blitzen," he said, indicating two of the four. He wrote the names above them. "You name the other two."

She took the pencil, still feeling the agitation in the air. Trying to find her way back to the feeling of a moment ago, she said, "This one name Dog."

"Write it," Howard said.

She wrote "D-O-G" slowly above the puppy.

"And that one?"

"This one name Howard," she said. "Because he bite."

Howard took the pencil and drew exaggerated fangs on the puppy named Howard. Then he took a new piece of paper and covered it with squares and filled the squares with a comic about a dog named Howard, the meanest dog in the world, a dog who was so mean he bit rocks, and ten minutes later they were both laughing.

But that night, dropping off to sleep, she saw again the look in his eyes.

THEN THERE WAS the drinking.

Howard didn't drink often, but when he did, he became someone else, someone sullen and quick to take offense. Twice they left a restaurant without paying because Howard, who had been drinking, said the food was bad and the dishes were dirty, although they'd seemed clean enough to Rose. She'd blushed furiously as he berated the waiter and pushed back his chair, and everyone in the restaurant stared at the two of them. The walk to the door seemed to take hours.

And then, the next morning, he apologized and told her he wouldn't do it again. Weeks passed before he did.

Other than the one time, he never aimed his fury at her. It was always something else—a taxi driver, or someone who bumped Rose on the street, or, one time, a shirt that had come back from the hotel laundry with a button missing. Howard had put it on and buttoned it most of the way up when he came to the empty space, and all of a sudden he was swearing and yelling, and he grabbed the shirt at the bottom and tore it open, sending buttons bouncing across the carpet.

"Goddamned fucking people!" he shouted. "Can't do fucking anything right!"

Rose said, "Which people?"

He'd whipped his head around as though just realizing he wasn't alone in the room. "The . . . the laundry," he said in his normal voice. He swallowed and steadied his breathing. "They've ruined half my clothes."

"That shirt," Rose said. "You ruin."

"Yeah," he said, looking down at it. "I did, didn't I?" He grins at her. "I'm a jerk."

After a moment she returned his smile.

So yes, there were signs, but she chose not to look at them. To be with one man, not to work, not to have to lie all the time, to know that her family was taken care of and her sister was safe. She wanted all those things. She wanted them too much.

19

The Rocks

Men have taken her to Pattaya before, and she hated it: the bars, the noise, the streetwalkers, the dirty water. But she's never been to Phuket. All the girls have told her it's much better than Pattaya, that the beaches are clean and the water is clear and the hotels are palaces. At any other time, she'd be excited about it, but she can't be, because she's focused completely on the second half of their trip. After five days in Phuket, Howard has promised her they'll go to the village and he'll tell her parents they're getting married and pay them the dowry.

She hasn't been back to the village since she ran away. And now, to return with a rich, handsome, good-hearted *farang,* a man who can take care of them all, is almost too much for Rose to believe. Her parents will have their new house. Howard has drawn and redrawn it, making it bigger and more solid every time. Airier.

Her brothers and sisters will grow up differently than she did. They'll have space and light and money for nice clothes. They'll have futures. And she'll be finished with Patpong.

In her mind she's already in the back of the orange taxi with Howard, slowing at the end of the village street, with the kids assembling to parade them in. She barely registers the flight south to Phuket, even though it's the first time she's ever been in an airplane. Her lack of interest tightens Howard's eyes and turns his gaze past her, out the window. She feels the change in his mood and puts her hand on his and says, "Thank you."

He says, sounding like a kid whose surprise fell flat, "It's like you fly all the time."

"Have happy too much already," she says. "Not have room for more."

He smiles at her, and the tension in his shoulders eases. He leans over and kisses her cheek. "We'll see about that."

ON THE MORNING of the fourth day, with only two more days before they leave for Isaan, he takes her to the dock, for the trip he's been talking about ever since they arrived.

He's seemed nervous the past two days. He's had trouble sleeping, and wherever they're going, whatever they're doing, he's always ready before she is, sitting on the couch, eager to move, while she scurries around getting whatever she needs. He doesn't criticize her, but his impatience is obvious: a tapping foot, an occasional needless trip to the door, just standing beside it so he'll be ready to open it the moment she's ready to go.

She feels as though he's trying to hurry time along. When she asks him about it, he tells her he's just eager to get up to Isaan, eager to meet her parents and arrange the marriage. They'll be married in the village, he says, and he'll throw a two-day feast for everyone. It seems like a dream, but still, the whole time they're in Phuket, she feels like she's running to keep up with him.

On the rickety dock, they stand side by side, his arm around her shoulders. One of the things she loves about him, she decides, is that he makes her feel short. She wraps her arm around his back and is surprised to find she can feel his heart. It's beating much more quickly than hers.

The boat rides high in the water, battered wood painted white a long time ago, with a faded, abstract brown eye on the front of the side Rose can see. About seven feet back from the prow are a big wheel and some controls, set behind a curve of plastic windscreen that has absorbed so much salt it's almost opaque. The engine is tilted up at the rear, its big propeller hanging almost a meter above the water, nicked and scarred.

An afternoon breeze, chillier than usual, blows in off the water.

"Little," Rose says, eyeing the boat.

"There are only two of us," Howard says. "Just you and me." He throws a suitcase onto the boat and turns to get the four big two-gallon bottles of water.

"This"—she levels a finger at the gray-blue horizon of the Andaman Sea, the water dark today beneath gray clouds—"this very big."

"Ahhhh," Howard says. "The Andaman is a swimming pool. Anyway, you're with me, and I can handle this thing."

"Not hard? Not hard to . . . to handle?" The new word comes out fine, but Howard doesn't acknowledge it.

He does arm curls with the water containers. "Easy as buttoning a shirt."

"Sometime you not so good with shirt."

Howard laughs. "Light a cigarette. It'll relax you. Oh, wait. I almost forgot." And before she can even react, he drops the water bottles to the deck, making it shake underfoot, slides his big hands under her arms, and lifts her straight up like she weighs nothing. She laughs and beats at his chest as though he's a monster, but he carries her across the pier, leans forward, and puts her down in the boat, which rocks enough beneath her weight to make her grab the side. "Trip wouldn't have been any fun without you," he says, watching her hang on. "You'll have your sea legs in no time." He turns back to the water containers.

"See legs?" she asks, raising one of hers.

"Not like 'see,' not like looking at legs." He's been pointing at his eyes to illustrate, and now he picks up a huge bottle of water in each hand and waves her away so he can lower them into the boat. "The sea," he says, nodding at the Andaman as he puts the water aboard. "That's the sea. You know, it goes"—he puts his hands in front of him palms down and makes wave motions—"like that. It can make you sick at first. When you get used to it, we say in English you've got your sea legs."

She sits on the wooden bench that runs around the passenger compartment and opens her purse. A cigarette sounds good right now. "Sea legs. You have sea legs?" She's taken to repeating every new term she hears so she can file it in memory, hoping to improve her English more quickly. In her imagination she sees herself in two or three years going to *farang* parties as Howard's wife, speaking perfect English.

"I don't need them," Howard says. "I'm a fish." Rose suddenly remembers Oom describing herself as "half fish" the night Rose—Kwan then—went with Captain Yodsuwan. It seems like years ago. Howard puts the other two water bottles aboard and bends to the dock to pick up the black rubber wet suit that looks to Rose like an empty person.

"Not cold," she says. She finds the pack of Marlboro Lights and shakes one out. "Water okay." She swam the day before for hours, forgetting for once about not getting dark from the sun, no longer worried about what the customers and the other girls would think. The water was much warmer than the shower back at the apartment. "Why only one?"

"You won't need one," Howard says, climbing aboard with the suit tossed over his shoulder. "And it's not for cold. It's for something else. I'll show you when I see one." He rolls the suit up and stuffs it beneath one of the benches, then straightens and shades his eyes, although the day's not bright, and squints up at the sky, dark gray in places but with one or two small, tattered patches of blue. "We left the rain in Bangkok."

"Maybe later," Rose says, watching him as she takes the first puff. He's right; the smoke makes her feel smoother. Howard, on the other hand, seems even more energetic than he has the past couple of days, as though his blood is carbonated, bubbling in his veins. There's something bristling, something sparky about him that reminds her of the first day she drank Nescafé. That buried kernel of energy. If she could see through Howard right now, she wouldn't be surprised to find a flame at his center.

In all the months she's known him, she's never seen him do a muscleman exercise like the one he just did with the water bottles. His body tells her he exercises often, but it's something he does privately, and although they've been together for three and four weeks at a stretch, she has no idea when.

Howard steps up onto the edge of the boat and makes the leap to the dock. The boat's stern swings outward behind him, but the prow stays put, anchored by a thick rope that's been passed over one of the vertical timbers that supports the dock. He pulls the loop of rope off the timber, tucks it under his arm, and jumps back onto the boat, which rocks alarmingly. He holds the rope out to Rose.

"Coil this," he says.

She says, "What?" This "coil" is not a word she knows.

"Circles," Howard says with an edge of impatience. "Just—" He makes a circular motion with his index finger, pointing down. "The rope," he says. He makes the gesture again, giving her the wide eyes she sometimes gets when she's too slow for him.

"Fine," Rose says, getting up tentatively. The boat is still rocking, and she has to put out a hand to steady herself. "Coil." She goes to the place where the rope has been knotted inside the boat and begins to feed the loose rope onto the deck in a circle. "Coil," she says again experimentally.

At the wheel, Howard mutters something and takes a long drink off a smaller bottle of water.

Rose says, "What?"

Without looking back, Howard says, "I said, Jesus Christ."

"Oh." She finishes making rope circles and drops the end, then nudges the rope with the toe of her flip-flop to make it rounder. "Why Jesus Christ?"

Howard screws the cap onto his water bottle, but he doesn't look at her. "Something I always say when I go out to sea," he answers without turning. She has to cup a hand to her ear to hear him. "Like a prayer." He turns a key beside the wheel and pushes a button, and the engine growls to life with a racketing sound, spewing gray smoke. "Sit down," Howard says, almost pushing past her. He goes to the back of the boat and releases a little catch that lets the engine drop into the water. The noise is cut in half, and the dock begins to slide by beside them. He returns to the wheel, and the boat points itself away from the dock. She grips the edge of the bench in both hands and turns back, seeing the widening V of their wake, churned greenish white in the center behind the propeller, seeing the island fall away behind them. It seems to get smaller very quickly.

"THAT WAY IS India," Howard says, pointing west. He's at the wheel, and he zigzags right and left. The boat's sudden wobble makes Rose dizzy. "The old Thai boats had the engine at the end of a pipe," he says. "The long-tail boats were steered by pushing the pipe right or left."

"I see before."

He gives her a lengthy look before he replies. "Am I boring you?"

"No. Just . . . cold." She glances at the sky, which has turned darker, partly because the clouds have thickened and partly because the day is beginning to dim. The island is far behind them now, although she can still see it rising, pale and irregular, on the horizon.

"So get a jacket. That's why we brought the suitcase, remember?" He passes a loop over the wheel. "Do you see this?"

She gets up, feeling the wind hit her, and finds the handle of the suitcase. "Yes," she says. "See."

"You're not looking. This holds us on a straight course."

Rose says, "Yes."

"Born to be on the water," he says. "The wheel makes the keel under the boat go side to side." He demonstrates by holding his right arm straight out, pointed toward the engine, dead center in the water. "When you turn the wheel to the right, the keel goes this way"—he shifts his arm—"and the boat goes right. Turn it the other way, et cetera."

Rose says, "Et cetera." She shivers. "Cold."

Howard shakes his head. "So open the suitcase. Oh, never mind." He picks up his water bottle, unscrews the cap, and drinks. Then he pulls the suitcase away from her, puts it on the bench, and rips the zipper open. He paws through a couple of layers until he comes up with the bright pink windbreaker Rose had bought the day before. "Put it on."

"Why you angry today?"

"All I want," Howard says slowly, "is for us to have a good time. I don't want to have to say everything ten times, I don't want you shivering with cold when it's eighty fucking degrees, and I don't want you arguing with me all the time."

Rose's stomach muscles tighten the way they would if she were afraid of being punched there. "Not argue."

"Good. You steer."

"Okay," she says, holding up both hands. "I steer."

She shoves her arms through the windbreaker's sleeves and goes to the wheel. When she has both hands on it, Howard says, "Turn starboard."

"Star—"

"Right, right, for Christ's sake." He clamps his hands over hers and twists the wheel, and the boat lurches severely enough that Rose has to sidestep to remain standing. *"Starboard,"* he says, pointing right. "Port." He points left. "Now turn to port."

"Port," Rose says, easing the wheel around. "Port, okay?"

"You know," he says, "I don't have to show you anything. I could just skip the whole fucking thing. Or do you want to learn something?"

"Want."

"Bow," he says, pointing to the front of the boat. He points back, toward the motor. "Stern."

"Bow," Rose repeats with a clamping around her heart that she almost doesn't recognize as fear. "Stern."

"COME HERE," HOWARD says. He's at the wheel. They are traveling in a straight line, at an angle to the island, now a hazy break on the far surface of the sea. While they were headed directly away from Phuket, they had taken the swells head-on, but now the swells are hitting the boat from the side, and the two movements—the boat churning forward, the relentless rocking from side to side—are making Rose uneasy. She can feel her lunch, a hard, heavy ball in her stomach. It's a little like the first three or four times she'd smoked a cigarette and the room had begun to spin.

Howard locks the wheel and moves to the other side of the boat. He makes a curt "hurry up" gesture with his hand, leaning over to look down at the water. Rose gets up unsteadily, feet spread wide, and waits for the boat to do its sideways rock, then hurries across and grabs hold before the next swell rises up beneath them. She knows she doesn't want to look down at the water. She has an instinctive feeling that watching it stream by will be the final ingredient in a mix of motion that's likely to bring her lunch back up into the light of day.

"Down there," Howard says, pointing. "See them?"

She looks down and then, immediately, up again. "I can't," she says.

"What do you mean, you can't?" The words sound barbed to her.

"I get sick."

"No you won't. Just look for a minute, and then I'll give you something to make you feel better."

"What?"

"A pill. I should have given it to you before we left. You're getting seasick, is all. The pill will fix it."

"Seasick," Rose says.

"This isn't a language lesson," Howard says, "and those fucking things aren't going to be out there forever. Look." He points toward the water at about a forty-five-degree angle, and Rose searches the dark surface.

She sees nothing but the Andaman. The day is on the way out now, the clouds an angrier, deeper gray that verges on black, and the surface of the water is powder gray and oily-looking. And then she sees rounded shapes, as though the water has thickened into spheres that are barely floating, only the very tops exposed to the air.

She rips her eyes away from the water and looks up at Howard, to find him studying her intently. "Like this?" she says, and she makes a little curved motion with her hand, as though running it over the top of a ball.

"Right," Howard says. "You can only see the top, but what you need to worry about is what's underneath. They're jellyfish."

"I know jellyfish," Rose says. "I eat. You have pill?"

"In a *minute.* These jellyfish are different. They're sea wasps. The tentacles are a couple of feet long—"

Rose says, "Tenta . . ."

"Tentacles," Howard says between his teeth. "You know." He holds up his hand, curved, with the fingers pointing down, and wiggles the fingers. *"Tentacles."*

"Okay, okay," Rose says. "Why you yell at me?"

"Can't even have a fucking conversation."

"I speaking English," Rose says, suddenly angry herself. "You no speaking Thai."

"Why the fuck would I speak Thai? English is the world's language. Nobody speaks Thai."

"I speak Thai." She's furious enough to forget she's feeling sick. "Maybe we go home."

"When I say we go home, we go home. The *sea wasps,*" he repeats with a bad imitation of patience. "When you brush the tentacles, they break off and stick to you, okay? They're poisonous. You know poisonous?"

Rose says, "Not stupid."

"No point in taking a vote about that, since there are only two of us. The sea wasps. You get stung once, you're going to get sick. Two or three times, you're dead."

Rose says, "Pill."

"They'll kill you."

"So I not go in water. They cannot jump in boat, *na*? Give me pill. Now."

Howard says, "In a minute."

"I do on you." Rose sticks a finger down her throat to make it clear, and Howard jumps back. He's swearing, she can tell that, but she doesn't know the words. He goes to the suitcase, opens the zippered compartment on the outside, and pulls out a small, foil-backed blister card with pills in it. He pushes two of the pills through the foil and hands them to Rose, and Rose grabs his water bottle to wash them down.

"No," Howard says, but it's too late. Rose takes a gulp, and then her eyes grow enormous, and she spits all of it, pills included, over the side. Then she leans over and is shudderingly sick, losing everything she ate into the Andaman. When she's finished, she wipes her chin and rounds on Howard, her fists clenched.

"You crazy? Drink vodka?"

Howard snatches the bottle from her hand, plants a hand in the center of her chest, and pushes. Rose stumbles backward until the backs of her knees hit the bench, and then her legs collapse and she falls on her rump.

"Sit the fuck down and stay there," Howard says. He points a finger at her, his eyes tiny with fury. "And *shut up.*"

It begins to rain.

THE SEARCHLIGHT on the front of the boat is like a finger pointing forward, making a long silver streak through the rain. They haven't spoken in more than an hour, and it's almost completely dark now, the sea barely darker than the sky, except for the trail of luminescence that's churned into a cold green glow in the boat's wake.

They're both soaked. Rose is huddled in a ball, shivering, her jacket and T-shirt a cold weight on her back and shoulders. Howard seems not to have noticed the rain.

He has drained the first bottle and is a third of the way through a second.

"Slow it down," he says aloud, and pulls back on the throttle, a handle positioned to the right of the wheel. Rose has been watching him whenever he's been turned away from her. Pushing the throttle down slows the boat. Pulling up makes it go faster. Throttle, wheel. Engine on the end of the pipe. Switch for the searchlight.

Off to the right—*starboard*, Rose thinks irrelevantly—is what looks like a small floating palace of brilliant white light. And behind it, or at least smaller, so probably more distant, is another. She has no way of knowing how far away they are, but they look like angels of safety out there in the dark, luminous points of refuge.

"Squid fishermen," Howard says, following her gaze. "Lanterns hung out all over the boat. Squid come to light like whores come to money." His tone is conversational, reasonable. He might be talking about the wedding. With his eyes on the distant lights, he takes another drink and looks at the glowing green navigational screen set into the wooden panel beside the wheel. Then he looks left and scans the dark surface of the sea. "Ought to be there," he says. "Don't want to find them before we see them."

He puts the water bottle down and leaps up onto the boat's side. Then, moving sideways, he edges around the plastic windscreen until he's next to the searchlight. At precisely the moment Rose gets her feet under her, her eyes on the throttle, Howard says, "Give me any kind of trouble at all, *any* kind, and I'll break your neck. Understand?"

Rose nods.

"Say it."

"Understand."

"She's learning," Howard says, as though there were a third person present. "She's actually learning." He sits on the deck beside the light, which is sending up ropes of steam where the rain hits the hot metal housing, and grabs the frame that surrounds it. He twists the light left and sweeps it back and forth. He says, "Damn, I'm good." Then he wiggles the light back and forth and says, "Take a look, sweetie."

Rose lets her eyes follow the beam through the darkness and the slanting rainfall until it bounces off something pale, not colorless but not a color that carries across distance, especially under these conditions. Tan, she thinks. Light brown. It's low and rounded, rising gradually out of the water, no more than a foot above it, and it's long, maybe eighty or a hundred paces in length. Smooth and featureless, as though it's been sanded down for thousands of years.

"That's the big one!" Howard shouts into the rain. "Over here is its little sister." He shifts the light to the right to reveal another stone, about half as long, and even lower, than the first, its sloping sides just peeking above the water.

"There's another one back behind the bigger one, but you can't see it. The Three Sisters. Also called the Bitches because they've ripped the bottom out of so many boats." He turns the light so it's facing front again and then scoots crablike back toward the cabin area. "At high tide," he says, "about six hours from now, they'll be underwater. Fucking everything's hit them for centuries and centuries. Chinese junks, Javanese pirate ships, the occasional fancy yacht. Great dive site, stuff all over the bottom."

He's back in the cabin, facing her. She hasn't moved from the bench. He looks down at her and then shakes his head. "You finally figured it out, didn't you?"

She responds, but her voice is almost a whisper. "Figured . . ." She closes her eyes, hearing Fon's voice: *Clothes folded by the door, shoes on top, just scoop it all up as you go.* She says, more loudly than she'd intended, "Oom."

"You're not as dumb as you seem," Howard says.

Rose says, "Why?"

"Because I can. Because God in his infinite wisdom has humored my little quirk by providing me with an endless supply of brainless whores to play with and cops who don't give a shit." He points a finger at her, eyebrows high, meaning, *Don't move,* and goes back to the wheel and does something that reverses the boat, pulling it back from the rocks. "Not a good idea to drift into them." He pulls the plastic bottle out from under again and drinks, then goes to the rear of the boat and picks up something heavy that's all points, on the end of a chain that's wrapped around a cylinder. He drops the object into the water and the cylinder spins as the chain unspools, the handle on one side whipping around so fast it's a blur.

"There," he says. "Finished with housekeeping." He takes a step toward her.

Rose fastens the snaps at the cuffs of her windbreaker. Maybe a layer of cloth will be enough to protect her skin. Not much she can do about her face.

"Still cold?" Howard takes another step and stops. He slips his right hand into the pocket of his jeans and comes out with a leather sheath that has a bone handle protruding from it. Rose hears the unsnapping of the little strap over the handle as loudly as she would a shot. Howard's looking at her as though she's transparent, as though he can see the bench beneath her, the edge of the boat behind her.

Shoes on top, Rose thinks.

With the same relaxed, unfocused gaze, Howard pulls out the knife.

Rose yanks her feet up, lifts them as high and as quickly as she can, pushes up with her hands against the bench, and rolls backward over the edge of the boat. Just before she hits, she sees, upside down, the golden glare of the squid boats in the far distance. Then she's in the water.

Her clothes grab at her, the jacket ballooning out, and she forces herself to remain under long enough to do the bottom two snaps. It's pink, it'll show if he shines a light down, but her long hair is black and it's billowing around her. The water feels very warm after the windy rain.

She forces herself down, pulling herself through the blackness until her shoulder touches the boat. She knows she's invisible here; the outward curvature of the hull makes it impossible for anyone on board to look down at the point at which the boat enters the water. She turns so the hull is against her back, trying to present the narrowest possible silhouette, and allows herself to float up until her head breaks free of the water. With her mouth wide open, she grabs some deep breaths while she listens to Howard banging around on the boat, throwing things and screaming either meaningless sounds or a marathon of swearwords she doesn't know. A moment later a beam hits the water two or three meters to her left and a good four or five meters away from the boat.

Not the spotlight. He's got a flashlight.

"Rose!" he calls. "Rose!" He plays the light over the water. "Come on. It's dangerous down there."

The light is moving slowly now, coming nearer, and again Howard says, drawing it out, "Rosieeeeee!" The light stops, and Rose's heart stops with it. Clearly silhouetted at her eye level, glistening in the beam, are the curved tops of several sea wasps. They're only a meter or two away. They hold the light, glowing as though from within.

"Look at those," Howard says in that same singsong voice. "You don't want to be in there. Lots of bad things down there. Underneath you, next to you, behind you. Not a place for a pretty girl." The boat rocks against her back as the light disappears. Now she can't see the sea wasps, and panic uncurls in her chest. She edges right, toward the front of the boat, then stops. For all she knows, there are a dozen of them right there. Frozen in place, she hears a splash from the other side of the boat.

Howard calls out, "That's the rope. Come on, get over here. You can pull yourself up. The rope's got knots in it. You can climb it like a ladder." The light stretches out over her head again, twitching left and right and left again over the water, pure, jittery impatience. "Come on, Rose. I'm sorry. You're right, I shouldn't have been drinking. Listen, I'm throwing the bottle overboard." Something flashes through the beam of light, and she hears a splash. It sends ripples toward her, probably bringing the sea wasps closer. "Please just get to the rope and come up. I'll help you." The light freezes at a point six or seven meters from the boat, and she can feel and hear Howard moving closer to the edge above her for a better look at whatever it is. After a moment he says, "Fuck," and the beam begins to move again.

For a minute or two, she tries to remain motionless as the sea lifts and lowers her. She peers into the darkness for the rounded shapes of the sea wasps. The boat rocks upward, which means Howard is back on the other side, probably playing the light in the direction of the rocks. He's swearing over and over in a low voice, like someone who doesn't know he's doing it out loud. Then she can hear his shoes on the deck, going past her toward the front of the boat—the wheel, she thinks—and for a moment everything is quiet. Then Howard says, "Hello?" There's a pause. "Yeah, got a problem here. How far away are you?" He waits. "How did that happen? Shit, you're no good to me. Okay, okay. See you when I see you. And leave your phone open, so I don't have to fuck around dialing you."

Rose knows she has to move. She can't stay where she is, but she can't think of anyplace safer. The water, which felt so warm when she entered it, now seems much cooler, seems to be leaching the heat from her body. And she's uncomfortably aware of the dark depths beneath her, and of the sea wasps, invisible for now, floating level with her face or just beneath the surface.

And then Howard calls, "Gotcha!" and the light shines right down the side of the boat, and Howard's face dangles down, pale in the reflection of the flashlight. He's managed to anchor his feet somehow so he can hang over the side, but the light is hitting nothing. It's focused straight down, near the motor, but Rose knows he can turn it toward her at any second, and she grabs a breath and ducks under.

If the sea wasps are like the jellyfish she dodged in Pattaya, she thinks, they usually stay on the surface or in the meter or so just below it. She forces herself down into the darkness, fighting against her buoyancy, until she can't hold her breath anymore, and she stops her stroke and lets her body right itself to the vertical again. Rising, she bends her head forward at the sharpest possible angle as her shoulders slide up the curvature of the boat, hoping that her hair will protect her if she's coming up beneath a sea wasp. When she breaks the surface, she lifts her head and grabs the biggest breath of her life, mouth wide open to make it as quiet as possible. Howard is banging around on the other side, and then she hears him go forward, probably to climb up near the spotlight and look down from the prow.

She wants to get to the stern. She pictures the stretch of black water between her and it, and suddenly she has a strategy. She pulls her hand back into the sleeve of her jacket so no skin is exposed, extends her right arm along the side of the boat, and then sweeps it stiffly away, elbow straight, toward the bright pinpoint of the squid boats. She's careful to stop when her arm is straight in front of her, terrified of sweeping a cluster of jellyfish into her face. Only when she's finished the maneuver does she ease herself right, almost as far as her arm had reached, and repeat the action.

The fourth time her arm encounters resistance, as though the water has suddenly thickened, and then she feels the dead, soft weight against her inner arm, just below the elbow. Her gasp is reflexive and, to her, deafening. She clamps her teeth together and keeps the arm moving, sweeping the cold, heavy, yielding mass aside. Then she pulls her arm down and holds her breath, shuddering violently and listening. It isn't until she hears Howard still lumbering around on the prow, not rushing toward the sound she'd made, that she moves into the space she's just cleared with her arm.

She's dizzy with fear, but there's a hard little bit of knowledge gleaming inside her: The sea wasps can't sting her through her clothes.

With three more swipes of her arm—finding nothing more floating in the water—she's at the corner, with her back still to the boat. The rain, which had lightened, begins to come down harder again, making the sea around her hiss as the drops strike. For several minutes, Howard remains relatively still, except for a couple of changes in weight, shifting from foot to foot, moving a few feet to one side or the other.

He grunts.

Grunting? Why? Lifting something? Lifting what? What's so heavy? And then she hears a sharp *snap,* and she knows what it is. It's the cuff of the rubber wet suit. *It's not for the cold,* he'd said. *It's for something else.* A second later there's a loud splash as he strikes the sea's surface on the other side of the boat.

The only direction that makes sense is the one she's most afraid to take: outward, away from the boat, away from the rocks, toward the fiery glow of the squid boats, maybe three or four kilometers away. She's sure he'll circle the boat first and then maybe swim toward the rocks to see whether she's clinging to the far side of one of them.

She can't endure the thought of swimming facedown, eyes and mouth open to the jellyfish coming out of the darkness, and she can't stay underwater for more than a few yards at a time. So she rolls onto her back and pulls herself away from the boat, looking up at the sky, the rain pelting her face, hoping once again that her thick, heavy hair and the jacket with its turned-up collar will protect her head and neck if she swims into anything. The rain is colder than the seawater, and she opens her mouth, letting it land sweet and cool on her tongue, closing her eyes against it and feeling it tap gently against her eyelids. She counts her heartbeats, since she has no other way to measure time.

When her heart has beaten two hundred times, she stops swimming and lets her feet dangle down into the cooler water below. Then she pulls some of her hair forward, to cover her face, which she knows will look pale above the water. She clears just enough hair from her eyes to see.

About a meter and a half from her are two or more sea wasps. She starts to move away from them but stops, reversing her arms underwater. Howard has come around the boat, swimming quietly from the bow toward the stern. She can see the light-colored bathing cap he's wearing—one of hers, taken from the suitcase—to protect his head. Halfway along the bow, he stops, apparently treading water, and then the flashlight comes on, and she realizes it's the rubber-coated one that had been upright in a bracket beside the wheel. Howard angles the light along the boat, pointing at the stern, and then slowly turns it in a half circle, and Rose pulls herself down.

Thirty heartbeats later, when she surfaces to look, Howard is gone.

She treads water, feeling the rain on her hair. He'll finish his circuit of the ship. She decides he won't swim to the rocks, as she thought at first, because it would take him too far from the boat. If she got aboard, it would be easy for her to keep him in the water—there are long poles with hooks on them, and she could swing one of those at him whenever he gets near. No, she thinks, he'll get back on board.

Through the rain she sees his head, still in the pale cap, on the deck of the boat. She hears the metallic, teeth-grating sound of the chain being wound in as he retrieves the anchor, and then the motor catches and purrs and then purrs more urgently, and the boat starts to move. Within seconds the spotlight comes on, and Rose's hopes die.

There's no way she can hide from the spotlight. Even if she were a foot underwater, he could probably pick out the bright pink of her jacket. If the spotlight hits her, he'll have her.

But the spotlight can't point *behind* the boat. She needs to swim behind the boat, following the man who's hunting her. At the moment he's heading to her right, parallel to the rocks, and she sees what he's going to do. He's going to make a circuit of the rocks, make sure she's not on them or behind them, and then he'll search the surrounding waters, probably in a spiral, until he catches her in the spotlight or until she's stung by a sea wasp and he finds her floating facedown.

She orients herself toward the biggest rock, closes her eyes, and starts to swim, expecting the fiery lash across her forehead and cheeks with every stroke. She's surprised at how clearly she can hear the motor when one ear is in the water. She's paying a lot of attention to it as a way of knowing how far from the boat she is, when the volume suddenly drops. She stops and orients herself again, feet downward, dark hair pulled over her face, and looks.

She's about halfway to the big rock. Howard has taken the boat behind the one to the right, which has intercepted the underwater sound of the outboard. There were three rocks, he'd said, the third hidden behind the other two. She closes her eyes and tries to visualize it. If she can get between them without swimming into a jellyfish, she might be able to stay out of sight. Even Howard can't see through rocks.

She follows the boat's route, knowing that Howard is glued to the wheel, eyes on the spotlight, carefully steering around the massive stones. He's going slowly, obviously dividing his attention between navigation and scanning the water in front of him. She realizes, as she lifts her head for a breath and looks ahead, that following the boat gives her an unexpected advantage: The wake directly behind the boat is free of sea wasps, pushed to the sides by the boat's prow.

She swims past the big rock, daring to lift her arms out of the water in an overhead crawl, knowing that she'll be seen in a minute if Howard goes to the stern and looks back. But she risks swimming a little faster anyway; the closer she is to the back of the boat, the less likely she is to swim into a sea wasp.

She pulls herself along until she's gotten around the bigger rock. She's swinging out to her right to get behind the smaller one when the engine stops.

In an instant she's floating vertically, hair pulled forward to mask her face. The boat rises above the low, flat surface of the rock, and in the stern she sees Howard, flashlight in hand, the beam transcribing arcs across the water. So it's occurred to him to look behind him after all.

Rose edges closer to the smaller rock just in case, but she stops at the sight of a cluster of sea wasps in between her and it. In fact, now that she's near enough to the rocks to see them more clearly, she sees that sea wasps have been carried to them from all directions by the water's motion. There's a ring of jellyfish, like a border of solid water, maybe two-thirds of a meter wide, wherever the rocks meet the sea.

There's no way she can get through it. She'd be stung a hundred times.

A hard core of certainty begins to form inside her. She will die here.

And something bumps against her from below.

The terror is instantaneous and all-consuming. She swims wildly, smacking the surface with her arms, not thinking about the noise she's making, swimming after the boat as though it were her refuge, putting the smaller rock to her left now and then accelerating beyond to turn around it, following in Howard's wake.

Once she's circled the second rock, she sees the boat, sliding around the far end of the third rock now, only the bottom couple of feet obscured by the stone's low-rising surface. As she watches, Howard cups his hands to his face and lights a cigarette.

All these months, she thinks, *and I never knew he smoked.*

The thought strikes her as absurd, and she lowers her face into the water and releases a bubble of laughter. He was like a fancy envelope, she thinks, with a toad folded inside it. She laughs again and loses some of the rest of her air. With both of her ears underwater, she's almost deafened by the grinding sound of the boat's hull scraping over rock, and she brings her head back up in time to hear Howard screaming a sustained, unvarying stream of obscenities and to see him running the length of the cabin and repeatedly slamming the side of the boat with one of the long poles, as though he's punishing it. Then he leans forward, facing her directly from the far side of the rock, shoves the end of the pole into the water, and grunts with effort. He throws his weight behind the pole again, and this time he lets loose with a scream that seems to come all the way from his belly, and as it dies away, the boat moves and he pitches forward, off balance, and has to catch himself with both hands, the pole slipping away from him and splashing on the ocean's surface as the boat floats free of the rocks. Howard runs to the wheel, cranking it hard right, accelerating to increase his distance from the underlying shelf of stone.

Rose floats there, watching him go. She thinks that he may just have opened a path for her, even if the path leads to a place she doesn't want to go. She reclines on her side and does a gliding stroke that carries her slowly down the full length of the third rock and then around it, her eyes on the receding boat most of the time, shifting only to check the surface in front of her and make certain she's not getting too close to the solid ribbon of sea wasps that surrounds the stones. As she swims, she visualizes the other side of the big rock, and slowly, methodically, like someone drawing a map from spoken directions, she assembles something that might be a plan. The idea, thin as it is, seems to buoy her up as she swims toward the place she least wants to go, the place she'll be most conspicuous, the first and last place he'll look for her. Toward the rocks.

AND THERE IT IS. Floating in front of her, maybe ten meters from the first and largest of the rocks, is the long pole with the rusted hook at one end that Howard used to push the boat free. She grabs it with both hands, a surge of exultation passing through her, and scans the surface near her for a sea wasp. Sees one, about three meters away, between her and the rock. She kicks herself toward it and then puts the end of the pole under her arm, resting it against her rib cage, wraps both hands around a segment of the pole she can reach with her elbows slightly bent, and slices it sideways through the water, just beneath the surface. The resistance pushes her in the opposite direction, but she scissors her legs to stay in place, and the pole continues to ripple through the water until it hits the weight of the sea wasps. It takes almost all her strength, but Rose is able to keep the pole moving, shoving the sea wasps aside.

Four or five minutes later, gasping with exertion, she has cleared a path through the band of jellyfish surrounding the rock, and she is on her knees in the shallows, only her head and her very pink shoulders above water. The boat is a few hundred meters away, making a wide turn that might bring it back. She stumbles forward, all the way out of the water, until she is facedown on the biggest rock. She stays there for as long as she dares, watching the light, gasping for breath and luxuriating in the sensation of a solid surface beneath her. Then, without much faith in what she's about to do, she goes to work.

Fortunately, what she wants is right at the edges. Lying down, so she's out of sight below the crown of the rock, she rolls onto her back and pops open the pink jacket, then works her arms out of the sleeves and rolls off it. Lifting her arms as little as possible, she peels off the T-shirt, and then she unfastens the jeans. She tugs them down to midthigh and then rolls onto her side and brings her knees up so she can inch the jeans all the way down. They're heavy and wet, and she's sweating, despite the cool drizzle, by the time she scissors her ankles free. Then she folds her T-shirt once for protection, tucks her hands into it, and begins to gather seaweed. She's worried there might be sea wasps, or at least sea-wasp tentacles, tangled in the weed, although she sees none.

Working as fast as she can with her hands trapped in the shirt, she stuffs seaweed into the arms of her jacket and builds a mound of it in the center. She does up the snaps, looks at it for a moment, and then jams handfuls of seaweed into the jacket through the bottom. When it looks about right, she crawls another couple of meters, dragging the bulky jacket and the jeans behind her, until she hits another mass of seaweed. With one hand in the T-shirt and the other holding the jeans open, she begins to stuff the jeans, starting with the cuffs and shoving the seaweed as far as the knees, and then turning the pants around and working in stuffing from the top until the legs are full. She zips and snaps them, then pushes the remaining weed into the rear and hips, all the way up to the waistline.

It takes her five or six minutes, with frequent peeks above the rock's surface to track the movement of the boat, but at last she has the jeans convincingly stuffed, and she picks up the jacket and places it above the sodden pants. It lies there, arms splayed outward, separated from the jeans by a few centimeters, looking like someone who's been cut in half at the waist. She wants to put the T-shirt back on, but it's lighter-colored than her skin, so she leaves it at the rock's edge as she pulls herself, flat on her belly and scraping every inch of skin on the front of her body, up the gentle slope. She drags the jacket and the jeans behind her.

The boat is on its way back from whatever spot Howard investigated. If he keeps to his course, he'll be roughly where they were the first time she saw the rocks in the searchlight's glare. It seems like a lifetime ago. If he points the light toward the rock she's on, he'll see her, but she has no choice—for the next minute or two, she will have to be visible.

Before she lifts her head again, she says a prayer, and it is immediately answered. The rain begins to bucket down. She can barely see the spotlight, and the boat itself is completely hidden from sight.

She's already visualized the pose, so she works quickly. Everything depends on where the boat will be when Howard finally looks. She's betting he'll begin his new survey somewhere near the original position, which seemed to be where he was heading. She turns the back of the jacket toward the boat, with both arms drooping away down the far side of the stone to mask the fact that no hands protrude from the jacket's cuffs. She slips the waist of the jeans inside the jacket, bending them sharply at the knees and putting the upper leg over the lower so its cuff faces toward the boat. She's almost sure Howard will focus on the jacket because it's so much brighter, but she takes off the one plastic sandal that hasn't slipped off and drifted into the depths and leans it up against the cuff of the jeans, hoping that the light-colored sole will obscure the fact that there's no ankle above it.

The rain emboldens her, and she gets up and runs, bent low at the waist, to the side of the rock where the boat will be. She needs to take a look. At this distance, which is thirty or forty meters closer than Howard will be on the boat, the clothes almost look like they have a body in them, but she goes back around to the far side, drops to her stomach again, and creates a sharper bend at the waist, pulling the top part of the jacket just over the crest of the rock, away from where Howard will be. From the boat, she hopes, it will look like her head is just out of sight on the other side.

Either it's good enough or it isn't.

Now comes the part that frightens her most.

She works her way back down the rock, heading for the pole that she left there to mark the area she'd cleared of sea wasps. She squats there with the pole in her hands and leans forward to clear the few that have floated into the empty area. Then, her heart pounding, she wades naked into the water, flailing the pole in front of her, knowing that now she has nothing, not a single layer of cloth, to protect her from the stings.

A moment later she is swimming slowly away from the rock, stopping and clearing the way with the pole every meter or so. Once the rocks are twenty meters behind her, she turns to her left and begins to work her way into the open water, toward the glistening masts of the squid boats. She keeps her legs drawn up whenever she stops, expecting at every moment that whatever bumped her before will come rushing up, all teeth, to tug her into the depths. The image is so powerful that she almost floats into a sea wasp and has to pull the pole back and bat the jellyfish away. She hangs there in the water, breathing heavily until she trusts herself to swim again, out beyond the point at which Howard dropped the anchor.

The boat is gliding past her now toward the rocks, about thirty meters away, and she treads water, her hair pulled down over her face, hoping that Howard's eyes are locked on the rocks. The searchlight is picking out the smaller of the two rocks in front, and as Howard cranks the wheel, the light slides left, but it's too low—it's on the water when it passes the larger rock—and the jacket and jeans are well above the center of the beam. They slide back into the dark, but then Howard shouts, and the boat powers down. She sees him jump up onto the bow and wrench the light back, stopping it on the jacket and jeans.

For what feels like a long time, nothing happens. Howard sits there on the bow, looking at the splash of pink, at the bent leg of the jeans. At the bottom of the sandal, bone white, which Rose can see even at this distance, even with contacts washed out by the salt water.

Howard stands and cups his hands to his mouth. He calls her name. He goes all the way to the tip of the bow to call it again. He stands there, hands on hips, staring at the rocks. He even bends forward, as though those few extra inches will resolve what he's seeing.

Then he turns around and goes back into the cabin. He's out of sight for a moment, bent over to get something. Then he's back, the pale shower cap clearly visible above the black wet suit. He leans over the side of the ship nearest to Rose and calls, "Rose! I'm not fucking around. If you can hear me, *move*."

He leans forward again, peering through the drizzle. Then he raises a hand, points it at the rock, and Rose hears a terrific noise and sees a spurt of flame from his hand, and a little geyser of powder explodes from the rock, several feet to the left of the jacket.

Howard shouts, "Next one will be closer."

He waits, and then he goes to the wheel, and Rose hears the motor thrum into life. Howard halves the distance between the boat and the rocks and then shuts down the engine and goes to the rear.

The instant she hears the anchor splash, she begins to move.

She can't keep the pole. It slows her progress. She dives a foot or two down, closes her eyes, and pulls herself forward, then again, and then again, until her lungs are bursting. Just as she breaks the surface, she hears the splash.

She knows where to look, and the bathing cap on his head reflects light, so it's easy for her to pick Howard out. He's swimming strongly toward the rocks. Too strongly, she thinks with a jolt of panic: She doesn't have enough time. She forgets about swimming underwater and strikes out for the boat, moving as fast as she can without making too much noise. The boat doesn't seem to get bigger at first, but Howard is nearing the rocks, and with a rush of terror she kicks so hard her feet break the surface, and Howard stops swimming.

She goes under again, trying to decrease the distance to the boat, pulling herself through the water until her lungs threaten to explode. She forces herself to take another stroke, and then another, and then, at the moment when she will inhale water if she doesn't surface, she points herself up and feels a long line of flame erupt down her left arm.

She screams into the water, emptying her lungs and reflexively sucking in seawater, feeling it pour into her throat before she finds half a pint of air somewhere to blow it out again, and then she's coughing spasmodically, wasting air she doesn't have, as she summons the strength to pull herself forward in a desperate attempt not to come up beneath the sea wasp. When she surfaces, it's floating less than a meter from her, and, whimpering, she propels herself away from it, with nothing in her mind but the pain and the sea wasp. She's put two body lengths between her and it before she remembers Howard.

He's swimming again, maybe ten or fifteen meters from the rocks.

And she looks up and finds herself at the boat.

She sidestrokes to the rope and grabs it with her right arm, but the left is sluggish and heavy-feeling, as though the pain were lead flowing thickly through her veins. She forces the arm up somehow, grasps the rope, and gets both feet on a knot. With agonizing slowness she pulls herself up until she's halfway in, her feet hanging over the side, the edge cutting into her stomach, and she just rolls and falls the short distance to the floor of the cabin.

Her left arm is a wildfire of pain, radiating up into the shoulder and the side of her neck. And she's finding it difficult to draw a deep breath, as badly as she needs the air. Her lungs don't seem to be working right.

In the searchlight's beam, Howard stands up and wades onto the rock, pushing through the sea wasps in his wet suit as though they're not there. Something glints in his hand. Rose has completed only two revolutions of the handle that pulls the anchor up when she hears his scream of rage.

She manages one more crank on the handle and then has to stop, gasping for breath. She sees Howard sprint toward her across the rock and then arc out, his body straight and arrow-true, and he hits the water and begins to swim.

He swims very fast.

She manages one more turn of the handle, and then she spins and runs to the wheel. *Turn ignition.* She twists the key, and nothing happens. She wants to scream again, but she can't seem to draw enough air. *Press ignition,* she thinks, and there it is, the button. She pushes it hard enough to shove it through the panel, and the engine powers on. The boat begins to move but then jolts to a stop, and she is flung into the wheel, her forehead hitting the Plexiglas of the windscreen. The anchor has caught on something.

She runs back and tries to turn the handle on the anchor crank, but she hasn't got the strength. She puts all her weight behind it, and yet she might as well be a breeze. It won't turn.

She can hear Howard knifing through the water. He can't be far.

She has no idea how to back the boat up, which would probably free the anchor. She knows how to do one thing, and she does it: She throttles to full power. The motor churns up a tremendous amount of water, but the boat doesn't move. There's a terrifying creaking from behind her, as if the anchor assembly is going to be ripped through the rear of the boat, and she has an instantaneous vision of it taking the motor with it, so she reduces speed and then powers up again, repeating the pattern several times, trying to rock the anchor free.

She can't hear Howard swimming.

She powers down again, and the anchor snaps the boat back, and something jolts forward on the cabin floor and strikes her bare foot. It's cold and it's hard.

The boat tilts sideways, toward the rocks. The rope—*why didn't she pull in the rope?*—goes taut.

From the water Howard says, "Ahhhh, Rosie."

She looks down at her foot. The thing that slid into her is an automatic pistol, short and black. The one he fired at the rock. So the thing in his hand had to be—

Howard's hand slaps the top edge of the deck. Then his left hand appears, holding the knife he'd flashed before. He heaves himself upward and puts both arms inside, hanging there by his underarms. He grins at her beneath the silly-looking bathing cap.

"Baaad girl," he says. He begins to pull himself the rest of the way in, and Rose stoops down and picks up the gun and pulls the trigger.

It jumps in her hand, so hard she thinks she'll drop it, and wood chips fly up from the edge of the deck. Howard freezes, his face all eyes, and he raises a hand to stop her.

And she takes the gun in both hands this time and aims and very deliberately squeezes off two shots, and one of them hits him somewhere, because he's flung back, away from the boat, and an instant later she hears a splash. She runs to the edge of the deck, pointing the gun down, but she can't see him, so she yanks the rope out of the water with her free hand and goes back to the wheel. She powers down one more time and then gives the engine full throttle, and with a screech of wood being stretched the boat strains forward, and the anchor pulls free, and the vessel takes a leap that puts her on her back on the floor of the cabin, but she's up instantly, grabbing the wheel and cranking it all the way to the right, watching the rocks grow nearer and nearer and then begin to slide aside, and she leans there, all her weight on the wheel, sobbing and coughing, until the boat is pointed out into the empty sea. Only when she's been in motion for several minutes does she throttle down and go back to the stern to wind in the rest of the anchor chain.

Once that's done, she has to sit. Her breaths feel like they can be measured in millimeters, as though her lungs are shrinking into nothing. A band of numbness squeezes her chest. She sits on the floor of the cabin, gasping, as the boat glides slowly forward. She needs both hands to stand, one pushing down on the cabin floor and one pulling on the edge of the bench. As soon as she's up and heaving for breath, she goes back to the wheel, and in the clamp that had held the rubberized flashlight, she sees the cell phone, open and blinking. She picks it up and listens. Nothing.

Her voice an almost breathless whisper, she says, "Hello?"

A man's voice says, "Did you get the bitch?"

Rose's arm straightens automatically, as though she's just realized there's a tarantula crawling on her wrist, and the phone flies out of her hand and over the side of the boat. She's hanging on to the wheel, shuddering, when she hears it hit the water.

Fighting for air, she turns and squints back at the rocks. The rain is still coming down, but she can see him standing on the biggest stone, the wet suit a black vertical against the pale of the rocks. She thinks, with a jolt of joy that literally makes her grind her teeth, *Tide's coming in.* And then the rain grows heavier, and it all disappears—the rocks, the man, everything.

But she can still see the floating fire of the squid boats, and she steers directly toward it.

TWO DAYS LATER she checks out of the hospital in Phuket Town, where she's been treated for the sea-wasp venom, and gets on a bus to Bangkok. Her breathing has improved, although it will be months before she draws a breath without thinking about it. She has all of Howard's money and the extra clothes she had packed in the suitcase she took aboard the boat. Except for the money, everything that belonged to Howard, including the wallet and the gun, are at the bottom of the Andaman. She had given one of the squid fishermen two hundred dollars U.S., plucked from Howard's wallet, to lead her back to Phuket. He'd taken one look at her arm and poured vinegar on it, and the sting had eased a bit, but her breathing was still labored. One of his crew had piloted her as she lay in the bottom of the cabin, gasping like a fish, across the dark sea to the lights of Phuket.

Once in Bangkok, she checks into a cheap hotel miles from anywhere and sleeps for twenty hours. When she wakes, she takes the longest shower of her life and then goes down to the hotel's overpriced shop to buy tourist clothes, including a hat into which she can tuck her hair. There's no way to disguise her height, but at least she can change how she looks from a distance. A taxi delivers her to her bank, where she withdraws every penny she has deposited. Back in her room, she adds it to Howard's money and finds she has almost four thousand dollars, nearly 160,000 baht. That night, at 5:00 A.M., she is waiting across the street from her apartment when Fon and the other girls come home.

Twelve hours later, around 5:00 in the evening, she gets off a bus in Fon's village in Isaan, where she will stay for nearly four years. She pays a small amount every month to Fon's parents and mails a little money to her own. She calls Fon every week to see whether Howard has come into the bar. She asks her mother in letters to tell her whether he ever comes to her village.

He never does.

After four years, Fon calls to say she's moved to the King's Castle. When Rose returns to Bangkok, she joins her friend on the stage of the biggest bar in Patpong. Three years later Poke Rafferty walks into the place.

20

Ordinary Feels Very Good

It's been light for a couple of hours. The apartment is getting hot.

At some point—he has no idea when—Rafferty apparently pushed the glass coffee table away from the couch so he could sit at Rose's feet and lean back against her knees; her words seemed to flow more freely when she couldn't see his face. So he's facing away from her now, in the long moments after she's finished talking, and across the room he sees the morning light picking out glittering splinters of glass in the carpet near the sliding door.

Eight stories above the morning traffic, all he can hear is breathing.

He twists around, getting a message from his lower back to slow down. He ignores it and rises to his knees, then turns to face Rose, accidentally bending the injured elbow and sucking breath through his teeth.

She is sitting limply, sunk into the cushions, with her head tilted back and her eyes closed. He wants to put his arms around her, but it would be awkward with her sitting as she is, and he's also reluctant to break in on her, wherever she may be. Her face looks bleached out and tissue-thin, as though it's been scoured from the inside and one more pass will bare the muscles beneath the skin. Miaow lies on her right side, her knees jackknifed almost to her chest and her head on Rose's lap. Her eyes are wide open, looking directly at him. He reaches over and musses the yellowish chop of hair, and for the first time he can remember since he met her, she doesn't protest.

Leaning against Rose on the other side, her eyes partly closed and her forearm thrown across Rose's lap so she's touching Miaow's shoulder, is Pim. She has the half-drowsy, half-abstracted air of someone reciting silently something she memorized long ago. Her eyes flick to him and then back down, and she rubs her cheek against Rose's shoulder.

His cell phone rings across the room, on the kitchen counter.

"That's twice," Rose says. She opens her eyes but keeps them on the ceiling.

"And it can ring until the sun goes down." Rafferty looks up at his wife, but the moment their eyes meet, she drops her gaze, and the gesture ties a small knot in Rafferty's gut. He thinks, *What else?*

But what he says is, "Coffee? Nescafé?"

"I think I'll try to sleep for an hour or two," Rose says. "If that's okay with you, I mean."

"If it's *okay*—" Rafferty begins.

Miaow interrupts him. "That's all you want to say? *'Coffee?'*"

Rafferty rises, his back cracking like a bag full of knuckles. "I want to say a lot of things, but some of them are things I only want to say to Rose. And some of them are things I don't know how to say. Coffee will help."

"Well," Rose says, disentangling herself from the two girls and putting her feet under her to get up, "you can say them to me later."

Rafferty says, "I love you."

"That," Rose says, standing and meeting his eyes for the first time, "*that* you can say now."

Miaow says, "Me, too."

Pim says, "You were so brave."

"I was stupid," Rose says. She stretches, arms up, then presses her fists against her lower back, and bends backward. "But no stupider than you. Find something else to do."

Pim pulls up her knees and rests her forehead on them. Then she wraps her arms around her shins, sealing herself into a ball.

Miaow says, "I want a Coke."

"That's all you have to say?" Rafferty mimics. "'I want a Coke'?"

"Phoo," Miaow says. She gets up with no effort, as though she'd been on the couch for only a few minutes rather than hours. Rafferty is watching with a certain amount of envy when he feels Rose's eyes on him. When he looks at her, one corner of her mouth is up in an almost-smile.

"Remember?" she says. "Remember when everything worked like that?"

"Everything still works," he says. "It just needs a little coaxing."

"Well, since you're so limber," Rose says, "I'll have some Nescafé."

Rafferty nods. "I'll make it."

"I know," she says. "And, Pim? As long as Poke is up and proving he's flexible, is there anything you'd like?"

Pim just stares up at her, mouth half open, looking as if the world exploded in her face.

"Right." Rose sits back down and wraps her arms around the girl. "Nothing for Pim just now," she says.

From the kitchen, safely out of sight, Miaow asks her question. "So you changed? From when you were in the village. When you were in the village, that's who you really were. The way you were in Bangkok, that wasn't." A pause. "Was it?"

Rose, her arms entwined around Pim, says, "Of course not."

"How? How did you change?"

"Slowly," Rose says. "One bone at a time." She rubs Pim's shoulders with her right hand. "Like that thing you say in the play. About the king under the sea."

"'Of his bones are coral made—'" Miaow starts, coming into the room.

"In Thai," Rose says.

"Mmmm." Miaow squints up at a corner of the ceiling and changes languages. "His bones are made of coral now, and his eyes have turned to pearls. Everything's changing because of the sea, because he's underwater."

"Like that," Rose says. "One bone at a time. Because I was underwater."

Pim says, "Like I am now," and burrows her forehead into Rose's shoulder.

"And after," Miaow says. "You changed again, into who you are now." It's more a challenge than a question. "Why? How?"

"I met Poke," Rose says. "We found you." She glances at Rafferty and then back to Miaow. "You were the big one."

Miaow returns her stepmother's gaze and then looks over to Rafferty. "Oh," she says, and she goes back into the kitchen.

RAFFERTY'S BEEN EXPERIMENTING lately with what he likes to think of as domestic time management, trying to work out the best order for different chores, so one thing can process itself while he does another. It feels good to turn his attention to the coffee-making routine he's worked out: putting Rose's water on to boil while he grinds his coffee and pours it into the filter and adds a shot of cinnamon—a new touch— measuring and then pouring the cold water for his own coffee into the reservoir of the coffeemaker as Rose's water comes to a boil, then spooning out the powdered Nescafé, half a teaspoon extra, and filling Rose's cup with boiling water, stirring the Nescafé into something that resembles coffee's highly challenged third cousin, while the real thing drips from the pot into the carafe behind him.

The whole procedure—the boiling, the grinding and stirring, the smells, the narrowly avoided collisions with Miaow as she barges around the tiny kitchen washing her hands, popping the top on her Coke, going on tiptoe to grab an orange—makes him aware how blessed he was yesterday, when all this was unremarkable, normal, everyday procedure, nothing that needed thought beyond boil the water first or grind the coffee first? *Ordinary,* he thinks. Ordinary feels very good.

He carries Rose's cup in and puts it on the table. She gives him the sliver of a smile, her arms still around Pim. Miaow pulls a stool up to the counter and starts to peel her orange. Rafferty stops in the middle of the living room, flexes the sore elbow a couple of times, and says, "I just want to go on record. I love all this. I may not say so every day, but I do anyway."

Miaow looks up from her orange. "That's a lot better than '*Coffee?*'"

"I even love you," Rafferty says. "It's like loving a cactus, but I do."

Miaow gives the orange all her attention, but he can see the color bloom in her cheeks.

He goes into the kitchen, feeling light-headed, and pours his own coffee into the mug he uses every day of his life. Every wonderful day of his life. Leaning against the cool of the refrigerator door, he inhales the aroma. Out in the living room, Rose murmurs something, probably to Pim, and the couch squeaks as someone gets up, and then the air conditioner cranks into life. Rose says to the world as a whole, "Time for a cigarette," and he hears the rasp of a match.

"Maybe," Miaow says, her mouth full of orange, "maybe you ought to check the voice mail."

"Me, me, me," Rafferty says happily. Despite the chain of horrors in Rose's story, he feels almost exhilarated. He knows what's wrong now; they can begin to fix it. He downs about a third of his coffee, scalding the roof of his mouth, and then tops up the cup from the pot. "Fuel first," he says to Miaow, toasting her with the mug and slopping some on his fingers.

She says, "Bean drink," with the special scorn she reserves for coffee.

"The phone, the phone." Rafferty gulps and burns his mouth again, puts the cup on the counter, wipes his burned fingers on his pants, and speed-dials his voice mail. The first call is a hang-up. Then Arthit's voice comes on the line. He sounds like someone five thousand years old who hasn't slept since the turn of the century.

"Your guy, Horner," he says. "He hasn't left the kingdom. He's in Thailand."

PART III

THE STORM

21

I Was Wondering
Where I Wasn't

Rafferty says, "Pack. Everything you'll need for three or four days." He's tugging at the hem of a new T-shirt, water dripping onto it from the tip of his chin, which he missed with the towel after splashing his face. His hair is damp from his having clawed through it with wet fingers.

Rose says, "Where are we going?"

"Later. For now, pack." To Pim he says, "This isn't the safest place in Bangkok. You should probably go."

Pim looks at Rose and then Miaow. "Can I help?"

Rose says, "I'll pack for me and tell you what to pack for Poke."

"Don't forget the Glock," Rafferty says, and Miaow swivels to stare at him. "Both clips."

"Where are you going?"

"Arthit's not in his office, and no one is answering at home. So I'm going to his house."

Miaow says, "With no one answering? Maybe he doesn't want to see anybody."

"Of course he doesn't want to see anybody. I should have gone over days ago."

HE HAS to knock three times.

Standing there with the morning sun beating down on his shoulders, he has more time than he needs to see things he doesn't want to see: The tiny dead lawn, the stunted line of brown scrub where the flowers used to be. Three yellowing copies of the *Bangkok Sun,* lying any which way on the fried, brittle grass. When Arthit's wife, Noi, was alive, this little yard was as green and as immaculately tended as a Scottish golf course. Even after she got too sick to care for it herself, she would sit on the porch and direct Arthit as he planted and trimmed and raked and swept, grumbling happily the whole time.

It's been only eight months.

He's knocking again, harder this time, when the door opens. Arthit stands dead center in the doorway, blocking access. The house is dim behind him, the curtains apparently drawn. He does not smile at Rafferty. He glances at the graying bandage on Rafferty's elbow and the one on his thumb and says, "What?"

"You're not at the office."

"Thank you," Arthit says. "I was wondering where I wasn't." He hasn't shaved or combed his hair, and he's wearing a dirty T-shirt and a pair of wrinkled shorts. The circles beneath his eyes have an actual depth; they look like they've been pressed there with the bottom of a glass. The smell from the house is as sour and musty as a bad secret.

"Well, I mean, you've been working time and a half since—"

"And today I'm not." He looks past Rafferty as though making sure that no one else is coming. "You got my message."

Rafferty smells alcohol on his friend's breath. It's 10:30 A.M. "Are you anything at all like okay?"

Arthit continues to look past Rafferty. "Did you come here to talk about me?"

"Not really."

"Good. Then let me start over. You got my message."

"Yes."

"That's why I left it," Arthit says. "Anything else?"

"What is it, Arthit?" Rafferty says, concern receding to make room for anger. "Is solitude calling? Do you have plans or something? Is this an intrusion?"

Arthit's eyelids droop and then close for a moment. He leans against the side of the door. When he opens his eyes, he says, "This isn't a good day for company."

"Sitting around drinking in the dark isn't going to make it any better."

"Poke," Arthit says. "Fuck you." He starts to close the door.

"Wait." Rafferty puts a hand against the door, expecting to have to push back, but the door just floats free of Arthit's hand and swings all the way open again. Arthit stands there, arms hanging down, hands loose at his sides, looking like a man who's just used all the strength he's been hoarding.

The pose is so naked that Rafferty can barely look at it. He looks down instead, at the porch between his feet. When it becomes clear that Arthit isn't going to spend any more energy trying to throw him out, he says, "Horner killed a girl. He tried to kill Rose. For all I know, he's killed a dozen of them."

Arthit doesn't say anything.

"I'm not expecting a rescue," Rafferty says. "But I could use some more information." He looks back at Arthit and says, "And you need to be doing something other than this."

"All you *farang*," Arthit says. He shakes his head. "You lack delicacy. No Thai would criticize me like that. Not at this time."

"I can't afford delicacy. And I have to tell you, Arthit, I'd probably be here kicking your door in even if I didn't have a problem."

Arthit says, "Precisely the point I was making. No Thai would."

"But I do have a problem."

"Wait," Arthit says. He squeezes his eyes shut and lets his head fall forward until his chin hits his chest. He takes a long breath and fills his cheeks and blows it out like someone surfacing from the deep, then lifts his head and shakes it back and forth quickly, the way a sleepy driver does when he needs to clear his head and refocus on the road. When he's finished, he grabs another breath, heaves a whiskey-laced sigh, and looks straight at Rafferty. "Tried to kill her."

"And did kill another one, another bar girl."

"Any chance at all she's wrong about him trying to kill her? Maybe he was just—"

"No."

Arthit steps back. "I suppose you should come in."

"PROBABLY," ARTHIT SAYS. He's sitting on the couch, next to a confused pile of clothes and magazines and DVD cases he'd swept out of his way before he sat down. "The pieces aren't hard to assemble. Immigration has the dates he was in the country, assuming he's using only one passport. And the cops down south actually do keep records of bodies that wash ashore, although probably not for more than, say, ten years. The problem is that nobody bothers about missing bar girls."

"No. Really?"

"It's not what you think." Arthit looks at the table in front of him, jumbled high with unopened mail, plastic utensils, and used paper plates, and then he says, "Well, it's not *only* what you think."

"What else is it?"

He rubs his eyes with his palms, almost grinding at them. "It's partly the girls. You know how it works. They go home. They go off with men. They get married to someone they just met. They move to a bar in Soi Cowboy or Nana Plaza. They decide it would be nice to work in Pattaya or Phuket and live at the beach. They get hired by a private club or an outcall service. They get sent to Singapore or Japan. They get a positive HIV test and don't want to scare their friends. They disappear all the time."

Rafferty says, to his knees, "Still." He's trying to keep from looking at the house, which is filthy.

"Yes," Arthit says. "It stinks. But that's how it is."

"Makes them ideal victims."

"Prostitutes everywhere. Half the serials in the world focus on them."

"No reason," Rafferty says, "for the Land of Smiles to be an exception."

"No. Because you're right. The other part of the problem, here and everywhere else, is that the cops don't care."

"Fine. So we forget asking about disappearing bar girls and concentrate on whether there's a pattern of women washing up around Phuket during or just after Horner's visits."

"You're assuming that he'd go back to the same place to do the girls."

"Can you suggest another assumption that gives us somewhere to start?

"You know," Arthit says, leaning back and lifting a bare foot. There's nowhere on the table to put it, so he uses the foot to sweep some of the junk onto the floor. Then he rests the foot on the table, the sole angled politely away from Rafferty. "I have to observe that this is suicidal behavior for a serial killer."

"What is? And why is this place so dark?"

"Because I like it dark. Coming back to the bar like that. He takes this girl—what's her name?"

"Oom."

"He takes Oom and does what he does to her, and a few months later he's back looking at Rose."

Rafferty says, "And?"

"And that can't be his pattern. No matter how lazy the cops are, someone, even if it's only the mama-san, is going to notice that every time this guy shows up, some girl vanishes."

"Lot of bars in a lot of places," Rafferty says. "Hundreds in Bangkok, God knows how many in Pattaya and Chiang Mai and Phuket, and who knows where else. He could snatch one per bar for years and years without ever repeating, without even getting within miles of a place he's hit before."

"That's what I'm saying, Poke." Arthit looks at the foot on the table and flexes his toes. "After Oom, why would he go back to the Candy Cane?"

"I don't know, Arthit," Rafferty says, feeling his face heat up. "Maybe Rose was special."

Arthit winces as though he's been hit, then lets his head fall forward so he can rub the back of his neck. "Of course. It's *Rose,* isn't it? Of course he came back."

Rafferty breathes deeply a couple of times to slow himself down. "Rose says the other one, Oom, was a real beauty."

"Cherry-picking," Arthit says. His face brightens a shade. "That should make the bar end of it a little easier. We don't need them to remember everybody who disappeared, only the most beautiful ones."

"I guess that helps."

"But like I just said, the girls move around. You'd figure he'd bump into some who remembered him."

Rafferty says, "I just spent six or seven hours inside a bar girl's life, and you have to remember that they see hundreds of thousands of men a year. Say they work three hundred fifty days and eight hundred men come into the bar each night. I can't do the math, but that's more than a quarter of a million. Unless Horner took one, she's going to forget about him in a week or two. They focus on the ones who give them money. The others are just scenery."

"The place for us to start," Arthit says, "is Phuket on one end and the Bangkok bars on the other."

"Not we," Rafferty says. "Me. And whoever else I can strong-arm. You lean on immigration, and I do the rest. You're working ten days a week as it is."

"I can do what I want," Arthit says. "I'm a public hero, remember?"

Arthit's been milking this ever since national television showed video of him killing someone who had just murdered a much-loved Thai millionaire.

Rafferty says, "Yes, but I mean—"

Arthit lifts a hand. "So I'll make the time."

Rafferty says, by way of preface, "Listen. And don't get mad at me."

Arthit shoots a glance toward the front door as though he's thinking about escaping through it. "I'm going to hate this, aren't I?"

"Look around."

"I don't have to. I see it every day."

"I mean, if you can make all this time, why don't you clean the damn house? It's not good for you, living like this."

Arthit says, "I don't want to move anything."

"Fine, fine. Don't move anything Noi touched. But this other junk, this *crap* . . . my mother, who has some good qualities, always says that even an angel can't live in a pigpen without turning into a pig."

"Does she," Arthit says. His eyes click on Rafferty's for a moment and then dart away.

"Well, no," Rafferty says. "I made that up. But you know what I mean."

Arthit nods slowly. "A moment ago we were talking about something important."

"This is important," Rafferty says.

They're both silent for a minute or two. Finally Rafferty reaches behind him and pulls the curtain open a couple of inches. The sunlight is merciless, and he lets it drop. "Jesus," he says. "At least ask Rose to get you a maid or something."

"I don't want a maid."

"Get a live-in. Her agency has a lot of women who need the work. You shouldn't be alone like this."

"This is exactly what I mean about *farang*. No Thai would be so presumptuous."

"That's what you get for making friends with me. Rose would be horrified to see this."

"But she'd have the sensitivity to leave me alone."

"Maybe, but this house didn't belong just to you."

A blink, almost heavy enough to be audible. "Your point?"

"It was Noi's house, too. It should be honored. What kind of way is this to honor her?"

"Poke." Arthit's tone is a warning.

"This isn't just sad, although Christ knows it's sad. This is the same as turning your back on her."

"That's enough."

"Who's going to say this if I don't?"

"Nobody." Arthit gets up. "And that'll be fine with me." He heads for the hallway. "I'll get all the dates from immigration. I'll get the picture, if they've got one, although all those pictures look like everyone. And I'll talk to the guys on the force in Phuket. I imagine you want this fast."

"Sure." Rafferty is still sitting. "He's here somewhere. He knows where we live. Rose and Miaow are home packing, scared half out of their minds."

Arthit stops walking, but he doesn't turn. "Where are you going to put them?"

"I don't know. Like I told Rose, the first thing is to get them ready to go. Some hotel in some obscure neighborhood."

Arthit says, "I'll be back."

Rafferty listens to his friend's footsteps, slow and heavy, the shuffle of a much older man, going down the hallway toward the kitchen. Then they stop. Without allowing himself to think about anything, Rafferty looks around. The dining room, always polished and immaculate when Noi was here, is a dim chiaroscuro, the table piled with dirty clothes, unopened newspapers, folded towels from the laundry, take-out cartons from restaurants, a few books, and several empty bottles labeled Johnnie Walker Black. Even the floor has junk on it, little islands of homeless uselessness, the kind of litter that's barely worth the effort of picking up and throwing away, the kind of stuff drunk people trip over. He can actually smell the dust in the air. It's impossible not to remember the bright, soft luster the place had eight or nine months ago—flowers, buffed surfaces, a gleam on the pale hardwood floors.

He comes to the present, realizing it's been a couple of minutes and he hasn't heard anything at all from the kitchen. No cupboards opening, no rattle of china, no running water. The house is so quiet he might as well be alone. A little foam of anxiety curdles in his stomach.

He gets up. "Arthit?"

After a moment Arthit says, "Just stay where you are."

Rafferty stays where he is, although he's got misgivings. To occupy his mind, he lifts the corner of the living-room drapes once more and lets the sun in. Depressed by what he sees, he drops it again. He decides he'll count to twenty and then go to the kitchen.

When he's reached eight, Arthit calls, "What are you doing for the next two hours?"

"Free as a bird," Rafferty says. "Get Rose and Miaow out of the apartment, find them a hotel, set them up, feed them. Plan the rest of my life. Other than that, nothing at all."

"Good," Arthit says. "Then you can give me a hand."

"Fine. I'll come back."

"No. Now." Rafferty hears the water run and then the sound of the teakettle being set on the gas stove, then the little *poof* as the gas ignites. Arthit comes in through the dining room. "We'll drink some Nescafé, and then you can help me straighten this place up."

"Any other time—"

"Don't be obtuse," Arthit says, trying to look cheerful and looking instead like someone whose smile is stuck in place and who's panicking behind it. "You'll bring them here."

CURTAINS WIDE, DAYLIGHT washing the room like water, floor wide and empty. The magazines have been stacked by size in two plumb-straight piles. Three white plastic trash bags have been stuffed with spoiled

food, cartons, disposable plates and utensils, used paper towels, empty
Kleenex boxes, and old newspapers. The dining-room table is bare and
shining. When Rafferty aimed the spray can of wax at it and pushed the
button, releasing the scent of lemon, Arthit froze in the living room,
bending over the coffee table as though his back had gone out and he
couldn't straighten.

Rafferty had said, "Arthit?"

Arthit stayed where he was for a few seconds, and then he straight-
ened, and with his back to Rafferty, he sniffled. "She loved that smell,"
he said.

"I remember. I never use this stuff without thinking of this house."

Now Arthit bends again as though to dust the table and then
straightens again. "I haven't been waxing much."

"Gee," Rafferty says, watching his friend's back. "You'd never
know."

"You have such a light hand with the irony."

"Want to do the kitchen?"

"Sure, it'll be easy. I've barely used it."

Rafferty picks up a couple of the garbage bags and throws them over
one shoulder. The kitchen, located directly behind the dining room,
can be reached either that way or through a hall that bypasses the guest
bedroom, the bathrooms, and the room in which Arthit and Noi had
slept. When Rafferty went past that room, half an hour ago, the door
had been standing open, and he saw the bed, made up but wrinkled,
with a little canyon on the bedspread and two dented pillows showing
where his friend had been sleeping on top of the covers. Rafferty had a
detailed vision, a tenth of a second long, of Arthit deciding every night
not to turn the blankets down, and his breath caught in his throat.

He crosses the kitchen and opens the back door, not looking at the
abandoned garden, and puts the bags outside. Arthit comes in through
the hallway with the other plastic bag and a wad of damp paper towels,
detours around Rafferty, and goes through the door to set them out.
He straightens and stands there for a moment, hands on hips, looking
at the wasteland that used to be a garden.

Rafferty runs water and passes a musty-smelling sponge under
it. The kitchen, as advertised, is relatively neat, although dusty. He
squeezes the extra water from the sponge and swipes it over the kitchen
counters. "We're going to need some more paper towels."

From the doorway Arthit says, "Under the sink."

Kneeling hurts Rafferty's back, reminding him that he was up, sitting essentially in one position, all night long. The pain sharpens his memory of Rose's story and brings a question to the surface. "He's here, Horner is. He's got to want to get to Rose, maybe all of us. Why hasn't he done anything?"

He opens the cupboard door and settles back on his heels, his question forgotten.

"Something to think about," Arthit says, coming in. He looks down at Rafferty, who's staring at the space beneath the sink and says, "Shit."

"This is impressive," Rafferty says. He pulls out a big plastic tub piled high with empty whiskey bottles.

"You should see the ones I left in the bars," Arthit says. He comes over to Rafferty. "Give me that."

Rafferty slides it over to him, and Arthit picks it up with a little grunt.

"Maybe it is impressive," he says, putting it down again and dragging it across the floor toward the back door.

Rafferty's phone rings. He stands, fishes it out of his jeans, and says, "Ahh, my skyscraper darling."

"We're on the way," Rose says. "All of us."

"Good. We're pretty much ready." He thinks for a second about what she's said, and he asks, " 'All'? What happened to 'both'?"

"All," Rose says.

Rafferty says, "Oh. Well, don't forget the circling and double-backs and all that."

"Thanks," Rose says. "I never would have remembered." She hangs up, and he folds the phone and turns to Arthit, who's coming back in. He says, "I'm sorry about this. I think we've got one extra coming."

Arthit stops, obviously processing the information, and then he tries on the smile again. It looks like he's got gas. "No problem," he says. "Invite everyone you know."

22

Generic Pictures
of a White Male

"Poke asked an interesting question a while ago," Arthit says. He's showered and shaved and changed into a white dress shirt, tan slacks, and an awful pair of tartan plaid socks. He has a huge collection of bad socks, given to him by Noi as a birthday joke every year. "He knows where you live. He painted the door to tell you he could get to you, and then he disappeared. What's he doing?"

"It's only been a few days," Rose says. "Since Saturday." She's sharing the couch with Miaow and Pim, whom she's apparently adopted permanently. Pim hasn't raised her eyes from the floor since the moment she realized she was in a cop's house. They've all got glasses of iced coffee, rich with sweetened condensed milk, except for Miaow. Miaow brought two six-packs of Cokes just in case and is working on her second can.

Rafferty, framed in the sunlight that's streaming through the front window, settles into his armchair, takes a polite sip, fights down a grimace at the sugar, and says, "You're the only one who knows him. Is he someone who sits around and waits for things?"

"No. He decides to do something and he does it. He wants things when he wants them. He's not careful, at least not about things that might be dangerous. He goes skydiving, he climbs rocks. And look at the way he came back into the Candy Cane to get me so soon after he took Oom. That wasn't careful."

"It was impulsive," Arthit says. "But if he's impulsive, why hasn't he tried to get to you? He had that guy, that guy—"

"John," Rafferty says.

"John. He had John following Poke—and maybe you, for all we know—just getting information. But he already knew where you lived. He and John, the two of them, could have waltzed into that apartment in the middle of any night of the week and done whatever they wanted."

"Not to be immodest, but I was there," Rafferty says.

"These guys aren't going to worry about a travel writer," Arthit says.

"Well," Rafferty says, "I'm not *just* a travel writer."

"Of course not." Rose passes her fingertips over the condensation on the side of her glass and pats the side of her neck with the cool water. In Thai she says, "But they have no way of knowing how lethal you are."

"You think he's a soldier," Arthit says to Rose, ignoring Rafferty. "But his visas say 'businessman.' And what kind of soldier gets so much time off?"

"He's a soldier," Rose says.

"Jesus, we're slow," Rafferty says. "He's both. He's a mercenary."

"The talon," Arthit says, sitting up. "I knew I'd seen it before. He's Grayhawk."

"They're both Grayhawk," Rafferty says.

Rose says, "What's Grayhawk?"

"Contractors," Rafferty says. "Hired guns. The guys who kill people on behalf of the Land of the Free when a war is unpopular and the president doesn't want military casualties. The guys who shot a lot of those folks in Iraq and are shooting folks now wherever freedom is threatened."

"That's a cynical attitude," Arthit says.

"Well, excuse me," Rafferty says. "And not to digress from the matter at hand, but I think all the world's professional politicians, every single one of them, should be herded together and imprisoned permanently beneath a giant glass bell jar and fed a diet of issues and causes. We could use the gas they generate as an energy source. Enough to light whole cities."

Arthit says, "That's hardly a digression at all."

"I just thought we should get it on the table."

"Grayhawk guys are not tabby cats," Arthit says.

"Howard is very dangerous," Rose says.

"Old John let me stick chili up his nose pretty easily," Rafferty says.

Pim says, "I was there. You were lucky."

"Yeah," Rafferty says. "I was." To Arthit he says, "Where do we start to look for him?"

"What hotel did he stay at?" Arthit asks Rose.

"The Royal Orchid. Always, at least when he was with me."

Arthit asks Rafferty, "Sound like a starting point? Not that he's likely to use the same hotel much."

"I'll check it out—"

"No you won't," Arthit says. His cell phone rings. "Yes?" He glances over at Rafferty and nods. "Thanks, e-mail it and we'll take a look. When will you guys be here?" He glances at his watch and says to Miaow, "What time is your rehearsal?"

Miaow's eyebrows go up in surprise. "Two. It starts in sixth period."

"One-thirty," Arthit says into the phone. "See you then." He disconnects and says, "Come with me, Rose."

Rafferty says to his receding back, "What do you mean, I won't check it out? Who will?"

Rose gets up and follows Arthit into the dining room with Rafferty trailing along behind, his question unanswered. Arthit lifts the lid on a laptop that's sitting on the dining-room table and brings up Gmail. At the top of the messages in his in-box is one with the subject heading HORNER. Arthit opens it and clicks on the first attachment.

A fuzzy, low-res black-and-white picture of Howard Horner fills the screen. He's got glasses on, and he's puffed out his cheeks with just enough air to change the shape of his face. He's also tilted his head back so the glasses are bouncing light into the camera lens, making his eyes invisible.

"That's not him. Is it?" Miaow asks from behind them.

"Exactly," Arthit says. He flicks through the other attachments. There are six of them in all, generic pictures of a white male in his early thirties. Beards and mustaches come and go, as do a couple of wigs and several pairs of glasses. "He's good at this."

"No one will recognize him from these," Rose says, and then she straightens and says, "Oh."

Rafferty says, "Oh?"

"We need to go back in the other room and sit down."

Arthit says, "If you say so," and he gets up, and they all follow Rose.

"Give me a second," she says, sitting back down on the couch. She picks up her glass of iced coffee and drains it, then closes her eyes for a second, and then she says, "He's got another one."

"Another girl," Rafferty says.

"Sure. That's why he was in Patpong the night we saw him in the restaurant. That's why he's leaving me alone right now. He does one thing at a time. He gives it—he gave *me*—all his attention. He's working on some girl right now. When he's finished with her, or when there's a natural break in the, the *courtship,* he'll get around to me."

"A girl in Patpong," Arthit says. "How many years has it been?'

Rose slides her fingertips around through the coating on the inside of her empty glass and then licks them. "He took me in 1998, 1999. He spent months with me, off and on, until he took me to Phuket. So eleven years, twelve years."

"Probably feels safe to him again by now," Rafferty says. "People have forgotten him. Lots of girls have quit, new girls everywhere."

"He likes newer girls," Rose says, with an involuntary glance at Pim. "They're dumber."

"This turns things around," Rafferty says.

Arthit says, "Not with what we just got."

Rose says, "What turns what around? And what did we just get? I hate it when you two do that."

"He doesn't know where you are, right now," Rafferty says, "but we know where he is, or at least where he's going to be. In Patpong, working on some girl. But we don't have a good—"

"Thirty bars," Arthit interrupts. "Five thousand *farang* men on any given night. We need a much better picture."

Rose says, "That's the other part of 'Oh.' I think I've got one."

"You kept his *picture*?" Miaow says in disbelief.

"I forgot," Rose says. "In the suitcase I took on the boat, I had a little camera, one of the old ones you use once and then throw away. I bought it for the trip and never touched it again. If the film is still any good, there are ten or fifteen pictures of Howard in it."

"Where?" Rafferty asks.

"In a cardboard box with a lot of things I never use, on the top shelf of the closet." She closes her eyes and says, "On the right. Behind the iron and that machine you bought to write down all the things you said into the tape recorder you were going to use for your writing."

"The transcription machine." Another burst of enthusiasm gathering dust.

"That. Behind that."

"One of those little cardboard cameras? Yellow or something?"

"Yes."

"I'll have it developed," Arthit says. "When Poke comes back from Miaow's rehearsal, he can stop at the apartment and get it, and give it to Kosit."

Rafferty says, "Kosit?"

"You remember Kosit. Older cop, leathery face, got—"

"I remember Kosit. Why will Kosit be at my—"

Arthit waves him off. "Because he's going with you. Also, a kid named Anand. Patrolman on his way up, if I have anything to say about it. He's the one—I think I told you about this—who gave me the money when all the other cops were looking for me. He found me trapped at the top of a flight of stairs in an apartment building, threw me all the money he had, and went down to tell his sergeant that nobody was up there." He swallows, cups his hands, and rubs his face with them. "That was the night Noi died."

Rafferty lets a few seconds creep by and says, "Arthit. You can't just assign cops to us like we're visiting Saudis."

"They're on special assignment," Arthit says. "To the national hero."

"Boy, are you squeezing that."

"Why not? It's not going to last forever. As soon as Thanom can stuff me into a box and nail the lid shut, he will. He hates that I get all the attention, even if he does jam himself into every picture." Thanom, Arthit's boss, is a guaranteed first-ballot occupant of the Police Corruption Hall of Fame, and Arthit has been a stone in his shoe for years. "Kosit and Anand will check the Royal Orchid," Arthit continues. "And they'll be wherever Miaow is. When you're with her, they'll stay out of sight on the assumption they'll be able to spot the watchers and get in the middle if anything happens. When you're not with her, they'll be visible, so nothing *does* happen."

"What about Rose?" Rafferty asks.

Arthit says, "Rose isn't going anywhere."

Rose says, "Excuse me?"

"Good," Rafferty says to Arthit. "*You* keep her in line. And call me once in a while to let me know how you're doing." He checks his watch and stands up. "If he's really found a new one, and if we can get a good picture, we might be able to turn this whole thing around."

Arthit says, "Maybe."

"Before he finishes with the girl," Rose says.

23

An Indigestible Lump of Exposition

Prospero's island, or at least the part of it that's visible to the audience, is a rugged, steep-sided rock that juts up almost vertically on the left and then crinkles its way down on the right, ending offstage. It lifts its craggy silhouette against the unbroken gray of a cyclorama, one long piece of seamless fabric that curves all the way around the back of the stage, from the floor to the top of the audience's sight line, and which is lighted the color of gunmetal for these act 1 moments following Prospero's magical storm. Later in the production, as the day wears on, different lighting will turn it turquoise, but for now the gray is fine, easy on Rafferty's tired eyes.

The vertical edge of the rock begins its thrust about four feet from the curtains on the left edge of the stage, leaving room for actors to come and go. That's *Rafferty's* left, as he faces the stage, but for the actors, who are facing out, it's stage right. Mrs. Shin, in giving direction, always means *stage* right and *stage* left, even when she says only, "Cross right" or "A few steps left." So: stage right; stage left; upstage, or away from the audience; and downstage, or toward it—the points of the theatrical compass.

Everyone in the room except Rafferty, and probably Kosit and Anand, understands it instinctively.

A big, irregular, dark-looking cave, Prospero's hangout, punctuates the rock face at about center stage, and a huge clutter of driftwood has been stacked just to one side. The pile of driftwood is on a hinge, and on the back of it—the side that's invisible to the audience at the moment—is a bunch of heavy canvas framed and painted to look like rocks. The unit will be swung around to provide scenery for the clown scenes—what Rafferty, who shortened them for weeks, thinks of as the *endless* clown scenes—and also to mask part of the cave.

Beginning high on top of the island, a rough-hewn stairway of sorts has been incised into the rock. It appears near the pinnacle and then angles back and forth all the way down to the stage floor. This was designed to be used by arriving and departing actors, but Mrs. Shin has been worried about the stairway since long before the set was built, anxious that someone might fall through it and get hurt. She's decided, as she sets the action of the play, that the stairway belongs exclusively to Ariel, since Miaow is by far the lightest child in the cast. Miaow has tried not to look smug at having an entrance only she can use.

Rafferty is sitting next to Mrs. Shin, about eight rows back from the stage, feeling like he's entered an enchanted world. This is the first time he's seen the entire set with most of the lighting, and it's turned the auditorium into a sorcerer's stony realm, completely sealed off from the urban friction of Bangkok and the real-life drama of the past few days. The school's theater accommodates about four hundred people in rows of hard, fold-down wooden seats—another reason to shorten the play—set in front of a classic proscenium stage, complete with a small orchestra pit and a curtain. For *The Tempest* the curtain has been festooned with cloth seaweed in half a dozen shades of green and brown, with sparkles glued here and there. Some kelpy pieces are ten or fifteen feet high, extending all the way from the floor of the stage to the top of the proscenium arch. Mrs. Shin was not allowed to sew the seaweed to the curtain, so every now and then Rafferty sees the glint of safety pins.

He likes the safety pins. They seem appropriate to the production, a bit of inexpensive practicality in the middle of all the magic.

The boy playing Prospero, a Chinese kid named Luther So, is on-stage now and is not having a good time portraying age. He's presenting Shakespeare's magician as a stiff-kneed hunchback who walks high-shouldered and bent over, leaning on his magician's staff and frequently grabbing his back as though in pain. Every time he takes a step, Mrs. Shin says quietly, "Oh, dear," and finds a way to keep him still.

"Why don't you just have him stand there through the whole play?" Rafferty asks behind his hand. "The other actors can hang hats on him."

"He speaks the verse very well," Mrs. Shin says. "He understands every word. And it's unusual for a ninth-grader to have such a strong lower register."

"And such a weak lower back."

"Shhh." But she's smiling.

Privately Rafferty thinks it wouldn't matter if the kid played the whole role stark naked on a unicycle, because no one, or at least no one who's male, will ever see him. Siri Lindstrom, who's been assigned the role of Prospero's daughter, Miranda, is an incipient heartbreaker, the kind of girl who seems to carry her own breeze with her. Her ash-blond hair, which falls to the middle of her back, is constantly in motion, framing a face having nothing wrong with it that's big enough to see with the unaided eye. The first time she came onstage, Kosit, sitting three rows back, said something that made Anand laugh. Mrs. Shin had twisted around toward them.

"My police escort," Rafferty said.

"What an interesting life you lead." Mrs. Shin looks up at Siri, who's huddled with Luther running through the lines of the play's eternal second scene, in which Prospero explains the whole backstory to his daughter, starting before she was born. It seems to take as long to tell as it did to happen. Siri's wearing a great many yards of muslin, draped in layers around her like she's just come from some celestial steam bath. All the actors are in working costumes, rough muslin approximations of their ultimate outfits, so they can learn how to move in them without falling on their faces. Siri seems to be having no problem with hers, but she could probably dance on pointe in full body armor. "Wait till they see her in the real dress," Mrs. Shin says, regarding her. "She's breathtaking."

"Miaow hates her."

Mrs. Shin nods matter-of-factly. "She's got a lot of company. Siri is not a girl's girl."

Rafferty says, "I'm just glad I'm not her father."

Mrs. Shin gives him a quizzical glance. "And Mia?"

"Well, Miaow's difficult sometimes, but it's a different kind of difficult."

"For the moment," Mrs. Shin says, and now it's Rafferty's turn to look at her.

"You think?"

"Absolutely. She'll probably never be tall, but she's going to be a beauty."

Rafferty looks up at the top of the rock, where he can just see the chopped-yellow crown of his daughter's head. She's sitting where she always sits, all by herself on the highest step of the metal stairway that leads to her entrance. "Really."

"Take my word. I'm an expert on how they'll grow up. I've been watching it for years." She leans forward and calls out, "Luther. Siri. Let's have it out loud and in your places." Luther hobbles downstage, and Rafferty can almost hear his joints creak. Siri drifts weightlessly toward center stage, which is her favorite place. "Ellen"—Mrs. Shin's voice is louder—"give me the cave lights."

The inside of the cave takes on a pale color halfway between a peach and the inside of a conch shell.

Rafferty says, "Pretty."

Mrs. Shin says "Shhh" again, focused on the stage. Luther has launched into the story, much shortened by Rafferty, of how his brother betrayed him and stole his dukedom, in connivance with the king of Naples, and how Prospero and Miranda wound up cast away on this benighted island. He is interrupted by dutiful interjections from Siri, as Miranda, who is herself interrupted by Mrs. Shin, who reminds her that the people in the back of the theater will want to hear her, too. It is, Rafferty thinks, one of the worst scenes Shakespeare ever wrote.

He says, "Still feels too long, doesn't it?"

"It's been too long for four hundred years." Mrs. Shin slips sideways out of the row and goes down to the edge of the orchestra pit at the foot of the stage. The actors break off and look at her. "I want you guys to pick it up by about ten percent," she says. "We'll move on now, but as soon as you're both offstage, I need you to run through it a few times, just speeding it up. Here's the motivation: Luther, you're eager to get through it so you can talk to Ariel and find out about the storm. Let the intensity speed you up. Siri, maybe you can cut him off with some of your lines, because as good a daughter as you are, you're a kid, you're impatient—"

"This is important material," Luther says. He was born to be forty. He's watched anxiously as his big opening scene has been snipped like substandard yardage. "The audience needs to hear it."

"They need to be awake, too," Mrs. Shin says. "You guys are doing great, but this scene is a big, indigestible lump of exposition, and we haven't solved it yet. Okay?"

Siri says placidly, "When will I get my real costume?"

"When it's finished," Mrs. Shin says, a bit shortly. She smiles, taking the sting out of it. "Siri, why don't you go backstage and think about how to hurry this scene along? That way you'll be ahead of Luther when he's finished out here."

Siri nods and floats off stage left, where a sun-dappled meadow probably awaits her. Even Luther, whose developing sexuality seems to be taking an interesting direction, watches her go.

"Okay," Mrs. Shin says, clapping her hands. "Lights ready? Ellen?"

"Ready!" a girl shouts.

"Mia?"

Miaow stands up, high on the rock, looking even smaller than usual, and says, "I'm here," and then disappears again.

"Then let's go."

Mrs. Shin backs up the aisle, still facing the stage, with her right arm behind her back, fingers crossed. The peach color inside the cave is replaced by a chilly steel blue, and the cyclorama darkens ominously to slate gray. A bright spot of light hits the top of the rock, where Miaow had been standing, and Mrs. Shin calls out, "Ellen. Not till you see her. Where's our sound?"

"Sorry," a boy says from stage right.

"Put the light on the cyclorama back the way it was," Mrs. Shin says. "I want to see this whole transition come together. Luther, you cue everything. Everybody ready?"

A general chorus of readiness from all over the theater as the cyclorama brightens, and then Mrs. Shin claps again and says, "From 'Come away,' Luther. Go."

Luther cramps his way stage left, toward the bottom of the stairway, and says, " 'Come away, servant, come; I am ready now. Approach, my Ariel, come.' "

The sky darkens and the onstage lights dim, and Rafferty hears a howling wind, punctuated by crashing waves, and suddenly there's a sunburst at the very top of the rock as Miaow, wearing a waist-length shirt of little mirrors above black tights, is transfigured by a pure white spotlight, and she lifts her arms high, the brilliant mirrors flung out like an exploding star, and says, " 'All hail, great master! grave sir, hail!' " and Rafferty gets goose bumps.

"*That* works," Mrs. Shin says as she resumes her seat. "That'll wake them up."

Miaow is maneuvering her way down the uneven, curving staircase as though she's been walking it her entire life, throwing off points of light as effortlessly as she throws off her lines. The spotlight follows her, and down below, Luther realizes he's not standing in his own light and makes the adjustment.

"Look at her," Mrs. Shin says proudly. "She doesn't even check to see where she's putting her feet."

"She's been in more dangerous places than this," Rafferty says.

"She's going to be wonderful."

Four feet from the bottom of the stairway, Miaow makes a flying leap to the stage floor, leaving behind the follow spot, whose operator hadn't expected the jump. Mrs. Shin, who hadn't been expecting it either, starts and emits a mild "Eek." Miaow is all over the stage now, owning it, swooping and diving ceaselessly as she describes the storm she caused, the storm that drove onto the island the boat containing Prospero's evil brother and the king of Naples. As he watches and listens, Rafferty begins to feel an odd kind of tension, the sort of low-level electrical charge he experiences in his scalp and skin when he's close to working his way through a problem. Despite the sensation, which definitely demands attention, he's distracted by something very different in Miaow's voice, a quality that's nothing like how she had played the lines when he helped her learn them. He looks up at the stage and then glances over at Mrs. Shin to find her leaning on the back of the row of seats in front of them, staring at Miaow as though the entire speech is new, something Shakespeare, against all odds, just wrote.

"What in the world is she doing?" Mrs. Shin asks, although Rafferty doesn't think the question is addressed to him.

Miaow is certainly doing something. The tale of how she bewitched the ship and made all aboard terrified that they were about to drown, how she drove them to leap into the raging sea, and how she dispersed them around the island in small groups, is told with white-hot fury, as tightly focused as the flame from an acetylene torch. When she assures Prospero that the shipwrecked courtiers are all safe on solid ground, their clothing not even wet, she sounds bitterly regretful, as though she'd rather report they'd been flayed alive one at a time and their skins hung over bushes to dry. When, in answer to a question from Prospero, she describes the king's son sitting and sighing on a rock, " 'His arms in this sad knot,' " she accompanies the words with a petulant crossing of her arms, and she gets a laugh from offstage. Somebody else whistles, perhaps at the sheer amount of energy Miaow has just generated.

There's a silence. Luther has been so busy watching Miaow that he's forgotten his line. Now he turns to face the audience and asks, "Is she going to do it like that?"

"Good question," Mrs. Shin says, moving back into the aisle. "Mia. Where did *that* come from?"

Miaow takes a step back and looks down at the stage floor, and the spotlight goes out, and she's just a little girl again. Rafferty thinks she's going to retreat into sullenness. But she says, "Ariel hates them. She hates all of them."

"Why?"

"They're bad. Look what they did. How they stole everything from Prospero. How they put him and the baby—I mean Miranda, who didn't know anything and never hurt anybody—into a leaky boat and tried . . . tried to drown them. In the ocean. Like kittens nobody wants."

Rafferty feels a blaze of love for his daughter, but that little zigzag of electricity returns. Something he's missing . . .

"But Ariel doesn't care about Prospero, Mia," Mrs. Shin says reasonably. "It doesn't really matter to her whether Prospero succeeds in trapping his brother. Remember, Prospero is Ariel's master. He enslaved her, didn't he?"

"But first he *rescued* her," Miaow says, and her eyes dart to Rafferty for an instant, and then she looks down at the floor again. "And he . . . uh, he taught her stuff. And he took care of her."

Rafferty wants to get up and vault over the orchestra pit and hug his daughter, but she wouldn't speak to him for days. He hears Mrs. Shin talking to Miaow, but he's not following the words, he's thinking about the play. Prospero brought his enemies to his island. He didn't search out his enemies. He brought them to him.

He brought them to him.

24

Little Designs Here and There

On the phone Arthit says, "We've found three so far."

Rafferty is jammed up against the door on the passenger side of the cab, the bandaged elbow lifted awkwardly over his chest so he doesn't lean on it. The driver's seat is pushed all the way back, so Miaow had volunteered to sit behind it, but now she's toppled sideways, her head on her arm and her eyes closed. She's probably exhausted from the energy she burned on the stage. Her yellowish chop of hair is inches from Rafferty's knee, and it takes an effort not to rest a protective hand on it. But he doesn't want to wake her, and she'd hate it anyway, so he concentrates on speaking quietly into the phone. "That was quick," he says.

"I found a Phuket cop who's been assigned to an inactive post, and I offered him money. You owe me ten thousand baht, by the way. And he's only started."

"Inactive posts" are a uniquely Thai way of saving institutional face while dealing with the inept or the haplessly corrupt who get caught in plain sight; they're assigned to an empty desk in front of a bare wall and have to show up every day to punch the clock and sit there as they slowly descend into madness. The poor guy in Phuket probably leaped at the offer.

"You think there will be more?" Rafferty is looking out the window at a surprising flow of traffic for 4:00 P.M. They're doing maybe ten, twelve kilometers per hour.

"What I think is that he found records of three dead girls in about four hours," Arthit says. "Horner has been coming in and out of the country several times a year for almost twelve years. So yes, I think there will be more."

"And they match his dates here."

"So far. All either while he was here or within ten days after he left. The one who was found late had been in the water longer than the others."

"Any identities?"

"No. But they're all in their late teens or early twenties. Right in the range."

Rafferty glances over at Miaow, whose eyes are still closed, and cups the phone, bringing it so close to his mouth that his lips brush it. "What about cause of death?"

"They all had knife wounds. No real autopsies, so we don't know whether they were alive when they went into the water."

"When you say knife wounds . . ."

"I mean carved. Thirty or forty cuts. Shallow, deep, straight, curved. Little designs here and there. Wounds that would have taken time. He enjoyed himself."

"There would have been a lot of screaming," Rafferty says, practically whispering. He feels the driver's eyes on him in the mirror, and he stares back. The man, a turbaned Sikh, returns his gaze to the road. "No wonder he keeps going back to those rocks."

Arthit says, "There *will* be more, Poke."

"Son of a bitch. He almost had Rose."

"And if she's right," Arthit says, "he's got another one picked out right now."

"I've got some thoughts about how to nail him. If he hasn't already killed the new one, I mean."

"Officer Inactive Post is looking now at the period of time when Horner took that girl Oom out of the Candy Cane. Rose says Oom had a little tattoo, a heart, on her shoulder blade. All the girls are tattooed these days, but it was unusual back then. Even without an autopsy, somebody would have made a note of the tattoo. He's going through the case files, such as they are. So we'll see."

"See what?"

"Whether we can make this official. Get cops on it, above the table, not like Kosit and Anand."

"I need to think about that."

"Poke, I'm a cop. If we've got a witness who says Horner tried to kill her, and a body that's got the same tattoo as a girl he took to Phuket, there's a solid case. I'm going to have to bring the department in."

"One thing at a time, okay?" Rafferty says, "So far you haven't got it all."

"But I might in about ten minutes," Arthit says. He speaks more softly, a sign he wants to be listened to. "And just to remind you, there may be a girl right now who's—"

"Hold it," Rafferty says. The cab is slowing and slanting left, toward the curb. "What's happening?" he asks the driver.

The man behind the wheel avoids looking in the rearview mirror and shrugs. He says, "Sorry."

"Sorry for what?" The car stops next to a black SUV, a Land Rover or some other hulk. "Why are you stopping?" Rafferty leans forward, over the seat back, and on the driver's seat, an inch or two from the man's thigh, is a small digital print of a color photo: him and Miaow emerging from Mrs. Shin's *soi.*

Rafferty grabs the driver's shoulder, but the doors to the black SUV open and two very large men climb out. They're wearing camouflage pants, tight T-shirts, and motorcycle helmets with reflective visors, and the nearest one yanks open the door of Rafferty's cab and wraps big hands around Miaow's ankles.

She comes awake with a scream, instinctively kicking at the man's hands, but the man manages to snag the cuff of her jeans, and then he grasps the leg in both hands and pulls, putting his back into it, and Miaow, flailing with her one free leg, starts to slide across the backseat as the cab glides slowly into motion again. Rafferty manages to get his hands beneath her arms and pull, but the door behind him opens, and he pitches backward until he bumps up against someone—the second man—and an unyielding arm goes around his throat. The arm tightens until it cuts off his air, and he reflexively reaches up with one hand to pry it loose. Miaow pops out of his grip. She's snatching at everything in sight, but she's no match for the other man's strength, and she slips away, toward the open door. Flailing wildly, she starts to scream again, but then her shoulders clear the edge of the seat and she falls, the back of her head striking the bottom of the door with a sound like a cracking egg, and the next thing Rafferty knows, she's lying faceup on the pavement. The car continues to creep forward.

The man bends down to pick her up.

Rafferty reaches behind himself and finds the handle of the open door. He bangs it repeatedly against the man who's choking him, hitting his bad elbow against the front seat each time, but he hasn't got a good enough angle to do any damage. Still, it's an irritant, and the man shifts his weight to yank Rafferty out, and instead of resisting, Rafferty jams his legs against the driver's seat and shoves himself backward with all his strength. The man behind him, prepared for resistance, is sent staggering, obviously into the traffic lane, because there's a squeal of brakes, and he lets go of Rafferty's neck.

Rafferty turns and grabs the man's nearer hand, yanks it into the cab, and slams the door on the wrist, which is full of delicate little bones. The door rebounds open, and there's a rewarding bellow of pain, followed by the clamor of crumpling metal and breaking glass as one car rear-ends another.

Rafferty's almost out of the cab, pulling himself through the door Miaow vanished through, but she's four or five feet behind now, because the cab has continued to creep forward. As he slips through the door, he leans over and slugs the driver as hard as he can on the nape of the neck, just beneath the edge of the turban. The man's head snaps back and then forward, and he instinctively jams on the brakes so that Rafferty, prepared to move forward when he hits the pavement, is left windmilling his arms for balance.

The man who pulled Miaow from the cab is crouching beside her, slipping his arms beneath her shoulders and knees, so he's defenseless when she rolls onto her side and sinks both hands into his trousers at the crotch. His knees straighten convulsively, and Miaow comes up with him, dangling from his testicles, as the other man, the man whose wrist Rafferty just tried to break, blindsides Rafferty and knocks him sprawling. Rafferty lands heavily on the asphalt, his head ringing, and the man sidesteps to Rafferty's midsection, lifts a booted foot, and drives it into Rafferty's solar plexus. Then he does it again.

Rafferty's head and knees snap upward as though he's being folded in half. He feels like he's been yanked inside out and everything he's ever eaten in his life is coming back up, and he's vaguely aware of the cab rolling around the corner of a *soi*.

He rolls to one elbow—the bad one—to vomit, but the man above him grabs Rafferty's hair with both hands, hauling his shoulders up off the asphalt, and Rafferty reaches back, squeezes the bad wrist, and twists, trying to rotate the damaged bones. The man roars and tries to yank free. The other guy is backing away from Miaow now, dragging her along on the road's surface, her hands knotted on his scrotum. She's emitting a high, earsplitting squeal, as even and unvarying as an electronic alarm. Her assailant brings up a hand and hits her with a heavy slap that rocks her head and loosens her grip, and she pitches forward onto her stomach. The man brings back a foot to kick her.

Something breaks through the edge of Rafferty's vision, more a blur than an image, and the younger cop, Anand, flies through the air and hits the man above Miaow low in the abdomen, with a broad shoulder. The man has one leg upraised to boot Miaow, and he goes down, landing with all his weight on his left knee. He lets loose a red, throat-shredding scream, as much rage as pain, and grabs the knee, trying to rise, and the man whose wrist Rafferty is squeezing brings one of his knees into Rafferty's spine, just beneath the shoulder blades. Rafferty yanks on the damaged wrist, pulling the man sideways, to his left, and then tugs the wrist straight down, and the man drops helplessly to his knees, his free hand scrabbling in the pocket of his jeans and coming up with a leather sheath, about six inches long. Rafferty sees the bone handle of the knife and twists the wrist, trying to grind the bones to splinters, but the man doesn't seem to feel it as he uses his forearm to raise the visor on his helmet a few inches and pops the clasp over the handle with his teeth.

The square jaw is enough to confirm to Rafferty that the man is Horner.

At the sight of that face, Rafferty feels himself double in size with pure, burning fury. Nothing hurts, nothing is stiff or sore. The day brightens before his eyes, and his mind is moving so fast he can see the specks of dust floating between him and Horner, so fast it gives him time to plan the move that brings the palm of his free hand up sharply beneath the tip of the leather sheath, driving it up, tearing Horner's lip and maybe breaking an incisor, then smashing into his nose. Horner's mouth goes wide with pain, and blood spurts from his nose, and Rafferty grabs the sheath and jerks it away, but the knife slips out of it, glinting in the sunlight, still in Horner's hand. Feeling as though he has all the time in the world, Rafferty slaps both hands on the sides of the helmet and lifts up, popping the helmet off like a bottle cap, and then he slams Horner's forehead with the heel of his hand, driving it into the door of the stopped car behind him, and when Horner's head bounces back, Rafferty does it again as the car's driver twists her own head around, looking horrified. When the head bounces this time, Rafferty can see the dent in the door.

But as he raises his hand to strike again, there's a scuffling sound, and he snaps his head around to see Anand with his arm encircling the throat of the man—it has to be John—who pulled Miaow from the cab. John uses the strength of panic to bend forward sharply enough to pull Anand off his feet, turning him into a sort of human knapsack, then straightens abruptly and brings his head back trying to smash Anand's nose.

Motion to the left, and Rafferty instinctively jumps away. Horner leaps toward Rafferty with a deep grunt of effort, the knife slicing air in a long arc that barely misses Rafferty's face and chest. All Rafferty can do is retreat as Horner slides forward without raising his feet, the knife cutting from side to side like jagged writing in the air, and then Rafferty feels his shoulder strike something or someone, and Kosit shouts into his ear, "Don't *move*!" He's beside Rafferty, his gun extended, pointing at the center of Horner's chest.

Rafferty glances over and sees Anand holding a gun on John as Miaow gets to her feet. Her cheeks are wet and shiny, and the left side of her face is scarlet where she was hit, but she seems more angry than frightened.

Kosit says, "Drop the knife."

Horner's eyes shift left and right, and he finds himself in front of the gap between the grille of the black SUV and the trunk of another car. Behind him the sidewalk is dense with people, even more than usual, since dozens have stopped to watch the fight and the rear-end collision. Horner takes a deliberate step back, between the cars.

Kosit says again, "Don't move."

Horner grins, his teeth large and square. He says, "Fuck you."

"I'm telling you—" Kosit says.

Horner retreats another step, putting him close to the crowd. People are trying to move away now, but they're held in place by the press of bodies behind them. "Nine-millimeter," Horner says, stepping back again. "Let's say you hit me. Odds are, it'll go through. You ready to kill whoever's behind me?"

Kosit says, "I'll risk it."

Horner clears his throat and spits at Rafferty. Then he says, "No you won't." With a quick, fluid movement, he's up on the curb, straight-arming his way into the crowd. His head, with its distinctive, short-cut helmet of hair, rises above the dark hair of the Thais, but there's little Kosit can do except watch him shoulder a path for himself until he's broken through, and then he begins to run.

Kosit takes off after him, staying in the street, and then something cracks against the side of Rafferty's head, knocking him sideways, and he looks up to see John run past him, only slightly favoring the knee he landed on. John dodges into traffic, and Rafferty sees the same broad back he had chased into the Beer Garden—how many days ago?

Across this very road.

Anand is already chasing John, but Rafferty grabs the back of his shirt and shouts, "Stay with Miaow!" then plunges into the traffic, in time to see John leap onto the center island, his arms extended to his left, palms out, to signal the traffic on the other side to stop. Miraculously, it does, and John darts across the three center lanes, still looking to his left when he enters the last lane, the reverse-direction lane where the traffic is coming from his right, and there's a tremendous rush of air under pressure, a loud, rasping horn, and a panicked squeal of brakes, and a bus slams into John, knocks him, limp-jointed, about eight feet, and then runs over him. The bus is still fighting to come to a stop when the truck that's following it hits what's left of John like he's a speed bump.

Rafferty is at the center island by then, and he realizes that Kosit is standing beside him, panting with his jaw hanging open. John is crumpled across the asphalt, his silhouette so broken he looks like clothes draped over a scattering of rocks. A wide pool of dark liquid surrounds his head.

Rafferty snatches at Kosit's sleeve and says, "Come on."

"But," Kosit says, "he's—"

"If you're a cop for sixty years," Rafferty says, "you'll never see any-one any deader. Let's get out of here."

He tows Kosit back through traffic that has come to a total stop as drivers gape at the accident on the other side. "Horner?" he asks.

"Gone. The cab was waiting for him."

"Well, hell." They jog over toward Miaow and Anand.

Kosit says, "When you tell Arthit about this, make something up. Something where Anand and I come out looking good."

"Horner's a pro," Rafferty says. "This is what he does for a living. There's one down anyway." Miaow sees him coming and drops Anand's hand. She runs to Rafferty and throws both arms around him. He hugs her so tightly she squeaks. "Are you all right?"

She wriggles free. "I have a headache."

"We'll get you to a doctor."

Miaow steps back to get a better look at his face. "It's a *headache.* I don't need a doctor."

"Well, you're going to get one."

"What's he going to say? 'Looks like you bumped your head'?" Then, with no transition, she's crying, and Rafferty kneels in front of her, his hands on her shoulders.

Anand comes up to them, seeming younger than ever. "Sorry, sorry. I looked at the one who ran first, and my guy clobbered me." He glances across the street, eyebrows raised in a question.

Rafferty says, "Over there."

"I heard the brakes. Dead?"

"By a broad margin." Rafferty rises, a hand on Miaow's shoulder. "Come on."

"We're cops," Kosit says. "We should—"

"You do what you want. I'm leaving. Although maybe Anand should stay and take care of having the SUV towed, get somebody tracing its papers. Anand, you don't know anything about the guy across the street, okay?"

Kosit and Anand exchange glances.

Rafferty says, "There's no way to explain this without bringing it all down on Arthit's head."

Kosit nods. "You didn't see anything," he tells Anand. He starts toward his car and says over his shoulder, "You'll both ride with me."

"Fine," Rafferty says. "Now."

Anand says, following, "Both of those guys, when we first saw them, did you notice?"

"Thanks for helping Miaow," Rafferty says, rubbing a circle in the center of her back.

"She was helping herself," Anand says. "Did you notice their clothes?"

"No. There wasn't time to—"

Anand looks questioningly at Kosit, who's opening the door of an unmarked car. Kosit says, "I didn't notice anything either."

"I did," Miaow says. She sniffles and wipes her face with her forearm. "The man who pulled me out of the car had blood all over him."

25

The Continent of Red

They're down to three now—Rafferty, Miaow, and Kosit, since Anand is waiting for the tow truck. Miaow takes Rafferty's hand as they cross the apartment-house lobby toward the elevator. After everything that's happened, he's not sure which of them the gesture is meant to comfort.

"Don't call Arthit yet," he says to Kosit. "I don't want him making a fuss."

"What's the problem?" Kosit says. "These guys should get caught, and fast, and we—I mean, the cops—are better at that than you are."

"I'll tell you and Arthit at the same time." The elevator doors slide open. "I know that your people can probably catch him. What I'm worried about is whether they'll hold him."

"What does that mean?"

"Later. I need to talk to someone first anyway."

"Who?" The elevator does its usual pre-ascent shudder of dread, and Miaow squeezes Rafferty's hand, a sure sign that she's still off balance. She's ridden this elevator hundreds of times since he and Rose adopted her off the street. He squeezes back in what he hopes is a reassuring manner.

"A guy with the American government, here in Bangkok."

"That little squeaker from the Secret Service?" Kosit has met Richard Elson and wasn't impressed.

"The very one."

"Why? What can he tell you?"

"I don't know. Right now let's just go into the apartment, get Rose's camera, and get out again. We need those pictures more than we need anything else."

Without looking up, Miaow says, "It's nice to be back."

"We'll be back for keeps in a few days," Rafferty says.

Miaow says, "How do you know?" and Kosit looks away to hide a smile.

"Good question," Rafferty says.

"Don't do that. I'm not a baby."

"Well," Rafferty says, "you're *my* baby."

Miaow says, "Ick." The elevator stops and the doors open, and she drops his hand and bolts through, into the corridor, where she stops like someone who's run into a punch. She says, "Oh, no."

Rafferty and Kosit shoulder each other getting off. They halt in unison behind Miaow.

The apartment door has been split down the middle. It sags inward crookedly, hanging by one hinge.

Miaow says, "The *floor*."

Rafferty looks down and sees a trail of bloody footprints coming out of the apartment, leading to the emergency stairwell.

He grabs Miaow by the shoulders and shoves her at Kosit, then reaches past him to stop the elevator doors from closing. "Get her downstairs," he says.

Miaow pulls away, but Rafferty pushes her back, not gently, and Kosit gets a grip on her this time. He says, "Take my gun."

"You keep it. You've got her with you. Go, go."

The elevator doors close, and Rafferty can hear Miaow protesting all the way down. Not until the elevator stops moving does he turn back to the shattered door.

He follows the bloody tracks with his eyes. *Blood all over him*, Miaow had said. There are two doors he needs to look through, but the one that terrifies him is the one leading into his apartment, so, moving parallel to the bloody footprints, he makes his way to the door to the emergency stairs. He yanks his T-shirt away from his belly and puts his hand inside it to turn the doorknob.

Footprints lead down, two pair, undoubtedly Horner's and dead John's, fading as they go. He lets the door sigh closed and turns back around and almost chokes on his breath. The door to Mrs. Pongsiri's apartment is wide open.

He feels enormously heavy, nailed to the floor by his weight. He can see it all. Horner and John kicking in the door, Mrs. Pongsiri— already alerted by having found the red X—hearing the noise and going to investigate. She comes down the hall and into the apartment. They're inside, knives in hand, ready to kill anyone who's there. She's seen them.

He can't face this. After everything that's happened in the past few days, he can't face this. He reaches for the phone in his pocket, thinking to call Kosit. Kosit's a cop. He knows how to deal with these things.

But Kosit's with Miaow, and he can't have Miaow up here. And then a wave of heat flows through him, and he thinks, S*he might be alive.*

He's running without even knowing it, and he plunges through the door and sees the small figure dead center in the continent of red that's been mapped onto the far end of his carpet. She's facing away from him as though she's reclining on the floor, idly looking out through the cracked sliding glass door. Her wig—he never knew she wore a wig— has been wrenched sideways, and the hair beneath it is steel gray and cropped as short as a Buddhist nun's. Her neck looks slender enough to break with a pencil.

She's not moving.

He tracks his way around the blood. She's so tiny. She's wearing a loose, flowery print dress that's multicolored on the top of her body but a rusty brownish red beneath. It's been torn, he sees, the hem ripped right off it.

When he's in front of her, he drops to his knees, trying to make sense of what he's looking at: The strip of cloth from her dress, wrapped around her arm, the arm outstretched on the carpet. The broom, which he had left standing beside the balcony door, protruding through the cloth, which has been twisted tight. The long gash in her arm.

It's a tourniquet. She made a tourniquet. It's held tight by the weight of her arm on top of the rigid broomstick. She made a tourniquet that wouldn't loosen even if she passed out. He leans in and sees her nostrils flare.

He jumps up, dialing the phone as he goes. In the bedroom he rips a blanket from the bed and drags it behind him into the living room, doubles it for extra warmth, and throws it over her, seeing the other cuts, five or six of them, as he does so. When the emergency response service answers, he gives them the address and the apartment number and then hangs up and dials Kosit.

"Get up here. Don't let Miaow come in."

He hangs up and runs to the closet, sweeps everything from the front of the top shelf, and stretches for the box. He's got the little yellow camera in his hand by the time Kosit comes in and freezes at the sight of the draped blanket in the circle of blood, the little head sticking out of it.

"My neighbor," Rafferty says. "They cut her a few times and slashed her wrist, but she's alive. Anything you can do?"

"I can call for an ambulance."

"I've done that." He hands Kosit the camera. "Take Miaow and get to Arthit's as fast as you can. I need the pictures from this thing now, whatever it takes. And tell Rose I need the women from her agency there, as many as possible, around six-thirty. Go on, go on, get out of here."

"What are you going to do?"

"Stay with her. Wait for the ambulance."

"What are you going to tell the cops?"

Rafferty says, "Go."

He hears a gasp from the doorway and turns to see Miaow, holding on to the jamb as though she's about to go down. She says, "Who . . . who . . . ?"

"Mrs. Pongsiri. She's alive. Kosit, please get out of here. Miaow, you're going with him."

"Where?" She's staring at the blanket, at the broadening stain on the carpet.

"Arthit's. I'll be there in a little bit." Neither of them moves. "Miaow, I need you to go with Kosit. Both of you, get out of here."

He turns his back on them and goes to sit in front of Mrs. Pongsiri. He puts his hand on top of her outstretched arm. When he looks up, they're both gone.

He stays there, holding the warm, smooth hand and willing life into her, until he hears the siren growl to a stop in the street below. Then he says to Mrs. Pongsiri, "They'll take care of you," and gets up. Being careful not to step in the blood, he goes back into the corridor and through the door into the stairwell. When he hears the elevator doors open, followed by the emergency medical technicians' voices, he climbs the stairs to the ninth floor and then takes the elevator down. He passes through the glass doors of the apartment house without a glance at the waiting ambulance and fades down the street, into the thickening dusk.

26

No Commonly Accepted
Index for Improbability

Arthit says, "You're putting me in an impossible position."

Rafferty has dried blood on his hand from when he pushed himself up from the carpet beside Mrs. Pongsiri. The sight of it makes him dizzy with anger. "Well, I'm sorry about that, but I don't know what else I can do."

"What *else* you can do? You're leaving a trail of bodies across Bangkok, and you won't even talk to the cops."

"Body," Rafferty snaps. "*One* body. Mrs. Pongsiri is alive. And the other one, John, fuck him. Anybody disagree with that?" He gets up from the armchair, too rattled to sit. "And would you like to tell me what I've done? Did I kill someone? Seriously, Arthit, you want to tell me how I'm responsible? And where are those pictures?"

He, Arthit, and Rose are in Arthit's living room, Arthit on the couch and Rose in the armchair that matches the one Rafferty just vacated. There's a clatter from the kitchen, where Miaow and Pim are unpacking take-out food and laying out plates and utensils. It's quarter past six.

"I only got them an hour ago." Arthit stands, too, unwilling to give Rafferty the height advantage. "They're on rush, they'll be ready soon. But I don't know whether I'll let you have them."

"Whether you'll—"

"This can't continue. It's time for the cops."

Several responses go through Rafferty's mind, all of them hurtful. He says, "Let me call Elson."

"Poke." Arthit stops, breathes deeply, and continues. "What in the world does an American Secret Service agent have to do with any of this?"

Rafferty says, "I want this guy to go down. Forever."

"And I don't? Every time the phone rings, there's another dead girl in those records in Phuket."

"They found Oom," Rose tells Rafferty. "The right time, the tattoo."

Arthit says, "You don't trust the police? The Thai justice system?"

Rafferty doesn't even think about it. "No."

His face reddening, Arthit says, "You're slandering a lot of good people."

"If the police are such crackerjacks, tell me how a dozen bodies, or however many it is, all killed the same way, can just wash up in Phuket, like Japanese glass fishing floats, with nobody hearing about it?"

Arthit's shaking his head by the time Rafferty is halfway through the sentence. "That's different."

"How? How is it—"

"Phuket is a tourist destination. It's still recovering from the tsunami. They're not going to publicize a serial—"

"Oh, well, that inspires confidence. Let the girls die, but, please, no bad PR."

"They were working the case," Arthit says, barely moving his lips. "But quietly."

"And look at all the progress."

Arthit holds up both hands. "You can argue with me until the sun comes up. The police are getting involved. Now."

"If you bring the cops into this, you'll regret it until you die."

"This country is not completely corrupt, no matter what you believe."

"If it makes you feel any better," Rafferty says, "I don't trust my government either."

Rose says, "He should be dead."

They both look at her. Arthit is expressionless, wearing what Rafferty thinks of as his cop face. "Obviously, I can't guarantee that," Arthit tells her. "But what are you saying, Poke? That if the police aren't involved, you're going to kill him?"

"Here's what I'm saying: Your colleagues may catch him, but they won't keep him. Where are you going?"

Halfway to the dining room, Arthit says, "You dodged my question. That's another reason for me to do what I should have done this afternoon."

"He'll never see a Thai courtroom," Rafferty says.

"I'm not a judge," Arthit says. He picks up his cell phone from the dining-room table. "I don't try them, I just arrest them."

Rafferty raises his voice, knowing it means he's losing the argument. "He killed four women— Wait, how many is it now?"

Rose says, "Five."

"All cut?"

"Just like Oom," Rose says.

"Okay, then, *five* women. Five that we know of. And you said it yourself, Arthit, there are going to be more. He tried to kill Rose. He and the other one cut and beat a woman in her sixties just because she came down the hall to see what the noise was."

Arthit says, "All the more reason to catch him."

"They tried to steal my daughter so she could lead them to Rose. What would they have done to Rose? What do you think they would have done with Miaow afterward? Buy her candy?" Rafferty hears the stridency in his voice but can't modulate it. "She's a *kid*, Arthit."

Arthit lowers the phone. "Listen to yourself. Look at the case against Horner, the one you've just laid out. Look at the witnesses: Rose, about both her and Oom. You and *two cops,* about what happened to you and Miaow today. Mrs. Pongsiri, since the doctors seem to think she'll make it. He'll never see daylight again."

"He'll never stand trial," Rafferty says. "He'll get sold."

Arthit says, "Sold?"

"Like the cheapest car on the lot."

"To whom, Poke?" Arthit's mouth is pinched tight. "Think about it for a minute. Even if my colleagues were corrupt enough, or stupid enough, to sell a serial killer after all the publicity this case will get, who'd have enough money? Because for that kind of corruption, we're talking seven figures, and I don't mean baht."

Rose says, "He only killed bar girls. That's not the same as killing *people.*"

Rafferty says, "Let me call Elson."

Arthit starts to reply to Rose and then looks from her to Rafferty. Something seems to unfold behind his eyes. He puts the cell phone on the polished table and spins it with his forefinger. Glances down at it and then back over at Rafferty. He says, "You're shitting me."

"Let me make the call."

Arthit spins the phone again, giving it all his attention. "You can't mean what I think you mean. But even if you do, it's not going to change anything."

"Then there's no reason not to call."

"This is your government we're talking about."

"Times have changed," Rafferty says. "My government has changed with them." He pulls out his own cell phone just as Pim and Miaow come into the room, each carrying a big tray full of take-out containers, plates, and glasses. Miaow has cleaned herself up from the scuffle of the afternoon and is once again the kind of shiny-faced immaculate that Rafferty always associates with her, but her eyes are a little too quick, a little too skittish. She looks as if a loud noise would send her diving through the window. Pim has discarded her garish street clothes in favor of one of Arthit's T-shirts as a dress, belted with a necktie. The shirt comes down almost to her knees.

Rafferty looks at the necktie and tries to lower the room's temperature by asking, "Are those snakes?"

"Cobras," Arthit says. "Thanom gave it to me for Christmas. I think there was some sort of threat implied."

"Can you make room on the table?" Miaow asks. "These are heavy."

Arthit says, from the dining room, "Over here."

"Listen," Rafferty says. "I need everybody to be quiet. I'm putting this call on speaker, but I'm not going to tell the guy I'm talking to. He'd have a heart attack."

He waits until Miaow and Pim have put down the trays, and then he waves everyone quiet again and dials. On the third ring, he checks his watch—6:21 P.M.—but then Elson picks up.

Rafferty raises the phone to his lips so he won't sound like he's on speaker. "Richard. Poke Rafferty."

Elson says, "Yeah?" He sounds like someone who expects to be asked for a loan.

"And a big hi to you, too."

"You're calling after hours. Means you don't want to talk on an office phone. How'd you get my cell number?"

"You gave it to me. Back when Frank—my father—was here."

"You should have torn it up."

"You should have changed it. But how's this? I'll erase it after this call."

Elson sighs into the phone. "What is it, then?"

"It's a hypothetical."

"I've been waiting all day for a hypothetical."

"Good. Then I'll lay it out and you tell me how probable or improbable it is."

There's a pause, and then Elson says, "Do you need a prompt to get started?"

"No. Okay, a guy working for a defense contractor, let's say Grayhawk or one of those, he's engaged on missions for the U.S. in . . . oh, I don't know, the Middle East, and while he's in a third country—"

"Third?"

"Neither the U.S. nor the country his mission is in."

"Okay."

"So in this third country he gets into very serious trouble. Let's say he kills several people. Kills them ugly. Let's say they're defenseless women. Let's say there are more than *several.*"

In the silence that follows, Rafferty can hear Elson doing something that sounds like jingling the change in his pocket. "Is this public knowledge? In your hypothetical, I mean."

"No. Nobody's heard a word about it except the people who are directly involved. And then let's say he's arrested in the third country and the American embassy is contacted as a courtesy, as they always are."

For a moment Rafferty thinks Elson has hung up. But then he says, "Yes?"

"How improbable is it that the U.S. would make a secret arrangement to spirit him out?"

"As opposed, for instance, to having a sensational trial that they can't control."

"Exactly."

"All right, let me make sure I have this straight. An employee of an American contractor, on a mission in, hypothetically, Afghanistan, does something horrific in another country, hypothetically Thailand, and the issue is whether, either in the State Department or in the Department of Defense, there might be a black-ops budget with minimum oversight, so nobody with any rank would be involved if the situation blew up in their faces, and whether that hypothetical budget has money in it that could be used to yank that contractor out of the third country before the media circus makes the U.S. look like bloodthirsty savages and the Senate starts demanding hearings into the war effort and secret budgets and the impeachment of the president. Umm, let's see, and that there are also people in the right places who have access to that budget and would be willing to spend it. Is that about it?"

"Very good."

"And also reopen the whole basic issue about contractors."

"Which issue?"

"About how they're not there because they were drafted. About how they volunteered and even competed for a slot where their basic job is to kill people. And about how there are always going to be psychopaths among them, no matter how stridently the people in charge deny it."

Arthit's eyes meet Rafferty's.

"Yeah," Rafferty says. "All those issues."

"And you want to know what, exactly?"

"How improbable it is that the government would spring a guy like that."

"Hmmm." Rafferty can envision the reflection on Elson's glasses as he lifts his chin, the man's thin lips tightening as he thinks. "Tell you what. There's no commonly accepted index for improbability that I know about. So why don't you give me an example of something improbable, and I'll tell you whether your scenario is less or more improbable than that."

Rafferty looks up to find Arthit's eyes still on him. Arthit mouths one word: *Frank*.

Rafferty nods and says, "Off the top of my head, okay? Let's say a U.S. government agency takes an Anglo man who needs to hide out for the rest of his life and assigns him a false identity that was originally set up for a Chinese man, without even changing the Chinese man's name, although the guy hiding out isn't Chinese. As improbable as that?"

"It's exactly that improbable. And you wouldn't believe how improbably large that budget would be, if there were such a budget."

"Improbable as it is, what would happen to the contractor after he was returned to the States?"

"Whatever it would be," Elson says, "you'd never hear about it. Are you finished?"

Rafferty says, "Am I ever," and hangs up.

From the dining room, Miaow says, "But that's what he did with your father. He gave him—"

"That's right," Rafferty says.

Arthit says, "I need to think about this."

"Think about it fast," Rose says, getting up and going into the dining room. "The girls will be here any minute. Miaow, we need more glasses and things."

Arthit says, "The girls?"

"I really need those pictures, Arthit," Rafferty says.

Arthit shakes his head as though he needs to clear it. "What girls?"

"From my agency," Rose says. "At least eight more glasses, Miaow. And, Pim, could you please make some tea?"

"How come you say please to Pim but not to me?" Miaow asks, heading for the kitchen.

Rose says, "Because I like her better."

Miaow makes a rude noise as she leaves the room.

"I don't need a maid," Arthit says. "I told Poke I don't—"

"You certainly do need a maid," Rose says. "This place is 'man clean,' but that's not the same as clean. Why don't you hire Pim?"

"Pim, Pim, Pim," Miaow says from the kitchen. Scarlet-faced, Pim flees the room.

Arthit says, quite loudly, "Everybody. *Stop.*"

Everybody stops except Pim, who runs all the way to the kitchen. The moment stretches out, totally silent. Arthit blinks in surprise.

Rafferty says, "What now, Arthit? Can we start again?"

"At least with the food and the glasses," Rose says.

There's a knock at the door. Rafferty pulls out his Glock, which has been tucked into his waistband ever since he got there.

Rose says, "What? You're going to shoot Fon?"

"You stay where you are. I'll answer the door." Rafferty puts the gun hand behind his back and crosses the room, and he finds Arthit beside him, his own gun in hand. When they get to the door, Arthit waves Rafferty aside so he'll be right behind the door when it opens, turns sideways to hide his gun and present a smaller target, and, with a nod to Rafferty, yanks the door open.

Fon takes a surprised step back and says, "Hi."

27

We're Going
to Create a Storm

here are nine of them in all, and Rose's partner, Peachy,
makes ten. With the exception of Peachy, who's wearing
enough makeup to sing opera, the women are scrubbed and
natural, their hair pulled back simply into ponytails or braids. Fon's
hair has been gathered on top of her head and rubber-banded, the hair
exploding straight up and then fanning out like a little black volcano.
Except for two of them, Fon and Rose, they retain little of the allure
they'd once projected onstage in the bars of Patpong. Some of them are
so determinedly plain it looks intentional, a way of erasing who they
were in the past.

They're sitting on the floor, most of them with their feet tucked politely to one side, each with a cup of tea or one of Miaow's dwindling
supply of Cokes. Five or six of them are smoking, as is Rose. Every time
Miaow comes into the room, she fans her hand and makes a face. A few
of the women blow smoke at her.

A piece of paper is being passed from hand to hand. One of the
women scans it and says, "The Kit-Kat."

"Good," Rafferty says, writing it on his own piece of paper. "That's twenty-seven."

Fon says, "What's that upstairs place up near Surawong? Used to be the Baby Bar?"

"The Lap Bar," Rafferty says. "We've got it."

"I'm getting old," Fon says. "That's where you and Arthit went to scare my little sister. I've blanked it from my mind. And it was only a few days ago."

"Poke terrified her," Arthit says from his chair at the dining-room table, where he's watching the proceedings with a certain amount of bemusement.

"He has that effect on women," Rose says. She looks at her own list. "I've got twenty-eight. The Lap Bar makes twenty-nine."

"The Butterfly," says one of the other women. "And Lolita's, ugh. And I think Poke's cute."

Writing the names of the bars, Rafferty says, "I think I'm cute, too. I've only got twenty-eight."

"So I've got one more than you do," Rose says to him. "Why don't I read my list, and everybody try to figure out if we're missing any."

"Sounds like a plan." Rafferty gets up from the floor, feeling as if every muscle in his body has been hammered by dwarfs. He walks stiffly down the hallway to the kitchen, where Pim and Miaow are tossing paper plates and scraping leftovers into Baggies. "This is what I like to see," he says. "The next generation of womanhood, turning its back on feminism."

Miaow shows him a white container that holds about an ounce of some kind of chicken with sauce. "Is this worth keeping?"

"Was it good?"

She shrugs. "It was okay."

"Gimme." He takes it away from her and picks up a used plastic fork.

Miaow says, "Eeeeewww. Disgusting."

"We are all one," Rafferty says, wiggling his eyebrows mysteriously, and Pim laughs. "You're right," he says, eating. "It's just okay. How's your head?"

"If we're all one," Miaow says, "you shouldn't have to ask."

"I guess that means you're all right." He scrapes up the rest of the chicken, which has turned out to be lobster. "You were great today," he says.

"When?"

"On the stage. As Ariel."

The hand in which Miaow held the food container is still extended, but she's forgotten it. She says, "Really?"

"Really. You're the best thing in the play, and Mrs. Shin knows it."

"Siri's good," Miaow says with a sideways glance at him.

"Miaow. She's awful. She's pretty, but she thinks she's in a silent movie."

"Are you really acting in a play?" Pim asks.

"Sort of." Miaow is suddenly very busy wiping her hands on her jeans.

"I always wanted to be a movie star," Pim says. She blushes a deep red.

"It's only a school play," Miaow says. She is talking directly to the tabletop. "Just kids."

Pim says, *"Still."*

"She's terrific," Rafferty says. "You can come with us when we go to see it."

Miaow straightens slightly, but then she gives Pim a quick look, sees just a normal, everyday, plump teenager in a T-shirt, and her shoulders relax.

"Can I really?" Pim asks. She directs the question to Miaow, not Rafferty.

Miaow says, "It'll be boring."

"Oh, no. I've never seen a play."

Rafferty says to Miaow, "And you know when else you were terrific today?"

Miaow almost smiles. "Yes."

"When you grabbed that guy's balls."

Pim drops a fork on the floor and stoops to pick it up.

"Street trick," Miaow says. "Boo taught me." Boo is the street kid who took care of Miaow when she was first abandoned on the Bangkok sidewalks.

"He'd have been proud of you."

"Oh, no," she says. "He'd have been a critic. He'd have told me I did it all wrong. He'd have given me lessons." She takes the empty container out of Rafferty's hand and reaches for the fork. Looking at the fork, she says, "The man got killed, didn't he?"

"Yes."

She drops the fork into the container and drops the container into the trash. "Good."

"And you know that Mrs. Pongsiri is going to be okay."

Miaow nods. "Yes."

"And you're sure your head doesn't hurt."

She finally smiles at him. "Leave me alone."

"I'm not supposed to. It's my job."

Pim says, "What is?"

"Being her dad. Not that she makes it easy."

Pim says, "I've noticed."

BACK IN THE LIVING ROOM, Rose says, "Volcano Bar," and two hands go up. She writes the women's names and says, "Bangkok Strip." One hand. Rose says, "Gosh, Nit, you really got around," and the other women laugh.

Nit, who has chiseled, highly defined hill-tribe features and pale skin that betray her Chinese blood, says, "If I had a thousand baht for every bar I danced in, I wouldn't be mopping floors."

"Well, we'd miss you." Rose looks down at the page. "So there are only six bars none of us ever worked in."

"That's kind of sad," Fon says, and the women laugh again.

Peachy, who's been sitting on the sidelines, says, "Were some bars better than others?" She's the only woman in the room who's never worked in the sex industry.

"Yes and no," Nit says. "They were like the houses we clean, but smokier. Some people are good to work for and some aren't. You know, some of them cheat you—"

"All the bars cheat you," another woman says.

"But some are worse than others. Some of them steal your drink commissions or say you missed days when you actually showed up, so they can fine you. Some of them want you to go with every man who asks you. They fine you if they think you said no too often."

Peachy says, "Oh, my." She clasps her hands in her lap, a gesture that always makes Rose think Peachy would be happier wearing white lace gloves. "What *about* the men?"

"They're the same in every bar," Fon says. "They're the same everywhere in the world."

"Not here," Rafferty says. "Arthit and I are princes."

There's a knock at the door. Arthit gets up, saying to Rafferty, "Sit. One gun is enough."

"A gun?" Nit asks.

"Joking," Arthit says, picking his way between the women. There's another, louder knock. "Cop," he announces. "Only cops are that rude." He disappears around the corner of the hallway, and they hear the door open. Arthit comes back in with Kosit in tow. Kosit is holding a large manila envelope.

Rose says, "Let me see them."

"Wait," Kosit says. He opens the flap on the envelope and sorts through the pictures with a fingernail, without removing them. Then he pulls one out and holds it to his belly so only the back shows, and he hands the envelope to Rose.

She lifts her chin in the direction of the one he's hiding. "What's that one?"

"Not Horner," Kosit says.

"Then who? I took the pictures, and I think they're all of—"

"You didn't take this one."

"Okay," Rose says, sliding the pictures out of the envelope. "Be mysterious." She flips through them, her face rigid with distaste. "These are better," she says. "This is the best." She holds up a color photo of Horner, a medium shot that shows him sitting at a table in what appears to be an open-air restaurant. He's wearing a T-shirt and leaning back in his chair, supremely confident. He'd been eating when Rose pushed the shutter, and he has a knife in his hand, point upward.

"Oh," Nit says, looking startled. "I remember him."

Arthit says, "Did he take someone from your bar?"

"A few girls, I think. I went with him once or twice."

Peachy fans herself.

"You're sure it's the same man?" Arthit asks. "After all this time?"

"He's handsome," Nit says, as though that explains it. "I went with him."

"Which bar?"

"Not in Patpong. Over on Soi Cowboy. The Play Room. It's closed now."

"Did all the girls come back? I mean, after they went away with him, did any of them disappear?"

"Maybe." Nit looks over at Rose and then back at Arthit. "Why are we talking about him?"

Arthit says, "Before you go any further with this, Poke, I want to cover two things. First, I want to make sure that everyone here knows that this man has killed at least five bar girls."

Peachy gasps theatrically, but the other women just look at one another. Nit, eyes narrowed, says, "Five's a lot."

"There are probably more," Arthit says.

"Her name was Ploy," Nit says. She shifts as though the floor has become uncomfortable. "He took her for a few weeks at a time for almost a year, and then he bought her out for a month and she didn't come back."

"Nobody worried about her?" Arthit says.

"She told us she thought they might get married and she wouldn't be working anymore."

Rose says, "Fon. Remember when we talked about me marrying him?"

"Yes. It was pouring. The rain ruined my hair."

"That was his idea. He said it would be good for me to talk it over with someone."

"So you tell Fon and Fon tells everybody in the bar," Rafferty says. "And when the girl doesn't come back, nobody pays attention."

Arthit says to Nit, "When did he take Ploy?" He's pulled a pad from his trouser pocket and is looking for a pen. Rose extends hers, and he takes it.

"Mmmmm, hard to say. Four years ago? Five? Maybe 2005."

"Do we have one in 2005?" Rafferty asks.

"In the first bunch he found," Arthit says. To the women he says, "We have a cop looking through unsolved cases to find women this man might have killed. What month did he take Ploy?"

Nit says, "I don't know. Summer, I think."

"She washed up in August," Arthit says. He puts his left hand on top of his right shoulder and rubs, hard. "God*damn* him."

Nit says, in a tiny voice, "Ploy was a nice girl."

"Here's the second thing," Arthit says. "I want Poke to tell all of you—and me, while he's at it—exactly what he's got in mind for you. What he wants you to do, and why, and how he's going to guarantee your safety."

"Fine." Rafferty sits. "We're going to create a storm, and we're going to wait for him to come to us."

"A *storm*?" Arthit says. "It must be nice to have the time to be metaphorical."

"Mapmakers used to use figures of gods or beasts blowing on the water to indicate prevailing winds and storm areas. That's what we're going to do, we're going to blow on the water. We're going to create a magical storm area just for Howard Horner, one that won't affect anyone else. We'll fix it so every bar worker and every vendor in Patpong, hundreds of people, will recognize him on sight. We're going to find the bar his current girl works in, and if he hasn't taken her already, we're going to spirit her away. When he comes into the bar, he'll be told she's gone out to eat and that he should wait for her. Then they'll call us. If he goes into a different bar, or if someone spots him on the sidewalk, they'll call us."

"Who will?" Rose asks.

"The mama-san. The girls. The only real problem is if he's already taken her down to Phuket, but I doubt that, because we just saw him and we hurt him."

"He's not going to slow down because he's hurt," Rose says. "As long as he can walk, he'll come up with some story and use it to make the girl feel sorry for him. Then he can flatter her, tell her only she can make him feel better."

"Even if he's on his way down there," Arthit says, "there are two cops at the airport in Phuket with these pictures. He won't make it out of the terminal."

"So," Rafferty says, "here's what we're going to do: In half an hour or so, we're going to go to the copy shop on Silom at the foot of Patpong and make about ninety color photocopies of the picture Rose is holding. Then the women here tonight, the ones who agree to help, will go into the bars they used to work in and talk to the mama-san. The idea is to get the mama-san to let you stand at the edge of the stage as each shift comes off and to make sure all the girls see the picture. Every girl, even the ones who are in the restroom. If girls are out on short-times, the mama-san will show them the picture when they come back in."

"And you think they'll all remember him if he comes in?" Arthit asks.

"If we tell them that he killed those women. That should get their attention." Rafferty looks back at the women. "Oh, I kind of messed his face up—"

"Good for you," Nit says.

"So you should tell them he might have some injuries, maybe even bandages."

Kosit, who's been standing near Rose with the photo still pressed to his stomach, says, "Wait a minute." He navigates between the seated women to the dining room and shows the picture to Arthit, then leans down and whispers into Arthit's ear. When he sees the photo, Arthit's upper lip lifts to reveal his teeth, and he darts a look at Rose. He turns his attention back to the photograph.

He says to Kosit, "Good idea."

Kosit says, "This is ugly, but you should see it." He holds up the picture as the women crane at it and, one by one, turn away. They look at the window, at the floor, at their laps, at each other. The room is completely silent.

"Girl number two, the second one we found in the files," Kosit says. "From 2007."

Even from where Rafferty's sitting, the photograph is a window into horror. The woman is colorless and cold-looking, with skin like white wax. Her eyes are rolled back as though she's seeing something high above her head, and her wet hair streams out onto the dented table. The water-puckered, fish-slick skin has been sliced to ribbons. The cuts, long bled out and laundered by the sea, open into more whiteness.

Rose gets up and goes to Kosit. She takes the photograph from him and holds it up to the room and says, "We show them this one, too. We tell all of them that he did this. We show them. Even the girls who are on drugs will remember."

"Will they believe you?" Arthit asks.

Rose starts to answer, but Nit pushes her way in. "We're sisters," she says. "Whether we like each other or not, we've all been through the same thing. We all have the same story. And we all know there are men like this one."

"They'll believe us," one of the others says to Arthit, "faster than they'll believe you."

Arthit nods and says, "You haven't finished, Poke. Go through the rest of it. And I mean step by step. What keeps these women safe?"

"First thing they do when they walk into the bar is say hello to anyone they know. The pictures will be in folders we'll get at the copy shop so no one will see anything until it's time. Second thing they do is sit for a few minutes with the mama-san and make sure he's not there. If he is, she never takes out the pictures. She just leaves and calls us from outside. If he's not there, they do the third thing, which is to show the picture of Horner to the mama-san and ask if she's seen him. If the answer is yes, the next question is when. If the answer is this evening, or recently, they ask whether he's been taking one girl regularly and, if so, whether she's in the bar. If the answer to *that* is yes, then the woman with the picture gets the girl's name and calls us and leaves without showing the picture around, and we go in a few minutes later and get Horner's girl. If the answer is no, then we revert to normal procedures and we make sure all the girls see both pictures as they come off the stage. These women will never get near any action, if any takes place."

Rose says, "Who here doesn't want to do this?" There are no responses.

"You keep saying they'll call us if he shows or if he's just been there," Arthit says. "Where are we going to be?"

"Right there, on Patpong. There are six bars that no one here worked at, so we'll take care of those. Anand and Kosit, if you'll let them, will show the pictures to the vendors in the street market and the touts working the sidewalk. If we don't get him tonight, we'll go back tomorrow, and the next night. My phone number will be written on the back of every picture."

Arthit says, "My phone number."

Rafferty nods, trying to conceal his elation.

"As if you didn't know I'd say that."

"Oh, well," Rafferty says, and then dumps the rest of what he was going to say because of the way Arthit's looking at him.

"If we find him, Poke"—Arthit's voice is soft—"what then?"

"You guys are three cops," Rafferty says. "I'm one me. I suppose it'll be whatever you want to happen."

"You know," Arthit says, "I could do this without you. I could forbid you from getting anywhere near Patpong."

"I guess you could."

"Will it be necessary?"

Rafferty says, "I'd be more comfortable about answering your question if I hadn't seen the picture of that girl."

"But you have seen it. Am I going to have a problem with you?"

It's almost a minute, with all the women looking at him, before Rafferty replies. "If you do," he says, "I'm sure you'll be able to handle it."

28

It Used to Be
a Good-Natured Sewer

Above the bright lights of the night market, the sky flickers chalky white and darkens again, like a loose lightbulb. A moment later a breeze kicks up, carrying the sweat of the crowd to Rafferty's nostrils.

"Could rain," he says.

"So what?" Arthit says, bulling his way through the slow-moving throng. "You afraid you'll shrink?"

"Rudeness one, small talk zero," Rafferty says.

Arthit grunts.

Rafferty says, "Not so busy, is it?"

"If you need to chat, it's not busy because it's early," Arthit says. "Only seven-twenty. It'll pick up."

Ahead of them Arthit watches Nit go into a bar called Bamboo, her folder held against her hip in a businesslike fashion.

Rafferty says, "Don't worry about them. They know what to do."

"You're the one I'm worried about." Arthit stops, the shirt of his uniform already wet in back. "*Look* at this junk," he says. "Patpong was always a sewer, but it used to be a good-natured sewer."

Rafferty looks over his friend's shoulder at a miscellany of murder weapons, gaily displayed in the shimmer of the spotlights: Gurkha knives, switchblades, gravity knives, nunchucks, brass knuckles, ninja throwing stars. Behind the display, a cheerful-looking woman sheds some of her smile when she notices Arthit's uniform and facial expression.

"They're just for fun," she says.

"You have an odd idea of fun."

She brings both hands up as though the items on the table were red-hot. "Me? I wouldn't have any of this in my house. They're for *farang*. The *farang* like to kill each other. Look at the movies."

Arthit says, "We shouldn't let you sell these."

"You could close some of them," the woman says eagerly. "There are four on this street and two more on Silom. I could pay you a commission. You close them down, and I'll give you one-third of the increase in my profits."

"No thanks." Arthit turns to go.

"Half," the woman says. "I couldn't give more than half."

Arthit says over his shoulder, "I'll think about it."

"Sixty percent!" the woman calls.

"The respect is so rewarding," Arthit says.

"If it's any comfort," Rafferty says, "I respect the hell out of you."

"You're nervous," Arthit says. "You don't usually natter."

"It's not nerves, it's plain old hatred."

"But you're going to do what I tell you to do."

"Oh," Rafferty says. "Sure."

Ahead of them Patpong runs from Silom to Surawong, the longest short block on earth, in Rafferty's opinion. Arthit's right: It's still early, and a lot of the people have come for the night market that stretches down the center of the street, rather than the bars. There are *farang* women everywhere, flushed pink with their own daring, holding blouses up to their shoulders, wrapping belts around their midsections, ransacking faux-Vuitton bags like manic customs agents, and bargaining amateurishly for the privilege of paying three times more than the whatever-it-is is worth. Looking around, Rafferty sees a lot of future buyer's remorse.

Two booths up, Anand is talking to a seller of counterfeit DVDs. He flashes both pictures, and the merchant grabs the iron-pipe frame of her stall for support.

Rafferty says, "They'll all remember."

"Here," Arthit says, heading left, toward the sidewalk and a dingy-looking door beneath a small, stuttering neon sign that reads BOTTOMS UP CLUB. As they approach the door, a dark young man in a T-shirt and shorts materializes from nowhere, opens the door just enough to slip his hand in, and pushes something. They're listening to the buzzer upstairs as he fades back into the crowded street.

"Don't worry," Arthit calls up the stairs in Thai. "No problem."

The stairs are vertiginously steep and so narrow that the walls almost brush Rafferty's shoulders. At the top he and Arthit find themselves in a long, dim, windowless room not much wider than a broad hallway with an unoccupied stage on one side, maybe two meters wide, adorned by a single pole that hasn't been wiped down in years. Palm prints fog its shine and dapple the broken mirror behind it, the lower right corner of which has fallen away and is propped against the wall. At the far end of the room, framed by incomplete strings of Christmas lights, a small bar blinks at them, decorated with plastic chrysanthemums, the perfect advertisement for alcoholic depression. The bottles behind the bar are the only clean surfaces in sight. Rafferty inhales the smell of a hamper full of dirty laundry that's been damp for weeks.

"Hello, hello," says a woman of indeterminate years, crammed into a tight dress, the seam of which has popped open on her left hip. She thinks her anxious grimace is a smile. She might have been pretty once, but she's used herself badly for a long time, and what's left of her beauty has been broken into random fragments—a nice set of cheekbones, a mouth that was probably plump before it got fat. There are four other women in the room, all overweight and, by Patpong standards, overage. They're all sheathed in the kind of tight, floor-length dresses that Rafferty associates with high gloves and big-band singers from the forties. All of them look nervous, but nowhere near as nervous as the two men sitting on the bench that runs along the wall facing the stage. They've obviously made hurried adjustments: One of them has half his shirttail hanging out of his pants. On the floor in front of each of them, a pillow has been placed. The pillows are permanently dented by years' worth of knees.

"You two," Arthit says to the men. "You need to go to the bathroom."

"You bet," says the one with half his shirt tucked in, jumping to his feet. He and his companion trot the length of the room and disappear into a dark corridor to the left of the bar.

"Give me some light," Arthit says.

The woman who met them at the top of the stairs nods to the shortest and youngest woman in the room, and the younger one goes to a wall fixture and snaps on an overhead fluorescent. The light reveals whole new frontiers of dirtiness, as well as masks of makeup as thick as toothpaste, and Rafferty thinks for a second of Rose, working to help women get out of the bar life before they end up someplace like this.

"Seen this man?" Arthit asks.

"Ooohh," says the youngest one. "Handsome."

"Has he been here?"

"No," says the oldest woman, who is obviously the mama-san. She looks at the other women and laughs. "And we'd remember. We don't get many like him."

"He's killed at least five bar girls," Arthit says. He holds up the second photo. The faces of the four older ones harden, but the youngest brings her fingers to her lips. "I want you to look at both these pictures. I want you to remember his face."

"I'll remember," the mama-san says.

Rafferty says, "He might have some injuries to his face, might even have bandages."

The mama-san says, "That would be nice."

"Get your cell phones," Arthit says.

The women go behind the bar and come out carrying purses, all of them battered and worn. Working ten-hour days on their knees in this cesspool, they're making barely enough money to eat. In a moment each of them has a phone out.

"Key in this number." Arthit recites his cell-phone number. "Save it. Name it whatever you want, as long as you'll be able to remember it if he comes in here. If he does, one of you goes back into the short-time room and calls me, is that clear? Just treat him like any other customer. He's never hurt a girl while he's in a bar, as far as we know. But call me."

The mama-san stores the number and takes another, longer, look at Horner's face. "If he comes in here," she says, "we'll kill him ourselves."

❦

BY NINE-THIRTY THEY'VE burned through all six of the bars on their
list and there's a light drizzle falling, creating flaring halos around the
lights in the night market and softening the lurid hues of the neon. Big
sheets of blue plastic have been stretched into place above the stalls and
tied to the metal frames to keep the merchandise dry, and water is running in the gutters, but the damp hasn't interfered with business in the
bars. The street is jammed solid on both sides.

Arthit's phone has rung eight times, with Rafferty practically jumping out of his skin each time. Six of the calls were sign-offs from the
women who were showing the photos, finished with their task. No one
had definitely recognized Horner. Some of the women had decided to
meet for a late meal at the Thai Room, a restaurant on Patpong 2. The
other two calls were news: Women had identified Horner as a customer
in the Kit-Kat and Bar Sinister, both relatively nice downstairs bars
that feature younger women, relatively new to the life. In both cases
he'd been there within a few weeks but hadn't been taking girls out.

The ninth call, coming in now, is from Nit, who had the longest list
of bars. Arthit listens and says to Rafferty, "The Office?" He squints
like someone trying to read small print. "The girl he's been taking out
works at the Office. Where the hell is that?"

"Patpong 2," Rafferty says. "But the Office isn't a go-go club. It's
just a hostess bar."

Nit hears his remark, and Arthit puts the phone to his ear and listens. "That's why she went there last," he says. "She almost didn't
bother." Into the phone he asks, "Is the girl there?" He looks over
at Rafferty, who's shifting from foot to foot, and nods an affirmative.
"You what? . . . Good, that's good. Smart of you." He puts a hand over
the phone. "She only showed them the picture of Horner. Thought
they'd give themselves away if they saw the other one."

"We need to get the girl."

Arthit points to the phone, which Rafferty takes to mean, *Nit's got
her.* To Nit he says, "Most of your friends are over at the Thai Room, so
you're close to them. Why don't you take her over there. We'll see you
in a minute or two. Stay away from the windows." He lowers the phone
and says to Rafferty, "Let's go. The Thai Room. If he goes into the Office, we'll be just up the street."

"Sure. As you said, away from the windows."

Arthit calls Kosit and, after that, Anand and tells each of them to head over to Patpong 2 once they've finished with the vendors.

"We should have sent people to all the hostess bars," Rafferty says.

"And we will," Arthit says. "Let's allow them a few minutes to eat, though. But, you know, men who frequent the go-go clubs don't usually visit the hostess bars. It's pretty much one or the other."

" 'Pretty much,' " Rafferty says between his teeth. " 'Usually.' I'm an idiot."

Seen from above, the Patpong district is a big capital H, with the two uprights being Patpong 1 and 2, named after the Patpong family, which has added considerably to its worldly riches, if not its store of good karma, by owning them. The cross stroke connecting the verticals is a nameless little stub of a street that's housed a long string of failed bars and restaurants, including one upstairs clip joint that changes its name so often Rafferty long ago stopped trying to keep up.

Patpong 2 is considerably sleepier than its big sister, with three or four struggling go-go clubs, a few restaurants, and six or eight decorous hostess bars, ranging from intimate to relatively vast. There's no night market. Where it can take fifteen minutes to plow through the people who pack the street from Silom to Surawong on Patpong 1 when the evening is in full swing, on Patpong 2 it can usually be done in one-fifth that time. Patpong 2 is less crowded. And a lot darker.

As they fight free of the crowd on Patpong 1 and enter the stub street, Arthit says, "I think we'll set up at the Thai Room. We can stay out of sight, and it'll take us less than a minute to get to the Office."

"Fine."

Arthit glances at Rafferty. "Problem?"

"Why was she there?"

"What do you mean?"

"Why was she working tonight? Rose said he was with her constantly when they were together."

"He had things to do today," Arthit says. "Bust into your apartment. Kidnap Miaow, and maybe you. Find Rose. Kill everybody. Big day."

" 'He does one thing at a time,' Rose said."

Arthit stops walking. He looks like he's studying the air in front of him. "Maybe he just decided to put things on hold while he got rid of the only person who could tie him to the killings."

"Then why not earlier? Why not the night he painted our door red? Why not just come in and kill us all? Why wait until now?"

"Rose said he was having fun. When he painted the door."

A very drunk Japanese man bumps Arthit from behind and backs away, bowing, until he bumps into someone else.

"There's someone who'll be lucky to have a wallet tomorrow," Arthit says. He starts walking again. "Don't worry about it. Your idea was solid. We found the bar. We've got the girl. Everybody in Patpong is looking for him. He'll show, and we'll have him."

"It doesn't work," Rafferty says. "He sees us in the restaurant, paints the door to scare us, and then disappears. Rose guesses he's got a girl and he's busy with her, and that's apparently true. But suddenly he's back, kicking in the door to kill us, trying to kidnap Miaow. I understand why he wants us dead. Rose is probably the only person who can tie him to the killings. What I don't understand is why he's suddenly got time to pay attention to us. I don't understand why that girl is in the club tonight." He pauses. "Maybe it has something to do with John?"

"How would he even know about John?" Arthit asks. You and Kosit said he was around the corner and in that cab, going in the other direction, by the time John got hit."

"I don't know," Rafferty says again. "But there's *something* I don't understand, because she shouldn't have been in that bar."

"So," Arthit says, "let's go see her."

They cross to the far curb on Patpong 2 and head left, past a decent French restaurant, a little hostess bar, a blow-job dump, and a pharmacy. On their left are a couple of open-air bars that do most of their business in the afternoon, before the go-go clubs open. The men occupying the stools constitute a representative assortment of *Caucasianus patpongus*, mostly in their forties and fifties, mostly overweight, mostly drunk. Someone who looks like Horner, Rafferty thinks, would have cut through the competition like a bright new scalpel. Even before he met Rose, Rafferty knew that some of the Patpong girls were as susceptible to a romantic fantasy as any starstruck teenager. For every ten who saw the customers as ambulatory ATMs, there was always one— usually a new one—who still had her illusions.

The Thai Room is cold enough to hang meat in. Five of the women from Rose's agency, plus Kosit, are huddled together for warmth at a long banquette. Trapped dead center in the row between the table and the wall is a girl of nineteen or so with the kind of whole-new-race beauty the Thai genetic stew sometimes produces. She has skin the color of maple syrup, luminous eyes that seem to have been imported directly from India, a tiny and perfect nose, and an impossibly long neck that looks like it was made to be hung heavily with gold.

"Warm it up in here," Arthit snaps at the waitress who greets them, holding menus of phone-book thickness. The Thai Room will take a slap at approximating any kind of cooking in the world, but their approach to the Thai food they cook for Thai patrons is more painstaking. "And bring me whatever you're cooking for them."

"They ordered a lot."

"Pick the two items you'd feel most comfortable serving to a high-ranking policeman who's in a bad mood."

The waitress blanches and retreats toward the kitchen, with a detour at the thermostat.

Rafferty grabs a chair from another table, and two of the women shift their own chairs so he can sit opposite the girl from the Office. She looks everywhere but at him.

He says, "What's your name?"

The girl doesn't answer.

"Her name is Wan," Fon says. "She's not happy to be here."

"You should be," Rafferty says to her. Wan is busy moving her utensils around, trying to improve on the arrangement, her mouth a stubborn line. The plate in front of her is empty. He turns to Nit. "How'd you get her here?"

Nit says, "I bought her out." Two of the women laugh.

"Where's Horner?" Rafferty asks.

Wan shakes her head.

"*This* man," Rafferty says, holding up the picture.

"I don't know him," Wan says in Thai.

Nit takes the utensils out of the girl's hand. "Everybody in the bar identified him."

"I don't know him," Wan says again. She tries to push her chair back, but it bumps the wall. "I go now."

From behind Rafferty, Arthit says, "Tell you what. You talk to us or I'll take you to the monkey house."

Wan says, "So?" But her eyes have widened at the words.

"Where's his hotel?" Rafferty asks.

She offers a shrug so packed with resentment that it reminds him of Miaow. "How would I know?"

"Why aren't you with him? Why are you working tonight?"

"It's my job," she says defiantly. "I work at the Office Bar."

"Wan," Rafferty says in Thai, "Howard is a killer."

"Don't know Howard," she says in English. "I go."

"My wife used to work in a bar. He tried to kill her."

She's shaking her head. "Don't know—"

"He killed a friend of hers. He killed at least five—"

"Why you no listen? Don't know Howard."

"His wife," Nit says, leaning in, "is one of my best friends. She's helped every girl at this table. Howard took her out into the Andaman—"

Nit breaks off because Wan has whipped her head around to face her at the word "Andaman."

Rafferty jumps on her. "Phuket. He was going to take you to Phuket. Wasn't he?"

The girl is shaking her head again, but the certainty in her face is softening.

"He took *her*—my wife, I mean—to the Andaman," Rafferty says mercilessly, "to Phuket. He told her he was going to marry her."

Wan says, "No," but the word has little behind it except breath.

"Phuket was the first stop," Rafferty says. "After that he promised her they were going to her village so he could meet her parents and he could—"

She says, "No, no, no."

"—so he could pay the dowry. But instead he took her out in a boat and tried to kill her with a knife."

Wan says, "Not Howard. Not Howard."

"Where is he?"

Her lower lip is moving as though she's going to say something, but she shakes her head and sits back. "Don't know."

"Where is he staying?"

She shakes her head again, and it's clear to Rafferty that she won't tell him.

"Is he coming to the Office later?"

A pause, then, "No."

"Why not?" No answer, and Rafferty stands, leaning on his knuckles on the tabletop. "Why aren't you with him? Why are you working tonight?"

"He . . . he doesn't want me."

"Why not?" He leans toward her. "*Why not?*"

Everyone in the restaurant is staring at them.

Nit says, "Poke." She puts a reassuring hand on the girl's shoulder. "Come on, little sister. It's not going to hurt anyone if you just tell us why he's not with you. Why he won't come to the bar tonight. And you know what? If we're wrong about him, you might help us get things right."

With no transition Wan bursts into tears, not genteel sobbing but big, openmouthed, gulping howls. She cups her face in her hands and then pulls them away and slams her forehead against the table, so hard that all the silverware jumps. She lifts her head to do it again, but Rafferty slips his hand in, palm up, in the spot her forehead hit. She stares down at his hand, and the sobs deepen. She says to Nit, although Rafferty can barely understand the words, "I have my period. He doesn't like it when—"

The restaurant door opens with a bang. Anand looks in, finds them, and says, "Something's happening. Patpong 1. Everybody's running."

Less than a minute later, having bulled his way through a dense crowd on the stub road with Arthit a step behind him, Rafferty enters the throng on Patpong 1 and sees hundreds of heads, all craning to see something to Rafferty's left. Rafferty, who is taller than most of the crowd, turns to look, and says to Arthit, "Holy Jesus Christ."

29

Perfume, Hair Spray, Dance Sweat

He's walking in the center of a red whirlwind, a whirlwind of rage and self-loathing. His bandaged nose and mouth hurt, and he raises his right hand and slams it open-palmed against his nose, sending an electric burst of pain vaulting through the circuits of his nervous system. His eyes watering, he's about to do it again—God knows he deserves it—but he realizes that it will start his nose bleeding again.

He looks freakish enough already, without blood all over his chin and shirt.

It's about two minutes to ten. He's chosen to come into the area through the Silom end of Patpong 2, the first block of which is always dark. Sidewalk vendors, closed at that hour, own the first segment of the road, so there is no one to see him there. A go-go bar scatters its neon into the night on the right, but he keeps to the left, hands jammed into his pockets, shoulders rigid with fury. John had been right. They should have killed Rose and the others that first night, just minced them where they slept. But they'd seemed so harmless, the wispy little half-breed husband and that ugly brown kid. And he was busy setting up the last act with Wan, and he'd thought he could have his fun with her and then have a little more fun with Rose and that patched-together, pathetic little family.

After all, it was *about* fun. It had always been about fun.

It humiliates him that John had been right. The accomplice, the sidekick, the guy Howard had always thought of as Tonto—even called him Tonto out loud a few times, knowing that John wasn't aware that *tonto* was Spanish for "stupid." Well, Stupid had been right.

And where the hell *is* Stupid? Did the cops get him? If they did, then he and Stupid are both as good as dead unless he moves right now. Faced with a bunch of Thai uniformed muscle in a concrete room, John will talk. Ten minutes later Howard's passport will be radioactive. No legal way out of the country.

And then, just to make everything perfect, that idiot Wan got her period. The day before the flight to Phuket and the dance on the rocks, the bitch got the curse.

Mistake after mistake, piled on the lethal sin of underestimating the opposition. Letting that wuss writer slap him around in the street, jam the handle of his own knife up his nose. No, he and John couldn't just follow them from the kid's school, the way John had wanted to, and then kill them wherever they were hiding. (John was right again.) *No, let's get the kid,* he hears himself say. It'll paralyze Rose. She'll come to us on her hands and knees. We'll make her call the hubby and bring him to us, we'll make her open her own blouse to the knife, as long as she thinks the kid will come out of it okay.

Right. *Who's* stupid?

He shakes his head and reorients himself. He can't let his alertness lapse. Patpong is no place for him to be right now. If he had a choice, he'd be on a bus heading for the Cambodian border. Find a place where he can walk across, rely on the fact that the Cambodian government hates the Thai government and will probably ignore any watch notice with his name on it. Fly out of Phnom Penh to Hong Kong, connect to Kabul. Get back to work. Put this behind him.

In a couple of years, he'll be able to come back. These people have no memories.

On his left is a massage parlor with no tout in front of it—there's never a tout in front of it, so at least he's right about one thing. Opposite it, brightening that side of the street, he sees a Foodland grocery store, blazing away like noon, full of squat little brown people buying their awful food. Bugs and peppers. Coming up ahead of him on the left, on his side of the street, is a large, dimly lighted hostess bar called the Presidential Club that he's never gone into. And lounging around in front of it on high stools, smoking and babbling at each other, are six or eight girls. Sucker bait. He heads for the far edge of the sidewalk, giving them as much space as possible, eyes on the pavement.

But one of them says, "Ow, honey, look like hurt. Me kiss it okay." He doesn't slow, but the hatred in his eyes when he glances at her pushes her halfway off her stool. The girl next to her grabs her friend's arm to hold her up and says to Horner, "Keep going. You no come here."

Half a block ahead on the left is the stub road that leads to Patpong 1. Patpong 1 will be much brighter. He puts on his sunglasses to hide the developing black eye and finds that they sit too high on the thick bandages over the bridge of his nose. He stops and forces the little pads farther apart, and one of them breaks off. He stares down at it for a moment, feeling the red heat at his center send out wires of rage, and then he deliberately breaks off the other one. He puts the glasses on again, and this time they sit almost low enough.

It'll have to do. The stub street is mostly empty, just a few men heading somewhere, some bar. Not looking at other men. Going from bar to bar as though the women were different from place to place. They are identical: stupid, greedy, dishonest, parasitical. Pick one, pick any of them. As identical as dolls.

Entering the teeming brightness of Patpong 1, he makes a left and keeps his head down as he pushes his way onto the sidewalk. He stays away from the vendors, who are, in any case, either bargaining a sale or trying to snag a passing customer. A couple of girls trolling the crowd at the entrance to the Throne Room look at him and then exchange wide-eyed glances, but he doesn't know them, and even if he did, he doesn't think they'd recognize him. What they see is a tall man wearing dark sunglasses to hide a black eye, a man whose nose is sheathed in a stiff white bandage. His upper lip has been stitched closed where Rafferty tore it with the haft of the knife, and it is swollen out almost an inch above the upper. He doesn't look like himself.

One of the women says something in Thai, and the other laughs.

All he wants to do is get off the sidewalk and into the Kit-Kat to wait for John. He hasn't heard from John since the debacle on Sukhumvit, and Stupid's cell phone seems to be out of order. They've been partners for years. They have their systems, whether they're in the firing zone or on vacation, and part of those systems is a series of fallback meeting points. The Kit-Kat is the third and last of the fallback points. John didn't show at the first two. If he doesn't show here within fifteen minutes, Howard will have to assume that they got him. Only after three fails can you abandon a partner. It will be time to run for his life.

The next bar he passes has no women working outside, and he turns into the next, which is the Kit-Kat. The usual crap music, the usual losers sitting on the benches nursing the usual beers. The usual whores on the stage, the usual demi-whores serving drinks. He's absorbed in locating an empty table, so he doesn't notice when one of the women on the stage checks him out as he comes in, her eyes doubling in size. She turns her back on him and scans the club for the mama-san but doesn't see her. One of the girls behind the bar looks at her expression and arches her eyebrows, and the first girl turns her head about a quarter of an inch over her left shoulder. The second girl glances over and gasps, although the gasp doesn't carry above the music.

Horner stares down at three fatsos who are taking up two tables, and without a word from him they snuggle up to free the table directly before Horner, a small table in front of the long upholstered bench that runs the length of the club's right wall. He eases himself down, looking for a waitress, not paying attention to the women on the stage. Across the room he catches a girl staring at him, her jaw slack, and he tilts his head down, embarrassed by his injuries. With his face downturned, the first thing he sees of the waitress is her feet. He lifts the eyes behind the sunglasses to her and says, "Singha."

Obviously ill at ease, she stammers a reply he can't catch over the music and wheels away from him, walking quickly, her back straight and stiff. He watches her go with a preliminary tickle of anxiety. She heads for the bar, but she seems to be looking all over the club for someone. Horner glances at her again and settles back to wait. He takes his first look at the women on the stage. Many of them glance away.

He sees the one he'd been buying Cokes for before he found Wan, and he tilts his head to her, just a hello, and she takes a step back, so fast she bumps the girl behind her. The girl she bumped doesn't turn around, but when Horner looks in the mirror on the other side of the room, he finds her eyes wide, aimed at his reflection.

In fact, all the girls in the row that's facing away from him are watching him in the mirror.

At the bar the waitress who took Horner's order is told that the mama-san has gone down the street to Superstar to chat with that bar's mama-san. The waitress turns and runs out of the bar as though ghosts are after her.

Horner watches her go and sits well forward on the bench. He surveys his surroundings, slowly and meticulously, and then he looks at his watch. Ten-twelve. In three minutes he'll know they got John.

He lifts his eyes from the watch and, one at a time, examines every face in the room. There is no one who seems familiar. The customers are the invariable ragtag assortment of big-gut assholes, most of them half tanked. Almost all of the women are now assiduously avoiding his face, as though some telepathic public-address system has just made an announcement. When he feels eyes on him and looks to check, the woman turns away.

The skin on the back of his neck prickles.

Outside, the waitress who took his order barrels out of the King's Corner and fights her way through the crowd to run into a bar across the street. She's followed a moment later by a girl and a ladyboy, who have left the King's Corner so fast they haven't even pulled on the wraps they usually wear over their dancing costumes. They split up, one running toward Surawong and the other heading toward Silom. People in the street jump aside and watch them go.

A song by Hall and Oates, an act Horner detests, blares through the speakers. Keeping his face expressionless, he pulls his feet, which he'd extended beneath the table, toward him and watches the women's eyes go to the movement. He stretches out an arm and feels the weight of gazes from all over the room. Then, very deliberately, he bends his elbow and looks at his watch again.

Ten-fourteen.

Slowly and loosely, keeping his gaze wide and unfocused to see anything that moves, he stands.

Once, years ago, Horner had been on a plane that was struck by lighting, and an actual bolt of electricity had rocketed through the cabin. That's what the bar feels like right now. He can almost smell the ozone. Some of the girls on the stage stop dancing, just hang on their poles and stare at him.

Hall and Oates give way to a snarl of static, and then a woman's voice, louder than the music, says something in Thai on the disc jockey's microphone. Two girls jump off their customers' laps and go out the door, moving fast.

Horner lets his eyes wander the room behind the sunglasses, without turning his head. There's movement everywhere. A dozen women stream toward the door and through it. Another eight or ten stop at the curtain. They turn to face him, avoiding his eyes, clearly terrified, but sharing a kind of group bravado.

Not good. And no John.

He takes two steps, and half the girls on the stage jump down and scoot past him to join the women at the door. They stand there, maybe twenty-five of them, five or six deep, blocking his way.

The disc jockey kills the music.

For a moment the silence seems even stranger to Horner than the band of women between him and the sidewalk. He's never been in a go-go bar when the music wasn't blaring. Somehow its absence makes the place smaller and shabbier, brings into sharp relief the cracks in the mirrors and the cobwebs above the speakers, the pieces of tape covering the rips in the fake leather upholstery on the benches.

The other customers are looking around as though they're not sure what has changed. One by one they turn their gazes to Horner, the only man standing in the bar. He dismisses them; there's no one there who worries him, but there are too many pairs of eyes. He says to the women at the door, his voice the sole sound in the room, "Get out of my way."

None of them move. A few of them raise their eyes to his face.

He takes a step forward, and they step back in time with him, forcing the ones farthest from him through the curtain and onto the sidewalk. Two more steps push more of them out of the bar until there are only five in front of him, in an arc only one girl deep and all of them looking at him, and when he makes his final move, those melt away outside, too, and no one is between him and the door.

He goes to the curtain. For a moment he fingers the cloth, and then he takes one final look at his watch. Ten-fifteen. Good-bye, John.

As he steps through, Horner looks behind him to make sure no one in the bar is coming at his back. When he's through the door, he drops the curtain and turns to the street. He has to blink to make sense of what he sees.

At least sixty girls stand there, shoulder to shoulder, looking silently at him. They've cleared a half circle with a radius of about six feet around the door to the Kit-Kat, so they're all just out of arm's length. He stands there, weighing options for a moment, and over their heads he sees a girl run into a bar three or four doors down. Twenty seconds later she comes out at the head of a stream of girls, maybe another twenty or twenty-five.

The Kit-Kat's door is opposite one of the little passages between the night-market booths that make it possible for customers to cross the street without having to go all the way down the block A large group of bar girls, all in their dancing costumes, are running through the passage, shoving their way toward him through the tourists.

Maybe forty of them. In all, he thinks a hundred and ten, a hundred and twenty.

The shortest way out is to his right, back to the stub road and then through that to Patpong 2. It's a distance of thirty or forty yards. He looks right and sees the sidewalk packed solid with women, with more of them pushing their way out of the two clubs he'd passed. Neon light bounces off bare shoulders and shining hair, glinting from the spangles and sequins on their costumes. He smells perfume, hair spray, dance sweat.

He can hear them breathe.

There are fewer girls in front of him, between him and the vendors' booths, so he takes a step in that direction, and the girls fade back, toward the booths. He grins, feeling the sharp tug of pain from the stitch in his lip, and takes two more steps, the women moving with him, maintaining their distance, and the fourth or fifth step takes him off the sidewalk and into the street.

Piece of cake. All he has to do is *walk* at them.

And he hears the curtains over the Kit-Kat's entrance rustle behind him, and he turns his head to see the remaining girls from the Kit-Kat come through it. Sees still more women from both sides of the entrance close in to join them until they're six or eight deep. He is at the center of a circle of women, and the circle continues to thicken in all directions.

Nobody says a word.

But he can hear the tourists complaining, their way blocked, until the oddness of the sight strikes them and they, too, fall silent. He sees a hand go up beyond the circle, now at least twenty women thick, and hold up a cell phone. It flashes as the tourist snaps his picture.

Horner stands absolutely still, his eyes roving over the crowd. He takes off the sunglasses to show them his eyes, drops them to the road, and steps on them.

In the silence the crunch of glass and plastic underfoot seems amplified.

When he's surveyed the women in front of him and on either side, he lets his head fall forward and he studies the surface of the road. He lifts his foot and looks at the shards and the twisted frame of his sunglasses for a long moment, seeing the tips of the dancing shoes and boots less than three yards away. He counts to eight, takes a long slow breath, and jumps.

He covers the ground to the nearest girls before anyone can make a sound. He slaps his hands on the shoulders of the woman directly in front of him and starts to pivot her so he can get an arm around her throat, but she reaches up and backhands his broken nose and then balls up a fist and hits him square on the stitched lip. His eyes fill with tears, and he lets go of her and brings both hands to his bleeding face, bending forward against the pain, and a searing flash of heat erupts in his lower back. When he grabs at it, he feels the hard shape of a knife. He tries to yank it out, but it's already being pulled away, and his fingers close on the moving blade.

He straightens, amazed, and stares at the ribbon of blood flowing from his hand. Fury seizes him and twists him around to find the woman with the knife, but he doesn't see a knife, just women backing away from him, stone-faced, and then something slams against the base of his skull, hard enough to jolt his vision, and he whirls to see a woman dressed like an idiot's erotic dream of a cowgirl backpedaling, with a set of brass knuckles on her right fist.

His lunge in her direction is brought up short by a stab in the back of his right thigh, and then a long burning river of pain down his back, a long swipe with the edge of a blade. When he turns this time, the woman with the knife is *right there*, and he wraps his fingers around her throat, ignoring her slashes to the backs of his hands, but then he feels a deep slice behind his right knee, severing one of the tendons, and he sags to the right and lets go of her and puts a hand down to break his fall, but he recovers his balance and stands there, his weight on his left leg, swaying slightly and starting to feel little sparkles in his head, a kind of fizziness that he knows means he is losing blood.

He lets his eyes rove over the line of women in front of him. There are knives everywhere, cheap switchblades and gravity knives, crap shiny Chinese steel that he knows will be sharp only once, will never take an edge after it's dulled, and he thinks a complete sentence: *It's sharp enough now.*

He pulls himself to his full height, leaning left. There's a scuttle on the asphalt behind him, and something else penetrates his skin, near his spine this time, the blow feeling dull rather than sharp, but he doesn't even turn. He just stares across the tops of the bar girls' heads to the tallest woman he sees, a full head above them, looking back at him. Looking at him as though he were already dead.

As the knife behind him seeks his spine again, she smiles at him.

RAFFERTY SEES HIM go down, sees the center of the circle narrow and almost close, like the iris of a camera lens. Women grunt and pant with effort, and there's a roiling at the center, heads darting in and then drifting back, replaced immediately by others. For a moment, out of the corner of his eye, he thinks he sees his wife, but then she's gone, and he and Arthit are plunging into the crowd of women with Kosit beside them, both cops shouting "Police! Police!" and tossing the women aside. The women in front of them turn back to face them, and then, slowly, reluctantly, jostling one another, they part.

In the center of the circle, Horner is on his back on the pavement. His arms are thrown out, and one knee is drawn up. His head lolls to one side, and his eyelids are half closed, but Rafferty thinks he can feel the man's gaze.

Arthit says, loudly enough to be heard to the circle's far edge, "None of you move. There are police coming from all directions. Anyone who tries to run will go straight to jail."

The women stay where they are, watching Rafferty and Arthit come. Rafferty sees the glint of steel in hands on all sides, and then, as the row of women in front of the night-market booths thins, he sees the unbroken expanse of white cloth where the knives and brass knuckles had gleamed in the light.

"You need to stay here, all of you," Arthit calls again. "Everybody in the back, tighten up. Don't let anybody in."

Rafferty hears feet scrape pavement all around him, and the circle becomes almost solid, women shoulder to shoulder, staring at him and Arthit, more interested than afraid. Horner is a still figure at the end of the path that's been cleared for them. Rafferty takes five more steps, and Horner is at his feet.

A knife stands upright in his chest. The blade had sunk in only an inch or two before Horner fell away from it, and four inches of naked steel gleam above his bloody shirt. At the edge of his vision, Rafferty sees that Arthit is looking at him, but when he turns toward his friend, Arthit slowly raises his eyes to the tangle of electrical lines above the street and stands there studying them. Rafferty waits until it is clear that Arthit is lost in contemplation of Bangkok wiring, and then, his pulse suddenly racing, he lifts his foot, puts the sole of his shoe on the handle of the knife, and presses down.

A sigh escapes the circle of women.

Without looking down at Horner, Arthit says, raising his voice only slightly, "Listen to me. Is there anyone who can't hear me clearly?"

No response. Women in one-piece bathing suits, flimsy wraps, bikinis, T-shirts, cowboy hats, all looking at him.

"You all came out here because there was a rumor that this man was— Who's your favorite movie star?"

A woman beside Rafferty—one of the heavy women from Bottoms Up—says, "Johnny Depp."

"Somebody said he was Johnny Depp," Arthit says. "You ran out here, and he wasn't. He was just a drunk *farang* who fell down in the street. Is there anyone who doesn't understand this?"

Once again no answer.

"That's what you tell *everyone*. The customers in your bars, the cops if more come around. You came to see Johnny Depp, but it was someone else. And get rid of those weapons, now. All of you go back to work, except for the ones who are right here." He makes a full circle with his finger. "Count the heads in front of you, in between you and me. If there are four, go away. If there are three or less, stay here."

The outer layers of the circle peel away, women heading back to their bars. Not many of them bother to look back.

"I need you to stay tight around us," Arthit says. "We're going to take him to Silom." He pulls his cell phone from his pocket, pushes a speed-dial number, and says, "Anand. Send Wan back to work. Tell her we're through for the night. Meet us in the car in two minutes." He repockets the phone. "Kosit?"

Kosit and Arthit kneel and get their arms under Horner. Each grabs one of Horner's arms and hangs it over his own shoulders. Then they tug him upright. Horner's head drops to his chest so sharply that Rafferty can hear his teeth snap together.

"Poke. Get that knife out of his chest."

Rafferty grabs the handle of the knife and pulls it out. He's suddenly dizzy with exhaustion, stranded by an outgoing tide of adrenaline. He has no idea what to do with the knife.

"Hang on to it," Arthit says. He raises his voice again. "You women move with us. Keep the circle tight. We're going to a car parked at the end of the street on Silom, and I don't want anyone getting close to us. If anybody asks, he's a drunk who got in a fight. Clear?"

A chorus of affirmatives.

"Here we go. One. Two. Three." Slowly and clumsily, the circle begins to glide toward Silom. "Make noise," Arthit says to the girls. "Talk, laugh." To Kosit he says, "Anand will drive. You sit in back with our friend here and make sure he doesn't die of his injuries."

Kosit says, "Got it."

"Poke," Arthit says. "Give him the knife."

Rafferty does.

"That's the knife we don't want him to die from," Arthit says. With a glance toward Rafferty, he continues. "If he does die, there's no point in taking up valuable hospital space, and we don't want to bother the Americans."

Kosit says, "The river."

"Why not?" Arthit says. "It's already polluted."

30

The Final Curtain

The level of audience enthusiasm, which had dropped off a bit when Ferdinand and Miranda came out for their bows, spikes sharply as Miaow runs onto the stage in her mirrored cloak. There are even some cheers, mostly, it seems, from kids. The follow spot hits her, making her the center of a blaze of light until the boy behind the spot snaps it off. He wasn't supposed to turn it on in the first place; it's Rafferty's guess that it's his way of applauding.

The whole cast is lined up now, and Prospero limps onstage, slowly abandoning his crouch as he goes, as though to amaze the audience by revealing that he isn't really an old man after all, but the flourish doesn't get the anticipated response. In fact, the applause drops off somewhat. It remains at a polite level as he takes his place in the center of the line, and then it increases slightly as everyone bows in unison, and the curtain falls.

They stand, Rose grabbing Rafferty's arm and hugging it to her. "Wasn't she wonderful?"

"She was," he says. "And what about that adaptation?"

"It was long."

"It was a lot longer before I got to it." He stands in the aisle as she slips out of the row, and they edge down the slope toward the stage, threading their way between the people heading up toward the exits at the rear of the auditorium.

Rose looks over at him, wearing his one jacket and tie, and then down at the clothes she bought herself for the evening, a loose, off-the-shoulder blouse in a silvery material and a pair of midnight-black velvet pants. "We're a handsome couple."

"You raise the average," Rafferty says.

She pats his cheek in a matronly fashion. "It was a great adaptation."

He takes her hand and leads her toward the stage door to the right of the orchestra pit. Even before they get the door open, they can hear the hubbub of voices behind the curtain.

Rose had sat forward in her seat when the lights went down and the curtain went up to reveal the shipwreck, played way downstage to the accompaniment of wind and wave sounds, with airborne handfuls of silver confetti to simulate splashing water. But after the sailors staggered off the stage clutching their masts and sails and the silhouetted black rock of Prospero's island had loomed in front of the gray cyclorama, she had sunk her nails into his wrist. Not until Luther and Siri were well into their eternal opening dialogue did she sit back and relax, only to claw him again when Miaow exploded into sight on top of the rock. Three or four minutes into Miaow's scene, Rose had wiped her cheeks with the backs of her hands. When Trinculo and Stephano had stumbled onstage, she'd laughed.

"You told me the clowns were terrible," she says as they climb the stairs to the stage.

"Well, they were until tonight. The kid who played Trinculo was great."

"He was the little one?"

"In the big yellow cape."

"He was funny. And he's almost as little as Miaow."

At the top of the stairs, Rafferty stops. "We've just seen the final curtain, right?"

"What's that mean, the final curtain?"

"When the play ended, just now. Everything was solved, everybody was saved, and all the secrets came out. Didn't they?"

Rose's face assumes an expression Rafferty can only characterize as complicated. "Yes," she says with some caution in her voice.

"So," he says. "Were you or weren't you in Patpong that night? And don't ask me which night."

Rose gives him a full and frank gaze and says, "You told me to stay at Arthit's. So of *course* I stayed at Arthit's."

They stand there, looking at each other and listening to the cheers and laughter from the stage.

"Well," Rafferty says, "I'm glad that's settled." He opens the door, and they step around a bunch of canvas rocks and find themselves far stage left.

"Oh," Rose says, staring up. "Oh, my."

From where they stand, the mighty rock is a jumbled construct of two-by-fours covered with heavy canvas, with three sets of roll-up stairs staggered beneath it to hold Miaow up. Looking at it from this perspective, Rafferty is happy he hadn't known how fragile the structure actually is. He wouldn't have been able to think about anything else whenever Miaow was on her path.

Rose says, "I wish I'd seen it this way first."

Clumps of people have gathered all over the stage, each attracted by one of the actors, and Mrs. Shin trots from group to group. Luther So stands, theatrically exhausted and literally mopping his brow, in the middle of a mob that looks like half the population of Chinatown, while Siri clasps a funeral armload of flowers, undoubtedly presented to her by the mob of adoring boys that presses on her from all sides. Her onstage lover, Ferdinand, is playing to a coterie of boys who seem to be wearing discreet makeup.

Rafferty hears half a dozen languages: English, Thai, Mandarin, what may be Swedish from Siri's parents, who are trying to elbow their way through the boys, Italian from somewhere, and a few he doesn't recognize.

"She's over there," Rose says.

Rafferty looks and sees first a bulky cape wrapped around one of the scrawniest little boys he's ever seen, a kid whose shoulders are barely wider than his neck and whose thick glasses, which he hadn't worn on the stage, are the size of silver dollars. His parents, not much bigger than he is but just as studious-looking, flank him proudly, and in the middle, her back turned to Rafferty and Rose, is Miaow, still wearing her mirrors.

"Trink-something," Rose says.

Rafferty says, "Wait a minute." He opens the program and runs his finger down the cast list. He comes to Trinculo and follows the line of dots to the actor's name: Andrew Nguyen.

He starts to laugh.

"What is it?" Rose says.

"Nothing." Miaow has heard his laugh and turned, and she waves them to her, her face incandescent with happiness. When they reach her, she hugs Rose and then Rafferty.

"Where's Pim?" Miaow asks.

"At Arthit's," Rose says. "Learning to be a maid. You were wonderful."

"Thank you," Miaow says politely, but it's clear she has something else on her mind. She steps to one side, inhales, breathes out, and inhales again. "Mom," she says. "Dad." She swallows and turns to the kid drowning in the yellow cape. "This is Andy."

Author's Note

This is a work of fiction, but it also isn't.

On the fiction front, the picture of U.S. defense contractors presented by Howard Horner and John Bohnert is absolutely not meant to be representative. I personally know a couple of people who are serving in Afghanistan right now, and they're motivated primarily by patriotism and belief in their mission. But anyone who has served with any of the companies who contract out this work will tell you that weeding out psychopaths is a constant, and not always achievable, priority.

On the nonfiction side, what Rose goes through in her transformation from village girl to sex worker is commonplace. Somewhere in some northeastern village, a young girl from a poor family takes the first steps on that path almost every day of the year. Particulars vary, but each of these women will endure a long process of change, leaving behind the names and the attitudes that once defined them and becoming someone almost completely new. The scene in which Teacher Suttikul and Mr. Pattison come to Rose's house to confront her father is based on an actual event. In that case, I'm happy to say, the girl was able to remain in school, although it might just as easily have gone the other way. And it often does.

There's a tendency in male-written novels about Bangkok to idealize bar workers or, in some cases, to demonize them: They're lost innocents on the one hand and flint-hearted gold diggers on the other. The only thing I'm trying to say about them in this book is that every Nit and Noi and Fon is a real person who has been given a very narrow range of choices. I think that most of them cope with their difficult situation with a certain amount of grace.

I don't know that we can ask much more of anyone.

Acknowledgments

I had a lot of help with this book—from individuals, from the restaurants and coffeehouses where I was taken care of while I wrote it, and from the artists who emerged from my iPod to get me through the process of envisioning the story and putting it into words (those are two very different things).

My previous editor at William Morrow, Peggy Hageman, gave the first draft of the manuscript the most sympathetic possible reading and made a number of suggestions that tightened and improved it, especially the last chapters. My agent, Bob Mecoy, put his finger on the book's potentially fatal weak spot at first reading, confirming the instinct that had me wincing every time I read certain passages. My wife, Munyin Choy, listened to the whole thing in its roughest, most raggedy form, and helped me sort wheat from chaff. There was a *lot* of chaff.

My current editor, Gabe Robinson, gave me the book's title over my wrongheaded objections, and supervised the development of the jacket and the page design.

I wrote the book in Los Angeles, Bangkok, and Phnom Penh, Cambodia. Thanks to the people at BB Cafe in Los Angeles and the Novel

Café in Santa Monica, who kept me caffeinated during the American stretches of the work. In Bangkok I fueled at Coffee World; and in Phnom Penh at Corner 33, K-Coffee, and the famous Foreign Correspondents Club, which overlooks the river just around the corner from my apartment there.

If coffee is one of my fuels, music is the other. This time around I was carried along by James McMurtry (yeah, "Choctaw Bingo"!), Bob Dylan (I must have listened to "Brownsville Girl" thirty times), Vince Gill, the perpetually beautiful Emmylou Harris, Mindy Smith, Eliot Smith, The Smiths, Pete/Peter Doherty, Van Morrison, the Soweto Gospel Choir, Randy Newman, Vienna Teng, Elvis Costello, Yeah Yeah Yeahs, Delbert McClinton (as always), Calexico, Franz Ferdinand, Aimee Mann, and a hundred others.

The long central section of the book, which is pretty much all women, was written almost exclusively to Tegan and Sara. I made a playlist of fifty-four Tegan and Sara cuts and just repeated it over and over. Almost the only exception is the chapter when Rose is in the water, which was written mostly to Ravel's Piano Concerto for the Left Hand, a piece of music that's got dark water running all the way through it.

Finally, several times when my courage flagged during the writing of the book, a reader sent a nice note to my Web site. Heartfelt thanks to all of you who did so. And let me urge readers who have that impulse from time to time to yield to it. You have no idea how much it can mean to a writer who feels like he or she is drowning and no longer has any idea which way is up.

CPSIA information can be obtained
at www.ICGtesting.com
Printed in the USA
LVHW08s0854050818
585933LV00004BA/26/P

9 780061 672279